THE WINTER SWORD

A NOVEL OF GERMANIA AND ROME
HRABAN CHRONICLES: BOOK 3

BY: ALARIC LONGWARD

HARDHILL
ADVENTURES

TABLE OF CONTENTS

Dedicated to Vanir Goddess Freya, who is said to champion war, love, and wisdom.

To my wife, who knows love and war are often closely related and has the wisdom to make it all work between us.

And for my brother Lauri, for the things we have missed.

A WORD FROM THE AUTHOR

Greetings, and thank you for getting this book. I hope you enjoy it and possibly also The Oath Breaker and Raven's Wyrd, books one and two in the series. I humbly ask you rate and review the story in Amazon.com and/or on Goodreads. This will be incredibly valuable for me going forward and I want you to know I greatly appreciate your opinion and time.
Please visit

www.alariclongward.com

and **sign up for my mailing list** for a monthly dose of information on the upcoming stories and info on our competitions and winners.

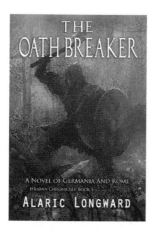 

OTHER BOOKS BY THE AUTHOR:
THE HRABAN CHRONICLES – NOVELS OF ROME AND GERMANIA

THE OATH BREAKER – BOOK 1
RAVEN'S WYRD – BOOK 2
THE WINTER SWORD – BOOK 3
THE SNAKE CATCHER – BOOK 4 (COMING 2016)

GOTH CHRONICLES - NOVELS OF THE NORTH

MAROBOODUS - BOOK 1

GERMANI TALES

ADALWULF

THE CANTINIÉRE TALES – STORIES OF FRENCH REVOLUTION AND NAPOLEONIC WARS

JEANETTE'S SWORD – BOOK 1
JEANETTE'S LOVE – BOOK 2
JEANETTE'S CHOICE – BOOK 3 (COMING LATE 2016)

TEN TEARS CHRONICLES – STORIES OF THE NINE WORLDS

THE DARK LEVY – BOOK 1
EYE OF HEL – BOOK 2
THRONE OF SCARS – BOOK 3

THIEF OF MIDGARD – STORIES OF THE NINE WORLDS

THE BEAST OF THE NORTH – BOOK 1
QUEEN OF THE DRAUGR – BOOK 2 (COMING AUGUST 2016)
QUEEN OF THE DRAUGR – BOOK 2 (COMING 2016)

'The Bear will roar, beware you gods,

for time is come to break the bars, sunder the rules, break the words.

The road from the shadow will begin,

the Raven to bleed on the evil, rocky skin.

A sister, a brother, wrongful act share,

a deed so vile, two children will she bear.

The Raven will find the sister,

the gods to look on as blood spills onto the Woden's Ringlet.

A raven will show the way, a bear is slain,

cocks will crow, men feel pain.

Youngest sister's blood is needed, her heart rent,

onto the plate of Woden, her life is ended.

Released is the herald, the gods will bow.

After doom, life begins anew.

A selfless act may yet the doom postpone.'

MAP OF NORTHERN EUROPE B.C. 12

NAMES AND PLACES

Adalfuns the Crafter – mysterious old man trying to help Hraban fight Tear. Will help Hraban three times if Hraban proves himself worthy.

Adalwulf – champion of Hulderic.

Adgandestrius – a Chatti adeling, son of Ebbe, brother to Gunda.

Adminus – Catuvellauni noble in Britain, brother of Togodumnus and Caratacus. A schemer and former exile in Rome.

Agetan – son of Tudrus the Elder, brother of Tudrus the younger, twin to Bohscyld.

Albine – daughter of Ebbe the Chatti.

Albis River – Elbe River.

Ansbor – Hraban's rotund friend, sarcastic yet staunch.

Ansigar – Hraban's scheming friend.

Antius – also Gaius Antius. A trader and negotiator, a servant of Rome who is plotting the downfall of both Germania and certain Roman nobles.

Aristovistus – in the past, a famed leader of a confederacy of Suebi. Tried to conquer Gaul 58 B.C. Defeated by Gaius Julius Caesar. Grandfather of Balderich, the old leader of Marcomanni.

Armin – Arminius, a Cherusci noble, son of Sigimer, husband to Thusnelda, foe of Rome, of Maroboodus and of Segestes.

Arrius Vibius Bricius – a Mediomactri Gaul noble living near Rheine, father of Cassia.

Aska – first man created by Woden, Lok, and Hoenur.

Balderich – grandson of the famous Aristovistus, grandfather of Hraban, leader of the Marcomanni.

Bark – brother of Wulf, priest of Freyr, foe of Maroboodus.

Bero – brother of Hulderic. Followed Hulderic from Gothonia to regain his ring and vengeance. Foe to Maroboodus.

Bohscyld – son of Tudrus the Elder, brother to Tudrus the Younger, twin to Agetan.

Brimwulf – an archer of Segestes

Burbetomagus – shared capital of the Mediomactri Celts and the Vangiones.

Burlein – youngest brother of Isfried and Melheim, noble of the southern Marcomanni.

Camulodunum – city of Camulos, the former capital of Trinovantes, now lorded over by the Catuvellauni.

Caratacus – Catuvellauni in Britain, brother to Togodumnus and Adminus.

Cassia – daughter to Arrius Vibius Bricius, a Gaul, and a healer.

Castra Alisio – a Roman fort in the lands of the Bructeri.

Castra Flamma – a Roman fort in the lands of the Luppia River near the borders of the Cherusci.

Castra Luppia – a Roman fort in the lands of the Matticati.

Catualda – son of Bero, cousin to Maroboodus.

Catuvellauni – a tribe in Britain, foes to Catuvellauni and Atrebates. Lords of Camulodunum, where Hraban is hiding Thumelicus.

Chatti - a fearsome Germanic tribe living north of the Maine River, south of the Cherusci.

Chauci – mighty Germanic tribe of the north.

Cherusci – a mighty Germanic tribe was living at Weser and Elbe Rivers.

Chariovalda – Lord of the Batavi, allies of Rome, client to Drusus and Hraban's captor.

Cornix – optio of the nineteenth legion, servant to Gaius Antius.

Danubius River – Danube River.

Draupnir – ring of Woden. Every ninth day this wondrous, dwarven-crafted ring would spill eight others.

Draupnir's Spawn – spawn of Draupnir, Woden's ring, and the influential ancient ring of Hraban's family. Also called Woden's Gift.

Ebbe – Chatti noble, father of Gunda and Adgandestrius, ever ready to oppose Rome.

Embla – first woman created by Woden, Lok, and Hoenur.

Ermendrud – daughter of Fulch the Red, lover to Hraban, then Wandal's wife to be.

Euric – father of Wandal, a blacksmith.

Felix – a Celt slave to Maroboodus and Hraban. Hraban's friend.

Fulch the Red – Warlord of Bero, father of Ermendrud.

Fulcher – Hraban's conscience and friend.

Gaius Julius Caesar Augustus – the first man of Rome, seemingly keeping Rome a republic, but in reality creating an empire where he would hold the power over the military and much of the legislative power. Tried to ensure the continuation of his line in charge of Rome.

Gaius Julius Caesar Augustus Germanicus – Caligula, the Roman Emperor whom Hraban sacrificed to elevate Claudius.

Gaius Sentius Saturninus – a Roman consul, supporter of Augustus. In the book, he is helping Drusus with the wars of 12 B.C. to 9 B.C. A fair ruler, a wise general. In reality, he would not arrive in Germania until 4 A.D. and would he replaced by Varus in A.D. 6.

Galdr – magic, spells, rhythmic spell singing.

Gau – a Germanic county, administrative area.

Gernot – Hraban's weak-willed brother.

Gnaeus Calpurnius Piso – son of famous Gnaeus Calpurnius Piso, a praefectus of auxilia.

Gothoni – old Germanic tribe from the Baltic Sea.

Grinrock – capital of the southern Marcomanni, home of Isfried.

Gulldrum – ancient abode and shrine of Tear's clan and god by Elbe River.

Gunda – a Chatti Noble, daughter of Ebbe

Gunhild – sister to Sigilind, Hraban's aunt. Daughter of Balderich.

Gunnvör – Burlein's archer, slayer of Guthbert.

Guthbert – Batavi rider of Maroboodus, brother of Leuthard.

Hadewig – Thumelicus's real name.

Hagano – Hraban's friend, youngest of the Bear Heads.

Hands – a Chatti bounty hunter.

Hard Hill – capital of the Marcomanni, oppidum hill next to Rhine.

Harmod the Old – champion of Hulderic.

Helmut – caretaker of Segestes's hall.

Hengsti – the war king of the Matticati, allies of Rome, famed riders.

Hermanduri – vast Suebi nation was covering much of the Weser River. Roman allies.

Hraban – the Raven, the Oath Breaker, the main character of the story. Son of Maroboodus, he is telling his story to Thumelicus, so he might one day have his fame redeemed, and his daughter Lif know him.

Hugo – a Cherusci warrior of Segestes

Hund – a Batavi signifier

Hulderic –Hulderic the Gothoni, noble of an ancient house, father of Maroboodus, grandfather to Hraban, brother of Bero.

Hunfried – a Vangione noble, son of Vago, brother of Shayla, Koun, and Vannius.

Inguiomerus – a Cherusci noble, brother to Sigimer and Segestes, foe of Rome, but envious of Armin's growing power and Armin's ability.

Isfried – lord of the southern Marcomanni, head of his large family. Ally to Bero, Balderich's lord. Brother of Melheim and Burlein.

Ishild – daughter to Tear, sister to Odo, she is a girl entwined in her mothers and brothers attempt to destroy the world. Torn between her family and her love for Hraban, she makes Hraban's life full of hard choices.

Ketill – a Cherusci chief, servant of Segestes.

Koun – a Vangione noble, foe to free Germani. Brother of Shayla, Vannius, and Hunfrid, son of Vago.

Leuthard – a Batavi warrior who served Bero, then Maroboodus. Brother to Guthbert, Maroboodus's bodyguard.

Lif – Hraban's and Ishild's daughter.

Lífþrasir – son of Odo.

Lok – a trickster, half deity, half giant. Bound by the entrails of his son for causing the death of Baldur, son of Woden, and for his chaotic nature.

Lothar – a Batavi Decurion of Castra Flamma and a servant to Segestes.

Lucius – a centurion of Castra Flamma, Hraban's friend.

Luppia River – Lippe River in middle Germany. Where much of the Germanic wars took place.

Maelo – famous opponent of Rome, Sigambri Germani noble.

Marcomanni – the border men, Suebi Germanic tribe divided into two gaus, counties. Led by Balderich and Maroboodus.

Maroboodus – son of Hulderic, father to Hraban and Gernot, husband to Sigilind, returning home after a long period, bringing with him war.

Marcus Romanus – a Roman exile living with Hulderic, teacher to Hraban. Servant of Maroboodus.

Mare Suebicum – the Baltic Sea.

Mare Germanicum – the North Sea.

Mathildis – daughter of Helmut, Brimwulf's love.

Mattium – famed capital of the Chatti, home of Ebbe. Oppidum.

Mediomactri – Gauls living west of Rhine River, opposite to the Marcomanni. Share their land with the Germanic Vangiones, foes of Maroboodus.

Melheim – brother of Isfried, brutal and treacherous. Noble of the southern Marcomanni.

Moenus River – Maine River, where Hraban lives as a youth.

Moganticum – a major Roman military base started by Agrippa, it kept growing into a naval base and a trade city. Mainz of today, located where Maine River combines with Rhine.

Nero Claudius Drusus – Stepson of Augustus, son of Livia, brother of Tiberius. The leader of the early wars against the Germani east of Rhine, and likely the greatest, best-liked leader of his time. Rumored to be a staunch Republican.

Nihta – a Germani warrior of the Rugii tribe, a harii, night fighter, and champion of Maroboodus. Deadly with a sword.

Odo – son of Tear, brother of Ishild. The driving force behind the god who wants to destroy the worlds. Hraban's nemesis.

Oldaric – the other Chatti lord, father of Albine. Stubborn and slow to oppose Rome.

Oril – Odo's servant at Castra Flamma.

Paellus Ahenobarbus – a military tribune of the XVII.

Pipin – a Batavi guard.

Quadi – a Suebi tribe, allies of the Marcomanni north of Maine River.

Radulf – a Batavi guard.

Ragnarök – the final battle of Germanic mythology, the end of most of the living things, the gods included.

Ragwald – a warlord of Segestes

Ralla – a völva at Hard Hill.

Rochus – a Cherusci noble, brother of Armin, son of Sigimer.

Segestes – also Segestes the Fat, a Cherusci noble, brother to Inguiomerus and Sigimer, uncle of Armin and father of Thusnelda. Roman sympathizer. Ruler of the Cherusci lands west of Weser River.

Seidr – magical power of Freya, the war goddess, mistress of seduction. Völvas use it.

Shayla – a half Celt, half Germani druid, an opponent of Tear, trying to steer away the prophecy of the end of the world. Sister to Vannius, Koun, and Hunfrid.

Sibratus – Quadi noble, brother of Tudrus the Older and Tallo.

Sigambri – old Germanic tribe was living around Lippe River. Always at war with Rome along with the Bructeri, Usipetes, Marsi and Tencteri.

Sigilind – daughter of Balderich, wife of Maroboodus, mother of Hraban and Gernot.

Sigimer – a Cherusci noble, father of Armin, brother of Segestes, ruler of lands east of Weser River.

Suebi – a vast confederacy of Germanic tribes stretching from Sweden to Danube River.

Svea – Suebi from the north, trackers of Segestes

Tallo – Quadi noble, brother of Tudrus the Older and Sibratus.

Tear – also called Zahar, the mother to Odo and Ishild. Reluctant servant of her old god bent on the destruction of the world.

Tencteri – Germanic tribe from the Lippe River.

Thumelicus – son of Armin and Thusnelda, rescued by Hraban. He is recovering in Albion, Camulodunum.

Thusnelda – a noble Cherusci woman, wife of Armin, daughter of Segestes and mother of Thumelicus.

The Three Spinners – norns, the Germanic deities, or spirits, sitting at the foot of the world tree, by the Well of Fate, weaving the past, the present, and the future of each living creature. Also called Urðr, Verðandi, and Skuld.

Tiberius Claudius Nero – son of Livia, stepson of Augustus, brother of Nero Claudius Drusus

Togodumnus – King of the Catuvellauni, Lord of Camulodunum where Hraban is hiding Thumelicus. Brother to Adminus and Caratacus.

Trinovantes – a tribe in Britain, foes to the Catuvellauni.

Tudrus the Older – brother of Tallo, nephew of Sibratus, a Quadi noble, and leader of the westernmost of the Quadi.

Tudrus the Younger – eldest son of Tudrus the Elder, the brains of the three Quadi brothers.

Vaettir – Germanic nature spirits.

Vago - king of the Vangiones, foe to Marcomanni and the Quadi. Leader of I Vangiorum, a Roman Auxilia unit. Father of Shayla, Koun, Vannius, and Hunfrid.

Vangiones – a Germani tribe serving Rome.

Vannius – a Vangione noble, son of Vago, brother to Shayla, Koun, and Hunfrid.

Varnis – Sigambri Germani noble.

Varus - Publius Quinctilius Varus, a supporter of Augustus, took over Germania from Saturninus. Did not understand how to treat the Germani, and Armin took ample advantage of Varus's shortcomings causing the destruction of three legions.

Veleda – the girl Hraban must find for Tear and Odo.

Visurgis River – Weser River.

Vulcan – a smith of Segestes, also called the Old Saxon and Heimrich.

Wandal – Hraban's ham-fisted, slow-witted friend. Son of Euric.

Woden – also known as Odin, the leader of the Aesir gods, one of the creators of men and the world.

Woden's Gift – spawn of Draupnir, Woden's ring, the influential ancient ring of Hraban's family.

Wulf – a vitka from the village of Hraban. One of the few who are trying to stop the prophecy that will end the world. Hraban's former tutor, foe to Maroboodus.

Wyrd – fate in Germanic mythology.

Yggdrasill – the world tree, where the nine worlds hang. Source of all life.

Zahar – see Tear.

CAMULODUNUM, ALBION (A.D. 42)

I had to dispose of a body this morning.

The man was a nothing. A Gaul of the Camulodunum, poor as shit, dirty as mud and only a tool for someone far higher. However, despite his low rank, I had to figure out how to make sure his death would remain a mystery. He would be missed, and I could not just drag it to the woods, for dogs scent corpses. It can take a surprisingly long time for wild animals to wholly devour a carcass. Some animals would save some of it for later, and that would not do. And, all of the scavengers tend to scatter bones and hair and clothing over a large area. A terrible mess; I have seen it many times. So I thought about burying him like many murderers do, but after I had considered it for a moment, I shook my head.

I am ancient and have no wish to shovel dirt. That sort of manual work makes me grumpy as an old, saddle-sore woman, and I knew there was no mead in the hall, which would have fortified me to attempt a burial. So, eventually I decided to let the crabs take care of the corpse, and I hope they did a thorough job. They usually do, they waste nothing, work uncannily fast and there will only be a skeleton left in but a blink of an eye.

I carried him to the cliffs, pushed the corpse down to hit the beach of the river below, squinted as I tried to fathom if he was close enough to the waterline and decided I had done a splendid job. I came home.

I was not sorry. Not in the least.

The man betrayed us or tried to, at least. I am not sure how much damage he managed to do in the short time I knew him, and I will go out to the town to find out, later.

As you recall, my wounded lord Thumelicus; we are, as ever, in peril. Our protector, the king Togodumnus of the mighty Catuvellauni and now of the beaten Trinovantes and Atrebates is facing plenty of harsh choices. That is due to Rome, of course, for what land is not reeling under the weight of their hobnailed caligae or at least fear their invasion? The whore wolf's armies are out there across the channel in Gallia Belgica, building strength, gathering ships and supplies, waiting to pounce. Here in Albion, the strange land my mad lord Caligula planned to take, what the cursed princeps Augustus hoped to annex, where Caesar god failed to conquer, we hide, my Thumelicus. The supreme chameleon Tiberius Claudius Nero Germanicus will sail here one day soon. 'That bastard pretender and a liar,' I whisper in fury, for Claudius is not the simpering fool he pretended to be, no. Where the court of the Palatine Hill used to throw rotten vegetables at him when Caligula wanted amusement, and the poor fooled thanked the Emperor piteously in return, now he is a glowering and calculating princeps of Rome, a rat no longer. He is a stammering tiger, and he fooled me, even. He fooled everyone, in fact. He ate mockery and drank tears, and now he has legions to bleed his enemies. To think I served Tiberius and Caligula for so long and missed the glint in Claudius's eye? Impossible. But there it is. I did. After I had left Caligula to die, I did not expect Claudius to have any spirit when he was raised to the helm of the great Roman ship.

It is a miracle I escaped.

It is also a miracle I managed to spring you from the gladiator ludus, Thumelicus, son of Armin. They want you back. Oh, they do.

I chuckle as I think how Claudius must suffer every moment the son of his father's great enemy, Armin, Arminius the Cherusci is free as a hawk. I wipe my face tiredly, for I have been thinking about my vengeance for years and years, ever since your father died, Thumelicus. After he had died, after some other unpleasantness, I went back to Rome, suffered, then served dutifully and forgot much of my past; my hopes and dreams and past lives. Then, just after Caligula died, and Claudius showed his claws, I

19

remembered my oath to your father. It was an oath we gave to save you and your mother Thusnelda after he lost you to the betrayal of Segestes, his traitorous, uncouth uncle. Rome took you, his family, paraded you in a mockery of a triumph, and we all promised Armin we would one day burn and slay and murder to give his family freedom.

It took nearly two decades for us to do so. Or for me. The others died long ago.

I am sorry you were grievously hurt while we saved you.

Wyrd, the fates made it so, and the spinners cannot be easily denied. You live yet; you are healing, and while we succeeded, there are many who died that day. I miss them. They were friends, good friends. Their wyrd was to go and yours to survive, at least for a while. 'Take them, Woden, and serve them roasted piglet and ale, warm their bones by your cauldrons and when they fight for you, give them a sturdy shield and a thick spear and applaud them as they slay in your games,' I said and breathed heavily. I hope my god still hears me.

You moan, and I shake myself from my somber mood. Old men are prone to such moods, but there is still much to be happy and thankful about. We are free. As free as an enemy of Rome can be. I will work, Thumelicus, to keep us free. I will bleed men and claw our way out of the traps of Claudius. That is why I killed the man that morning and why I hid him.

I glance out the open door of our ancient hall, the hall Togodumnus gave us near his city and squint at this seat of his power.

The oppidum, the walled Gaulish city I see at from our hill, the city of Camulodunum the god of war was once the mightiest city of the Trinovantes. This was before the father of Togodumnus; the fey Cunobelius took it. Now Togodumnus rules the uneasy land, and while Cunobelius was one to send humble and submissive embassies to Augustus and Caligula, they never fully received pardon for destroying the weak Trinovantes, Roman allies since god Caesar's time. Rome does not trust Togodumnus. And there is more, of course, for the brother of Togodumnus, the young warlord, Caratacus, drove the Atrebates into ruin, taking Calleva with sword and spear. The worm Verica of the Atrebates was in Rome soon after Calleva fell, an exile. I know for I saw him there. I remember the fat bastard sweating and licking his thin lips as he went to his hands and knees and begged like a child to mad, mad Caligula for aid and accolades. He got none but was allowed to stay and amuse my mad lord.

Bah, I thought, *Claudius inherited the dog, no doubt.*

In Rome, my Lord, I also saw Adminus.

Adminus is the youngest brother of Togodumnus and Caratacus and their father Cunobelius drove him away, the thieving dog that he was, and he visited Rome, as well. Rome is where all the exiles end up, in hopes of finding legions to reinstate them to the power they have lost. He is Roman now. I know it.

He is here.

He is in Camulodunum with Togodumnus and Caratacus. He is here, not in Rome. And as Claudius is looking for you, the lost son of Armin the Cherusci, the Legion Eater's spawn and for me, the Oath Breaker, then one should be worried.

And I am.

I'm as worried as a clever merchant when he spies a fat publican approaching. One way or another, no matter our common enemies, our worries will seem paltry to the king. We will weigh nothing at all in the scales of Togodumnus. Even if the mighty Celt gave us shelter after our flight from Rome, granted us this rotten hall on the hill next to Camulodunum, he might wither from his promises and break them if Rome finds us here. Rome might make direct demands for our rebellious heads, no matter if the legions come later anyway. He is a king after all, and kings think about their people and throne. He has inherited the kingdom of Cunobelius, perhaps, but can he defeat thirty thousand Romans in battle? Forty thousand? More?

No. Of course not.

He might pray Taranis to sink and mangle the enemy fleet when it appears on the coast, but should they land? The triple axis of Roman legions will push his men to red ruin. And he will be king of refugees. Or dead.

The man I killed this morning worked for Adminus and so the snake is aware of us, and we are being watched. Adminus will scheme to give us away to Claudius.

I'll not allow that, no.

And who am I to deny these whoresons, nobles and lords of the Catuvellauni?

I am Hraban, the Raven, the Oath Breaker, the Bone Breaker, and I did fight for and against Rome and the Germani both when your father Armin still lived, Thumelicus. I was a Marcomanni noble and the red hand of Tiberius and Caligula. I have enemies across the lands and few friends, but in here, we are out of the clasp of Claudius for now, and I intend to keep it so.

I try your forehead with the back of my hand. The fever is gone, nearly so. The druid who administers to your wounds might be a rude, gruff beast of strangely clean clothing amidst grime and dirt, but he knows his business. He has yet to speak to me, but I think he gave me a hint in the form of a happy grunt. You will survive your wounds, after all.

I pull forth the codex, the wondrous thing of glued together pages and stare at your thin face. Before I go to the town, I will write again, for I have a past I wish to share. There are few in Midgard who love the Oath Breaker, but I have a daughter, somewhere in Germania, perhaps with the Cherusci, possibly still holed in the Godsmount. As a favor to me, Thumelicus and should we survive the upcoming ordeals, you will travel to her. You will find the fine woman called Lif, now over forty and perhaps and hopefully, my grandchildren, and you shall tell her and them of Hraban. If you do, I pledge to serve you humbly in the afterlife. I shall travel there first, no doubt and win you a seat near Armin, your mighty father, and there I shall sit in dust at your feet, wallow in mud and hay and do your bidding if you do this one deed for me.

Find Lif. Take her this Codex. Read it to her if she cannot decipher Latin.

If you feel no gratitude for your savior and you do not travel to find her, I will torment you in Valholl. I will. Each day the Einherjar gather to meet in battle, I shall cleave through a legion of shields to get to you if you turn out to be an ungrateful little cock. You will quake, for Woden's blood runs wildly in my veins and his raging spear dance grants me speed and agility. I'm a berserker, Lord, and I doubt you are. Armin was a tactician, the brains. I was the spear.

Heed me, Thumelicus. Lif must learn of me.

And what will she learn of me? She already knows I am a traitor. I am called the Oath Breaker. They still sing about me out there over the Rhenus River, and they do love their tales of fallen heroes and traitorous curs. But she must learn that I, like any, was a man of some finer virtues. What the Germani cherish, fame, I have none. I am infamous. However, I loved her.

I stare at the pages of the Codex and my spidery handwriting. I wonder at the stories I have written while you healed. I am not a deft writer, mind you, my back aches and fingers groan from the herculean effort, but I have managed it so far, and I wonder how many times I should have died after my father betrayed me.

I slam the book closed and stare at it.

Imagine, Thumelicus, the first families of men. They were born Gothoni far in the north and Woden made them, breathed life and purpose into the two lifeless bodies of Aska and Esla and took Midgard as his own. Imagine Lok, Woden's brother cursing these men while giving birth to his family, in mockery of Woden's, under the root of Gulldrum. Imagine such families being tied together by a curse, a sibilant prophecy that might come to pass and would cause the world of Woden to perish, the gods to topple and Lok's brood to rebuild Midgard. That is the story of our family. Father was the Bear; I was the Raven, and there was a prophecy that tied us all together with Lok's family, especially foul vitka Odo. When Maroboodus came home from his exile in Rome, Lok's servants sensed the prophecy was moving. And it was.

Had I left when I learned of this curse, all would be different.

However, Father returned, I stayed, and many things took place. The Bear came home and met the Raven, and Lok's prophecy was running rampant. But that was not the only thing to worry about. For Father was a traitor.

As you recall, at this time Augustus reigned.

He reigned more wisely than god Caesar had and built his legacy slowly and resolutely. It was a legacy that would destroy the Roman Republic as it was. But Augustus would die one day, and who would then take over? The ancient Republic and its Senate? His sons? Someone else?

Father came home to Germania with a mission. He had agreed to help a high woman in Rome to be rid of those who would have Republic. He would combine the tribes of the Germani, a near impossible task as the Germani are willful and proud, and he would slay the greatest supporter of the old Republic. Nero Claudius Drusus, son of Livia, stepson of Augustus.

To do this, he used his family first to gain control of the Marcomanni.

My grandfather Hulderic died, Sigilind fell and Gernot and me? His sons? He used brutality to scare us, then pretended affection and love for us and fooled us both. In the end, he ruled the Marcomanni, and we were cast out. Balderich, our other grandfather and leader of the Marcomanni, was ousted, Maroboodus's cousin Bero sacrificed, and Father even worked with Lok's cursed creatures, for he did not fear the prophecy. In the end, Gernot went to serve Odo. I was to die, but escaped his plans, killed my many foes, learnt of Father's Roman nature and raised the southern Marcomanni against him. I wanted my fame back, my place and a hall of my own.

It was not to be.

Friends died, Father won and though I had delayed his plans, he was stronger than before.

I forgot about my fame.

I had a child. With Ishild, Odo's sister. And it changed everything. Yes, it is Lif I am talking about, the same woman I want you to meet. I lost her in Father's pursuit of us, and she was taken to Godsmount, where the final steps of the cursed prophecy would take place. Odo did not know where it was, but I, the Raven was to find her. It was inevitable. I cared not. I wanted her back.

However, to get her back, I needed allies.

I found Nero Claudius Drusus, the man who was to fall to Father. His cause became mine, and I learned of honor rather than fame. I fought for him; I fought father's henchmen, and I fought Armin, the rival to Maroboodus and enemy to Drusus and there we were, Thumelicus, when I last quit writing.

I sighed and rubbed my face as I watched you in the throes of some odd nightmare.

While I had no hope or even will of becoming a Germani again, I had Drusus and his dreams to follow. And I had to find Lif. She was in the lands of the Cherusci, your father Armin's lands, and Drusus was going there. I had men to kill; my murderous father, who did not love me, perhaps yours, Armin, for he had tried to use me to slay Drusus. Father's Roman contacts Antius and Cornix were out there, still working to slay Drusus, and there was also Catualda, a relative who had worked with Father and wanted the Woden's Gift, our family's perilous, ancient ring for himself. It would grant one power amongst Suebi, and it was something Armin desired as well, for it would give the Cherusci peace from the Suebi Semnones of the east, for they revered the ring. Also, I wanted to murder Odo, the one who desired Lif, tried to find Godsmount and Veleda to end the world and who stole our ring. I had to deal with Gernot, my brother, another victim of Father, also serving Odo. And likely Ansigar, my former friend, who was with Gernot.

I had a lot of bloody goals, Lord.

I had lost a lot of friends for these goals. I only had a few left. I had my grandfather's ancient sword, the Head Taker, something I had ever loved, and it whispered to me of vengeance. Not of fame, but blood.

I followed Drusus against Armin as I tried to settle my scores, and I knew they would all soon come together, my foes, for Drusus was their goal and my sword was his. This story is about what I managed to achieve, what I failed in, and of my sword, what Cassia, my lover, called the Winter Sword, the weapon that was the symbol of my drive for vengeance. The sword was my curse, my bane, and I will tell you how that turned out.

Sleep, Lord, as I sit and write and fight for our lives in Camulodunum. If I fail in that, then you need not worry. You will be dead.

That day, we were standing amidst a wreck of a battlefield, and we had been victorious

BOOK 1: THE TROUBLED HILLS

'It yearns for blood. It's a sword that drives you to vengeance, I think. Is it evil?
Perhaps.'
Rochus to Hraban

We had won a great victory against Armin and the Germani tribes of the Luppia River. However, the price had been very high. It was unusually high for the disciplined Roman army fighting undisciplined Germani. More, there had been three legions in the battle, and auxilia, and still it had been a close call. All that was thanks to Armin.

The three legions that took part in the battle that had no name in the lands of the Bructeri still had a war to make. In our rear, the troublesome Tencteri and Usipetes were harrying the half built Roman castrum that had been set to supply us on the Luppia River, and far in the east, there was one castra guarding the land against Cherusci. It held one pristine legion, and beyond it, the nation that was now an enemy. The cavalry was very spent though the Batavi and remaining Thracian auxilia got on their bedraggled horses bravely. The foot auxilia, Thracian, Aquitanian, and Germanic? They had suffered so many losses to Armin's surprise, there were but some two thousand left of them.

But the enemy had lost more. Far more. Their dead littered the ridge and the trampled valley.

The Bructeri lost Wodenspear, their great chief. The stubborn Sigambri had lost many great champions in the desperate battle to break the V Alaudae Legion and in the ensuing, chaotic rout. The small Cherusci army had been shattered. The Marsi was all but decimated, always a small tribe. The lands south and north of Luppia River were to be Roman, but we knew that was but a dream. We would hold the river and its fertile valleys, but the woods would still belong to the deadly warriors whose dark gods lived there with them. No Roman went there willingly. The enemy would take a long time to recover, and Rome would give them no time to do so.

Armin's skills gave every Roman a pause. There was a thought planted in their heads. *They nearly lost.* It was a bothersome, irritating thought for a Roman soldier, one that made the mouth sour, and the belly churn. The war was not over, and the horrid possibility of ignominious loss snaked easily into their minds as they prepared to go east.

And Nero Claudius Drusus, my Lord? Did he know he had nearly been beaten?

He knew it as well.

Armin the Cherusci had fought him and done very, very well. Armin, the young Cherusci adeling had prepared the battle to a minute detail. He and his father Sigimer had schemed, bullied, and forced tribes unused to set piece battle to suffer hunger and losses and hardship to give Rome one surprising, supremely mighty and coordinated push at a time of their choosing. And that push had very nearly separated many Romans from their Aquila and heads.

I'd had a part to play in the battle.

I had nearly obeyed the Cherusci Armin to slay Drusus before the campaign in order to get my daughter Lif back, a baby whom Armin had found as I had been forced to give her to Hands, a bounty hunter. In the end, I refused Armin and joined Drusus, and nearly killed Armin.

Lif.

She was out there, in the lands of the Cherusci. She had been spared thrice already from death, and she was but a babe. I had saved her from my father when we fled the south. Then from Odo, the vitka of Lok and then again from Leuthard, beast of Maroboodus, whom Father had sent to kill me and Armin both. Maroboodus, my black-hearted father, wanted Armin dead, for Armin was stubbornly being a greater warlord than Maroboodus was, and one Nero Claudius Drusus considered his greatest enemy. And how was Maroboodus then to slay Drusus if Armin did? That was Father's secretive Roman mission. To slay Drusus in war and smother the thought of Roman Republic for good and then he would gain a kingdom. If Armin managed it, perhaps his master in Rome would not reward poor Maroboodus, whose hands were red with the blood of my family, his family, the family he did not want. The beastly killer of Maroboodus, the wolf-faced Leuthard had died at my hands after the battle. I bore wounds from that fight and had nearly died.

And then there was Odo. I spat as I thought of the Lok's vitka. Our family and theirs. A mad god was trying to end the world, and so many of the lines of that foul prophecy had come to pass. I was the Raven, Father, the Bear, and we were all coming together in lands of the Cherusci. He thought I had led them to the final trail by saving Lif. He had taken our ancient ring from me, thinking that was Woden's Ringlet and had ridden after Lif.

If he found her?

He would not slay her, no, for she was important. She was to marry his son and survive the end of the world to populate Midgard in Lok's name. *Mad, mad*, I thought. Odo would try to make it so. If he found Lif, he would also find völva Veleda to whom Lif was being taken to by Hands, the bounty hunter. The prophecy of Ragnarök would be proven true after the dirty, and mad Odo of god Lok sacrificed Veleda on our ring. Worlds would end. At that I smiled, for only I knew our ring was not Woden's Ringlet of the prophecy. No. It was not golden, and our ring was. Odo did not know that. But then, I did not know what Woden's Ringlet was.

I did not care.

Lif. I had to find her. And I had to keep Father from killing Drusus. And I had men to kill.

I was snapped from my thoughts as buccina blared. The horns called the ragged legions to attention, and the only things to spoil the pristine moment were the moans of the wounded in the castra erected in the middle of the former battlefield. The army was due its honor, it was drawn up on the shredded field, and many men were well rewarded. Some received the Golden Crown, others torcs and phalerae for their armor.

Centurions were promoted, the bravest men of the Legion taking up the traverse plumed helmets of their predecessors who had died in great numbers.

Then I was startled. I was, even if I expected it.

I was called up in my turn, and I walked forward. My Lord Nero Claudius Drusus was short and fey looking in his grimy armor, once shiny sculpted metal and now rusty in places. His strong jaw, piercing dark eyes and curly hair was that of a Roman, but his spirit did remind me of Hulderic, my grandfather, for he had a commanding presence that made one instinctively straighten one's back. I reached him, and Drusus embraced me. He turned to the lean, savage faces of the soldiers, and I turned to stare at them, as well. Having gotten used to being spat upon by my fellow Germani for my father's manipulations, lies, and I admit, even my weaknesses, I was surprised. I saw respect there in those wolf-like faces. Respect. That was something I had decided I no longer cared for, but I did. They were soldiers; I was one, and we shared the hardships and glory. Drusus lifted my arm to the air. 'Hail, my boys, the brother and a friend who led the beaten to the glorious, golden victory! The slayer of the Cherusci!'

And they did.

They cheered me wildly, calling me "a confused boy soldier," "a witless Germani oaf," and other insulting, but in truth endearing words, and I smiled. I heard one call me "the slayer of kings" though I had killed no kings that day, only opened up Armin's brother Rochas in a mad melee to spare the legions from being cut in half. In truth, I was a refugee, a Marcomanni exile and now a dirty Batavi Decurion though I had no men. 'The Oath Breaker!' someone yelled.

My mind darkened at that, for that was the name The Germani knew me by. *Thanks to Father. Thanks to my orlog, the decisions that make up one's wyrd, fate,* I thought. Drusus whispered at me, smiling on. 'Even that is a praise. Harsh life is what they know, and many have joined the army to escape their broken oaths and failures. They love you, so you just smile and thank them.' I smiled and tried to quell my uneasiness at the sight of such a glorious, blood-spattered army regarding me so high. They saw a man in bloodied lorica hamata, Leuthard's beautiful chain mail. I was taller than most men, wide at the shoulders as a boulder, my hair and beard were raven dark, and I wore the helmet my friend Tudrus the Old had given me once, an Athenian bronze helmet that covered my face. Some of them called me "god Mars," and I felt my pride swell, only to remind myself I was Woden's champion, and that god was wickedly unpredictable. *He might give me suffering if I let the praises go to my head,* I thought.

'As long as he breaks skulls as well as oaths, I'm happy!' an optio yelled from the side, one of the V Alaudae, the legion I had spared many losses. And so I forgot my shame, let the praises go to my head, and I grinned, damning Woden. I saw Fulcher, the dark, long-haired man with the Batavi auxilia, still weak from his fall. He had his revenge with Bricius dead, the slayer of his son. Far, somewhere out there, helping the Romans in the Rhenus River and Castra Vetera was Cassia, the Celt noble, a healer and my lover. I wished she was there. But she was not. It had been unexpected love, for all I had cared for was my fame and place, my vengeance, but she had stayed with me, and she should have been there to see my honor. My eyes sought Ansbor, and then I remembered he had died. He had, for he had loved Cassia, and I had taken her. He betrayed me. He paid.

Wyrd.

I had a cause. I eyed Drusus, and I smiled at him, and he embraced me. I loved him like a brother. His cause was mine.

Lif. The voice said her name in my head, and my face darkened again. I forced a smile on my parched lips, for while I served Drusus, Lif was ever in my thoughts.

More insults were hurled at me, mostly to do with my wild looks and heritage, but Roman jokes were different from the Germani ones, much cruder but also ironic and so, soon, I learnt to appreciate them. They were all brothers, and I was one of them. I was to lead some of the Batavi, perhaps. Of course, I was, for Chariovalda had made me a Decurion though that was a position one earned by leading men in long, dangerous campaigns and by faithfully serving Rome and not by saving a day in a single wild melee.

That thought of leading men made me feel uncertain.

I had ever wanted to be a ring giver, a warlord, and the spear of the thiuda, of the War King, and that meant leading a large band of men. I found to my surprise, I was happy I had no men, save for Fulcher. I had led many in battle, but to lead them out of it? I was not sure I could. I had failed poor Burlein, had I not? Father had killed the southern lord and routed the lot of us, and I had not been able to save the rebellion. In any case, Chariovalda, the father-like Batavi had given me no men, for he had none to give.

Drusus let go of my hand and handed me a precious golden torc and a silver spear, a miniature prize for putting down Armin's tall brother before they could break to the rear of the legions. He had fought well. So had I. I bowed to Drusus. 'Don't boy! It goes to his head!' someone shouted from the ranks, and amidst waves of laughter, Drusus's voice amongst them, I went to stand with the hulking, grinning Batavi contingent. I felt tired, yet proud like a stag of the deep woods. Men still cheered, and I raised my arms in the air for the honor until the next man was called forth.

I had a home, I thought.

But most of all, I wanted to march for Lif. And she was in the lands of the Cherusci.

That night Drusus spent in the mud-spattered praetorium tent with his generals, planning under the Aquila of the legions. Later that night, the troops were awakened, and everything was packed. Scouts rode out to recall troops chasing after Bructeri, Sigambri, Cherusci, and Marsi refugees. The next day, I got my wish as the army marched. We were aiming for the land of the Cherusci.

Drusus, despite the army's condition, wanted to flash his sword at them.

CHAPTER 2

'Poor bastards,' Fulcher said as we sat on our horses. The Tencteri had surrounded the supply castra of Alisio and a savage thrust by Drusus had left a hundred of them dead. In a day's time, Alisio was freed from the Tencteri, who fled without a further fight.

Some ten such former warriors were chained at the side of the fort, guarded by the Batavi.

'Poor bastards,' Fulcher said again as I had not responded. 'They had as little food as we did out there. Are you there, Hraban? Did you swallow a bone?'

'I'd chew the bone if I had one. But now we will gorge ourselves. The fort's full of it. Wheat, oil. We'll knead bread until our knuckles bleed. The bastards of the XVII are fat.' I chuckled. 'Did you see the cheeks of that supply immunes and the tunic of the Questor? Smeared in oil. I swear they were.'

'They will have to give it up now,' Fulcher said maliciously and saw how the army was emptying the castra amidst bitter complaints of the camp praefectus who was bodily fighting to keep at least a part of the reserve in reserve.

'I wonder what is happening down the river,' I said, gazing down Luppia River for the far west where the Uspietes had burnt the warehouses of Castra Vetera. 'And I wonder how—'

'She is fine,' Fulcher said, knowing I worried about Cassia. 'I never thanked you for giving me the head of Bricius.'

'I didn't take it. The beast did,' I said and shuddered at the memory of the not so distant night. It had ended with Odo taking my ring and following Hands and Lif for the east, Armin and Thusnelda escaping, and Briscius, who had been serving Father dying at the hands of their own commander, the bald beast of Leuthard. *Had he been a wolf? A Lok's beast? Hati's spawn? Or just a very savage, thick-skulled warrior who Father sent to nip Armin, Hraban, and Lif from this life?* He had slain Ermendrud, my lost friend and Wandal's betrothed, the woman I failed to protect. She had been so afraid; then she had been brave and then dead. *He had gnawed on her. I had seen it. No man would do that. Or would they?*

'He is dead,' Fulcher said. 'Forget him.'

'I'll never forget Leuthard,' I told him. I patted my swords, the Head Taker, my grandfather Hulderic's long, ancient spatha. My fingers brushed Nightbright, the leaner blade I had won in battle, and finally the spear's head of Wolf's Bane, now aptly named. It was the broken spear of Aristovistus, given to me by Balderich, the former lord of all the Marcomanni and my grandfather. I wondered how he was. We had saved him, and he had left the land as Burlein and I faced Maroboodus.

Perhaps he could have made the difference in the battle for the Marcomanni. He would have. He would have commanded the troops, would have summoned some of the northern lords to join us and things could all have ended differently.

Wyrd.

Burlein wanted to be the War King and had distrusted Balderich. It was his fault as well that we failed. 'Come, Hraban. Let's find something to eat. I can feel my spine in my belly,' Fulcher spat.

'You sound like Wandal,' I told him as I guided my horse after him. 'You whine like a rotten, spoiled girl when the winter is long. He always got depressed when hungry.'

'I hope to meet him one day,' he said pleasantly. 'Wandal sounds like a likable fellow.' I as well, for Wandal was lost. I had lost him in battle, and none knew what happened to him.

'So you will stay with me now? And not go home yet?' I asked, as I was curious. I needed him, his help, and wisdom, and steady spear, but he had a family. Briscius had taken his boy, but Briscius was dead now. Fulcher had pissed on the skull, and his boy was at peace, but he had a wife and a daughter far south.

'Perhaps,' he mumbled. I stared at him, and he withered. 'I want to. I don't wish to go back to my land, tilling the damned soil, breaking my back on the fields and burning woods for a new one. I hate the fucking cows; I hate the misery of bad crops, and I enjoy ... travelling these lands. What wonderful poems I will tell when I am old.'

'You won't live to see such old age, Fulcher while you travel with me. You must have missed how many have fallen in my wake. Not all were enemies.'

He huffed and waved his hand, dismissing my fears. 'I've seen myself die in bed, old and bald.'

'Not your sights again!' I cursed as we dodged some archers running for their auxiliary unit. 'I wish you had sight of where Lif is!'

'Gods do not cut adventures short like that, Hraban. It would bore them,' he said seriously. 'I love to travel with you. Yes. But I will fetch them. My family. Maroboodus rules there now. He will have some ugly warlord guarding Grinrock, and so it might get perilous. They know I am your man.'

I snorted. 'Not even my father can keep track of wives and children of all the men who hate him,' I told him with some amusement. 'We have to fetch Euric, as well. Though I am not sure he wishes to travel with us. He is old. But if we find Wandal, he will want Euric with us. He loves his Father as much as I hate mine.' *Maroboodus. Father. The Roman bastard,* I thought and chuckled. We served the same land now, though different lords. I was a man of Drusus. He served someone who wanted Drusus, the frightening Republican, the simmering, growing opponent to his stepfather Augustus dead. I would stop Maroboodus, indeed. Not for my fame, no. That was beyond recovery. For Drusus, I would fight Father.

But like ever, I still had to save Lif.

Ishild, Odo's unhappy sister and my one-time lover had left Lif. She had left Lif to my care and finally told me why she was drawn back to Odo, her brother. Odo had whelped a son on her, named Lifspsavir. Just like the prophecy dictated, the sibling had shared a filthy act though I called it rape. I shook my head at the people arrayed against me and rode on and saw the legions were already moving, furcas on their shoulders, helmets swinging on their chests, laden with gear. They marched to the east. They would go and march to the Castra Flamma at the springs of Luppia River and from there, we would take the sword to the Cherusci.

I noticed the blond Chariovalda, Drusus's Batavi client sitting by a fire, reading orders. He noticed me and smiled, his infectious grin filling me with happiness. I had plotted on killing Drusus for Armin, and he knew it. He had forgiven me. 'Fox,' he said.

'Hraban means raven,' I told him, confused.

'No, you idiot,' he told me drolly and tossed pieces of hard meat up to us. 'They call Armin the Fox now. They are trying to suppress the number of losses we endured but, of course, that is impossible. Drusus will have to recruit in Italy for these legions, and the poor recruiting officers will probably stare at the orders for a long time in silence, their mouths hanging open before they comprehend what is needed. Augustus does not want him here anymore, never did, but under his eye and this will fuel that wish.'

'So we go after the Fox while we can, eh?' I asked and winced as I tried to take a bite out of the meat. 'Shit. Is this saddle?'

Chariovalda grinned at me again. 'They gave us the old, mummified stuff. It could also be saddle, I know not.' He nodded at the XVII still staffing Alisio. 'Bastards. Fat buggers. I ate well enough yesterday, a bit of a horse from a Cherusci that surrendered, but it will be harsh going.'

'We will eat when there is food and go faster for the hope of it,' Fulcher sang.

36

'Yes,' Chariovalda agreed miserably as he tossed a pebble at Fulcher and then pointed a finger at my friend. 'I hate him. Too cheerful, and I want mead. None to be had. Not a drop. And Fulcher is happy. But he is right. We go on and eat men if we must. That is the way of war.'

'Not with the Germani,' I noted. 'They will split up quickly if the food runs out. They'll go home and have a feast.'

'They didn't under Armin,' Chariovalda said glumly. 'They starved while they waited for us. And so we have to make sure Armin will no longer entice them to act so uncharacteristically wisely. Too bad he got away. Too bad.' He glanced up at me with a raised eyebrow, and I shrugged.

I spat out an inedible part of gristle and poked a finger his way. 'I led the Beast to him. I left that golden haired bastard with Leuthard. I had Lif to find. And what I did, leaving him with Leuthard? That was a near death sentence, and they fought, they fought hard. Leuthard butchered Briscius and his men, some of the Cherusci but still Armin got away. So did his woman, Thusnelda. I cannot capture everyone. I only have two hands. A Jotun would fail killing all these people we have to kill. And Drusus will want even more heads, now that I serve him. Armin is gone. Now we have to find him. He lost, his men are scattered and Drusus—'

'About that,' Chariovalda said, rubbing his face and then getting up with a groan. 'By the wrinkled balls of Hercules. I'm getting old!'

'Yes,' I agreed, and he gave me the evil eye. 'About what?'

'He want's a word with you,' Chariovalda said. 'Go and have it.'

'Where?' I asked for I knew he was speaking of Drusus.

'At the castra,' Chariovalda nodded at the gate of Alisio. 'Hurry. Not much time left before we dash after the Fox's tail and end up buried in some sad wood somewhere, starved and hacked to bits.'

'I'd rather hear Fulcher sing than you mope.' I grinned. 'We will chase the Fox and see him run.'

'This fox shows its teeth occasionally,' said a burly Batavi Pipin as he held Chariovalda's horse still.

'I'll make a necklace of them if I can,' Chariovalda told him. 'Ride after us. When you can.'

I nodded and headed for the fort. Fulcher was following me on his horse, nodding at legionnaires readying for the march. I stopped and dismounted before the gate and adjusted my chafing lorica hamata, the fabulous chain mail of Leuthard, one with a bronze beast head on the chest. 'Its too big for you, isn't it?' Fulcher wondered. 'He was the size of a horse. You look like a child in it.'

'Child or not, I'll not let it go after slaying the thing,' I growled. 'Boot the ass,' I told the gate guard who had heard the day's watch phrase so many times his face no longer twitched.

'And kiss it after,' he said tiredly and nodded inside. Fulcher giggled, and we gave him an incredulous eye. While he hated hunger, he had turned from the somber, melancholy bastard into a merrymaking poet. Pissing on the skull of the killer of his son had done him good. *Or he had hit his head too hard when he fell from his saddle before the battle*, I thought.

'I'll wait here and you go ahead. He is your Lord, and I don't want to intrude on your ass kissing or even the booting part,' he chuckled. I cursed him and hiked up the Via Principalis, the guard elements of the XVII Legion lounging near their contubernium tents. I slapped some stray mules, dodged a procession of slaves carrying amphorae of wine for the departing troops, and stopped before the praetorium, where Drusus was dictating a scroll. On the side, the principia tents were shuddering for many officers were running around in absolute madness, and a quaestor, the supply officer was in tears by his tent. Drusus noticed me, and there was a ghost of a smile as he finished his dictation. Then he walked to me, his lictors with their fasces over their shoulders were following near. Those men trusted me like none else. *I had jumped before Drusus and arrows once, had I not?*

'I've got some supplies,' he told me. 'Not enough, but some. I'm tempted to rage at the camp praefectus, but I'm too tired and dignified to do so.'

'You have tribunes for that. And legates,' I stated as he turned me to the main gate.

He snorted. 'I know. But I still need the supplies.'

'They burned many of the warehouses back in the Castra Vetera.'

'I know that as well,' he said and rubbed his tired face. His signum, a tall pole adorned with a purple cloth with intricate, golden lettering and topped by an eagle was carried past, and a host of military tribunes followed it. He shook his head, waved at a bothersome fly and laughed bitterly. 'I'm the urban praetor of Rome for the year, and right now I should be holed up in the Palatine, gorging myself with bribes and feasts. Would be so simple to govern the city compared to this shit. I suppose this is how they made their name in the old days? By sweating, dodging horse turds, enduring wounds and flies, and starving. Taking the Alps with my brother was a breeze compared to this Hades. I would love nothing more than call this victory, for it is one.' He looked like he was swallowing a fistful of ants. Then he sighed and shook his shoulders, jumping up and down, releasing the tension. 'Yes, it would be nice to see my wife and family. But your friend Armin is still at large, and I cannot settle down to rest until I have bled more men of his and his father's, just to explain we finish our grudges. Sigimer? He has to answer for his son's actions. He had that Raven ax?'

'Yes, he is the one with the famous ax. And Armin is not my friend. I don't know Sigimer either. His brother Segestes I have seen, and Inguiomerus—'

He interrupted me. 'Yes, we all know of Inguiomerus. The Lord of the eastern Cherusci, master of Albis River and the man who once flayed Roman traders and diplomats. That too is something I will remedy one day. With luck; soon. But now, I will raid the lands of Sigimer and his son and piss on the smoldering ruins of their hall.'

'I hear the Castra Flamma is being extended,' I noted. 'In the east.'

'Yes,' he agreed. 'They are making the agger and the fossa more formidable, and the vallum are built from thick wood by now. They are doing well though they are raiding the undefended Sigambri lands as well as building. Now that the Sigambri men are out here, trying to go home, our Ubii have been taking much loot from them across Rhenus River.'

The Ubii, formerly Germani, now Roman allies were having an excellent year, I thought.

Drusus read my mind. 'And we will have a good time, as well. I hear from the exploratores that Armin and Sigimer are summoning much of the western power of the Cherusci to battle. Not all obey, of course, but the major lords will. Sigimer is the thiuda and they should, in theory, obey him. There will be thousands of the scoundrels. And they have so many rivers in that bastard of a land it will be hard as Hades to get anywhere. We have to cross Visurgis and beat Sigimer at least before going home for the fall. We will stay in Luppia, of course.'

I snorted. 'Our reluctant allies the Chatti will see that as an offensive move, as you know,' I said sourly. Indeed, the Chatti were nominally Roman allies and those of Maroboodus as well and had warned Drusus not to stay in Luppia River.

'They have a choice to make, no?' Drusus growled, unwilling to show the thought scared him. The Chatti were feral warriors, long bearded and savage, and likely the hardiest of the Germani. And my people, the Marcomanni lived to the south of them. 'If your father riles them up against us, I know what to do. But we have to beat the Cherusci before the fall. We have great Ebbe as a hostage and the Chatti won't go to war this year, at least.' *Ebbe*. Father of Adgandestrius the Chatti, my friend, whom Drusus took a hostage in his Thing, treacherously. *And foolishly*, I thought. He slapped my shoulder to get my attention. 'But we have no food. And so I shall have to cajole and beg for it.'

'From whom?' I asked as we reached the gate. 'Will your Mars shit us some bloody sausages and venison if your chicken priests so beg?'

'I'd eat their chickens first, of the damned pullarii,' he stated seriously of the chicken observing priests. 'But no. From the Cherusci,' he grinned as we dodged under the weak gate.

'What?' I blurted as Fulcher brought my horse forward. 'Lord—'

'You call be Drusus,' he reminded me. 'You always go 'Lord,' when you are afraid of calling me an idiot. There is the third leader of the Cherusci. You mentioned him just now.'

'I did. But I don't see why he would supply us,' I said sullenly. 'Segestes the Fat trades and sympathizes with you. But to betray his kin? He would roast after we left.'

'With us,' Drusus noted laconically. 'You are with us. You are an auxilia Decurion of Batavi and Rome and no Germani.'

'I'll learn,' I told him apologetically, unsure if I would. 'But how is one to convince … Segestes is Sigimer's and Iguiomerus's brother.'

Drusus kicked a stone, apparently unhappy at having to put so much at stake in Segestes. 'He is fat fucking rich from trade; commands wide lands west of the Visurgis River and yes, he has answered the call of Sigimer. But his heart is not in it. I doubt he enjoys a fight in general.'

'Are you sure?' I asked him with some concern, for I had noted Drusus had a way of downplaying facts that hampered action. It had nearly cost him a legion and more.

'No,' he told me. 'But you will go and find out if I am right.'

I looked mortified, and Fulcher quaffed. I began a desperate argument. 'His daughter is to marry Maroboodus. He agreed to help Father against Rome. He does not know Father is Roman, but he was there when Father made plans for all the Germani to fight Rome.'

'None of that matters if I give him Sigimer's lands. He is a toad. A fat, lazy frog and loves the deep, rich end of the pond and can only stare at it enviously, as other frogs own it. We will help him take it. He will be given Sigimer's lands. He cannot resist such a fine promise, no matter if he is related to the braver frogs. Say yes,' he grinned.

'Yes, Lord,' I told him rebelliously, sure I was going to get killed at the hands of Segestes.

He frowned at me and patted his horse. 'I will have dangerous work for you in the future, Hraban. We have the world to conquer, and we all face risks. But you will have respect and home as well as dangers. And my love. And I will bury you well if you fall.' He grinned again, Fulcher laughed. 'Come, soon we have to find out how your father and Antius aim to slay me. Now, we have to eat.' *He was right in that.* Whoever had sent Father to ally the Germani to fight and to kill Drusus was someone we would have to deal with eventually. It might take a civil war if that someone was powerful enough. Drusus loved the idea of Republic. His stepfather Augustus, princeps, his mother Livia's husband was out to change all of Roman history, hoping to take Rome back to the era of the kings. Even if

41

there was a Senate in Rome, it was practically giving lip service to the old traditions. It was all a sham.

Unless Drusus brought back the old ways.

Whoever wanted Augustus's vision did not want him or Augustus in the picture. One day, Drusus might have to lead armies south. And I had promised to help him.

I bowed deeply to him. 'Yes, Drusus,' I said, and he smiled like the sun. 'Shall I go now? Better to die sooner than later.'

'No, you don't know where to go!' he laughed. 'You would meander around like a lost Syrian in the alleys of Viminal and end up clobbered and robbed.'

'You have no idea where this lord is currently?' Fulcher blurted and went silent as the great man of Rome turned to him.

'Fulcher, right?' My friend nodded with respect. Drusus always remembered the names of the soldiers. 'No, I do not. But there is someone who does know.'

'Oh?' I asked him, suspicious for there was a nervous twitch in his eye. 'Who?'

He sighed, ready for a fight. 'This man is in charge of the annona militaris. He is one of the lazy fucks who are supposed to feed this army. He worked in Moganticum but knows the tribes here as well, much better than the negotiatores in Castra Vetera. So he has been summoned.'

'Antius?' I breathed. 'The lard pot? The one who is the go-between for Maroboodus and whoever it is—' He raised his hand and eyed me with a warning. He did not want to share that bit of information with the lictors or any prying ear. I bit my lip.

'Yes, him.'

'He tried to murder me,' I hissed. 'Cornix, his supply optio? He stood in the same room where Ansbor died, and I think he smiled. And they have been plotting against us before. You know this.'

'Yes, and you will accompany Antius and take some men with you, your Fulcher included, to meet Segestes the Fat.'

'He was party to killing Ansbor, Lord,' I said again with a low, threatening voice, and my lord stared at me with impatience.

42

'We know why you were in the shrine, Hraban,' he retorted, his face stone hard. 'You were there to slay me for the Fox. For Armin. You had a reason, yes and owed us nothing. Your daughter is out there, and you did it for her. You changed your mind and elevated your soul from a murdering Germani into that of a noble Roman, boy, but you are not innocent in the slaying of Ansbor by the beast of Maroboodus. Eat it, Hraban, the guilt. Eat, chew, and swallow and know I have made many choices in my life that make me suffer every night. As a soldier, I would hang him. As a politician, knowing him my enemy, I need him near me. Near, Hraban. But you are right.' He waved some lictors away as they had shuffled closer. 'You are right in saying Antius is guilty of treason. He is guilty of many things, and his man Cornix is a hunted man. His is an enemy to both of us. And so,' he stepped near me and whispered, 'when you have agreed with Segestes on getting us fed as we march east of Castra Flamma for Visurgis River and Sigimer, you will kill him. We need him to find Segestes and to set up this deal, but after? No. In this, I will be a soldier. It is my gift to you, and the food will be a gift to me.'

I opened my mouth and closed it. I wiped the dark hair strands off my eyes and smoothed my short beard. My eyes traveled to Fulcher, who looked away, happy to let me choose our course of action. I nodded carefully. 'You once told me you need men like me to deal with men like him. And this is what I shall be. A tool for your house. It is not honorable, but as you said, I'm a Roman now, and your cause is just.'

'Peregrini,' he corrected. 'A non-citizen, but that will change. Like it was with your father after he saved Augustus in Hispania. And for a just cause?' he smiled like a ghost. 'The victors shall determine what was and was not a just cause. Kill him on the road back to the army. And you will give Segestes this,' he told me. 'This is important.' He handed me a thin scroll with sealed ends. It felt heavy and official.

'Yes,' I told him and nodded, my eyes twinkling.

'You will not ask what it is?' he asked with some irritation but waved the notion away and explained. 'River Visurgis is one wide, deep river to cross. It takes preparation and ships to get over the damned thing, and the enemy will be there to make life miserable for us. We don't have the supplies to maneuver far and build and wait around, twiddling our thumbs. We have to be over the damned thing. Two to three smaller rivers form Visurgis, however, running from the southern woodlands, from the Hercynian wilds and these rivers come together in the lands Segestes and Sigimer share. There, I'm told; there are shallow fords across the three smaller rivers, and they allow for an easy fording to get to Sigimer's lands over the Visurgis. They will meet us there, at that ford. I am sure of it. This year, Armin has no more tricks to spend. All he wishes is to use the winter rebuilding and gathering new allies. I have a chance to make all that a dream if I capture him there. And I have to go over those fords.'

'And Segestes is already giving you food. Perhaps. And he might ...' I ventured and he nodded. *Segestes might not fight at all, leaving the Cherusci army. Or, he might pretend to fight, but abandon the army and leave it vulnerable,* I thought. 'I see. And you are bringing all your cavalry. All of it.'

'Yes, all of it,' he said happily. 'I should leave it here; harry the Sigambri into weeping desperation, but no. I want it. And I guess you guessed why, you devious little Marcomanni. They will have a job.'

'Yes, Drusus.'

'So, at Castra Flamma, you will escort the bastard Antius there, let him feed us and then speak with Segestes on your own. Do not fail me. This will save us a lot of blood. Perhaps my noble blood.' He punched me to make it clear he was joking.

'We wish to spare your thin, noble blood,' I said, and he grinned and crushed me in a hug.

He stared deep into my eyes. 'We live only this one time, Hraban. Guess what I dreamt of last night?'

'Your wife?' I hazarded a guess.

He frowned with suspicion, for apparently; he had, and he was as superstitious as any man. Then he shrugged and spoke. 'That, of course, for I am a man without a woman on a damned campaign. But this was different. I dreamt of lying on the bottom of a boat and the water around me was dark and still. It was not unpleasant, nor frightening, only somewhat sad and a sword was laid on my chest, my hands folded across the hilt, but even the weapon felt meaningless. There were low hanging, pale green leaves of spring rustling in the wind, and I suppose it would have been chilly, had I been alive. But I was dead.'

'Lord ... Drusus' I breathed, my face pale from such a terrible omen.

'The Parcae will spin our life's threat out for us, and should Morta take me, I want it to mean something. Help me, Hraban, to meet my foes and be my sword in the dark. Perhaps if you do well enough, it might be so that my wife and I die happily in our bed, old and senile one day far in the future. The dream was a warning; Hraban, and I shall heed it. So go and make a dream slayer of yourself.' He pulled himself on the horse and rode away.

Fulcher's face was ashen gray, and he did not smile nor sing. He stared at me, and I knew he had had a sight. I cursed his sights and then clapped his back, and we rode through the lands that had belonged to the Bructeri but were now Roman.

At least for that summer.

CHAPTER 3

Wr hile the army marched east, the cavalry rode out on the flanks. The Thracian and Batavi alae were ranging everywhere, burning, killing, and enslaving. The slavers following the army grew rich in human flesh, and the enemy suffered horribly. While staring at a burning village with formerly fine halls, now blazing across a wide field, I could only wonder at what point one stopped calling them enemies rather than victims.

'They'll survive,' said the foppish prafectus Gnaeus Calpurnius Piso, leader of the Syrian and Parthian auxilia unit, forever lost in the west after accompanying Augustus home years past. His men were firing sagitta at some young Bructeri warriors gazing on at the destruction of their village from the edge of the wood. One such man screamed piercingly, and Gnaeus bit unhappily into his apple. 'They lost hundreds, but they will come back and collect and save what they can. They hid most of their skeletal cows in the deep woods anyway, and no sane man goes after them in there. Liable to get eaten if you go under those boughs.' He gazed at the deep woods covering the retreat of the Bructeri warriors, who were dragging a wounded boy with them, their colorful shields flashing. A Syrian rode after them. 'Idiot,' he said happily as if watching a play in the

Theater of Marcellus. 'Going to get eaten. I didn't like that one much anyway. Farts and laughs like a hyena.'

'What is a hyena?' I asked him as the Syrian was pulling an arrow, grinning foolishly as he guided his horse forward.

'Never mind,' he told me. 'He is gone. Dead. Want to bet?'

'No, thank you. How many can you spare?' I said with some worry. His horse archers were very useful, but growing fewer.

He chuckled. 'He will be a useful example. And I like the Parthians better this week anyway, and he just gave me a reason to berate the Syrian bastards.' His men were archers in chainmail, carrying powerful composite bows and were beastly killers the lot. They had saved us from the Tencteri once though I had thought I was doing them a favor. Gnaeus might look and sound like a wastrel, but he was a fabulously brilliant soldier.

A scream came out of the woods, and I could see some dozen Parthians laugh at their Syrian comrades, who had just lost one of theirs. 'Mars give me only men of one tribe to command. Or rather get the lot killed so I can go home,' he cursed. 'I better get the slaves moving. We will travel at speed now that the ships are again bringing some supplies.'

It was true.

Ships had been supplying the army soon after we left Alisio. There was not much, but the situation was slowly repairing itself, and we would be able to march instead of scavenging the vegetable gardens of the enemy. But it was nowhere near enough for a campaign that should breach the wide lands of Sigimer.

There was no sign of Antius yet. And so, we rode on.

It took five more days for all opposition of the Luppia valley to crash totally. The Bructeri and the Marsi, with some of the Usipetes, rode to us as the army was heading for Castra Flamma. They sued for peace, giving hostages, including the children and wife of poor, brave Wodenspear and Drusus marched east with relative peace on the northern banks of Luppia. But no Cherusci approached us, and none of the Sigambri from the south, and I saw many emotions in the face of Drusus. He was, I think, both relieved and enraged. He desired the surrender of the Sigambri and Maelo, but only the heads of the Cherusci. A day before Castra Flamma, Drusus sent the remains of the XVIII Legion to ravage Sigambri lands, which had already suffered heavily under the Ubii. Later, we got news that dreaded Maleo, Baetrix, and Varnis had fled across to the river and fought to spare Sigambri lands from the Ubii and the XVIII, but many villages were burned anyway. Drusus was tired of the Sigambri resistance. The decade-long battle to strangle off the most quarrelsome of Roman enemies was growing tedious, and he wanted a peaceful, cowed frontier for whatever it was he would have to face next. Rome and his stepfather Augustus? Further wars east? The Sigambri had no wish for peace.

So they would burn.

Soon, we saw the Castra Flamma. Its fires glowed far in the horizon on the night of the last camp and men were chatting excitedly around the temporary forts the legions always built at the end of the day's march.

'Food. Then a few days of rest and repairs,' Chariovalda confirmed happily as I helped dig a fossa for the temporary camp. 'Flamma is a large fort with thick walls and they have sent vexillations south and north. They are well prepared. A sort of a harbor is being built as well. So, you will go out for our patron?' he asked me, mirth playing in his eyes. 'I hear you will take your Fulcher and some ten of my men. And they told me to give you men who keep their mouths shut.'

'Impossible, with the Batavi,' I grinned as I climbed out of the ditch. 'Either they are gorging on something or complaining.'

He snorted and continued with a serious voice. 'I have some thin wolves who will help you out. I hear there will be someone joining us? Someone we dislike? Yes? So I suppose we need to bring a rope.'

'We do not like this man,' I confirmed. 'And we will need the rope. Thin and still very strong. Painful, but something that gets it done.'

He frowned. 'Do you think I make ropes for a living? I'll tell them to take anything they have. Antius might be too heavy for any rope, though?' Chariovalda said with a thin grin. He knew whom we talked about.

'This bastard might be, indeed,' I said with burning hatred. 'In all honesty, I don't care how he dies. But his corpse should be hidden.'

Chariovalda blanched. 'I doubt it is needed. Too much trouble. The land will be riddled with corpses anyway when the army heaves through it.' His eyes were glinting with Hel's fire under his eyebrows. He knew about the plan, as well. He would. He was a client to Drusus and his friend. Had been for long years. He nodded at the Castra Flamma where torches flared in the distance. 'Drusus will take two legions east soon, so we had better move as soon as Antius gets his lazy ass here. He will be surprised, no doubt.'

'Have you seen Cornix?' Fulcher asked, chewing on the gristle of a bone.

'No, the half-faced piece of cancerous shit is gone since he led that Leuthard creature to Castra Vetera.'

'He was not with Leuthard when I killed him,' I said unhappily. 'We had better be ready for him.'

'I'll send good men with you. They know how to think and use spear. You need more than lumps of muscle,' he assured me. 'Be careful, Hraban.'

'I'm always careful,' I said and endured his mocking laughter. I groped at my chest, where the wound given by Leuthard was slowly healing and my broken finger was slowly healing as well. I didn't look like a careful man. Chariovalda nodded and looked away. I loved him, the Batavi noble, and friend of Drusus. He was my only real ally in addition to Fulcher and Cassia.

Next morning the buccina and the trumpets sounded, men gleefully ate what they had, for they would have more very soon. The legions marched the final stretch of the muddy river. We could see the hazy hills and deep green forests separating the lands of Luppia River from the lands of the Cherusci and even the Chatti to the southeast. The men witnessed ships traveling back to Castra Vetera with the sick and wounded of the I Germanica Legion, men, who had been fighting the Sigambri in small skirmishes ever since the castra was built. The marching XIX and V Alaudae cheered the wounded, who cheered back as they were being rowed back in the navis lusoria craft of the Roman navy based in Moganticum and Castra Vetera. The army arrived, built more temporary castra and set up to rest.

That evening, Fulcher nodded to the east, and I nodded. 'How far that road takes a man, I wonder?' Fulcher breathed. Seeing the vast, misty hills and deep green woods stretching to the east made one uncertain. It was the unknown horizon of new things, strange people and myths. Crossing the huge rivers of Visurgis and perhaps Albis? No Roman legion had been that far before. Few Germani of the Rhenus River had seen them and I despaired, for Lif was somewhere out there, and I had to find her.

And these were the lands where Odo's family was spawned. In Gulldrum. *This was their land. Their home*, I thought glumly.

Fulcher grunted and apparently read my mind, scratching at lice. 'Didn't your family come from far Gothonia? These are just like any hills, the trees do not walk, and rivers are composed of water, rocks, and scaly things. We will find her.' I wondered at his astuteness and nodded careful thanks.

By evening, the loudest and most rebellious of the silvery soldiers began seeing signs of doom everywhere, and complaints were whispered in the darkness. The Cherusci was a vast nation, famed, old as time, and it could be seen even in the faces of men like Saturninus, the new legate of the XIX Legion, that they had reservations about going to fight a man like Armin with depleted legions and the dregs of the auxilia. Leading his people, in the lands where Romans were like lost lambs? What could Armin and Sigimer do? *Much,* I thought.

Unless we turned Segestes.

Perhaps he did not need much turning, for he was a shifty rogue, and Drusus was right.

That day Drusus mingled with the restless men and laughed with them, belittling the dangers, acting as if he had few cares in the world. He trusted his troops, and they loved him like a fat child loves a cone of honey. They would die rather than let go of him, and even the most depressed lifted their chin at his approach. He shared their meals, made fun of their misfortunes and told them harrowing tales of his wife, all of which I thought were lies, for he truly loved her. He promised them more supplies.

It meant Antius was to arrive soon.

Men rested for a few days, repairing and re-equipping, and the army numbered around nine thousand with the auxilia included, the legions each around three to four thousand, having suffered greatly at Armin's brilliant battle. It was early Quintilis, and the weather was still beautiful. The campaign would go on.

The next morning, Antius arrived. There were many ships rowing out of the foggy river.

'It's him,' Fulcher told me with spite as we sat on our horses in the morning light.

'Yea,' I agreed with barely suppressed hatred as we saw the bastard Roman negotiatore amble down a gangplank of a light navis lusoria. Some mariners were helping him down, and he smiled at them happily, his heavy jowls hanging. I had seen him the day grandfather and mother had died. After that event, he had helped father take over the Marcomanni. So had I. But his crime ran deeper. He was a foe to me, to Drusus. I hated him with an unbridled passion. He was not wearing his customary, sweaty toga, but a huge tunic and sturdy caligae and that made him seem somehow more dangerous. He was more than a fop and a corpulent schemer. He could get his hands dirty. 'Let's go down there and eyeball the bastard,' I said icily and Fulcher nodded and let me lead on. I pulled on the famous, fabulous Athenian bronze helmet Tudrus the Older had given me. The Quadi chief was my father's victim, his thousand refugees holed with the Sigambri. I hoped he had survived the battle, for he had been there with his three sons, my former friends. *Perhaps not former*, I hoped. I had not killed any of the Quadi in the battle, so there should be no feuds.

We saw Drusus walk to Antius with some officers and many civilians of his officia, all of whom were gesturing excitedly for the fat trade ships approaching the harbor, save for one, which stayed out. Antius greeted Drusus with humility and fawning and Drusus made his military tribune and Questor take stock of the new ships with Antius while he said nothing to the man, who was surprised by the coldness. Antius fidgeted; Drusus let him sweat and then, finally they spoke at length, and to my satisfaction, I saw the eyes of Antius go as large as plates as his face turned to stare at me. He was shaking his head empathetically as he gestured for me and then, finally I saw the fight go out of him. Instead, he brooded, his mind going over the many implications of the commands of Drusus. He bowed stiffly to our commander, and Drusus gave terse orders to a scribe, who set about writing down lines for Antius to deliver to Segestes. Drusus removed his entourage from the harbor and left. He quickly nodded at me, gave me a small, vicious smile, and I nodded back. 'We leave this evening,' I told Fulcher darkly. 'Go and tell Chariovalda to get the men ready.'

'Yes, of course,' he said with no surprise. 'Are you in the command?'

'I'm going to command, yes,' I told him with a nod.

'Gods help our poor bones,' he joked, and as I did not find him funny, he coughed.

I continued. 'We move this evening under the cover of the night. And now I'm going down there.'

'You are not going to do anything ...' Fulcher began and cocked an eyebrow at me, but I shook my head. 'Good. You know your part in the act. Don't let him goad you.'

'Thank you, Mother,' I laughed at him. 'I would love to take him to the woods and eviscerate him slowly there. I wanted to do that after he told me everything about Father and his plans and the part he had been playing in the game. But I can do that later, can't I? I will, in fact. Now, as you go to Chariovalda, go also to another man,' I whispered to him at length, and he nodded vigorously. 'Can you do that?' I asked.

'I suppose so,' Fulcher said unhappily. 'If he says no?'

'He won't,' I assured him. 'If he tries, tell him he will be sent to the furthest, shittiest hole of an outpost, far in the lands of Parthia if he fails.' Fulcher nodded and went away, frowning.

I rode down, and Antius saw me come. His eyes were in thin slits as he regarded my descent, but he did not seem afraid. Finally, I stood there, with my helmet on my head, my eyes shaded and tilted my head at him. He nodded at me as a young Questor was pulling at him, and Antius turned to deal with him. There was a quarrel broiling over the supplies. The questor had an imperious air about him as he nodded at the ships. 'Wine. I hear there was wine, plenty of it in Castra Vetera. There were many amphorae of that Gaulish shit in Alisio, but you bring *none* with you?'

Antius dismissed his words with a wave, but he also had a nervous stutter, while his eyes were glancing at me. 'There is *no* wine to be had. The wine *your* legates hoped to enjoy here in this damned hole in the woods was indeed something we once possessed. I'm not sure who told you there was some left in Castra Vetera? That is curious, very curious indeed, since I come from Castra fucking Vetera and you do not. What was there is gone. Now the Usipetes tribesmen are gleefully enjoying it, and I think they deserve it since *your* soldiers failed to protect it. It was looted from the warehouses that were supposed to be kept safe for us humble merchants. I wonder. I do wonder at your near accusations, as I think I have not failed at all, but you have totally.'

The young man just shrugged. 'Garum? There is no fish sauce either. You bring us flour and weapons, but no luxuries. Men need luxuries in war!' he said, a noble clearly used to such finer things.

Antius snorted and put his thumbs under his ample belt, his belly heaving. 'It is true. Men need luxuries. The Usipetes are men and enjoy your luxuries! As I just told you. Though I am not sure they kept the garum, as they hate it. No doubt they thought it horse piss.'

'But—' the Questor fought on stubbornly.

Antius tore his tunic in anguish. 'Look around, man! I'm not hiding any under my tunic! I'm not carrying these luxuries with me! This is it! I spent the whole miserable spring collecting, no, purchasing such supplies. Sometimes at my *own* expense. There was plenty of wine, weapons, horses, and mules, from Gaul, from Germania! There were to be benna to transport it, castra to hold it all in. There were supposed to be loot and cows from the Bructeri. But they were waiting for you. More, they took most all we had. And the Gauls? They are not selling what they need to survive this winter. Would you? We had what we had. It's gone. It is most all gone. And now you want luxuries! Why didn't you guard them! Usipetes are not likely to pay for them! You ruin me!' he cried, eyeing the Questor as a starving child would a glutton.

Men chuckled around him, and the Questor cursed, still giving a token of a fight. 'The pila. Why are there so few pila here on the list? And arrows?' He asked, still looking around the mooring ships to find even a single amphora of wine.

'Pila! Pila! The pila adore the flesh of the Usipetes! Remember? They attacked, the soldiers used the pila, and they are bent or broken! You have the armor smiths with the legions, the weapon experts! Immunes of skill! Why will you not straighten the pila you used? Did you wish for me to go yank them off the Usipetes flesh?' Antius asked with icy derision.

A nearby younger Tribune lost his patience and charged to the aid of the beaten questor. 'If the pila were used to repel the fucking Usipetes, then why don't you have wine? Or garum? Surely, an average Usipetes with a pilum in his gut does not run very fast and far and certainly, such a rancid creature does not carry away the wine with a pilum in his ass? Don't you have any of the Gaulish one at least? Biturica? What is that last ship doing?' he asked, eyeing a fat trade ship keeping out of shore.

'Ah, they have a sick man aboard. Cannot risk putting him to the shore, might infect the whole army and then you would fry with fever. No doctor can cure fever. The ship carries flour, just that, I think,' Antius said with a worried look. 'They will unload it tomorrow, maybe.'

The Tribune was also wavering, and so I decided to take part in the discussion. 'It's very low on the water, Antius,' I said, dismounting and stepping up from the ring of onlookers. His eyes looked like animal's eyes as he stared at me with hatred.

'Hraban, well, well. Guarding the horses? Or shepherding prisoners? Why don't you go back to that duty?' he said smoothly, but there was a string of sweat on his brow.

'It looks like it has a lot of weight, I stated again, spying a man moving an amphora.

'Ah, the young wolf who does not understand ships. Let the Tribune and the young man do their work. They will pay me, and then we shall discuss our mutual trip,' he said laughing, trying to dismiss me.

'We know ships, and those are not carrying flour,' I said with a growl.

He stammered. 'Yes, of course. You know ships as well as you speak Latin, eh?' He turned to the young officer. 'I do have some specialties for you that might interest you, but only after we are done here—'

The Questor, apparently emboldened by my support threw down the scroll with lists of packaged goods for the army. 'You work as one of the negotiators and traders for the army. Your job is to supply it. You feed us, but you do not make the men happy. You sailing this shit up here will make them satisfied, but they deserve something more than flour as they march east. Why didn't the Usipetes take that? Flour. They took fucking fish oil, you claim, but not the flour,' the Questor snarled.

The Tribune nodded. 'Pay the man. Half.'

The Questor shook his head, clearly disgusted at having to pay at all and pulled out a pouch of coins. He hefted it in his hand and viciously opened it, pouring only some silver and gold out, leaving the rest inside. Antius opened his mouth but closed it fast, apparently thinking better about fighting a lost cause. Also, the last ship, I was sure, was loaded to the brim with precious wine, and he would sell it on the side, for the legions carried heaps of treasure from the fallen enemy, mainly rings. It would make him a lot of coin in the end.

Antius took a long breath and walked over to me. 'Well, Oath Breaker. That's what they all call you now. I sat with the Chauci the other week, and there was a pretty, young boy singing about you. Not the sort of song you would like to hear, I am sure. Would drive you mad as a slapped hornet. But you do look good, like a warrior,' he told me while eyeing the ships getting unloaded.

I spat at his feet and got his full, unbelieving attention. 'We are going on a trip.'

'And why are you coming, I wonder,' Antius huffed, shuffling away from my spittle. 'His lordship was most adamant that a barbarian who hates me should provide me with an escort to Segestes. And yes, I can find him. I know the woods and the villages ahead and can likely find where he is holed at. But you? Useless as a dick without balls, but dangerous to me, maybe.'

'Coming from a man with no cock nor balls to fight his fights up front, that is quite an observation. You know what Antius is. I was to die when you told me about Maroboodus and Drusus. You played with a caged wolf, and the wolf is no longer caged. One day you will see the beast in the woods, and you will not have a friend in the world. But not today,' I lied.

'As for the reasons why I'm coming along? He needs a man he can trust. He does not wish to starve when he goes out to give the Cherusci battle.'

'Ah,' Antius smirked. 'You are to make sure I do my duty, eh? Fine. And you are bringing Batavi to guard me, no doubt?'

'Yes, they will suffice,' I told him coldly. 'He told me to keep you alive. It is an insufferable test and yes, he is testing me. He wants to see if I can be trusted with matters that are more important later on. He does not trust you, Antius. You know it. He thinks there are many plots being hatched against him out there, men moving in the shadows to kill him. He thinks you are a fat, useless thief, a liar, and a traitor, but he also needs you for this particular job. His campaign is in peril, and you can save it.'

'You are his lapdog, are you?' Antius said softly. 'Must be irksome not to be able to filet me, eh? And you will be a lord in his service, one day? Hopefully you will not fail his … test.' His eyes flashed. 'Here. This will change his life. And yours.' He showed me a scroll.

I grabbed it.

'What are you …' he choked with a panicked, high-pitched voice, trying to grab it back from my hands, but I pointed a finger at him, and he calmed down. I ripped it open, breaking the seal. Antius sucked in his breath, his face red and then visibly calmed himself. 'Do you understand what it says?' he asked snidely. 'I can translate it. Of course, it would be embarrassing to open a scroll meant for another and then ask the person you stole it from to tell you what—'

'No need, I get the idea,' I said as my eyes went over the text, thanking Woden for Marcus Romanus, the exile who had taught me Latin. 'It says it is from a man called Verrius Flaccus—'

'A scribe in the employment of Augustus,' Antius interrupted happily. 'This man is instructing the golden grandsons of Augustus in many things. But he also writes letters when his lordship requires it though Augustus often conveys his letters. It says—' Antius explained, and I interrupted him in my turn.

'How is it you know of it? The contents?' I asked him.

'I …' he stammered.

'I'm sure a slimy thing like you can unseal and reseal anything, worm,' I laughed at him. 'You could probably steal a god's ball hairs and sell them back to him as a beard.'

He bowed, not ashamed in the least. 'Many skills are useful in this world and unsealing scrolls not the least of them, boy.'

I read the text and spoke, my voice dripping with boredom. 'It warns Drusus not to cross to the Cherusci lands,' I said. 'Why is Augustus sending such—'

Antius was wringing his hands, snapping his joints, bored. 'Drusus is here, exercising the imperium of Augustus. Augustus can do what he will with Drusus and *his* armies, Raven. He owns the armies. To be exact, he rules the provinces the armies belong to. He is the master of men of violence, and Drusus is only one of these men. He was unhappy with the way things went in the Thing of Drusus. He has heard rumors of the losses inflicted on the legions by the young Cherusci. Now, the war continues. Augustus does not approve of this.'

I threw the scroll at his feet. 'I doubt the old man dare test his strength in this matter. And we are going this evening.'

Antius smiled as he picked up the scroll, though he was nervous. 'Does not dare? He dares. The more Nero Claudius defies him, the more determined Augustus becomes. I think even our young general sees this. Perhaps we won't travel, after all.'

'Unfortunately,' I grinned, 'we need the food, no matter if the army marches or not. Usipetes took it, I seem to recall.'

Antius stopped at that, his face ashen white. 'Be careful, Hraban, not to choose the wrong allies again. You are running very low on them, are you not? Perhaps you should just disappear?'

'I have my swords as allies, and you know I can crawl up from Hel, alone and naked if I need to. You helped temper me to such a fine edge, didn't you? Take care, Antius and meet us at the Porta Decumana this evening. Do take your scroll to him, but I'm sure you shall be there nonetheless. And the army shall march, for the men love him. And his causes.'

He nodded carefully, anger and doubt playing on his fat face. 'Fine. If that is so, pack up some food and water. No Legionnaire gear on the men, none. No words of Latin are to be uttered. Best you don't say anything at all out there and that shall be a relief, I tell you. Make sure all your merry boys know this. We shall ride due east, follow the trade route. The very same route the army will surely be using as they go east. They could cross the great Visurgis, but it is steep and harsh to build on, so there are three rivers to the southeast from here, shallower rivers. They call the first one Bhugnos, the Buck. Then there is Mödasg, the Angry One and finally Weihnan, the Holy Water. We shall stop at a village near Bhugnos, and there we shall wait.'

'What do they call Visurgis?' I asked.

'I don't know that. I am no teacher. I'm your enemy. I just told you all I know, and I hope you won't get us killed by your foolishness,' he noted. 'You have a history of bad choices.'

'We shall see, Antius the Fat, what you can accomplish with your scrolls and lies. But yes, the army will tramp for Bhugnos,' I said and decided he would not appear at the gates. He was very suspicious. If he did, I thought, he would be prepared. But so was I. I turned to go. 'Go and try to spare yourself the trip. Tell Drusus I opened it up for him.'

'I will,' he called after me. 'And we shall see where we shall all travel. Soon.'

CHAPTER 4

The men were killers.

There were nine of them, wearing little armor, armed with Germani shields, oblong and square, made of sturdy wood frames and thick leather, and painted with fantastic figures of moons, stars, and animals. Some were punctured; others were spattered with mud and blood. They were taken from the slain. All the men had cudgels, axes, and some held bows. Most carried the typical Germani spear with short iron tip, a framae. Fulcher had his heavy cavalry spear, and I had Nightbright girted on my hip and a round shield. None of us had chain mail, Roman gear, and helmets. Grimwald, a Decurion of the 2nd Batavi nodded at me as I approached, holding his hand out and I grasped it. We did not speak as the guards near the gates stared at the ragtag band, whispering.

Then we waited.

The sun went down, and stars twinkled. I was fiddling with the scroll Drusus had given me and hoped Antius had not managed to swindle himself out of the trip.

He had not.

Fulcher slapped my hand and pointed at the shadows of the harbor. There, a man on a huge horse trundled closer. He had two tall servants and three horses full of gear, and it was Antius indeed. He wore a heavy cape and had a pair of Roman pugiones, daggers on his wide belt.

'I take it Drusus is going east?' I asked him sweetly, and he did not answer but rode past us. I pushed my scroll into a bag and rode after him. 'Hold!' I yelled, and he stopped reluctantly.

'I recall you wanted to go, Hraban, this very night?' he asked sweetly. 'The night does not dance and tarry to your pleasure. We going or dallying here?'

'What is all that?' I asked, pointing at the horses and the two Gauls accompanying him.

'My gear,' he hissed, exasperated. 'I'm a to be a lord of the Chauci, this time, and no lord of the rich Chauci will travel like a beggar.'

'And what else?' I asked, feeling reluctant to let him take anything but his ass east. 'Comforts rather than gear we need?'

'Drusus is in need of food,' he said spitefully. 'It costs money. I am taking a fortune of coin with me. Most all Drusus had in his war chest.'

'Fine,' I said. 'But you don't need your damned rugs and wine.'

'My rug? Ah,' he said, displeased. He had used one to sit in the woods when I saw him the very first time, disdaining the discomforts of Germania. 'You want me to sleep on the ground as you do? Is that important to you, Hraban?'

'I've slept in a cage smeared with mice shit for you, Antius,' I told him and rode close to the packhorses. 'So yes, it is important for me. And I want nothing extra with us. Nothing.' The Gauls, two large, wiry men scowled at me, but I growled at them as I pulled Nightbright and poked at the gear.

'Fine. Leave that one,' Antius said with a hurt, tired voice, and one of the horses, laden with comforts was left with a slave. 'Together on the road, finally,' Antius whispered. 'Shall we?' I nodded and led the way.

We rode hard, and I was surprised by the hardiness of the fat man. He glanced at my wondering eyes and shrugged. 'I've been a soldier in my time, Raven. I have seen the world. I've ridden sturdy camels in Numidia, huge elephants in Parthia and suffered my share of discomforts before I found my place.'

'You served twenty-five years in the army? You look around forty,' I asked him, interested despite hating him.

'No, only fifteen, Hraban. I had talents that were needed elsewhere,' he whispered.

'Are you in the army still? Though not in one of Drusus's.'

His eyes widened, and then he looked away. 'You are a most perceptive bastard, are you not? But that does not matter. Here I am but a negotiatore and your charge, am I not?' I nodded at him and the Batavi around me gave him dark looks, for they were no fools. We would not underestimate him. He was not only a spy, but a soldier. A clever, dangerous one.

The night ride took us far from the camps, and we took to trails that were well traveled. We passed a Roman patrol coming back home and then soon, there were nothing but shadowy trees ahead and around us. The night was full of sounds, an owl hooting, our horses neighing, trees swaying and their leaves rustling sorrowfully. The hills were dark around us, and when the sun peeked, we found ourselves on top of a tall hill. We slept, and in the afternoon, we took to the lower ground between valleys, the game trails running south and east.

We encountered Cherusci or even Chatti, often hunting in pairs and hailed them somberly. Antius would approach them and trade news in a perfect Chauci dialect. They nodded at him, pointing around with their framae, and so we traveled on. We encountered some poor peasants, herding noble horses. He spoke for a time; they nodded, and he spoke some more. Finally, he pulled out something bright, then another such bright thing and handed them to a pale young man who took them eagerly. Then the youngster rode off on a skinny horse.

'What was that?' I asked him when he turned to continue the trek east.

'I set a messanger pigeon flying, Raven. He knows someone who knows where they are,' Antius told me while thinking deep. 'You need not bother yourself with such intricate matters, Raven. Let me do the thinking part and you just concentrate on brooding.'

Dog, I thought and we trekked on.

We skirted great settlements and major roads and so it went on until a few days later we found ourselves staring across a field at a great river. The field had been burned to the woods sometime years past. It had been a field of barley and wheat, and our horses nibbled on wild crops as we stood there. Antius was speaking with a rich looking Cherusci, seated on a large horse. The man had a long beard streaked with gray and was crippled in the leg. He was gesturing widely, and finally, Antius bowed to him and rode to us, reluctantly.

Antius glanced at me, and our day-long silence was broken. 'Your lord—'

'And your commander,' I reminded him.

'And my lord commander, urban praefectus Nero Claudius Drusus and the sun behind our victorious armies was right. Armin and Sigimer and even Segestes have summoned some ten thousand men to defend Bhugnos and the fords. They aim to keep our Roman boys out of Visurgis River gaus, and if they do, they will claim that was a victory. They hope to fight a more aggressive war next year. Inguiomerus is busy in the east, far in the east where your kinsmen Suebi are again pressing across Albis.'

'And Segestes is near?' I asked him.

He pointed his fat finger. He trailed the great green and blue River Visurgis stretching from north to south and then the myriad of rivers that made it up to our southeast. 'He is camped across Visurgis near the bit of delta heaped at the confluences of the rivers. They are camped separately until the Roman army comes here. It will be tough for Drusus to break through the ford. But he is a bullhead.' His eyes briefly traveled my gear, and I knew he thought we had a plan. He smiled, but said nothing about that. 'There,' he added and pointed a finger at haze rising from the bank of Visurgis. 'That is a village called Oddglade. And we shall wait there for Segestes.'

'I don't like it. We wait outside it and only enter when he does,' I said suspiciously.

'I agree,' Fulcher added.

Antius stared at him for a moment and then shook his head at me. 'Tell the thick skulled fuck to be quiet, Hraban. Now, listen. Segestes is the son of greater lords of the Cherusci. His line is ancient, and he carries the favor of the gods. He is one of the three men who can be the thiuda of the

62

Cherusci. The Cherusci are the power of the north. And you, a near damned peasant expect him to come if we are skulking outside? As if he was a common criminal? No, we go in, respect the lord, trust his well wishes, sleep in his beds, drink the wine and wait for his pleasure.'

'And if he is not interested in helping us in our plight and only wants to take the gold and silver? And our heads?' Fulcher growled.

'Then we need not worry about the silver and the gold and will go to the afterlife poor,' Antius grinned. 'But he is too greedy to settle for this paltry sum when he might get so much more. And I do believe you are to give him a deal that will make him rich and affluent in these lands.' He patted the bag on my horse, laughed hugely and whipped his horse. He had touched my scroll, and I cursed him.

CHAPTER 5

We rode to the village, passing halls and shacks on the way. Dogs were barking, we were grimy from the trip and our shields were dusty. We were not in a great mood, but the thought of foaming ale and a warm hall gave us the strength to be polite and patient. Some men approached us carefully, and I nodded grimly at the largest one of them, a man with a huge hasta spear. His beard was dark brown, and he stood on the road leading to a multitude of halls and sheds. I approached him. 'Hail,' I told him. 'Donor's blessing to you.'

'May Woden's spear Gungir give you strength,' the man said cautiously and squinted at us. 'Where are you off to?'

'Why, we hope for hospitality. We are to meet a man here,' I told him.

He laughed roughly. 'Hospitality is a gift most men deserve, but I want to make sure you are like most men. What man are you meeting?'

Antius rode forward. 'Your Lord, first. And then his lord, the mighty Segestes,' Antius nodded respectfully, pushing in front of me. 'Take us to your Lord Gerlach. We know each other.'

'Lord Gerlach is dead,' the man said brusquely. 'He knows nothing now, except the kisses of the Valkyries. Died in the battle beyond the hills. Died defending Rochus as they broke the Roman lines.'

'I have heard of the battle Rochus fell in,' I said and nodded reverently. 'We did not quite make it to Armin. And we had to flee the Batavi after.' My rogues nodded and spat at the mention of the Batavi.

The warrior before us echoed their sentiment and nodded. The leader spoke. 'His hall is half empty and you are to wait there. Gerlach's son is serving Segestes in the mustering. Sigimer is our thiuda now for this year, and they are—'

'Yes,' I agreed. 'We will likely join the army.'

'To fight the southern dogs,' the warrior concluded and tapped his finger on his spear, a suspicious look conquering his face. 'So how come you are to meet here and not at the rivers camp? In fact, are you sure you did not flee the battle earlier and now try to restore your honor by lies? I doubt Segestes would come here to meet scoundrels such as yourself.' Men were emerging to stare at us. Some had shields; all had framea. There were thirty of them, and they had dogs.

I jumped down from my horse and stood face to face with the man. 'Are you calling us cowards?'

'I'm not sure what I'm calling you,' he whispered as his bloodshot eyes took stock of our weapons. 'Strange you are. We have men here to guard the land and the halls, but you should be at war.'

'We meet Segestes here,' I hissed at him. 'He is coming. We captured Roman gold from their greedy slavers, killed Roman soldiers doing it, and I do hope to become a warlord of his with that gold. If I take it to his camp, Sigimer might want a cut.' I looked at Fulcher, who nodded and kicked the chest on a packhorse. It jingled happily, and the horse nearly bolted.

The man frowned, apparently thinking about taking the gold but relented, knowing Segestes would find the coin no matter if our bones were lost. Such an amount of coin would not easily disappear. 'The hall. There are servants and slaves to take care of the horses. Do not go to the northern side of the building. There is a party of wounded men there, resting.'

I bowed my head, and we rode through the silent groups of men and children, who had come to gape at us. Antius chuckled. 'Oddglade. They trade here in Roman coins and know the sound of it. That man is Ketill and a famous thief in Gerlach's former employ. Had better be careful with the chest and pray Segestes is coming.

We settled in and waited.

Antius enjoyed the food; venison and fat trout and so did the Batavi, and I drank ale and ate modestly, too nervous to enjoy the feast. Fulcher sat with me silently until I got up and went to the door that took one to the stable part of the hall. I turned to look at the shadows beyond the fire pit and saw three well-armed Cherusci staring at the merry company from the doors of the sleeping area. Fulcher grunted. 'Must be an important lord. Some of them have chain mail.'

'Yes,' I agreed and went to the stable. There stood our horses and then a dozen more, for it was a large, prosperous hall, and the stables were spacious with very well tended stalls. There were fine warhorses, well bred and tall, unlike normal Germani horses that sometimes looked like large hounds. I growled at a thin, bushy-haired slave who was startled from his sleep in the corner and stepped to one of the horses and let it nuzzle me. Then I spied wounds on its legs, healing. 'Been to the battle?' I asked the man. The slave was keen enough to smell profit. He kept his mouth shut and smiled.

Fulcher flipped him a copper coin.

He looked at it and shrugged. I put my hand on Nightbright's pommel, and he brightened. 'They were indeed. The lord who came from the great battle had to rest here. Near death, he was.'

'Many lords are near death.' I laughed and nodded. 'And his name?'

'He shared no name and had no standard,' the slave told us.

'But do you know his name?' Fulcher said.

'Yes,' the man agreed with a small smile, his hand out.

But at that moment, a great number of riders arrived at the yard and the slave blanched and ran out. In the hall, I could hear benches screeching as men pushed up. Fulcher and I walked to the door and headed for the middle of the hall. A warrior in a steel helm popped his head through the door, then Ketill came in. 'Stand at ready. The Lord Segestes is here.' His voice sounded terribly disappointed, and his eyes went to the chest that was placed next to Antius.

Ten men entered.

They were warriors, well dressed in practical leathers, shiny chain, and rich furs, most wore helmets, and their shields were painted with stags. They spread out in a semi-circle and silence reigned. Grimwald and the Batavi sat down and were soon taking swigs of their ale, their blond beards foamed, but they were near their weapons.

Then, the man I had seen in the Thing of Drusus, the failed meeting of the tribes before the war, entered. I had hard time deciding if he was fatter than Antius. He was red of face, his red and blond beard was plaited in silver, and he carried a huge, round silvery shield of Roman make, sculpted with figures of animals and embossed by beasts, especially that of a snake-haired woman; the Medusa. It was far too heavy to be used in battle by him, but it was a gorgeous thing, and his expensive sword with a golden hilt suited the shield well as a companion. His clothing was Roman and Germani, rich and embroidered with silver thread. His eyes took me in, then Antius, and the men. After him, came a champion, and I knew the man and groaned.

It was Ragwald, the wide-faced, ring mailed brute of dark hair and irascible demeanor.

He had been drunk in the Thing of Drusus, and I had struck him down. Then I had pissed on him in front of the lords of the Germani.

He stared at me with an open mouth.

I grinned, gathering bravery. He had boasted of having fought a hundred duels and even if just a part of that was true, I would be in trouble. I had my Woden given gift, the berserk rage, but most fights end badly for the less experienced. 'You!' he shouted thinly.

'Oh, you remember me,' I told him with a lopsided grin. 'After all, the last thing you might remember of Hraban was his cock over you and then the rain—'

'Hraban! The Oath Breaker! Gods' laugh, but this is my day!' he shouted hoarsely and swung out a huge two-handed ax. Segestes slapped a hand over his chest and other men grabbed his ringmail armor. The Batavi smirked at him, and I grabbed a horn of ale and took a long swig, staring at the barely constrained beast.

I saluted him. 'I had better drink more. My bladder is empty, and if the needs arise, I will empty it again on your flat face.'

'Well,' Segestes said with humor. 'You will not. Relax. I welcome my friend and the Raven.' He meant Antius and me. 'I heard an interesting tale not a day ago of Roman gold as a young man came to me in the camp. I was bored, the mosquitoes were making me crazy, and then I realized I could be feasting and making friends. And so I'm here.'

'I'd have words with you, Lord Segestes,' I told him with as much respect I could muster, which was not much.

'We shall have words,' he agreed. 'But first, we shall eat, feast, and make merry.' He ambled in and let Ketill give orders to the servants and slaves. Mead and ale were brought in from the cellars, cold meats as well, and I heard people yelling for more to be roasted. Antius brazenly walked to sit next to him, and there was no room left for me as Ragwald sat down on his other side with a huff, his feral eyes never leaving me. I shrugged and sat down with Fulcher to continue our meal though suddenly we both felt left out like naughty children given a lesser table at a feast. I gave Grimwald a sharp look, and he made a nearly imperceptible nod. We would be ready.

The day turned to evening, and the men enjoyed themselves.

Segestes was happy as he was chatting with Antius, now apparently about worldly matters for Segestes was Roman minded and yearned to hear of the lands beyond his borders. His lands were apparently very well stocked to help out our beleaguered troops. Ragwald was drunk by the time the sun had set, and he had not smiled once. 'He will be trouble,' said the sober Fulcher. 'I can smell it.'

'All I can smell is vomit,' I told him, for one of the Cherusci was throwing up by the wall into a bucket. The guards on the north door had not budged one bit, their eyes taking in the strange meeting. 'But I agree.'

Then, Antius got up, and Segetes sighed as he looked at me. The fat Roman left the corpulent Germani as he came to me and nodded gravely. He leaned down to me. 'So, Hraban. Tomorrow I will ride out to the Roman army and tell your Drusus the good news. I just bought us a month's worth of food and feed. And now he will discuss whatever it is Drusus wants to discuss.'

68

'Now?' I asked.

'Go, fool. And be polite. He might look luxurious, insolent, and ugly, but he is a lord and thinks deep. Make no mistakes that will cost us dearly,' he told me and went to sit at the end of the table. I got up and dragged the scroll of Drusus from my bag, avoiding the eyes of Antius that were sure to mock me. I felt clumsy and foolish, but I did manage to smile as I approached the Lord. He made an impatient motion with his thick hand, and I sat on a bench next to him.

The Lord was nodding at me sagely, and then he burped. He thunked his chest with his fist and smiled. 'Well. It is a while since you sat at your worthless brother's feet in the hall of Maroboodus. You have come a long way since. From a fool into a Roman. I do admire sensible choices, boy. You know where you belong now and can make a living for yourself. Your father loathed you. What does he do now?'

'I have no idea, Lord,' I answered. 'Are you not marrying Thusnelda to him to cement the alliance in war against Rome?' I asked him with a faint sneer. Father had once summoned many high lords to help him with his plans, and the fools did not know he would betray them to Rome after Drusus died. I did not bother educating him.

He giggled. 'What a strange world this is. That was an option, once. Now, perhaps not? I do not need Maroboodus's Germani alliance nor did I ever wish to fight Rome. I think you are here to give me something that might prevent such a marriage?'

'Yes, Lord. A strange world it is. And as you guessed, I'm here with a scroll.'

He stared at me for a time, his face featureless. Then he groaned. 'Well, must I beg for it? Dance and sing to receive it? Let me have it then,' he said with despair. 'I think I already committed myself to your Nero Claudius Drusus by selling him food, but Romans will go home after the war and I will remain and should my family find I made riches by keeping our enemy in fighting peak? I might learn to regret it. So whatever is in this scroll ... ' he said and grasped it off me, 'is likely agreeable should it also involve killing or capturing my fool brother Sigimer.'

'Yes, Lord. It will make your heart content,' I told him, and he nodded sagely. He opened up the scroll after sniffing it like a dog would excrement and then he settled over it, and I thought his eyesight might be terrible for he leaned in very close. He groped for some sausage as he read the lines and guzzled down rich mead, and I felt Ragwald's eyes on me as I ignored him.

He was nodding, and his finger was going over the words. 'I hear my damned nephew tried to get you to kill the young eagle.'

'He did,' I agreed. 'I did not.'

'And he had your daughter held? A baby, only a child, no?' he was chortling in apparent disgust.

'He did,' I said hollowly. 'Though he did not threaten to kill her.'

'And I hear there are men looking for her,' he told me. I stiffened and said nothing. I yearned for any news to be had of Lif. He glanced at me, annoyed. 'You wish to know?'

'Yes,' I said.

'These men live near our lands. Not all that far, in fact. And I know a man called Odo leads them. We, Sigimer that is, chased his men off our land weeks past. And I know he is after your baby, I do. I have spies with Sigimer, you see. Be happy! This Odo has not found her. The man and the baby escaped and are likely in the Godsmount. Now that is not a tall mountain, perhaps more a series of high hills but only the very keenest of vitka and völva know its secrets, so your Odo is stuck. They are holed in some nest of vipers now, brooding. She is safe,' he told me as if he had chased Odo's men singlehandedly off the land.

'Thank you,' I breathed, happy as a bird.

'Antius!' the fat Segestes yelled, and the room went quiet. I noticed the fat man was standing by the door, and Segestes got up, ignoring me. He walked to the fat Roman and nodded. The Roman gave me a wide smile and left. Men entered the room. Twenty, thirty. Others got up, and the Batavi sprinted up from their seats as they noticed something unexpected was taking place. Segestes turned my way. 'I'm not a cruel man, Hraban. That is why I told you your daughter is alive as far as I know. I'll not go into details why you must die. I am sure Lord Drusus will believe you were waylaid by Armin's men and died well enough. And I agree to help your Lord as well. You did well. But I cannot let you touch my friend, Antius. How would I get the rest of the gold he just promised me if he were dead?'

'Segestes,' I yelled as Fulcher pulled me up and pushed my shield into my hand. The Lord had left, chatting outside with Antius about the hunting season. 'Wall! Shield wall!' I yelled, and the Batavi grimly built one around me, covering the corner. The men confronting us made a thick wall on either side of the fire pit, bristling with spears and axes. Ragwald was walking back and forth in front of them. Men were throwing tables and benches to the sides to make room for the murder.

'Shit,' Fulcher said. 'Shit and bother. We are dead. I wish I had taken a piss earlier.'

'Take it after the fight,' I told him feverishly. My eyes turned to the men confronting us. They were warriors all. Well armed and grim, their beards jutting, eyes keen, and I realized they had been far less drunk I had thought. Ketill was gesturing at us, wordlessly urging Ragwald on to finish the business. But Ragwald was shaking his head, apparently very happy to have met me. 'So, you vermin riddled carcass,' I told him. 'Do you have something to say?'

'Piss on me? Shall you beg? You have ten men, Hraban,' he said spitefully. 'This will be easy. Perhaps too easy. So, make it entertaining at least. Beg!' And he was right. There were more than thirty men there now, all staring at us hungrily, some making hushed bets on who would die last, who first, and who would get a first pick on the loot. They would simply lock shields, herd us to the corner, push, push, and push us tight and hack and stab and eventually have slaves clean up the mess. Ragwald pointed his ax at me. 'But I hope you survive the battle. I will scald and stretch you. Then I shall have all my men piss on you. I'll buy a skillful poet's services, and he shall sing of your pathetic, piss sodden death across the land.'

I swallowed my terror and squared my shoulders. 'I am the Oath Breaker. The Raven. I am the slayer of the Usipetes Lord Ingvar. I am the killer of King Vago! I burnt my father's hall and slaughtered his men. I struck a spear through the skull of Leuthard, Ragwald. You know of him.

71

The champion. He was no man, no. He was a beast, Hati's spawn. You are a giggling infant in comparison. And you will slay me like a common thief in the sad shit of a hamlet called Oddglade? Murder me like you would a thief? No. Instead, you will elevate me, you piece of dung, by your cowardice. I shall think of the songs they sing about Ragwald, the *pig* of Oddglade. I think you will fix my fame, Ragwald, for men will hear of this, and where you expect to see faces saluting you after this poem of yours, they will stare down to the floorboards. They rather look at mice turds than an animal like you.'

Men murmured angrily as Ragwald's face twisted with uncertainty. He opened his mouth to refute me, hesitated and eventually shook his head in defeat. He stretched out his arms and the huge two-handed ax to silence his men and pointed it at me. 'You and me then. The winner walks out free.'

'Don't,' Fulcher warned.

'Have sight on how this will end?' I asked him.

'No, you fucking idiot,' he whispered. 'But common sense says we should fight together. They won't let us leave, anyhow.'

Grimwald grinned and pushed me forward. 'He is right, but at least we will see a fine show. Die well, Lord. We will be along shortly.'

I grinned at him and pulled Nightbright. The brute's ax was huge, and I wanted to be fast and so I left the Head Taker in the sheath. Ragwald went into a crouch and staggered a bit as he eyed me. He, unlike most of his men had drunk too much, but he was also experienced, and so it would be a terrible fight. 'You are what? Eighteen?' Ragwald asked as the war band around him made a circle around the corner of the hall. Our men pressed into a tight shieldwall by the corner. 'Will never know another girl, will you?' he mocked me and made a cutting motion over his groin. 'I'll make sure of it.'

'I'll fight one today, though,' I grinned and felt the fear and disappointment give way to rage and battle lust. I felt Woden's call, saw a shadowy figure with a twin dragon helmet pound the ground in a savage, feral dance, spear thrumming up and down, and I knew I had his gift. I would be fast, hard to kill and dangerous, and Ragwald would not easily walk out of the hall.

'I'll send Drusus your lips. He can have them kiss his rear one more time. That is the Roman way, no? You boy loving shit.' His men laughed dutifully at that, and Ragwald walked to the side.

I spat as I circled him. 'I hear your wife has lovers, Ragwald. They all whispered about it in the Thing,' I taunted him with the crime that was so deadly in Germania. For that crime, there was no wergild to be paid, only death. 'They toasted with you, then called you a sad cuckold behind your back, and they pitied you for a fool. The men who toasted with you had tasted her, Ragwald, your wife. Is that why you have fought so many duels? To kill men who touch her?' I laughed at his face and took mocking dance steps before him, baring my chest to him as I flung my shield aside.

He sucked in his breath, mumbled incoherently in a drunken rage and charged quickly as a wolf. The ax was coming from the side so fast I realized I had underestimated him, and I had no choice but to fall on the floor as the wicked blade cut the air. Skillfully, the bastard followed with the swing, the blade swishing around to an overhead position. I cursed, dropped my shield and grabbed his buckle as I fell back. He hollered incoherently and fell over me to our men's feet, and I struggled from under him, bringing the short, slim blade of Nightbright to stab his leg or back. I missed. He held onto his ax, clawed at my face and rolled away. I spat and got on my feet, Woden's dance demanding blood, and we faced each other. His ax was ready, his eyes bulging, and I thought he was fast enough to deal with my berserk rage and perhaps, he too, felt Woden's call. Yes, it was possible. There were others, many others and Woden enjoys such battles. The One Eye was a god of strife as well as wisdom. He was chaotic and generous, depending on the day. He was like the men he had created.

'Come old man!' I goaded him, blood oozing from my face where his finger had cut me.

'Yes, I shall,' he yelled, preparing and stomping my shield to pieces in his rage.

His foot was caught in the frame as he charged.

He staggered, stumbled on it, and I slithered to his side as fast I could, and his face betrayed fear as Nightbright was hissing for his ribs, his ax block too late.

Ketill kicked me.

I nearly fell, and my strike went past Ragwald as I stumbled over his legs. The Batavi hissed with disgust at the cheater.

Ragwald grinned as he turned to see me slipping, trying to regain balance. 'You might be Leuthard's Bane! But you are also Ragwald's Prey!' He made a mocking attack and pushed me with his other hand, and the ax swished in. I jumped back, cursing, and his ax came down fast, splitting my tunic and slashing my buckle so the metal showed a bright scratch. He was herding me into the corner, and his men were scattering as he did, his longer, surprisingly fast weapon threatening me relentlessly, and he sensed his victory for he was smiling in an unholy joy. The ax came up again, and he stepped forward, the blade came down in a spine shattering strike as I pushed my blade at his face. I hit his chest, drawing blood, and his ax strike was made incomplete as he flinched and dodged away, but he came back very fast and kicked me against the wall. The ax went up stubbornly. I had no room to maneuver.

I would not be able to survive it.

I could punch the blade at him again, but he would take the wound, the ax would come down, and Woden knows how that would end.

I prayed and threw my sword.

It was a mad, idiotic move. You never, ever throw a sword. The sword is what keeps you alive, and any Roman drill officer would have killed himself in disgust at what I did, but it was also a very unexpected move. And I knew my blade, and the act served me well.

Ragwald screamed.

His ax thudded to the floor before me, and he was no longer holding it. His face was twisted in supreme agony, surprise, and horror, and I saw Nightbright was sunk on his shoulder, blood oozing from a wicked wound. His arm hung uselessly on his side. I stepped forward, grasped the hilt and pulled it out savagely. His eyeballs went white as he crumbled on the floor, shuddering, and I kicked him for good measure. I put the blade on his throat and eyed his men. 'Well?'

'Well what, cur?' Ketill asked.

'We are leaving. Give way,' I snarled.

He shrugged and laughed. 'No. Come now. Don't be a fool, eh? We missed the coins of your Antius, Roman, but I bet you are not poor.'

I retreated to stand next to Fulcher, and the Batavi covered me with their shields. Ketill nodded, the thick shield wall tightened and men hefted their spears overhead. We would die, and I regretted not killing Ragwald, who was moaning on the floor.

'Enough,' said a voice from the guarded door. Everyone turned to look at the man who was leaning weakly on a doorframe. He was tall and wide of shoulders, his beard and hair were nearly white, and his skin was pale. He was bandaged around his torso, and I remembered the terrible wound he had taken from my sword, the Head Taker, running from his armpit to his hip, rending armor and flesh. That he was alive, was a miracle.

He was Rochus, Armin's brother, and the man I had fought not so long past. His eyes glittered in spite at Ketill. 'You kicked him in a duel.'

'He is our enemy. A Roman!' Ketill hissed.

'And what business did your Lord, Segestes *the Germani*, have with him?' Rochus asked with grim mockery. 'Segestes is all but Roman and was only going to do some fighting out of fear for Sigimer.' He spat on the floor, and some ten men of his came out to support him. I recognized some as the ones who had dragged him away from the battle.

'Lord—' Ketill began.

'Get the Hel out of this hall you claim to guard, you mead thief,' Rochus said with such malice Ketill went white from the face. 'Take the moaning bitch and go. Or I shall have you executed without a Thing and judges and mercy.'

A hollow promise, for death was a rare punishment in Germania, and Rochus only had ten men. But Ketill knew he was Armin's brother and Armin had suddenly grown to match his father Sigimer and the high lords of the Cherusci in fame. Ketill bowed stiffly and his men dragged the groaning Ragwald off. We waited until they left the building, and Rochus was whispering to his men. Some nodded and ran to the stables, and I could hear our beasts were being made ready. 'Come, sit,' Rochus said and staggered to the table by the fire pit. 'I will, for my part. I'm hurt, you see. A filthy boar gorged me.' His eyes laughed as he was complimenting me, and I liked his face, calm, clear and intelligent.

I walked over and sat next to him while staring at him. I took a deep breath and bowed to him. 'Thank you.'

He snorted. 'Thank you? I suppose you should. You took my damned standard in the battle, nearly eviscerated me and now I saved you? In the battle, I even told you where your daughter is to be found, and I hear you saved her, even if you lost her again. You should indeed thank me. You should kiss my wart ridden ass and smile like a child who just received his first mug of ale.' I smiled at him, but I doubt it resembled anything like a child with a horn of fresh ale, but rather like a child trying to hold down ale for the first time. 'Never mind,' he groaned. 'You look like a fool. Just stop smiling.' I did.

'I am thankful, Rochus. I might hate your brother and our relative Catualda, the man whom my father schemed with, but not you. You fought well.'

'Your great uncle's son and our distant relative,' he nodded. 'I dislike the worm. He wanted your family's great ring, this Woden's Gift so we could be free of the Suebi wars. I know he stole it from you and your Father and brought it here. I saw it, held it even. Then you took it back. Armin should not have sent it across Rhenus to sway the Roman Germani. I hear he ran into you? Ever since, Catualda has been growing arrogant, fey, hard to trust. He is a toad.'

'Yes, yes, I know,' I said. 'But now I lost the ring to Odo.'

'Ah!' he said as he groaned in his seated position. He stubbornly stayed seated, even if I saw he would have loved to lie down, and I admired the pale warrior's toughness. 'Armin would kill for it.'

'Yes, I know. I nearly did kill Drusus for him. He wanted the ring back and would have handed me Lif. He also offered me a place with you.'

'I'm happy you did not kill the Roman General,' he said, his dark eyes probing me.

76

'You are? Why?' I asked, surprised.

'You chose to be a Roman. Why?'

I shrugged, confused. 'I would never have found my place with the Germani again. My mistakes make it hard to find acceptance this side of the river,' I told him honestly. 'I came back after I dealt with Vago. I burned Maroboodus's hall, raised a war against him and ruined his reputation like he ruined mine. But my fame was gone. Then I had Lif, and nothing mattered anymore. Only she did. And my honor. Which Fulcher there,' I nodded at the tall warrior standing and staring at me, 'taught me is not the same as fame.'

'Wise man,' Rochus said and grinned at Fulcher. The man grinned back. He rarely smiled at people, and now he grinned. Rochus had that effect on people.

'Why did you save me?' I asked him bluntly. 'I doubt Armin would agree. I tried to have him killed after the battle.'

'I have not seen Armin since we fled the field,' he laughed painfully. 'But I hear you did. I spared you for I respect you and your honor. I stayed here, as I know Drusus will be near soon. Is that not so?'

'Yes,' I agreed, wondering. 'We bought food and Drusus hopefully bought us a victory in the battle that is sure to take place on the rivers.' I looked at him and wondered if I had just ruined all the plans of Drusus.

'I think you are right,' he agreed. 'Segestes hates Armin. For Thusnelda, his daughter, for his jealousy for Sigimer, his brother. He has a desire to be more than the least martial of the brothers, and I think Drusus will give him what he wants. I know not. But I wish to surrender to Drusus.'

'I see,' I told him, wonder filling my voice. 'And you need a sponsor?'

'Do you think he will have me?' he asked anxiously. 'And are you a good sponsor? You might have spilled wine on his lap or tried to seduce his daughter?'

'I've done nothing of the sort,' I grinned and then sobered. 'Why do you wish to go?' I stared at him, and he gave nothing away. 'You have everything here. You are a mighty man with men to command. Riches and lands and women to choose from.' There was a note of worry in my voice. *Was this another plot of Armin to kill Drusus?*

He leaned closer and put a hand on my shoulder. 'I am not Armin's creature, even if he is my brother. I'm the second son. I am Sigimer's least favorite boy and Hraban? I wish to see the wide world. I wish to be rid of the itchy woods and icy cold rivers and see what there is out there for me. Sun, adventure, riches? And fear not. I am no murderer to tell you lies and then attempt to slay Drusus. I know that is what you fear. Will he have me? I am Armin's brother, and it will embarrass my brother, at least.'

I looked into his eyes and saw the desire there. *He truly wished to be away.* 'Drusus loves warriors, Rochus. And I'm sure he will have you.' He grinned fiercely and hugged me happily, and I thought life was so strange.

'Shall we?' Rochus asked, getting up. His bandages were seeping, and I scowled. He rolled his eyes. 'I have a mother, Hraban; you don't have to scowl like that. I'll bleed a bit, or a lot and will survive. It's not infected. You keep your swords clean, I think, and its not as bad as it probably looked.' His eyes went to the Head Taker on my side. 'Old and famous weapon that,' he said.

'Fulcher does it for me,' I admitted, and Rochus bowed to Fulcher again, and the idiot grinned back. 'Cleans it.'

'Mighty weapon, clean or dirty,' he agreed, bending to touch the hilt. I let him. He pulled away as if startled. 'It yearns for blood. It's a sword that drives you to vengeance, I think. Is it evil? Perhaps.'

'It's a sword,' I growled. 'It is my tool, not the other way around.'

He nodded thoughtfully, hesitantly, and that made me scowl. My sword was the gift of Hulderic, my grandfather. Then Father had taken it. It had carved a scar into my face, deep and wide. It had been used to dupe us into believing Maroboodus was dead. *True, I had killed with it. But it was only a piece of metal.* Rochus smiled thinly to dispel the sudden somber mood. 'Who was that fat bastard with you?' Rochus asked as his men brought his gear. His chain mail was still rent, his spear and shield in fine condition, and they packed like maniacs.

'Antius. An enemy Nero Claudius Drusus used to gain Segestes's support. But I was to kill him after we left,' I told him as I tried to dispel his words about my sword.

Rochus smiled. 'I like your Drusus. Or was it your idea? His? Ah, this Antius anticipated his sad fate and nearly had you killed instead. The seedy, seemingly helpless bastards are always surprising,' Rochus said with a wince as he swooned from pain.

'Before we left, I asked for a friend to follow us. I doubt Antius got far. It was an … insurance.' I said that word in Latin.

'What is that?' Rochus asked. 'An insurance?'

'It's this fund you pay into, and then when you die you can get buried and your family will be taken care of. I thought he might try to get me killed, and I wanted to make sure he died no matter what happened here.'

'Well,' he smiled. 'You have made me an insurance for yourself in the future. I will not forget your help. I hope he didn't take a boat,' Rochus said with a groan.

'We will see,' I told him, now worried Antius had indeed gone by ship.

We left the village and scowling Ketill behind, and I smiled as I heard Ragwald raging in terrible pain.

In a bit of a day, we found Antius. And Gnaeus Calpurnius Piso.

Gnaeus was wearing his red cloak and a chain mail. His bored face had a rare hint of interest as his cursing Syrians and Parthians were struggling with the worm-like writhing mass of naked Antius. We sat on our horses near the army of Drusus. The dust of the two legions could be seen clearly, and I sensed Rochus was getting anxious. I reassured him with a smile and turned back to the face of Antius. It was not easy to get the huge man to sit on the sturdiest horse Gnaeus had brought, especially since the fat man was putting on a fight. His face was lathered in sweat, and his eyes were agog in incomprehensible terror. 'Is the rope thick enough?' Gnaeus asked. 'Patrax?' The Syrian called Patrax was cursing as he began pummeling Antius's midsection to calm him down. Antius threw up all his breakfast on the neck of the poor horse that tried to bite the Syrians hovering around it. They finally managed to slip a thick rope around the neck of Antius and men tightened it until the Roman could only sit still. The Gaul servants were hanging nearby, their faces ashen and dead and gave Antius a good idea what was in store for him.

'It will do,' Fulcher said happily from the side.

'Hraban? Anything you wish to say?' Gnaeus asked inanely, looking at his fingernails. 'I caught him for you though he nearly got away. Rides surprisingly fast, the bastard. Had nothing of worth so this is good fun only.' Gnaeus had no conscience. *In this case, he needed none*, I thought.

I rode around Antius, dodging the auxilia and hated the man despite his plight. 'I have nothing. I have precious little to tell you. You mocked me once when Vago took me, and you have ever tried to hurt me and my family, but I don't even know you. Only that you deserve this. Anything you wish to say, Antius?'

'I hoped you would ride far and live happily,' he said with a strangled voice. 'Remember?'

I shrugged. 'I will go, one day. You will not.'

He stuttered and visibly calmed himself. 'Did you wish to know about Drusus and my mistress?'

'No, not really,' I answered him. 'Drusus has a good idea who it is. I don't care.'

'You will regret not listening.' Antius grinned. 'And you will regret this.' I saw Fulcher frowning and knew he had a premonition. I hesitated, shook my head at him, and enjoyed the hope dying on Antius's fat face.

I smiled up at him. 'You underestimated me, Antius. People who do, tend to find trouble, and some fall victims to their arrogance. I might regret many things in the future, but you will not see me do so. You will see dark shades of Hel.'

'I'll haunt you, son of Maroboodus,' he said with resignation. 'I will.'

Gnaeus nodded lazily at his men, and the man called Patrax whipped the horse savagely. It bolted, and a Parthian rode after it wildly.

Antius swung around, his stubby legs trying to find a spot that would spare him his fate. There were none to be found. His face went red, his lips were thin, and the rope burrowed deep into his neck as he choked. The tree was groaning, and the Syrians and the Parthians were smacking their lips in some strange form of approval. I shook my head at his slow death and rode away.

In the evening, we marched through the vast camp for the praetorium of Drusus. He grinned at me and tilted his head at Rochus, trying to place the face.

'I have seen you,' he wondered. 'You were with … ' He stopped to think hard.

I nodded at Rochus. 'He is Armin's brother. He wants to join you.' Drusus grinned even wider and walked over to the young, wounded man. He looked at me over Rochus's shoulder, and I nodded. Antius was gone and yes, I trusted Rochus.

So, we had a feast for the food was beginning to roll in, and I told Drusus Segestes had agreed to help us in the battle. We were full of hope as we marched on for the Bhugnos River.

BOOK 2: THE FOX AND THE PIG

'In order for a young lord to become the leader of such a nation as this one, he has to become its oldest lord.'
Thusnelda to Hraban

CHAPTER 6

Chariovalda came to check on the guards at the next march camp. He spotted me staring east in the last evening light and smiled thinly as I was leaning on my horse, in the middle of caring for the beast. 'You recruited the scoundrels of Gnaeus?'

'They make good scouts,' I answered, rousing myself and stroking the horse down. I gazed again at the far away river land that was heaving to sight from under a thick layer of fog.

'And the Batavi do not make great scouts?' he said with some jealous disapproval. 'You know we are in a fierce competition with the Thracians and those eastern bastards. Next time take more of our boys.'

'Yes, Chariovalda,' I told him. 'I have no men of my own so I took the ones you gave and added a bit of fun to it. Gnaeus is one ruthless man.'

'He is half mad,' Chariovalda said, grinning in agreement. 'But so are you so perhaps you did make a good team. But use the Batavi next time, yes? I do not want to see them grow fat and lazy. Though I think we will see action soon.' He scratched his chin. 'So, you are a Decurion in my troop. I had no say on it, I was just told that is the case, but I suppose you earned it. A Decurion commands twenty men. I will give you none of mine. Not right now. I cannot as I don't have any to spare. Can you get your own? We lost a lot of men,' he said unhappily and then scowled at my silence. 'Your daughter?' he asked. 'That's what is making you timid like a virgin maiden meeting a drunken suitor?'

'Taken to the Cherusci lands. Godsmount.'

'Then we will see her soon,' he said cheerfully and scowled again as I made no sound. 'Your Ishild and Odo?' he asked carefully.

'Segestes said Odo is hiding in his ancestral home somewhere near. They did not find Lif,' I told him. 'As they did not find her, then he is likely seething and regretting letting me go.'

'This prophecy,' he rumbled. 'What part is unfulfilled?'

I shook my shoulders. 'It is not certain if the final road has begun. What is certain is that Odo and Ishild made a child, so did Ishild and I, and I have bled on a rocky skin. That was Leuthard's hand. Odo said it is so. Now he followed her to the east, thinking I had led them to the final road. He took my Woden's Gift, or Ringlet like the prophecy calls this mysterious item, and here we are.'

'There was a raven and a bear,' Fulcher called from the side.

'Sneaky bastard,' Chariovalda said and waved at the man. 'Go on.'

'There is a raven and a bear,' I told him. 'But as for Woden's Gift, the goddess speaking with Bero dying lips said it is not golden. So I think the ring is meaningless. If they pour Veleda's blood on it, we will not be destroyed and no cocks will crow. That is part of the lines, as well. Cocks will crow ere the end. I suppose they will raise the armies of Ragnarök or something similar.'

'Veleda will not likely enjoy the bleeding part, no matter if the ring is golden or not,' Fulcher added.

'Thank you, Fulcher!' I yelled and went silent for a time. 'A bear is slain, a raven will show the way. The whole prophecy and its lines are not in any real order but likely spewed out by Lok's drunken lips in haphazard, double meaning order just to make us all crazy. And one last thing. A selfless act may yet the doom postpone.'

Chariovalda stared at me, and I sighed. He slapped my hand. 'And you think if you let Lif meet whatever fate is waiting for her, it would stave off the inevitable?'

'Yes,' I said with spite. 'The gods are such cruel turds as to demand us mortals for something like this. I am sure they would giggle if I forgot about my daughter and let Odo eventually find her. I would be holy and high, no doubt, if I sacrificed my child. I hate all the vitka and völva, who love such tragedy so much. I serve Woden, but I think he enjoys our struggles far too much, as well. No matter if he spawned men.'

Chariovalda reached down and pulled me around. 'I think nothing truly matters, but the fact you look for her. No matter what, remember she is the one thing a father can never ignore. Piss on the prophecy. And one more thing.'

'What?' I asked him miserably.

'You are not alone in your story.' He smiled. 'The prophecy does not actually say you have any real part to play in this game of yours. You play it, trust your sword, fight well and in the end, I am sure this will all blow over either in an orgy of death or in some other more boring manner.'

I opened my mouth to refute him but did not. I nodded instead. *It was true.* I might have been too absorbed by my part to consider those of the others. There were many players in the game. Lif mattered. She was my charge. 'I will try.'

He understood as he shifted in his saddle. 'As I said, I want you to hire men, when you can. Two hundred and fifty to sixty denarii is the pay, and if I cannot have the officia of the ala pay them right that moment, you tell them they will get paid. They will get gear, all of it. They get a commission in the 2nd Batavorium and so will you.'

I nodded. 'Yes, I will.'

He looked at me hard and shook his head. 'Do *not* do anything rash, Hraban. I like you, but you are like a trapped, young wolf, and I worry about you. Have patience and don't go blundering around where I cannot help you. Things will be all right.'

'If I get the men's heads I crave for and Lif survives, then you are right,' I said thickly, and clasped his forearm. 'If Armin is caught, then perhaps I can find Godsmount, where they are, reputedly. Lif and Veleda.'

'Just do not make the mistake of going there alone,' Chariovalda said gravely. 'You are a soldier now and soldiers obey orders. Have you seen a

Roman legionnaire run ahead alone for the enemy like a headless chicken? No, they are boring and kill them together in a controlled manner.'

I grinned. 'I saw an order for Drusus to go home. And here we are.'

'He is not a soldier. He is a patrician, a noble, Hraban. His game is much more difficult and chaotic than a soldier's,' Chariovalda breathed. 'Patience.'

'Yes, I will try,' I told him, and we bedded for the night.

Tuba rang harshly in the camps the next morning. Men crawled out of their tents, and they assembled at the meadows, near a spring, standing in lines, their armor cleaned, beards shaven. I did not hear it, but Drusus held a passionate speech to his men, who were happy with the easy march and surprisingly full bellies. It also appeared many had had wine that Antius had sold in the night, for great profit. The last ship had held a treasure hoard of it after all. I snickered for Antius had no need of gold and silver. *That poor tree bore one nasty, rotten fruit*, I thought and thanked Woden for Antius's death.

That afternoon, we crossed the wood-covered hills, saw abandoned villages, which we promptly burned, and we came down to the lands of Segestes, west side of the Visurgis River, running north towards the distant sea. Oddglade was not that far, and it was just one of the wealthy settlements in sight. The land of the Cherusci was dotted with woods, as was most of Germania, but the land across Visurgis was rich, full of gentle hilly meadows and deep woods with many kinds of trees. But there was also far more flat land with rich soil than in the lands of the south, more plains with colorful flowers, and one could see much further away, sitting on one's horse. The exploratores and a few traders knew many places where to cross that great three-pronged river, but the best place was some forty Roman miles to the southeast, where a great trade route ran from the distant Albis River to Rhenus River and that was where the army was headed. The Batavi rode far before the army, and I joined Chariovalda as he led his men to scout the road itself.

The land opened up suddenly, the forests disappeared, and we stared at a group of surprised Germani riding for us. They stopped their horses, whipped them, and turned savagely. They rode for the clear waters of

Bhugnos River, the water reaching to the knees of the horses as they rode wildly over the river. Then horns were blowing across the woods. Many horns. We had found Armin and Sigimer. *And* Segestes.

'Go and get the leading elements of the army,' Chariovalda said calmly to a young Batavi as we stared at the sudden activity across the shallow ford. 'Hard to cross, isn't it? Not deep, but perhaps not so wide?'

'I think it will be a butchery if we cross under ten thousand spears. We have some seven with all the vexillations and castra we are manning,' Fulcher complained, and I agreed with him. Across the river, an army raised itself to look at us. Thousands of men and women got up. More horns joined the ones that had been blasting and some were tall carnyx of Celtic make and their deep, long blasts made our blood run thin. Fantastic standards of many makes could be seen as the men of Sigimer and Segestes formed their clans and war bands into many a tight cunus bristling with spears and strode forward to see what we were doing. I could see thousands of bearded men hefting framea, sword, ax and cudgel and the barritus yell was ringing from savage moths covered by the rims of their shields. It was quite overwhelming. I swear I could see Segestes and his shield out there on their right flank and told myself he had better be careful should he hang around for the battle.

Chariovalda looked around at the twenty Batavi around us, then back again at the thousand strong enemy lines. 'We should feel privileged they all come to say hello, I guess. But I am worth a thousand men, am I not? They look formidable enough.'

'They think we are here to lure them out,' I said.

'Probably. Let's wave to the bastards,' he said, and we did. They kept staring at us like a huge pack of wolves but did not send men over.

In an hour, it was too late.

We heard the stamp of many feet and turned to look at the V Alaudae and XIX Legion marching up. First came the engineers, clearing way, pushing trunks out of the road, hacking down bushes. Then auxilia cavalry followed, savage Thracians swaying on their horses. Then the elite First Cohort of V Alaudae hove to sight, savaged by the campaign, but the cohort's signum was proud and glittering in the sun, a warning hand topping it as if a warning from the gods. The phalarae and the hand atop the signum were gloriously presented at the enemy as the cohort marched and stood in guard, facing many times its number of men across the river. 'They would be wise to dash over now,' Fulcher noted.

'Probably too drunk, and Armin and Sigimer hope to hold the ford,' Chariovalda noted, bored already. 'But perhaps it would be wise of them.'

They stayed put.

The cohorts began to dig a fossa and build an agger for the inevitable camp. A simple vallum wall was erected though in places there were only stakes on top of the agger. The men were sneaking glances across the ford at the famed Cherusci. Few had fought them, and we all saw the proud, tall Germani men, bearded, savage, ancient as any people in Midgard and richer than most tribes. We all heard the fierce thrum of their shields and spears hitting each other rhythmically as their various chiefs exhorted their men, pointing us out, likely mocking our feebleness, and there were white clad vitka dancing at the fords, cursing us.

The legionnaires smiled and laughed at the sights of the vitka, an unnerving sound in itself, their eyes also mocking the ten thousand strong horde of Cherusci. Nothing makes a legionnaire smile like the prospect of loot and victory. The Cherusci were by now stretched in a huge horde across the other bank. They would stop Rome there if the Romans should even dare to attack. If Rome failed, Sigimer and Armin would grow powerful and dangerous, more so than they already were. The barritus yells were again ringing through the woods as the Roman army settled in, and I suppose they thought we would attack immediately. But no, we were in no hurry.

And Drusus had a plan.

I turned my horse away from the Cherusci and followed Chariovalda. He was grunting. 'Drusus is moving slowly. He will keep the bastards up all night by using small units while the army sleeps. Tomorrow, we will make mockery of them.'

'The champions of the Cherusci will wade to the water to taunt our men into a duel,' Fulcher told him.

'A tempting offer,' Chariovalda grinned. 'Let them stand there and freeze their balls. But the Roman discipline is such they will not accept such contests though many a man would love to make a name for themselves and earn an award. Come. Let us go and prepare for what must take place soon. Segestes was not promised lordship of the land so he just stands there doing nothing. He will have to earn it.'

'About half the troops there are his,' I said with some disapproval, for I hated the thought of Segestes ruling anything. 'The rest are Sigimer's and probably some Chatti as well. They live to the south and cannot resist a fight.'

'It will be a sad day for Armin and Sigimer,' Chariovalda laughed, brushing his yellow beard that was jutting from under his helmet. 'They will be very, very alone all of a sudden if things go just right.'

We waited for Drusus and finally, a military tribune summoned us. We rode to the edge of the march camp and skirted the muddy fossa for the western end of the fort. There we found a congregation of troops, the grim lictors standing in a huddle and enthusiastic officers rushing about like headless hens. We came to where our lord was hunched over a table full of maps and there was a tall Germani scowling at the activity around him. Drusus's eyes met mine and he nodded, waving at Chariovalda. They spoke at length and Chariovalda nodded many times. The big Germani grunted at Chariovalda, apparently answering questions. 'Man of Segestes?' Fulcher whispered.

'Yes, I think it must be,' I answered. Chariovalda was giving some terse comments to Drusus and finally, after many officers ran to the gloomy evening, Chariovalda turned my way. He hesitated and looked at Drusus, who apparently gave permission for him to speak with me first.

The big Batavi leaned closer to me. 'Hraban?'

'I have snot on my beard?' I laughed nervously. 'What?'

'He will ask you for a deed,' Chariovalda said heavily.

'What deed?' I asked him. I had a heavy premonition of impending doom.

'All he wants is Armin, you see this?' he said. 'And so if you fail, I will never see you again, lad. I thank you for the merry times. I'll take care of

Cassia.' He nearly made a lewd comment about *how* he would take care of my woman, but decided against it. It was unlike him, and I worried even more.

'What?' I asked, and he crushed me briefly with a huge hug and went.

'Hraban?' Drusus yelled, and I went to him. He pulled me aside, growled at his lictors to stay put and pulled me further to the side, under the shade of a tree. 'Hraban.' He looked bothered and feverish. 'I have a need of you.'

'You are worried that despite Segestes, Armin escapes once more,' I stated. 'And so you will ask me to find him.'

'You and Fulcher,' he said heavily. 'You are Germani and can pass under the most heavy scrutiny.'

'You know, Marcomanni are Suebi, and they don't like Suebi here.'

He smiled. 'Suebi wear a knot on the hair. And—'

'And my speech is different from theirs. They will know the difference.'

He nodded and looked away briefly. There was an unusual look in his eyes; one of worry and uncertainty. 'I am facing treason back home, as you know. I face the ire of the Chatti next year. I am already at war with the Luppia tribes no matter their promises.'

'The issues with the Chatti are partly your fault, Drusus,' I told him blatantly. 'Holding Ebbe hostage is an insult.' His eyes flashed in anger, and I held my peace. His hands twitched, and finally, he nodded.

'They echoed your father's plans during my Thing. If we stay in Luppia after the war, they will fight us. They said this. To my face, defiant and rude. Now, they dare not,' he stated.

'Adgandestrius will take his father's place. Oldaric will lead to have vengeance for his brother,' I said and briefly wondered what Gunda, Oldaric's daughter with whom I had once been betrothed to, looked like. She seemed to have a long distance affection for me, at least according to Adgandestrius and was sure we would marry one day. That made me smile briefly, and I cursed myself for a dog. *I had Cassia.* I missed her and looked over to the west, where I had to leave her after Ansbor had died and we rode to bring word of Armin's plans to Drusus.

Drusus had looked at my face and shook his head. 'First angry, then arrogant, then smiling and finally brooding. I think your face might fascinate me for years to come, Hraban.'

'Yes, Drusus,' I told him and hoped it was so.

Drusus took a deep breath and massaged his neck. 'All the more reason we must not fail. The legions are depleted. Brave as ever, yes, but they only have a battle or two in them now. It is here where something final must take place, something so very final that we don't have to come back next year. I want dead Cherusci nobles. Heaps of them. I want that lump of Segestes to rule and Armin taken or killed and Sigimer as well. So. The cavalry will ride north this night. Quietly, very stealthily by the routes that traitorous bastard will show us,' he nodded at the tall Germani of Segestes. 'You will swim across this river and come to hit Sigimer on the side as we clamor and make ready to assault them in the morning. We do not have siege gear so we will use archers and then just march over. The horns will blow, Segestes will run, and the butchery will begin. You know Armin. You know Sigimer. Find them in the chaos and kill them. Capture them if you can, but only if you can. You will be richly rewarded for many things, but do this, and we will conquer the world. Fail, and we will be here for years, dragging our feet through swamps and mud.'

'I will, Lord,' I said.

'Drusus,' he said thinly, for I was a slow learner and called him lord when I disapproved his plans. He leaned closer. 'Armin will have vitka who know where your daughter is held. Where Godsmount is. Someone will know the trails there. He and Sigimer are the key to your dilemma, as well.'

'I've not told you about Godsmount,' I said.

'Fulcher did,' he told me, and I turned to stare at the tall, dark man who shuffled his feet uncertainly. 'He is ever looking out for you and reminded me of your plight.'

'Yes, Drusus,' I told him and kneeled before him. 'I'll do my best. But if I do not return ...'

91

'I will not forget Lif,' he told me. 'If you do not return, we will try to find you. Even to burn your body and bury you and to do you honor.' This time he was not jesting, and I was worried.

'I am yours, Drusus,' I said, got up and turned my back on him. I felt his eyes on my back as I mounted my horse, and Fulcher nodded at me. I wanted to growl at him but ended up patting his back. 'Thank you.'

'We will go then?' he asked with some apprehension.

'We will, but we will break from the attack and hunt for Armin,' I answered.

'Just the two of us?' he asked with some panic in his voice. 'Is he doing this because of what I told him about you? Is he trying to be rid of us and our requests? I only told him Lif is held in this mountain and he should not—'

'He needs me, for he knows I will stop at nothing to get Armin,' I assured him. 'He has plenty of men trying to kill the higher Cherusci nobles, but he wants me to go for Armin and Sigimer. I will. One way or another, we will catch the Fox, at least.'

'Tiw help us,' Fulcher breathed as we guided our horses to where the Batavi and the Thracians were gathering, deep in the woods.

'Woden has helped me so far, but you just go ahead and ask the other deities just to be sure,' I said with a grin. 'My god is probably getting damned bored with the constant hassle and trouble.'

'He enjoys it, Oath Breaker and needs you. They are making wagers in his feast hall every night whether you will join them or not,' Fulcher said and grinned, and he was likely right. Also, if Odo was right, we were going to decide whether Lok's children shall populate the new world and if Woden's realms topple to the sea. *He needed me indeed*, I thought. *He had better help me.*

The cavalry moved under the cover of darkness.

CHAPTER 7

We had scouts out, patrols trying to flush out any spies Sigimer and Armin might have skulking around. Seeing this, the tall Germani of Segestes snorted at Chariovalda. 'There are men aplenty in these woods. They are simple farmers and only wish to serve their lord Segestes. And as for the spies? I'm the spy. Stop fretting.'

'Fretting has kept me alive since I was born,' Chariovalda grumbled. 'Where will we cross?'

'At the confluence of the rivers,' the spy said. 'It is a dreadfully harsh place to cross with a very strong current, but I'm sure you will manage. They say the Batavi can run their horses on the bottom of the sea.' He laughed at the thought, but Chariovalda was not happy with our mission.

'And there are no Armin's men out there?' he asked the spy.

'Yes, there are,' he told Chariovalda while dodging a low hanging branch in the dark. He did not quite manage it and was left bleeding and cursing. 'But they should be dead by now.'

'The Fox is a night animal,' Fulcher grunted. 'Rarely asleep when the moon shines on the sky. Perhaps he is riding around?'

'Then you will be fucked,' the spy said cheerfully. 'Fucked properly. You just try to relax. That way.' He pointed for a path and the cavalcade followed us as we rode on. We rode north for an hour, out of sight, the exploratores ranging ahead. We saw nothing save for deer and owls, some sleeping cows and a body of an unfortunate man one our scouts had apparently encountered in the woods. Finally, we reached the shore, and the river was surging and churning in the moonlight, almost peacefully. It felt like the army was making terrible noise as the horses were nervously neighing, anticipating what we would ask of them. The spy rode forward, stopping his horse in the water. He whistled sharply and from the other side a trio of Cherusci rode out. One waved his hand and the spy turned to Chariovalda. He nodded and rode to the south, singing softly. Chariovalda sighed audibly, and he nodded at the Decurion to his right. Then, the army moved.

We were twenty miles upstream from Drusus and the waiting Cherusci army, there was no time to waste, and so, the four hundred men bravely guided their horses to the river. The horses immediately sunk to their bellies in water, the armored men holding on grimly and guiding the desperate beasts for the shore across. The horses whinnied, men cursed, and if there had been any men of Armin's or Sigimer's out there waiting, we would have failed in our surprise. Drusus's money was well spent, however. The river was so full of swimming horses that one with enough skill could have easily skipped to the other side by jumping from man to man, but nothing alarming was taking place across on the other side. While shivering, I remembered Moenus River and the day I lost Ishild and Lif. 'Perhaps this is a sign I'll get them back?' I asked Fulcher, who was apparently thinking of the day as well as we approached the edge of the river.

'Yes, or lose more,' he spat as the cold water made him gasp. 'It was not a good trip. No.'

I cursed him and followed him. The water had a strong current and men and horses steered north helplessly, but most Batavi and the Thracians grinned bravely, prayed desperately and whipped the horses to struggle on through the dark water, swimming in full gear. Inevitably, some did not make it, losing their grip in the saddle and armored in chain; some men could be heard drowning as the horses swam on, and we prayed to Woden the beasts would endure. Most did.

'Forward and form in your units!' Chariovalda was exhorting men as we entered the land again. The alae of cavalry slowly formed up, Thracians to the left and behind, the 1ˢᵗ and 2ⁿᵈ Batavorium took the point with some of the men of Segestes. It took a long time to get the men in shape. The woods looked ominous and cautious whistles by officers caused dutiful scouting to take place immediately. A shady bank of clouds covered the moon, and we ploughed on. The men of Segestes could be seen discussing with Chariovalda and the praefectus of the Thracians, a young Roman who was apparently unhappy being under Chariovalda's command. After some ten miles, Chariovalda lifted his arm. The army stopped.

'Eat, wait,' the call came out, and the shivering men dismounted in a small cops of woods, posting guards. It was night, and the morning was still a ways off.

'We need a guide,' I said with clattering teeth, for the wind was chilly, and we were all damp.

'What will you do?' Fulcher asked.

'Get me one of those men of Segestes,' I told him. 'I'll get us some wine and meat.' I was rummaging in the saddlebags and pulled out suspicious strips of meat Fulcher had packed up and begged Grimwald for wine and that is when Fulcher escorted a young man to me. His face was full of pockmarks, and he carried his shield uncertainly. He had a curious look on his face, and he tilted his head so his long, light brown hair fell forward. 'What is your name?'

'Hugo,' he said with a steady voice. He was young, younger than I was.

'Didn't you find an adult?' I asked Fulcher as I threw him some of the meat.

Hugo's hand whipped out, and he grasped the flying meat from the air. 'I'm young, Lord, but hardly incapable.'

'Hugo, eh?' I asked him as he stuffed the meat in his mouth to Fulcher's horror. I got up with a grunt, walked over to Fulcher and gave him some of my food and the wine. 'I won't risk him going hungry, Hugo. So you are a man of Segestes?'

He shrugged. 'I got my spear and shield last year. I was fifteen and had killed a cattle-thieving man of a rival lord. I got mine in Yule feast and Tiw, they say, approved.'

'Fast, no?' I asked him. 'And fast to think?'

'Fast enough,' he agreed. 'Why am I here?' There was a clever look in his eyes.

'Who is your lord?' I asked as I sat down and stared at him. He was quiet, thinking hard, and I brushed my dark hair aside to see his struggle more clearly. My helmet was on the side, its dark eyeholes staring up at him. His eyes flicked that way, and he was thinking deep. 'Boy?'

'Man. I am a man, Lord Hraban,' he said with some challenge in his voice. 'I have no lord. I follow my father, a warrior in the band of on Angvir.'

'And what do you think of Armin?'

He stopped at that, swallowing hard. He shrugged. 'I admire him? I hate him? I do what my Lord Segestes does, of course, and we would not be here if he loved his nephew.'

'And you know Rome seeks to catch the Fox, don't you?' I flicked a coin between my fingers; a silver denarius and his eyes appraised it, apparently knowing its worth. He was greedy enough, I decided and knew the difference between silver and copper.

'Yes, I do. Moreover, I do know where he is camped. His father's fires are in the middle of the lines of their clans, but he stays on the side. He has no standard in the battle and seeks to survive it. He did not approve this stand.'

'I see,' I nodded. 'And would you guide me there?'

'You are to slay him, then?' he asked suspiciously, and I flicked the coin for him. His hand grasped it and his eyes settled on the next coin playing between my fingers. 'Does not matter,' he decided.

'I don't ask you to do anything but guide us as we ride. Soon.'

He looked beyond the woods, hesitating. Then he gave me a curt nod. 'I'll help. I'm sure Segestes, our lord would want me to.'

'I'm sure he would, yes,' I agreed and flipped him the denarius. He grabbed it with uncanny skill and gave me a small bow.

An hour passed. Another. Men were silent, tense.

Then, a Decurion ran through the camp kicking the men up. Most were asleep, which said something about the fiber of the Batavi, men able to sleep at the jaws of death, wet and hungry. They woke up, prayed to their gods and found their weapons and horses. All our gear was moist, covered in dew and cold to the touch. The army was shivering in their saddles. Far in the night, early morning really, we heard the Roman camp awaken to tuba. Then cornu blared, for they were ordering the standards out and that meant Drusus was swiftly preparing his two legions for a battle.

A low rumble was heard as the distant Cherusci were whipping themselves into the battle formations. They had had a terrible night, being constantly awakened, but now there was no doubt Rome was attacking. Many a cunus, a battle formation formed like a boar's tusk, were taking shape, no doubt, or perhaps they would make a thick shield wall? *Likely the latter*, I decided, for all Armin and Sigimer had to do was to keep the Romans out for long enough, then harry them as they retreat.

'Move!' yelled Chariovalda, and the army was startled by his bellowing voice. He was done with stealth.

'The bastard scared the shit out of me,' Grimwald said nearby. 'Hope he isn't drunk.' The hypocrite was taking a long swig of mead, which he handed to me.

'He is drunk,' Fulcher rumbled. 'But so are most of the foe.'

'No, I really did shit my pants,' Grimwald complained, and we moved our horses away from him. 'Ate something rancid yesterday.'

'Change your pants later and wash your saddle,' I instructed him as the Decurions waved their spears in the air, Grimwald echoed the commands and the belligerent riders moved through the light woods ahead that soon turned into a wide and flat beach.

The land was thrumming to the sound of the hooves. Horses were forming into two very loose arrows; one for the Thracians, one for the Batavi. The men were looking for any trouble ahead, the scouts rushing at the edges of the woods. Few saw anything, and so Segestes had probably kept his word. Miles passed. Not very far, the tumult of men screaming, cajoling each other and the Germani barritus began to drown our own noises away. A thin scream was heard. Likely, the archers had began lobbing their sagitta at the brave Cherusci who were mocking the Romans, no matter how many arrows found marks and how many deadly slingshots crushed bones. A warning horn signal blared ahead, a Thracian scout waving his hands at the leading elements of the cavalry. He was gesturing madly, his hands pointing in different directions ahead.

The enemy was close. Only a few miles away.

But something else was happening.

'Look!' Fulcher hissed and pointed south east.

There, a massive movement was apparent. Thousands of men were running for the east. Segestes had abandoned his brother and his men to face Drusus.

We whipped our horses, men were laughing in terror and giving oaths to their gods, their spears held overhead, shields tight in their fists. 'Break them! No dismounting, no shield walls. At them and throw them in Hel's waiting arms, you rascals!' yelled Chariovalda. The 1ˢᵗ and 2ⁿᵈ Batavorium with the Thracians rushed forward; heedless of the noise, not caring if we were observed. A young Cherusci stepped out of the woods and stared in horror at the impending doom rushing by. None cared for him, and he was left behind, his half-eaten apple forgotten in his hand, his pants soiled in fear.

I turned to look at our guide.

The young man coughed in the dust and pointed to the left, at the backs of the escaping Cherusci of Segestes. 'That way, skirt the running rabble and then south in the thickets. Though Armin's sure to be in the battle!'

'They will run soon enough,' I said through my gritted teeth as we broke off the arrow of riders for the east. I saw Chariovalda turn in his saddle and nod carelessly; I nodded back, and then we dove to the woods.

There, thousands of men were running right ahead of us to all the directions save the west. Many were on horses, most on foot, but they were not stopping. I saw a look of incredulity on some of the bearded faces, braver warlords turning to look back at the direction of the battle, feeling betrayed. We rode on and witnessed the milling mass of Cherusci facing two legions in triple axis formation across the ford though only a cohort at the time would be able to ford the river. Arrows were raining down on the covering shield wall of the Cherusci, and I saw the men around the bronze shield standard of Sigimer take the brunt of them. There, the old warlord was pulling at men, pointing at the running Segestes and hoping to extend his five thousand men to the right, where only the trampled grass now marked what had been a worthy battle line of fellow warriors. I did not see Armin, his blond hair and god-like face hidden in the bearded mass of warriors, all confused by the sudden retreat of Segestes.

But I saw Sigimer's face as he saw the mass of riders thunder to his sight on his right flank.

It was twisted in nearly a hurt surprise as if he was a man robbed of honor by cowardly thieves. All energy left him briefly as his shoulders slumped, and he knew his reign as the Cherusci thiuda was nearly at an end.

'This way, Lord,' Hugo yelled, indicating we should go deeper to the wood. And we did, staring at the hundreds of desperate Cherusci rushing to form a wall to face Chariovalda.

We rode in the shallow beech forest to the south and saw scores of Germani women were yelling encouragements for the men to fight. They saw us and hissed at us, likely thinking we were running from battle. I heard Chariovalda scream, the cornu blared as 1st Cohort of V Alaudae rushed to the water across the river. The legionnaire cavalry, some fifty was preparing to follow them, then more cohorts. The Syrian and Cretan archer auxilia began lobbing their remaining missiles at the edges of the Cherusci shield wall. Chariovalda's heavy horses charged for the forming line of men.

'Are they going to dismount?' Hugo asked with huge eyes. 'Surely they must?'

'No, they will not,' I said with a grin as I guided my horse by some scared women, all backing away from us. They were tall, lithe women, their faces covered by cowls, and they were whispering. They had knives, and Fulcher kept an eye on them. 'They can fight in the saddle,' I added as I kept an eye on the belligerent women.

'Surely they will lose their horses? They will hack at the legs and bellies and—' Hugo continued as the hundreds strong army rushed for the bracing line of Cherusci.

'They will take yours after your people are routed,' I told him and pulled him roughly closer. 'I see Sigimer, but where is Armin?'

'He must be anchoring the other end?' he said.

'Where is his horse?' I continued.

'Oh!' Hugo said and winked. He showed me deeper to the wood. There, we passed slaves and women packing gear, pulling at panicking horses, preparing bandages, and my bronze helmet gave most all a start as I guided my horse amongst the remains of a camp. 'Over there,' he told me, pointing to a tight grove of beech trees, and sure enough, under them there were plenty of bigger, stronger horses leashed to the trees. And with them, there was one with silvery reins and a dark leather saddle. A Roman four-horned saddle. I got down, pulled some rope from Fulcher's gear, and bent down to do a deed that would give me Armin. Then I mounted again.

'Oh, you are one evil vermin,' Fulcher said, eyeing Armin's horse. 'Poor beast.'

'We wait,' I told him and Hugo. We guided the horse to the side under the shadows of some low hanging branches.

To the west, men died.

We heard the impact of men charging the shield wall, the strange groan of wood and metal and flesh meeting violently. We heard the encouragements and screams of men fighting, people being trampled, and could nearly imagine the coppery, thick smell of blood and intestines, piss and shit. The legions wading across the waters did not have a chance to test their swords against the fierce Cherusci by the ford.

For the cavalry routed the enemy.

Chariovalda's charge completely toppled the right flank of Sigimer's oath's men into a red, chaotic ruin, and so we heard the thin blare of the distinctive horn, the same that had ringed across the hills when we last met Armin. It was a sound the Romans had learned to fear, for each such blast had signaled near doom for our armies. Now, though, the blare was desperate, going up, then down, and up again.

Armin was hoping to save the majority of the clans.

The Cherusci ran.

Around us, the slaves lifted their heads. Women were screaming encouragements to each other, horses were neighing, and in the distance, men could be seen flitting through the woods.

'Stay still,' I hissed at Fulcher and Hugo. 'They won't see us in the shadows.'

'Hope he gets his horse,' Fulcher grumbled.

'I would, it is priceless,' I said.

Warriors were seen. Some had arrows in their shields, others were bleeding from wounds, but most were untouched. A constant din of battle could be heard as the Roman drove to the backs of the army, and there Sigimer held firm, buying his men time. I could dimly see him in the glaring morning light, dissipating fog, and billowing dust. He was under the bronze standard reaching high, high above a thick, brave shield wall. I saw Roman pila coming down on the wall in droves, then the tromp of charging legionnaires and ultimately, the fall of the standard. The wall held, buckled, and broke as Chariovalda's men had circumvented to its side.

It was chaos.

In that battle, some twenty Romans died, most of the losses of Rome that day, and the Cherusci were scattered. They were running for us and with them, no doubt, was Armin. Pockets of resistance all over the fringes of the wood hampered Roman forces.

'Can you see them?' Fulcher asked Hugo.

'Armin?' he said softly, stretching his head in all directions as hundreds of men were beginning to pass us in panic. 'I see only beards.'

'A blond one and a dull handsome face,' I hissed. 'Let there be one,' I added, cursing at the dust, the vegetation and the hundreds of men streaming away. Screams made it hard to speak. Hard to think, even. There were many men fighting in the woods, for lord's honor forbade retreat and some actually held true to that creed. Some women fought, even, for Cherusci women did not fall prisoners easily.

101

'Ware!' Fulcher screamed, and a pilum embedded itself on the tree next to our shadowy cops of woods.

Then a group of well-armed men ran for the horses.

There were three men. Two were clad in brilliant ring mail, and one had a long vest of bear fur. He clutched a short, fat horn on his hip, and there was a long spatha, a heavy sword on his belt. His eyes were bright blue, his face well boned and strong, and he was cursing as he pointed out to his men where to go. One ran to pull at some women, cajoling them to hurry, another jumped on his horse, holding a spear and helped Armin control his horse. The horse was nervous, and it was not all due to the battle.

I hesitated.

I should not have hesitated, not after Armin had so many times tried to use me for his ends. His ends were the freedom of his people, and despite my love for Drusus, despite the admiration for the Roman army and my new friends the Batavi, I could not easily move against him.

He was a hero.

He was the one man, likely the only one I knew, with the vision to beat the foes of the Germani. *Unless you counted Maroboodus, my Father, who would kill Drusus, yes, but only to profit Rome in the end,* I thought. And I knew, despite my new allegiance to Rome, that all of Germania would suffer under the yoke of Drusus and Augustus. The land would change, and perhaps not for the better.

'Hraban,' Fulcher whispered, and I nodded at him. *My ladle is in the soup of Drusus*; I thought, *no matter how many innocents die, I shall eat from that soup.* I hefted my spear, breathed deep, and threw it. It spun in the air; it spun true. The man guarding Drusus saw it; his mouth fell open, and he fell across Armin, the spear through his belly. Armin grasped the man, cursing and making vile oaths, and I rode up from the shadows, my helmet tilted as I watched the man's astonished face. The Cherusci around us were fleeing in panic, little heeding their lord's plight.

'Hraban?' Armin said with a whisper, and I enjoyed the brief bout of fear in his face.

'I aimed for your leg, but perhaps he saved your life. It was a little high,' I told him with a guttural growl. 'So. Here we are. Again.' I pulled the Head Taker's massive blade from the sheath on my side.

'I have no time for this,' he told me irascibly, letting go of his man. 'You have the ring? We can still—'

'No, we cannot,' I told him bitterly. 'I lost the ring. To Odo. After I killed Leuthard. After you escaped him. We have common foes, but I do not trust you. Nor Catualda. I have a home now, and I shall take you home with me. And you will tell me how to get to Godsmount.'

His eyes betrayed frustration. 'I never meant to keep Lif from you. Nor do I now. She is no longer part of this. I will find a man to lead you there. I have one. One you would love to meet. But for now, I'll leave. We have to fight them, and fucking Segestes will pay.'

'He was already paid and expects the rest of the payment.' I grinned. 'Your lands.'

Armin shook his head in god-like anger, roaring and whipping the horse.

The rope that had been hidden and bound around the horse's foot went taut. There was an audible crack; the magnificent horse flew on its face, and Armin spilled painfully from it. I charged, and I was not sure if I would have killed him as he struggled to a seated position, but I did not get a chance.

My horse fell as well, and I was stuck under it so quickly I could not understand what had taken place. I was praying my foot was not broken. Fulcher bleated an oath as he engaged the other man of Armin's, the one by the women who were now rushing to the scene. Hugo hid behind a tree, and two new Cherusci ran for Armin. One spat in my direction, blonde, red hair spilling from under her hood. Her, for I saw the golden band across her brow, the high cheekbones and tall frame of a woman. It was Thusnelda, daughter of Segestes, lover of Armin, and she had thrown a spear that had downed my sturdy war horse. I cursed Woden, laughed in frustration and tugged at my foot as Fulcher speared his opponent, who still managed to grab his foot to stop him from moving. His horse was dancing around in wild circles, the dying Cherusci getting dragged behind.

Armin was up. He gazed at me in wonder. There was a man next to him, who wore a full metal helmet. He pointed a spear my way, demanding something, and Armin considered it. The warrior was tall, wide and terrible and cursed audibly. Finally, Armin shook his head, and the warrior held his head for a moment. Then he nodded and lifted Armin, and both staggered off to the woods. Thusnelda followed them.

Now some fleeing horsemen rode after them, and I heard Thusnelda screaming for Armin.

Fulcher had freed himself, and he and Hugo came to me and dragged me free. The fallen horse broke my sandal, but all I could do was scream in frustration.

'Find me another horse!' I yelled.

Fulcher did, and we rode after the refugees. It took time, of course, and they were long gone.

We were not alone. The Roman army surged to cut off the escape of as many of the Cherusci as they could. There were two more rivers to cross on the trade route, and Roman legates wanted to make sure there were not two more battles to be fought.

Sigimer had escaped, I heard the Romans screaming. Armin had as well, and I sobbed in rage.

And so, I rode after him. For the east.

CHAPTER 8

I rode so hard the horse was a sullen, resentful, and suffering piece of flesh in but a few hours time. By early afternoon, I growled at Hugo to show me the next crossing across the River Mödasg, the Angry One. We crashed through woods, dodged running warriors and bewildered local people who were witnessing the sudden, terrible rout of the Cherusci. This trek took all day, and we crossed the river in the afternoon. I was staring around wildly, ignoring all that Fulcher was saying and demanded Hugo to find out if Armin had been seen. A weary, wounded war chief told Hugo Armin had already passed that way. I cursed bitterly as the chief was cajoling his men to carry him. I rode on, Fulcher and Hugo with me and now there were the occasional Batavi and Thracian around us as well. They were scouts, brutally hedging the scattered enemy, avoiding any larger, organized groups of warriors but mercilessly pounding on the wounded and the cowards. I was sure I saw some of the Parthians of Gnaeus as well but lost the sight of them soon.

Night fell. The sun ran away from the sky, and I lost hope.

'We will never find him,' Fulcher said timidly while stroking the horse. 'Even Woden's loved one Hraban can occasionally fail. He got lucky.'

'He had Thusnelda save him. She does not seem to believe in luck,' I yelled, holding my head in anger. 'The bitch skewered my horse.'

'It did not even have a name yet, Hraban. Your horse,' Fulcher said with a small chuckle. I turned to stare at him with incredulity. He shrugged and spat. 'You have to admit it seems likely the gods wanted him to live, not strung at the end of Drusus's noose as he rides home. Perhaps it will be good for us, as well. Perhaps he will save us one day?'

'Regretting becoming a Roman?' I asked him, staring around at the woods filled with the noise of running dregs of an army and women and their pursuers.

'I'm your oaths man, Hraban. I have no doubts about our new allegiance, but perhaps Armin will have to live to balance the odds set against the Cherusci. Gods wish to see strife, not surrender. He is like you. Men love him and die for him. And spear throwing women fight for him. You are lucky she did not hit your manhood,' he said laughing. Even Hugo quaffed at that, and I sighed deeply.

'How in Hel's four names shall we find him?'

Then, as if the gods had heard me, a woman shrieked nearby. There were guttural yells of men, horses whinnying and then crude laughter as I heard the Thracian language being spoken. I gazed at Fulcher, and we both remembered the way we had met. I had killed the men who held him and raped his wife. The men had killed his son. His eyes flashed, and we rode for the sound.

And found Thusnelda.

There, in a small clearing, two burly Thracians were struggling with a tall woman on a bank of moss. She was breathing hard, her eyes agog with terror, and she tried to kick and bite at the two would-be rapists. They had half stripped her and were laughing at her futile fight until she scratched one of them, and they decided to finish the games and get to the point, and I saw the terror in the moonlight on the face of Thusnelda as one tried to kiss her savagely.

Without thinking too long about the matter, I got down from my horse and walked over with the Head Taker bared. The bigger of the two had just managed to tear the last clothes from Thusnelda's body when they noticed me in my armor and helmet.

The smaller one turned to me. 'Rome?'

'Yes,' I answered in Latin. 'A Batavi. What juicy morsel do you have there?'

The large one snorted as he tried to pry Thusnelda's feet apart, stripping his belt at the same time. 'Find your own fun Batavi dog. This one's ours, and we will not share.' I did not wish to share either so I slashed him through his neck so hard and so fast he did not realize what had happened. The other one was looking up, his open mouth full of foul, rotten teeth and the blade took them and his life. He screamed, and the blade visited his skull through his mouth. He fell back and died on Thusnelda, spraying blood on her nude and bruised body, and I dragged him off her. She backpedaled to the darkness, blushing and raging angry, hissing like a hurt lynx. Her hair was hiding her other eye as she looked at me apprehensively.

I ignored her for now, my mind awhirl with the implications of my prize.

I searched the corpses carefully and found some bracelets, Germani made, silver and bronze. I threw them at her. She didn't reach for them. 'Not mine. And I should think you know I rather use a spear than wear finery. Give me one of theirs?'

'No,' I chuckled. 'I rather not. Your aim might improve.'

'Wasn't trying to kill you,' she hissed.

'You tried to kill me after the battle in the lands of the Bructeri when I came for Lif,' I said. 'So why not now? Or when I wanted to take your pretty lover prisoner?'

'He needs the ring,' she said sullenly. 'That is why he has used you. He respects you. So I respected his opinion of you and spared you.'

'Don't have the ring, I told him.' I found her diadem, a thin golden thing and showed it to her. She spat in anger and then nodded though reluctantly. I grinned and threw it into her lap, and she instinctively grabbed it, forgetting to cover herself. She cursed, mumbled something uncouth about men and put the diadem on, little heeding our eyes. I sighed and nodded at Fulcher and Hugo, who had been sitting on their horse, stupefied by the beautiful female. They turned away.

107

'Tell me what do you think about your father's bid for power?' I asked while rifling the belts of the Thracians.

She shook her head. 'I'm with Armin.'

'A good daughter is to obey the father. You might not be betrothed to Maroboodus, my father, anymore, but should you not obey the fat piece of gristle?'

'I escaped him,' she said sullenly. 'After he ordered the retreat.' She cleared her throat. 'My ... clothes?' she asked hopefully, and I flicked the torn clothes to her.

'You only needed to ask.'

'You are paying me back for the spear. And my earlier belligerence. Are you not?' she asked as she pulled at the torn clothing with her feet, scowling at Fulcher, who slapped incredulous, sneaky Hugo on the back of the head. The rogue had been glancing at her, and he turned away, mumbling apologies. She was dressing up, and I laughed.

'Perhaps I am,' I agreed.

'He does not hate you, no matter if you do betray your people,' she said softly.

Armin, she was talking about Armin. 'No, I do not think your Armin truly hates anyone. He can sacrifice anyone at a whim, wipe his tears and say how sorry he is for having manipulated them, but he does not hate anyone,' I said and got up.

She shook her head. 'He hates your father.'

'For you?' I asked.

'For me.'

'Maroboodus is both my father and my foe,' I told her with some difficulty, for the thought of Maroboodus was burning me. I lifted my helmet and ran my finger across the scar he had given me after I burned his hall and nearly killed him. 'And as I told Armin, we have common enemies. But few common allies.'

'Fancy,' she said, indicating the scar while struggling with her tunic. She had been wearing men's clothing under her dress. 'He did that?'

'He did it. I would have done worse to him, as well. I will, one day.' I was walking back and forth as she was struggling. 'You had better hurry.

This is not a safe place, and I do not wish to explain why I skewered the two whoresons.'

'I thank you for that,' she said with some emotion, fear perhaps. 'I know you have had harsh times, Hraban, but you ride with the Romans now,' she chided me as she finished pulling on her pants.

I went to my hunches before her. 'So, do you think he truly cares for you? Armin? Or do you think he would have tried to topple Maroboodus, my father, anyway since it seems Maroboodus is trying to rally all the tribes against Rome just like Armin is? Even if he has surprising masters, Maroboodus does,' I asked her.

'He is a Roman,' she said bluntly. 'Like you.'

'A Roman but not like his son,' I said. 'I serve Nero Claudius Drusus, who is a fair man. He serves schemers and traitors and murderers. Do you think—'

She sighed, adjusting her hair. 'If you take me to him, he will reward you. He would reward you with Lif,' she told me with a smile. 'She is a beautiful girl, Hraban.' I stared at her sitting there. She had taken care of Lif when Hands the bounty hunter had fallen in Armin's hand while escaping Odo. 'She cuddles when she has eaten, and I swear she smiles at her name.' I looked away from her, holding my head. She came forward and placed a hand on my shoulder. 'Take me to him. And perhaps you will finally find a way to reconcile.'

Lif. I could get Lif back. *And perhaps I could find home again with Armin? No*, I thought. *Never again.* But I would be close to him. I could, perhaps, take him to Drusus. Or even slay him and then escape. I felt filthy as I stared at Thusnelda's eyes. 'Yes. Fulcher?'

Fulcher rode to me cautiously, trying to fathom my mood.

'So. Are we Germani again?' he asked, gesturing at the corpses and Thusnelda.

'No. I just don't like rapists.' I pointed my thumb at Thusnelda. 'I'm taking her to Armin. For Lif.' I held his eye for just a moment, and he knew what I was thinking about. *Lif. And perhaps Armin as well.* 'Don't mention the Thracians as you go.'

'Don't think anyone misses them,' Fulcher said and spat on the corpses. 'Bastards. I'll take the youngster with me then and wish you luck with your future, my Lord.'

'And I wish you the same, Fulcher,' I said and grinned at him. 'If we should not meet again,' I said as I fixed a hard eye on him, 'then you go find your wife, and Euric. Take them to Batavorium. As we agreed. Chariovalda will let you serve him. Try to find Wandal if you can. And tell Cassia—'

He snorted. 'No need for you to twist your jaw trying to admit it. I'll sing her a song of love, and I will tell her you are doing what you must.'

'Here,' I said as I gave him the bloodied Head Taker. 'If things go sour, keep it safe. It is ancient. It should go to Lif one day. And this.' I gave him the end of the spear that had killed Leuthard. 'Wolf's Bane, spear of Aristovistus.' I kept my helm and my armor. I also kept Nightbright.

He leaned close, and we embraced. He whispered in my ear. 'Make sure you survive. Remember your honor. I'll come and find you if you are lost. I'll tell Drusus you are doing your best.'

I nodded, swallowed my fears and clasped his forearm. He gestured for Hugo, and they rode off. I watched him go and turned to Thusnelda, who was smoothing her clothes, unsure what would follow. 'I guess you learn to run faster the next time the Romans butcher your army.'

'I got separated from the army in the dark and ran the wrong way, not too slowly,' she said and sniffed indignantly in the dark.

'Where is Armin then?' I asked. 'Somewhere beyond the trade route and the rivers?'

She laughed, not taking my hand. 'I will never tell you before we get there, my dear Roman friend and the Oath Breaker. But I am grateful.' I mounted the horse and then reached down to her and grabbed her hand. 'Do not make me regret this, Raven,' she said, and I pulled her up to me. We managed it with a struggle, and she was seated uncomfortably in the saddle that seemed too small for both, her hips tight against me. She glanced over her shoulder at me and raised her eyebrow. I cursed, let her have the saddle and slithered up beyond the four-horned saddle and slid to sit on the horse's rump.

'Where to, Princess?' I asked her.

'I was lost, oaf, remember?' she huffed and then gestured around. 'If you find the Weihnan, the Holy River to the east, I can find him. He is likely to be in a village of his father's warlord, not far from the ford. Perhaps a day's ride to the east? No doubt getting men together after the disaster,' she said so softly it could have been a forest mouse sniffing, but I nodded. 'Hoping to kill my father, perhaps,' she added.

'Then, there we shall go,' I spurred the horse.

We rode to meet Armin.

CHAPTER 9

We traveled through the long morning. The sunlight was peeking through the many holes in the canopy of the forest, lighting up mossy boulders, and the happy sound of birds made one almost forget the thousands of dangerous men traveling the land. The trip was strangely peaceful, and I enjoyed it, partly because I now had a plan. A filthy and dangerous plan, but one nonetheless. By midday, things got more interesting. We avoided bands of Cherusci still flitting through the forest, hid from the leading elements of Roman cavalry, all scouting around us but soon, some hours after midday, the Romans disappeared, and Germani alone could be heard talking in the dark shades. I pulled off my heavy Roman sagum cloak and threw it aside. I stared at the tunic over my armor, took that off as well, and cursed myself for not picking up a patched up garment with a hood from the occasional wounded men. We crossed a smaller stream, then another, and my belly churned with hunger at the sight of lazy fish resting in warm ponds, amidst smooth rocks of the brilliantly flowing waters. We rode through the midday and the poor exhausted Thusnelda managed to sleep on my shoulder, despite the discomfort. I wondered what Cassia would think if she saw Thusnelda there, and I chuckled at the thought of her thin eyebrows raised in divine fury. *Gods, I loved the woman*, I thought. Her love had cost me Ansbor, my sole remaining companion from childhood, but it was his choice. Wandal, I had lost before that, gods knew where he was. Ansigar was with Gernot, my brother serving Odo. *I had Fulcher. And Chariovalda. And that wonderful woman*, I mused as I adjusted Thusnelda's head. She mumbled in some discontent and settled down. *I would meet Cassia again*, I decided and rode ahead, a hollow feeling of fear in my belly.

Then, when the afternoon was nearly over, we came upon Weihnan, the Holy One, the last of the three rivers that ran to make up the mighty Visurgis River. Predictably, as I guided the horse out of the trails to a bank of sand, there was another ford not far and men were running across it. I rode that way and saw a motley crew of Cherusci warriors, their leader in leather mail and a wolf pelt guarded it. I rode down to the water's edge, the green and blue water churning on a very shallow ford. There I sat with a Cherusci princess on my lap and my quite distinctive helmet on my head, which I had forgotten to hide.

The two hundred men across the ford had been guiding refugees there all night and day. Seeing us did not give them a pause at first, but then a man shouted, pointing at the helmet, and the men, after a moment's incredulous silence and some excited whispering, charged in a haphazard mass, their leader attacking the churning water first. A herd of horses could not have churned and thrown up more water as the ferocious band. I grimaced as they came forward, and their steely faces held no promise of friendly hugs or happy banter. 'Would you mind?' I asked Thusnelda, who was rubbing her eyes, looking drowsily at the specter of my death.

She immediately jumped down, resolutely strode forward, and screamed: 'Hold, you! No! He is friendly today! Do not sully your honor!' and reluctantly they did as she hopped energetically before them.

'Did he do that to you?' one man asked with a dire look my way. He was pointing at her torn clothing.

'No! He saved me, please!' she cajoled and slowly, very slowly they went quiet.

The wolf garbed leader advanced on her, and I could hear her speaking in hushed tones, her hair covering the sides of her face as she leaned over to the man, and he was nodding and grunting, and the one word I could hear was Oath Breaker, and the men around her stirred and looked at me unkindly. Eventually, the warrior gestured at me, and they walked forward carefully, climbed out of the river and soon I was surrounded by ten strong men. All had spears pointed at me.

'Weapons,' said the leader. 'Give them over.'

'I am not a prisoner. I am a guest,' I retorted with a bored voice, and the effect was not positive.

'An unwelcome guest, like a plague. Give them your weapons,' he growled. Thusnelda gave me a begging look and sighed. I shook my head.

'Armin will be safe,' she said, glowering at me.

The leader snorted. 'Oh yes, they will surely see the wisdom of letting the damned Oath Breaker keep his sword. They will reward me with cones of honey, silver rings, barrels of mead, and a herd of fat cows if you are wrong,' the leader spat. He looked at Thusnelda, whose eyes were huge and wet, and his comments died in his throat as he squealed and grunted like a pig. His honor demanded he held onto his demand, but few could ever deny Thusnelda anything and so he hung his head and gestured for me to ride on, to the scorn of his men. So I did, rode over the river, to the lands of Sigimer. My horse neighed as the cold water reached its belly. Far behind, the Roman army was marching, and we heard the cornu ordering the cohorts onwards.

We rode north through waving fields of wheat and barley, through rich vegetable gardens and lonely halls that would soon be flaming husks. We constantly saw the ragged bands of Cherusci warriors streaming off to north, south and east. The army was disintegrating like sparrows at the approach of a hawk. The Cherusci escorts grunted in disgust at the chaos in the army, and the leader glanced at me. 'Segestes and Sigimer are in disagreement. What remains, will stop your masters,' he said glumly.

I snorted. 'Segestes is the lord of the land soon, and he won't stop us. And I am not sure Sigimer is alive, even.'

'Shut up, Hraban,' Thusnelda said softly as the men around us grinded their jaws together in rage. We rode through men lounging in the sunlight, resting, all of whom were eyeing the west with worry, seeking signs of the

Roman cavalry approaching. Some men would point at my helmet and armor, and whisper. There were some wounded men, and I saw burly men guarding some Roman prisoners, evidently over-eager legionnaires who had gotten lost in a pursuit.

Then we came to a farmstead.

It was a huge field with a simple hut in the middle, and there were many nobles sitting on horses or crouching on their haunches, speaking animatedly. Amongst them stood, to my surprise, the gaunt brother of Segestes and Sigimer. It was Inguiomerus. He was no longer warring against the Suebi in the east, but he was there. I could see his gangly arms wheeling in the air as he was explaining something to a crowd of chiefs, men easy to recognize by their expensive armor and better weaponry, ornaments of golden and silvery splendor. They were mostly old men, rich men, men with everything to win or lose.

There was no sign of Sigimer.

But Armin was there, standing with his arms crossed, tired to the bone as he stooped to the side, and his blonde hair was matted with grease, dirt, and blood, his armor and bear tunic torn at the hem, a bloody scratch showing underneath at his hip. He was straddling his father's standard, forlornly sprawled in the dust. The once mighty Cherusci were all dark-faced and gloomy, and as Inguiomerus saw us approaching, he whispered to Armin. Armin turned his head. On his face, there was a look of utter, blissful relief and a hint of tears, and I knew then the bastard had this one weakness. Thusnelda. She blissfully beamed at him; at her cousin, whom she loved with as much passion as he did her. Reluctantly, he tore his eyes off us and turned back to address Inguiomerus. We stopped our horses behind the nobles. Armin pointed a finger at his uncle. 'Inguiomerus, I still do not understand why you come here to berate us when you had no part in it. Did we fail? Segestes failed us both. But you do not lead my father's men.'

'Perhaps I should, from now on?' the gangly Cherusci said thickly. 'This plan was utter idiocy. You fight on a hill, not at a ford.'

Armin agreed, though only partially. 'I hated the plan, but Father wanted to fight there. I agree we should not have fought there. We should have forced the enemy to march and tire itself out. But I don't think we should have met them on any hill either, now or later unless we had some surprise in mind.'

'Uphill battle, Armin, is hard even for a Roman,' Inguiomerus told him with a lecturing voice.

Armin spat. 'No. It is a deathtrap. Only surprise works. Such surprises take the time to plan properly. We could have drawn them after us, harried them day and night, all over their columns. We could have cut through their army at night and denied them sleep and with ten thousand men harassing them thus it would have been very tiresome for the Romans. They would have withered. Their cavalry would have been slowly slaughtered. Then their infantry would have had to carry the wounded. Their trains of mules would have been scattered. Parts of their army would have built castrum and stayed to guard them, and they would have slowly split themselves to the winds. But it is done. Now we have to replan this whole thing. You go and fight with the Semnones. Go. You brought a thousand men, and while I thank you for doing so, it is not enough now,' Armin told him with a hint of a command in his voice. Inguiomerus scowled at that, and Armin took a deep breath, spread his hands in a gesture of peace and continued with more respect. 'Best take them and spare their lives, and we shall endure the ravages and get ready for the next year.'

'What if Rome builds a castra here?' a tall Cherusci warlord asked.

'They won't,' Armin snorted. 'They have the Castra Flamma already. They cannot support anything beyond Luppia. Not this year. What they build each evening will be abandoned.'

Inguiomerus snapped his fingers, and the attention turned to him again. 'Yes. It was Segestes and Sigimer who failed. I do not say you did badly. Had they fought elsewhere and our traitor brother done his bit, we would have slaughtered them there. I do not approve of such cowardly plans as you just shared. Tug at their tail? No. A hill. That is where we can win.'

'We, Uncle?' Armin asked tiredly. 'They are armored and disciplined and can march up a hill easily enough.'

116

The gaunt man scowled as Armin was not easy to manipulate nor threaten. Inguiomerus's finger pointed towards the west. 'They are not gods; they are men. They can be killed like the Suebi, or the Chatti, or any other man, so I say we gather your men while there is still time. We will find a good hill indeed, and I shall lead and men will flock—' he was saying in a strained voice, his beard jutting aggressively.

'No,' Armin said, and I saw many of the remaining war chiefs disagreed with him. 'No,' he said again, empathetically. 'We are scattered. We have two thousand men able to fight. Not all have weapons. The Romans have endured too few losses. It is too late now to fight them head on. We could have, had we not lost Segestes and half our men. This war is lost.'

'Germani fight! They do not run!' Inguiomerus said with a malicious, deep voice. 'Where is your honor?'

'My plan,' Armin said softly and dangerously, 'lies in beating them when we have most of the advantages! We nearly destroyed three of their legions and all their auxilia, and—'

'Nearly,' Inguiomerus sneered. 'It's like nearly marrying a pretty noblewoman but ending up with a toothless slave girl.' Men laughed at his words, and Armin glowered.

Armin was glancing at us, enduring the mockery, and his eyes met his love. She nodded at him encouragingly, and he took a deep breath. 'Stand in set piece battle with them now and you get slaughtered unless we have thrice the men. Ten thousand? We would lose anyway, but then we could try. Like we did in the river, before Segestes left us,' he said. Then he leaned closer. 'And Segestes is at large. He has thousands of men ready to do battle. But not for us, no. You wish to see if he loves you like he loved Sigimer? My father? You wish to risk that? I'm sure he will turn his face your direction soon enough, and he won't be smiling. He has been promised these lands. Why would he let you keep yours?'

Inguiomerus did not give up. 'Because I can defend mine. Because he hates to fight and to take my lands would lure the Suebi out in hordes. He does not want that, no. And now? You say we run. A flight? Then, later schemes and surprises? That is not the way of our fathers. You fight, and you win or die. That is the way to do battle and the way to save tribes from the displeasure of the gods, not to mention the Romans,' Inguiomerus was saying, explaining it as if to a child, but he was staring around the woods, perhaps wondering where Segestes was.

Armin looked around at the gathered chiefs who seemed troubled. 'Since Sigimer is lost, I am the thiuda, Inguiomerus. I should lead this war. It has been decided.'

'No, we will not make you the War King. I said you did well, and Segestes and Sigimer failed, but perhaps this is all your and Sigimer's fault, indeed. Why did you go and help the fools anyway? The Sigambri and the Bructeri? Foolish! Had you stayed at home, there would not be a mad army of armored enemies setting up to burn our lands.'

Armin growled and stepped forward. He poked a finger into his uncle's chest. 'We went because we would have fought Rome the next year. And we could have won this year. I had a brilliant plan; father had the chiefs and men all working together, and it was a chance for us to–'

Inguiomerus sneered and pushed the hand away. Some men grabbed their weapons, and he scoffed at them. 'What you did is you turned the Roman army into an enemy army, one which is in your lands. Your plan lost our allies thousands of men, thousands! Dead and wounded. Chiefs in their dozens. They may never recover! And now we also have a civil war on our hands,' Inguiomerus said savagely and enjoyed the approving looks he got from several more prominent chiefs. 'You, Armin, are useless against Rome.' I coughed. I could not help it, but I did not like Inguiomerus. The chief escorting me tried to stop me, but I slapped his hands off and all turned to look at me.

I cleared my throat, sorry I had made the noise. I spoke nonetheless. 'And yet, the one thing the Romans fear is not Inguiomerus on a hill. It's Armin's horn in the woods.'

Inguiomerus looked at me in disbelief. 'Hraban?' he said. 'That helmet is his, no?'

'Yes, Lord,' I agreed.

'You! Slave to the Batavi and the Romans! Oath breaking cur and slayer of our kind. God's cursed walking corpse. How dare you show your face here?' he bellowed.

I shrugged. 'After we split your army, I found this woman in the woods. I decided to bring her home.' I looked at Armin, and I could see him struggling. He wanted to go to Thusnelda, but his honor forbade him. 'Or should I take her to her father? Where is Segestes?' I continued viciously, and Armin flinched.

Inguiomerus spat at the ground and pointed a gnarly finger my way. 'Armin. If you wish to carry the burden of the War King, you have to be ruthless. I say have him killed. He is a traitorous dog. Nail his skull on a tree by the fords and let all Romans crossing the Holy One gaze at it,' Inguiomerus dared Armin, and there were wagers made all around to see if Armin would.

Armin looked at us and spoke heavily. 'Hraban. Ever appearing to cause chaos and sow discontent.' He turned to the chiefs. 'I would love to have his head on my saddle. I would let it hang there as I ride around the land, giving people hope. And why not? He has failed me each and every time I have dealt with him, choosing his father, then Nero Claudius Drusus over the causes of the free people.' He took a deep breath, and I was about to rebuke him, but he let out a sigh and pointed at Thusnelda. 'But he is here now with my cousin, and so the storm raven is redeemed in my eyes. He shall keep his head.'

Inguiomerus spat. 'Yea. He shall live. All the Romans shall, in fact. And you call yourself a thiuda?'

'I am a thiuda, Uncle,' he laughed with his head up high. 'I am a man of honor. I do not easily slay men who fight for their daughter. And that is what Hraban has been doing. He has no home, none. Even Rome will leave him cold, in the end. All he wants is his daughter.'

'I do want her,' I said softly. 'And I thank you for sparing her when Hands was being chased by Lok's minions.'

'You are welcome,' he smiled. 'As for Lif, it was my duty.'

'Your duty?' I asked.

He smiled and shook his head at me, ignoring Inguiomerus. 'Later, Hraban. Now, I wish Father was here. Did you see what took place with him?'

'I saw his standard fall.' I nodded at the once brilliant, beautiful thing in the dust. 'Then I tried to capture you and saw no more,' I told him. 'I am sorry.'

'We shall speak more, Hraban, soon,' Armin said heavily . He was tired but still handsome as a young god and I felt compelled to bow to him from my saddle. I cursed myself and asked Woden to keep my head clear. I had failed to slay Drusus for him; I should not fail to serve him to Drusus. After I had Lif, I would. He owed me. I did not owe him, I reminded myself.

Armin turned to speak with Inguiomerus and a short Cherusci came to lead us to the side. We followed him, were served some fish and rich ale. I watched the great, coming man of the Cherusci deal with the fey Inguiomerus. Armin was a few years older than I was. He had schemed against Father, afraid Maroboodus would marry Thusnelda and raised a Marcomannic civil war to topple my father, though Father had wanted him to do so to be rid of his rivals. Armin had then fled and captured our ring with Catualda's murderous help, though Catualda, a relative had a claim on it. *The fat-lipped turd,* I thought and wondered where he was. I did not see him and cursed aloud. Then I waved the warrior away as he thought I had complaints about the food.

I admired your father, Thumelicus.

I eyed him, tired and fey, arguing for his right to rule. Not only the plots against Father, Armin had gone home and plotted a whole winter and spring to do battle with Nero Claudius Drusus. I shook my head. It was no small feat he had managed to bring together all the Luppia River tribes to grab a near victory over three legions in a pitched battle. It would not be easy to duplicate that near success, of course, for Drusus would never again ignore Armin's capacity for a surprise, but it was a bleeding wound in a Roman heart. Now, Armin had lost the support of Segestes, his father and brother, and there he was, his back straight and demanding the right to rule.

I hated and admired him, and that was the first time I began to wonder how far was he trying to reach. *Was he to be the savior of the Germani? Free, happy, noble, and generous? Or like my father, did he wish for the ultimate power? Was there any difference between the two? Did he desire to be a king? King of the*

Germani? An abhorrence of the free men of the tribes, yet something we would all have a desperate need of, should we fight Rome. Us. Them, I thought, groaned and drank my ale with an angry grunt.

'He is a complex man,' Thusnelda said from the side. I had forgotten her.

'We are all complex. I just think I have not had time to plan anything for myself so far, except for regaining what I have lost. He is reaching for kingdoms, and I am always just one step ahead of death,' I cursed.

She hesitated and blushed. 'He does not wish to be a king. Do not be absurd.'

'How do you know?' I asked her with a smile.

She swatted at a fly, irritated, and scowled. 'I know him.'

'Nobody knows Armin,' I mused, half to myself and even Thusnelda stared at the man. After a while she spoke.

'In any case,' she mumbled and flinched as Armin was now angrily shouting at Inguiomerus. 'I will help you find Lif. I know she is to stay with this Veleda Hands told us about. You are her father and have to see she is fine.'

'They say I will risk the world if I find Veleda,' I mused with amusement. 'That Odo will slay her and pour her blood on Woden's Ringlet and thus will incite the events that lead to Ragnarök. I have decided to risk it. But you will still help me?'

She smiled. 'I'm not a great believer in curses and prophecies. I think men will destroy Woden's world indeed, one day, but not your family. Nor Odo's. Do not be absurd. And I know you will fight for Veleda. I've seen you fight. I will ask Armin to help.'

'He needs help, apparently,' I said with some concern, for Inguiomerus hurled his cup before Armin and strode away, taking a good number of Sigimer's warlords with him.

'He will survive. His lands will not, but he will,' Thusnelda said sadly.

The rest of the chiefs argued for a time, and in the end, Armin gave some terse orders. Apparently, the army was split in two. Inguiomerus took his few men and some of Sigimer's back home towards the east. He rode for the distant lands of Albis River and did not look back. There

121

Inguiomerus would fight the Suebi tribes of the Langobardi and the Semnones and wait until the Cherusci begged for him to save them from Rome. Armin was left with Sigimer's remaining lords, some rogue troops of Segestes. Hundreds would slink home to save their life stocks from the relentless legions.

There would be no fighting Rome in the lands of Sigimer.

Armin stood there for a time. If you ever saw a man in throes of desperation, gathering strength, begging the gods for patience, then you know what I saw. Finally, Armin looked at us, his face white with fatigue, and he nodded heavily. 'Follow us. We have to move.'

And we did.

Armin took his men north through verdant fields and pastures. His men ran after him and rode their powerful horses, most looking back where now halls had begun to burn near the ford. We were making great speed, and I rode behind Armin as he gently talked with Thusnelda.

'He is smitten with her, is she not?' a young Cherusci asked me with hushed tones as if he had made a great discovery. He was blushing.

'Yes,' I said simply, and Armin turned to me. He was looking at my eyes, and I looked back steadily. He said nothing, but he was thinking and apparently, Thusnelda had made a request on my behalf. We stopped as the night fell, the little over one thousand men eating what they had, the women feeding them, tending their wounds and blisters. During the night, many more would leave the army, going home.

I was brushing my horse when I noticed Armin approaching. He stood near and looked at some men being fuzzed over by their women. He snorted, clapped my shoulder and pointed at one of his men. 'That fat one, he has his wife carry all the food, the daughters the drink, and he has four slaves trapping and hunting for him, and he is not even a chief. I have never seen him lose any fat though he fights like an irate bear.'

I grunted. 'Wandal used to eat like a glutton. He fought like a hero the day I lost him.'

'Wandal, eh? Have you searched for your friend? I am sorry for Ansbor,' he said, neutrally.

I shrugged, bothered by his care. 'Wandal is a slave or a corpse. I have had no time to search for him. And when I find him, I have to tell him about Ermendrud.'

'His woman?' Armin asked, half smiling, though it was a sad smile.

I nodded, rubbing my face. 'I let her down. Him as well. I let her die to Leuthard. As for Ansbor? There was fault in me. In him. In life. Wyrd.'

'Gods fuck us sometimes, Hraban. Wyrd,' he agreed.

'Where is Catualda?' I asked him. I hated the bastard. He was one of the men I had sworn to kill.

He nodded as if expecting the question. 'Catualda is a clever man. Cruel, but clever. But he is not so useful in battle. I have used him to keep an eye on Segestes. He is riding after the traitor now, trying to see where he takes his army. Don't worry about Catualda.'

'I will always worry about Catualda. Did he not lie to my face and betray me so many times? His Father Bero?' I informed him.

'Did you not betray Bero for Maroboodus?' He smiled.

I did not answer his question. 'For now, I only worry about Lif.'

'Only about Lif?' He smiled again. 'You chose Drusus. And Drusus wants me. Tell me, Hraban, am I helping my would be captor? You tried once already.'

'I might be lucky, Armin,' I grinned and lied, 'but I have no desire to try my luck beyond a breaking point. I doubt I could carry you to Drusus.'

'You felled Rochus, they say,' he mused with some steel in his voice. 'He is not dead, is he? I have not seen him after the battle. I could use his help.'

'No, not dead,' I agreed, bothered by his question. I liked Rochus.

'He was supposed to be home already,' Armin stated darkly. 'If they—'

'He is with Drusus,' I said reluctantly.

'What?' Armin asked me. 'Captured?' he stated more than asked.

'He ...' I began and thought of telling him to give himself up if he valued Rochus. He might, or might not. Likely not. 'He betrayed you.'

'Hraban, he is my brother,' Armin said, his hand clutching a long spatha on his side. 'You cannot claim he would ... He fought well, didn't he? For me!'

I nodded and pointed a finger at him. 'He was in Oddglade where we bought Segestes. He saved me from your uncle, with whom I had a small unfortunate misunderstanding, and I took him to Drusus. They embraced, laughed, and feasted together, and he was tended to by Roman chirurgii and medicus. He is as Roman as I am now. Perhaps more. For he had a choice. I did not.'

'Rochus,' he breathed, holding his head.

'Perhaps he is called something else now,' I said viciously, and then regretted it. 'I am sorry. He chose thus. Strange it is that I am here, and he is there, eh? Especially after the battle where we championed different sides.'

'Different sides,' he said as he was trying to collect his dignitas. 'To get back to my earlier thoughts. I am not sure what side you are on. You killed Roman troops to save her?' he asked me, rubbing his face.

'I did. It was ... wyrd. It happened. And so, I have no home now. But I could not let them rape her,' I said truthfully, for I would have done so even if I had no orders to find Armin. 'Even if I did leave you and her with Leuthard that night and she might have died in the unpleasantries, this was more ... personal. I hate rapists.'

'I hang them without a Thing or settled wergild,' Armin agreed. 'I will help you find Lif.'

'You will?' I asked him, my voice crackling with hope. 'I am grateful. That is all I have left. Hope of finding her. I have lost everything else.'

'You will see her before Yule. I will send a war band with you to Godsmount and a man who will know the way. I will tell the man how to get to the two-pronged mountain.'

'You know the way?' I asked him, wondering.

'I do,' he said. 'It is a tricky path up the mountain, and the shrine to Woden is well hidden. There is Woden's Plate and before that, a Woden's Finger and gods know what else of Woden's. Perhaps he pissed up there when he took Midgard under his banner and there is Woden's lake as well. You know, they said Woden created men in Gothonia—'

'Yes, and they say my blood is of the first family.' I showed him my black hair.

He nodded. 'Yes, you are. But you see, you are not alone. While men were spawned in the frigid shores of the northern sea, making Aska and Esla strong and hardy, he took some south. But enough of that. You will learn more later. Did you know it was on the summit of Godsmount he claimed Midgard.'

'Really?' I breathed, wondering how he knew so much about the matter.

'Really? I know not.' He grinned. 'They say it is so. Wyrd knows if it is true. They said he stood there after feasting and sacrificed part of his soul to bind Midgard to him. Thus, he gave birth to stone, wood, and plant and created the balance of the life, and this world became real. His. And so it would make sense it is there it can all be unraveled. They say a great völva guards it, but now this völva is perilous. It is Lok's blood running through the veins of this Veleda.' He smiled mysteriously. 'And she defies Odo. Just like your prophecies say.'

'She is Tear's daughter. The youngest one, the one who has to die. I will go and see Lif safe. If you provide me men, or this man, Veleda will be safe.'

'What will you do with Lif, Hraban?' he asked me.

'I will … ' I began and went quiet. 'I will ...'

'See she is happy and safe. Is she safe with you?'

'No,' I said immediately. 'She is not.'

He placed a hand on my shoulder. 'Fine. As for your rootlessness. Come and fight with me. Guard the land and be a Cherusci. Guard her, visit her and make Odo a corpse. I will help. When I can.' He gazed around in distress. 'Imagine, we had ten thousand men. Now? Nothing. But I will rebuild. The men are still there, even if Sigimer's death has made them uncertain cowards. We have tens of thousands of men. We need fewer lords' He spat, grumbled darkly and squeezed my shoulder.

'I suppose that is a good offer. Yes,' I lied and felt my honor was sullied by the words.

He gazed at me and smiled. 'I'm happy we have an agreement. For a change, it is one that does not cost us anything. No? Unless you are still Roman. But we shall see.'

'You trust me, Armin?' I asked him, and cursed myself for bringing it up.

He chortled. 'I trust no one, Hraban. And I will not be left alone with you. Not ever. I will not share my plans of disrupting your Drusus's army either. And I don't expect you to slay nor fight him, for you love him. I will have plenty of work for you other than killing men you have fought side by side with. We will conquer. But you will be spared dishonor.'

'A bold claim for someone on a run.' I laughed. 'But yes, I do love Nero Claudius Drusus. He gave me home, but I cannot abandon Lif. I am happy I managed to spare Thusnelda. Give me what power you can of will, Armin. I will help with what I can and gods help us find a way to work together without compromising our honor again.' *Fucking liar*, I thought of myself.

'Yes,' he mused, 'the gods must forgive a lot in our case, no? And in your father's.' His eyes flickered at me, and I saw there was doubt and rage there, as if he was considering a past hurt.

'Yes,' I agreed.

'Odo has your ring, no?' he mused with a small smile now, his fey mood having evaporated. 'You told me and Thusnelda, as well.'

'Yes, he has it,' I agreed.

'And your friend Drusus will go home for the winter. After raping and burning a bit in my homeland,' he stated with gritted teeth.

'Yes, likely so,' I agreed, knowing it was true.

'We have the winter to find Odo. Perhaps getting the ring is a common cause that harms neither you nor me,' he said happily. 'Inguiomerus was very bitter, Catualda ... I lost it.'

'I would be honored to, Lord,' I answered, and my heart fluttered in anticipation of seeing Odo's scrawny body ravaged by Nightbright. 'Know you where he is?'

'I know where his scarecrows are most often seen. Due south of the battle of the rivers. In the wilds and unkind lands just south of where we lost my father. I will send men to find him. I have never had reason to find this home of theirs, but now I do. I need the ring. Even Inguiomerus has to see its worth. It will free him from most of the Suebi wars. If I have it, the

126

Suebi chiefs will see it as a sign of great favor. Some might join us. What is the name of the place?'

'Odo's ancestral home? Gulldrum. Under the stone, he said. A cave?' I wondered. 'He had a lot of men last year when he tried to take me.'

'But less after?' Armin grinned. 'I heard from Catualda they most all died.'

'Yes, the day Catualda killed my friend Koun for your ring. Mine.' He glanced at me and nodded. We had a sad, dangerous past. I went on. 'A friend died, and the ring was gone, and I did not regain it then, but later. Yes, most all of Odo's men and women died. But Odo is sure to have more such creatures.'

'You will treat with Catualda and settle your scores,' Armin said with a warning. 'Carefully. With time. Within the laws and the rules. He cannot defeat you in battle, Hraban. Think about that.'

'He helped Father have my mother and grandfather killed. He betrayed his father, Bero. All for his glory and the ring. And Armin, I should not wonder if he had plans beyond helping you with the ring.'

'He has a right to the ring.' Armin sighed. 'Your grandfather stole it from his father, Bero. I am asking you to think hard, Hraban, what you shall do when the time comes to deal with him. For now, he is useful to me. And yes, I know of his ambitions. He wants a kingdom. I don't, but he does. In the north? With the Suebi? In the south where Marcomanni rule? He is here, gathering wealth and fame, but in truth he wants to rule the Marcomanni, I think.'

'Really?' I asked, surprised. 'He told you this?'

'He speaks to men when he is drunk, and some of those men are there to spy on him,' Armin said, grinning. 'I trust no one. He should go north with the ring. There it can summon an army of the old families in Gothonia and Svear coast. But life is harsh up there. Winters are deadly. Svear and strange Nomads of the East raid in the summers. No, he knows the Marcomanni. And he seems confident he might one day find power there. Here? As you see, we have many mighty men here and all hate each other, and there is no room for strange new lords. Wait, Hraban, should you see him. I need him.'

I shuddered, cursed softly and bowed to Armin. 'Yes, Lord.'

He gave me a sideward glance and smiled. 'We will see if you have learned patience.'

'Patience for a Marcomanni, Lord, is as likely as a wolf enjoying berries,' I grumbled.

'You are a wolf, Hraban, but eat berries for awhile.' he laughed. 'He must be a great man for you to admire him so. Nero Claudius Drusus.'

I felt tired and made a gesture to the West. 'Drusus is not unlike you. He cheats and lies like a vicious, clever child, but for Rome. For ideals. Cicharni Germani, our Ubii and Vangione brethren across the Rhenus look at him and admire him just like your men adore you,' I said, and Armin smiled.

'Vicious child?' he grinned and shook his head. 'Perhaps so. Perhaps he shall make you a king for the Marcomanni, after all. A useful client, perhaps?' Armin smirked. 'If I die.'

I shrugged. 'He has many battles to win.' I felt a cold hand squeeze my heart and feared for my lord Drusus for a second. I cursed such omens and prayed for Woden to help him.

He smiled and guided his horse around some jagged stones. 'Must keep this horse alive. You killed the one I loved. I forgive you. You have seen a lot in one year. Much more than most men twice your age. Your father truly changed everything. Whole nations are moving. I will lie and cheat as a child and fight like a wolf for our people. I will fight your pretender father and Drusus and any general they might replace him with. Even my brother if I have to. And Segestes if he can give me no explanation.'

'He sold you out, Armin,' I said tediously.

He snorted. 'But it might not be polite to present him such an accusation if one is to renew our relationship.'

'He was sold your lands,' I explained, not sure if Armin understood.

'Yes, but I will make life hard for him, should he try to claim them,' Armin smiled coldly. 'I will make it very hard. Let him come each summer. We do what the Sigambri do. Hide and fight and kill and few men will call him the Lord of the Cherusci when they see his halls in cinders each spring.'

'You just need an army,' I spat and shrugged apologetically.

'I'll seed one if I have to,' he said darkly.

'Thusnelda would not approve. Or do you mean to whelp an army on her?' I laughed.

He grinned. 'No. I will never betray her. She is better than gold in my palm, and I need nothing but her if not the freedom of our people. That is the one thing I treasure above her. Here. I have to go and see the Falcon's Hall ahead. Talk to you soon.' He whipped his horse, and far ahead I saw a hall of high splendor, two layered and with thick doorposts like mine had once been. There were many men mounted in the yard; people were agitated and confused as they ran around. Some women were herding scared cows; nervous dogs were barking, and there was a cat staring at the confusion with an alert look.

'I am Kuno,' said the Cherusci chief who had escorted us to Armin. I was startled but nodded as the large man rode next to me.

'You know my name,' I said glumly.

'I know what they call you,' he said cautiously, his face unhappy under his bushy beard. 'But I also see Lord Armin treats you with respect and you speak as brothers. So I ask for your name.'

'Hraban. Of the Marcomanni. A lost soul in a sea of lost souls,' I told him, looking at Armin gesturing at south and west, speaking to a grizzled old Cherusci.

'Ride on,' someone called ahead. 'We are going north.'

Thusnelda guided her horse next to me. 'Did you agree?'

'Yes, we made a pact,' I told her. 'Though I am not sure I will fight Rome for him.'

'Good. Keep the pact, Hraban, and I'll be your friend,' she told me with relief.

I nodded, swallowing bile for my dishonesty, and the cavalry rode on. Men were breaking off it all the time, hiding away, or being commanded to take messages. We rode until a bank of clouds covered the moon, and a fog rose from the river. Then men rode from the dark and people were yelling questions. Kuno was rising upon his horse's back, trying to see to the dark. 'It a messenger. We are near Sigimer's hall, the Glittering Oak.'

'Armin's orders?' Thusnelda asked, clutching her cloak.

'Yes, I think so,' Kuno said uncertainly. 'Yes.' He noticed a man beckoning for them and pointed to the north. Hundreds of others rode east. Kuno rode forward and consulted a bit with a thin man who was gesturing around wildly, and then the lord of our escort nodded. He came to us, looking gloomy. 'Armin wants us to ride for Sigimer's hall. There is some strange cavalry probing to the east of it. Enemy cavalry. Short spears and fur hats.'

'Thracian cavalry,' I guessed. They were causing chaos as usual.

'The men will deal with them,' Kuno said with jealous pride, for he would have loved to go with the men who now whipped their tired horses. The riders were happy and grinned at the chance to fight back. We were left with ten men.

'Let us go then. Over those two hills?' Thusnelda said, squinting to the north.

'Three hills and that yellow and green valley full of moose and deer,' he told her.

'Used to follow Armin there to hunt when we were but children.' She giggled. 'A boar nearly got us once.'

Kuno nodded and laughed, and we rode to the dark until we entered a hauntingly beautiful valley full of fields and lone trees. In the moonlight, it looked eerie and silent. 'Where are the deer? Many here usually, when it is night.'

But there were none.

They had fled. For there were men in the valley.

CHAPTER 10

There were a hundred men, to be exact, and they had fooled us to chase after enemy that was not in the east after all.

All were well armed, rising from grass and moss all around us. Many had bows and arrows, and before we knew what had happened, Kuno screamed and fell from the saddle. His horse bolted, and I ripped Nightbright out, hit the flanks of the horse and aimed the beast at a man just getting up from behind a rock, his eyes confused. I stabbed down, he hissed and fell on his knees, and I forgot about him as spears flashed around my horse. They probed me, pushed me and the horse, and I could not get close to any of the men. Thusnelda screamed, and I looked her way to see the last of Kuno's men beaten down in a tangle of grass and twigs, his face open from an ax swing. Hugo was above him, and I paled. The young man smiled at me with vicious joy. Thusnelda was surrounded on her horse though the men around her did not point a spear at her.

I cursed and got ready to die, but I did not.

'Hold him,' a thin, mirthful voice demanded, and I gave a strangled voice as I knew who it was.

'Catualda,' I whispered and saw Thusnelda was staring behind me. I turned my horse, holding on to Nightbright and saw a man on a fat, white horse push back his hood. There, the blond young man with supremely thick lips stared at me.

He bowed ironically. 'Hraban. It has been a while. Last time we saw you, you were about to kill Vago the Vangione and made quite a mess of our plans. To imagine, you would escape his prison? Unbelievable. But here there is no escape.'

He was right, I cursed. Fifty men were gathered around us, many with bloodied weapons. Others rode around in the dark, making sure we were not disturbed. There were now ten warriors between Catualda and me, and I contemplated again throwing the weapon, but I doubted I would be as lucky as I had been with Ragwald. Thusnelda cursed him. 'He is with Armin now. You killed Armin's men. Not his! You dammed idiot.'

I spat on the ground and pointed my sword at Hugo. 'So. Is Fulcher alive?'

'I don't know,' the young man said with a shrug. 'Sorry, but I did tell you I serve Segestes. I left your friend horseless as he was taking a piss.'

Catualda bowed to Thusnelda, just slightly. 'I am here to take you to your lord father. I'm afraid he is very worried about you.' The cur was staring at me with hatred even as he spoke with Thusnelda. I had wounded him, tried to kill him, and he enjoyed his moment of triumph like a cat would enjoy mauling a crippled mouse. And he had been waiting for us.

'I command you ...' she began.

'Let it rest, Thusnelda,' I said heavily. 'He has betrayed Armin.'

'He is your relative!' Thusnelda scolded him, shocked. 'And you betray him?'

'Armin is my relative,' he nodded. He held onto a long spear and pointed it south. 'He has given me his love and his hall. But I have other relatives. You are one. And so is Segestes.'

Thusnelda grimaced in anger and nodded. 'I'll not go!'

'He desires you to follow his army under his guarding eye,' Catualda said with seemingly innocent concern, manipulative and treacherous. 'And so we shall go that way. That Hraban is here as well? It is a wonder. I hardly could believe it when Hugo told Segestes. I was happy to set this up, and it worked splendidly. And yes, you will go, Princess. Bound or with honor.'

'He will come as well,' she hissed, pointing at me. 'You will not kill him. Do not overplay your importance to Segestes. He has sold us to Rome, and Hraban is a friend to Nero Claudius Drusus. At least he should be spared your vengeance.'

Catualda was weighing the words of Thusnelda. A burly warrior approached him, and he was whispering and pointing his ax to the southern woods. They had no time for a lengthy stay. He finally nodded and pointed at me. 'You, Hraban, will come with us. Give your sword to him.' He pointed his finger at a young man approaching me with apparent fear, and I nodded heavily. I dropped the blade and glowered at Catualda.

'Shall I wear shackles as well?' I asked the dog.

He laughed. 'No, but you will be well guarded. Hold him.' Men approached me, spears out. They aimed their weapons at me, and I was surrounded by spears, their tips inches from my body. Catualda guided his horse forward. He held out his hand and took Nightbright from the young man. He held it up, wondering at the blade in the pale moonlight, and I saw his eyes come to rest on me. There was something dangerous there, he hesitated. He was contemplating on slaying me anyway. I held my head high and cursed him. Woden was whispering to me to kill him, to kill them all and die trying, but I held my mouth shut. *Patience*, Armin had said. Catualda's horse stopped in front of me. He used Nightbright to open up my tunic and whistled as he saw Leuthard's old chain mail. He tapped the bronze beast head on my chest with my sword. 'A fancy armor, eh. You keep them. Your armor and helmet. You keep them. That way you are known amongst our people. But beneath, it, you will have a mark.'

He pressed Nightbright on my neck and slowly slashed the edge across, drawing blood. He kept the weapon in the wound as I trembled with pain and rage. Then he dropped the sword. He leaned down to whisper to the young man who picked up the sword, and that man grasped something from the ground beside the blade and handed it to Catualda. Catualda stared at me and poured something from one hand to another. I saw he had filth, horse turd and dirt on his hand, and he crushed it together. Then he spat on it. He leaned over and rubbed it on my wound and smiled. I trembled in anger, and he saw it and smiled at me with pity.

'Since you are a friend to Segestes's Roman friend, I shall spare you. Next time I see you, Hraban? If ever? You should run. I will have many men following my banner,' he smiled inanely and nodded at a burly Cherusci, who waved his hand to the north. Catualda left me and rode away, and the Cherusci around us were preparing to leave. I gazed at Thusnelda, who shook her head at me. She was my only ally, and I calmed myself.

It was hard.

He had spat on the dirt and the turd. Woden was dancing inside my skull, and I kept staring at Thusnelda, who kept shaking her head. I breathed deep, trying to calm down.

Only Lif mattered. Armin, if I could get him. Later. Catualda would hold. He would hold.

CHAPTER 11

The sun came up as we rode northward. Fifty men rode with us to guard us and Catualda guided his horse carelessly around the troop. Thusnelda was giving him withering looks, but he ignored them. 'Your father will give me many men. He is a visionary if you are wondering why I am leaving your lover.'

'I did not wonder at all,' Thusnelda informed him disdainfully. 'My father has many plans and as ever, finds vermin to execute them. You are a Roman now. Like Hraban there.'

'It is strange,' I said darkly from under my helmet, 'that you once fought for Armin's dream of uniting the tribes and so easily abandon them.'

'Oh come now!' he chided. 'Simpleton. Today's submission to Rome is but a safeguard under which to grow strong. Give Rome an alliance, and they will fortify lightly. Give them resistance, and they shall build many castrum here. Best be friendly when you can. I still love my people best.'

'And you think you will rule the Marcomanni one day?' I teased him.

He was silent for a time, and then he agreed. 'Armin? He thinks he knows my plans, yes? Perhaps he does. The south is rich, Hraban. And I have the blood of great men running wild in my veins. And I am still a Germani, not a Roman, as I said. They will respect me and love me.'

'You would fight Father for the south?' I mocked him. 'You?'

'I will have to see what opportunities open up, Hraban,' he gloated. 'It will be a very interesting few years. Perhaps I need not fight him at all to gain power there. Or here. We will see. I'm at the top of my world; possibilities spread left and right under my gaze! And as Lord Segestes rises, so shall I. Perhaps over Rome, one day!' I remained silent at his gloating words. He spoke very freely in front of a Roman soldier. He had no plans to let me go. Thusnelda gave me a worried glance, and I knew she had thought about it as well.

The sun climbed higher as we followed the river. The light illuminated the land, the horizon white and golden and the fog dissipated. Forlorn birds sang, and men working on fields stopped to look at us. Some were imperceptible, almost, working on the edges of the woods, and none offered me any hope of escape. There was to be another perilous day for the Germani as the relentless Drusus would chase after them. As if to answer my thoughts, far, far to the south, I thought I heard the aneators of the legions blow their horns. The legions were up and awake, and the cavalry were already out and about. Many Cherusci villages would burn. Perhaps Armin's own. We ate in the saddle, napping in restless tiredness as our horses took us north. The horses were going at a steady gait, the legs carrying us over a flat land, the river banks, and small hillocks. Thick patches of forests spread to our right, with wildflowers filling meadows with their colorful wonders, hares popping their ears up at our approach, eagles and hawks stalking the sky for morsels for the bellies of their ever hungry offspring.

Behind us, the first smoke pillars of the day arose in the sky.

I grew tired of the silent company and spoke with Thusnelda. 'It is a shame the Romans reached this far. Drusus is implacable. This is rich land, with plentiful crops and beautiful, rarely burned villages. See there, that hall is fabulous,' I told her, nodding at a hillside to our right with a white hall and a village surrounding it.

She nodded. 'It is a shame we missed the Glittering Oaks. That one belongs to Sigimer, Armin's father. There Armin grew up, amidst the flowing wheat, and the great flocks of cattle. His mother was almost a mother to me as well, for mine is dead,' she said mournfully.

'Ah, and there you got your first kiss from your cousin as well.' I grinned, looked at her face, and she blushed. 'How much power do you have over Segestes?' I asked her carefully. 'Is he a father or just a bastard? Does he grant you wishes? Because, I think, I might have to call on you for a favor.'

She shrugged and waved her hand towards Sigimer's holdings. 'Favor? You know I will try. And power? As much as I have the power to save these homesteads. Not much. He might have abandoned the idea of marrying me to your father, but he has plans to marry me anyway. I have a brother, but he does not share his power with him either nor ask for advice. So, he is just a bastard, to answer your question. But he is a careful bastard, and I will try my best.' She looked away and shook herself, trying to sound confident. 'He will release you. He has to. He is allied to Rome.'

'Hah,' I said bitterly. 'I hope he fails and falls on his face,' I said, despite that being a reverse in the plans of Drusus.

She laughed. 'Armin will fight, and we will rise again.'

'We?' I grinned.

She smiled back. 'Armin. Thusnelda. Perhaps you.'

'Great,' I cursed.

'I will try,' she said, touching my hand. I nodded. 'Wealth is more than halls. The cows are hidden, horses in war, women will make bandages in the woods and many of Armin's foes will die, no matter my father and his betrayal. Armin has none lord over him now. I wouldn't be surprised if he managed some victories this year still. It is madness, Hraban, but he might surprise them all. My father will be surprised, I am sure.'

I snorted. 'If Segestes has his way, the cows will pay for Roman taxes, women will seed children to Roman soldiers, and the men will serve Rome far from here,' I told her morosely. 'The end might not be as glorious as you might think.'

'No,' she said more quietly, yet with determination. 'But it is better to be forgotten and dead people than grasp for straws like my father does. I do not wish Roman ways or Roman laws to enter our sacred halls. I speak Latin, I know of the enemy because my father wills it, and I know their gods. I do not wish to know of them, but I do. Instead, I pray to Frigg for

137

wisdom, and I think Armin would never let Drusus go home if all the brave men followed him. He will do anything to stop them.' She glanced at me. 'We must try our best to help him. And fight to the end. Perhaps this is how it must be. For a young lord to become the leader of such a nation as this one, he has to become its oldest Lord.'

I sighed, for I was, in truth, a man of Drusus. 'That, lady, may be true. Yet, I wonder, did not the nations of latinium, of Gaul, of Hispania and the mighty Greeks think to fight to the end? If only one would lead, they would be free. And one did lead, like Vercingetorix, like, in recent years, Ambiorix of the Eburones in Gaul? Pyrrhus? They paid the prize for trying,' I said, staring at the rich villages all across the land. 'I used to think fame was most important thing in the world. But perhaps the life of your children is.'

She nodded at my words, with little conviction. 'I have no children. Should I have some, perhaps I would think differently. But you speak of people who are vanquished. They are not vanquished as long as you have heard of them. If they did what Father did, nobody would speak of the Gauls and Latins and Greeks. Glory will resonate through the times, cowardice will be forgotten.'

'Children care nothing for the glory of centuries past when they laugh and run free over the hills. But perhaps you are right, and they will not run free if Roman slavers set up shot here.'

She was nodding and then leaned on me. 'You know of the world? How do you know of such things? You are, but a hay smelling Suebi brute from the south?' she said, teasing me.

'Father did not love me, but he had me taught by a Roman tutor, an exile. To know my enemy, I thought,' I said. 'But now they are my friends. Wyrd. I will help Armin if he does not demand I fight Drusus.' I looked away so she could not guess at my true thoughts. 'And if I should survive this tragedy.'

'He is a mighty man, your father. Perhaps he taught you in case you would be useful, not a hard-headed lump of muscle as you are. Or to make a presentable hostage to Rome? Rumors tell he is forsaking the old ways, the gods; the rituals and men still follow him because they fear Rome. You tell me he will eventually betray the Germani for Rome. But I would not marry him if he were a finer man than Armin is,' she said. 'As you said, I kissed Armin and never will I love another. I will fight. For you and me as well. Be at ease. I will try to set you free. You did save me.'

'I will suffer, lady,' I told her, and she did not deny it. Had not Segestes tried to kill me once already? For Antius, perhaps, but now he would have other reasons to do so.

We reached a camp of Segestes that evening.

The scouts of the Cherusci lord rode up to us, looked us over, saw Thusnelda, and rode off. Late in the afternoon, we saw the glowering, fat man on a huge horse perched on a hill, lush with barley. He had hundreds of men around him, men finely decorated with silver torcs and some high women with fine earrings made in the Roman style. Expensive tunics and finery were the norms of those he seemed to hold in high esteem, yet most were sporting the beards of the Germani. Contradictions and savagery, for the man next to him, was Ragwald, his arm limp, and a savage glee spread on his face as he saw me walk my horse uphill. I did not look his way, but I was scared shitless.

'Are you all right? Why did you leave my camp in the battle?' grunted Segestes to Thusnelda, his fat jowls flapping under his short beard. She nodded and rode up, and I wondered if there were any men present who would not wonder how such an ugly beast could spawn such a beautiful creature as his daughter was.

'I am fine, Father. I was with the army that fought when the Romans attacked. Hraban here found me, saved me from rape and murder and brought me to safety,' she said, casting her eyes up to him, deliberately not mentioning Armin. She tilted her head and spoke to him sweetly and with obvious derision. 'I had no idea the plan called for your sudden retreat. A masterful maneuver that, Father.'

Segestes ignored her barbs. 'Brought you to safety? Not to Armin? He is in charge of Sigimer's troops, after all,' said Segestes, fully well knowing the truth. Ragwald was fingering a spear with his left hand, barely able to hold his peace in my presence.

139

'Armin was there, yes. Why?' she asked and looked at the grizzled man, the former champion of her bodyguard with worry. Ragwald's arm was bound and limp, and his eyes were fixed on me. She eyed me, and I shrugged. She rolled her eyes, understanding I had recently met Ragwald and left him a cripple.

Segestes looked at her, then me. 'Are you not with the Romans, boy? Why didn't you take her to Drusus?'

'I was. I killed Romans for your daughter, Segestes,' I said gloomily. 'And I know Romans do not always respect their female prisoners.' She would have been safe with Drusus, but he did not know it. 'And I had no idea where you were to be found. Hence; Armin.'

Ragwald snickered. 'Worried for women. Should worry for yourself,' he stated with relish.

'I saved your daughter, Segestes,' I told the lord squarely. 'And now I should return to Nero Claudius Drusus. Your liege lord.'

Segestes brushed his shiny metal shield absentmindedly. 'I have a hunch you had a reason to save her, so perhaps I should not fall on your feet in gratitude. But I am grateful, nonetheless. As for my liege lord? I have none. Our family has held this land for as long as your family has been lurking in Gothonia. You might not think so, but the poets say it is so. No Roman is my liege lord. We are allies.'

'And you shall be skinned alive,' Ragwald spat. 'Our Lord Segestes has already once condemned you. Now—'

Segestes shook his head heavily. 'Hold, yes, I am discourteous as I let my disgruntled lord here insult our guest.' Ragwald's eyes shot open, and he stammered but held his silence as Segestes went on. 'You are not welcome here, Hraban, but I thank you for bringing my daughter back to me. It would be remiss of me to deny you my hospitality, despite the unfortunate affair with Antius. After tomorrow, you will leave my camp.'

He turned his horse.

'And the insult to my honor?' I asked.

'If you meet him out there,' he said, pointing to Ragwald and then to the woods, 'discuss it with him.'

'And my sword?' I hissed.

Segestes smacked his lips as he regarded me. 'You shall have it when you leave. Catualda? Give it here.' The fat-lipped man snapped his fingers, the sword was brought to him. He rode to Segestes and their eyes met as he handed over the thing. Segestes leaned to give Catualda some advice and the bastard left, not looking back at me.

The retinue rode off, and I could see Thusnelda talking with her father, angrily, gesturing towards the woods to the east. Segestes ignored her and left her fuming as we rode on. That evening many more smoke pillars touched the skies in the lands of Sigimer. Villages burned as the Roman army snaked forward, and there were reports that auxilia cavalry had been sighted near Segestes's troop, and I prayed for Chariovalda to appear.

He did not.

Instead, the army of Segestes took to looting. Warlords gleefully detached themselves from the army that I now estimated to be some six thousand strong, and the lands of Sigimer were ravaged as the pig of a lord took a chance to relieve Sigimer's people of their halls and cows. By the evening, he stopped at a village formerly held by a lord of Sigimer and set up a feast in the hall. Men drank, women laughed, and slaves worked, and there was a general feeling of festivity in the army of Segestes, except for Ragwald, who eyed me with a manic intensity. I ignored him as best I could, begging Woden to hand me a good shield and Nightbright back.

By late evening, Segestes was drunk, not overly so, but in a merry way and spoke Latin to his relatives, made jokes about Germani customs. He seemed to travel with the excessive amount of silver and gold and drank wine served from a beautiful green glass horn, trimmed with silver. I sat at the end of the table, nibbling at some pork and tasted ale frugally and waited. Men around me were speculating on the amount of wealth Segestes was wearing. I stared at the traitor lord with hate, his white tunica covering his ample belly, his thick, hairy neck adorned with silver and gold chains, hung with tiny emeralds, and his hair was held in place with a gold circlet.

Segestes eventually noticed my stare. He pointed at me. 'So, tell us, boy. Since we have new allies,' he yelled and some Germani in the table looked down in shame. 'Tell us how it is serving in the Roman army?' he called out.

'Come, tell us!' voices yelled.

I pretended I was a bit drunk as I shook my head, but they were relentless.

I felt malicious and shrugged. 'Men like any, I suppose. They have rarely lost a war. That is—'

'What? Speak up!' Segestes yelled.

I shook my head. 'Your nephew Armin nearly showed them defeat because he knew what to expect. But they do grind a normal Germani column down fast enough. But not Armin,' I said reverently, and the damage was done, men were whispering about Armin. Segestes clearly regretted having asked me anything, and I felt gleeful as I was determined to glorify Armin.

'Tell us of the great battle? Hraban? Do tell us!' A man was asking, giving me a drink of mead.

I got up and waved my hand. 'Armin was brilliant. Drusus ran after him in the valleys and woods of the Bructeri homelands and foolishly led the Romans to a killing field. Armin then inspired them, the Bructeri, and the Marsi to hold the enemy. Roman cohorts went up, full of fire, but soon they were wallowing in the dirt on the bottom of a trap he had dug. Armin, Sigimer's mighty son, was able to hold the indomitable Roman iron fist in place while the Sigambri charged for the enemy, committing all the Romans into a terrible battle.' Men were staring at me, their mouths open wide. I slapped my hand on the table, and they were all startled. 'And when the time was right, his horn! It blew!' They stared at me totally enraptured, and Segestes was looking at them as if he did not know them. They were his men but also Germani, no matter how much wine you poured into them, and how much Latin they had been taught. 'He blew the horn, by Woden, by Donor! With the hard work he had laid down in the spring, and Sigimer's few thousand men led by Rochus, they split through the legions and took some iron-willed cohorts down! They took their standards and pissed on them, and Armin led his men to slaughter more of the Romans!' I said, and men roared, proudly.

'And how, then, did the pup lose the battle?' asked Ragwald spitefully, and men were quiet.

I sat down. 'He lost because our kind will not work together. We quarrel, we argue and they, they work, tirelessly. And I, of course, fought them.'

Men laughed and roared at my bravado as Ragwald glowered at me. Segestes got up wearily.

'And what did you do in the battle? Serve Drusus his meals?' asked Ragwald with spite, and Segestes was about to shut him up when a blushing man got up. He was young, very young, and I saw he held a thick piece of silver in his hand. Then I spotted Thusnelda inching away from him and realized he was a poet.

'Asgar?' Segestes asked, slumping. One did not silence a poet.

'With your permission, I was at the battle and know it. I made a song after we made our way home.'

'No!' Ragwald spat.

'Let him.' Segestes sighed.

And he sang.

If you have heard a work of Horace, Lord, you will know a power that a true orator and a poet hold over men. A poet of the Germani is no different though he knows no letters, nor can he sway men far away, across the nations and time with written scrolls. But he is what the Germani are. He is a vessel of living history, spreading the past, weaving the present through their songs, giving birth to memories of humor and valor. He gives pain and regret a voice. A singer can silence kings and warlords, and woe to a man who cannot pay for such men.

The man chanted, his fine voice reaching the rafters, and all men were silent.

'The steel fisted foes snaked through the woods,
and the Fox ran across the land with the tribes and their goods.

Easy victory they sought, the southern lords,
but to seek to undo a young god of Sigimer, is to meet the angry swords.'

143

Weeks they marched, many they slew,
and much they burned, laid forts and made ever thinning stew.

The Fox smiled, the men cheered, in the night their arms were sharp.
Ditches they dug, stakes they cut and in the mornings, they raised the ale jugs.

Then, finally, like a cloud of a storm, the enemy followed the bait like a steely
swarm.
The horn was blown, the men braced, to Woden their yell was raised.'

He had a beautiful voice and sang about the battle, of Armin, and of Drusus. He pictured the Romans as fearful warriors, men far from home, obeying the oaths they have taken, and Drusus, as a young hero, reckless and relentless, looking for glory, and he praised his honor, his courage and his carefree attitude when danger threatened. He then sang of the Germani heroes. He sang of Maelo, Varnis, and Baetrix, charging from the forests, and the men who stoutly held in place the metal clad men of the legions, of Wodenspear and the Bructeri, and the clever Marsi, slayers of so many of the best men of the legions. He sang of sad heroes, and of mighty champions, men I did not see that day, and sometimes men would toast a name they knew. He sang more of Armin, the young lord sitting on ridge, facing ten thousand legionnaires and auxilia and directing the free peoples in their fight, men drunk on honor, mead, and blood that day. He sang how the men around him surged forward, wearing no armor, against men carrying swift death and how Armin led them, his horn a terror of Rome.

And then, incredibly he gave verses to me.

He sang how Chariovalda had failed and how I rallied the weak hearted, routed auxilia, harassed them into manhood and how I, the champion of the Dead Wall of Castra Vetera broke the Cherusci, and how the hero Rochus fell in my hands, a young man still, Woden's favorite. The last bits about my heroics were added to the song at the moment, I was sure, for Thusnelda had paid him silver for them, and he did an admirable job. He finished the song with some stammering as he gave me credit for bringing Thusnelda to Segestes, safe from harm.

I smiled at Thusnelda, thinking the poet would die for that. The men were singing his song, toasting me happily and should I disappear, many men would know I was cheered thus in Segestes's own feast and some would remember the last verses. Men do not forget a poet's fine songs. Thusnelda looked down, and I knew she was afraid for me, having tried her best to spare me humiliation and pain. The poet was pale as a sheet. The room was quiet, all staring at the lord of the hall.

Segestes took a step forward unsteadily, threw a gold ring to the man who caught it clumsily. The fat lord's face was dark with fury as he turned and walked out, looking at me. I nodded and bowed to Thusnelda. She gave me a nervous, wry smile. The party went on, the poet being bombarded by questions. I walked out in a few minutes and nodded at some guards following me. I pulled on my helmet as I exited the hall, found my horse and turned to look for Segestes, but there was no need. He was there, sitting on his.

'We ride,' he grunted, and I followed him.

We rode up to the hill nearby.

He sat there quietly, looking over the dark, fertile Cherusci lands, fields and sparse woods and dark hills. The moon was up, and we could see the silhouettes of distant halls. The west and south were full of fires.

'It is our land, Cherusci land,' he said sadly. He gestured around him. 'I will not enjoy seeing so much of it burning down these coming weeks, but Armin, like it was said in the song, wishes to be a hero. And the fools admire him,' he said, taking a swig of a gourd on his hip. 'Is Armin as good as he said?' Segestes asked, with a note of worry in his voice. 'And as you claimed. Just to spite me, of course, but did you lie?'

I shook my head. 'If the men fought like the Romans, with better discipline and had been better armed, not a man of the legions would have escaped that field unhurt.' He stood there on his horse in silence, waiting. 'Your daughter seems to think he is a great warrior,' I teased him, and he spat.

'She is to be married to your father. That is her role and not to voice her opinions. She was always too quick to speak out and ready to disagree. I hear your father knows how to break a mare?'

I sat still, thinking about his words. 'My father is not a friend to Drusus. And you are now ... allied, as you said, to Drusus.'

He quaffed. 'Your father, Hraban, serves a noble cause of Rome. He is out to kill Drusus. You know this. I know it. In return, he will be awarded. And given lands in the south.' The way he said it made all the warmth in my body disappear.

'And that, Hraban,' said a gruff voice I hated, 'leaves the north untended. It needs a king while your father rules the south. And Maroboodus does need help if he is to slay our friend Drusus.'

I turned to look at Antius. He was seated on a huge horse, swathed in a dark cloak, and his throat was covered with a white scarf. 'You.' I shook my head in disbelief.

'Yes, it is I.' Antius grinned, his eyes glowing with unholy light. 'Had I died, Segestes still would have dealt with my masters and mistresses in Rome. Cornix would have mediated with him.' There, near him a shadow moved. Cornix, the mad, green eyed Roman with a bear-like, short stature and half melted face came forward. He tilted his head but said nothing. I had last seen him when Ansbor died in an ambush set up by the two rats, and I did not expect to survive him now. He clutched a wickedly sharp gladius.

Segestes grunted. 'Of course, your father always wanted to see Armin fall. It is his job to kill Drusus, not this upstart of ours from the hay hall of Sigimer. So, I was happy to help. Sigimer and Armin are soon dead, and I will lead his men. I will help Drusus in his conquest of the Cherusci, he will learn to trust me, and one day soon when the time is right, I will help Maroboodus kill Drusus. Then, we will take over Germania and Rome will rule here, and we will rule in its name. I thank you for Thusnelda's life though and that is why I denied Antius his request.'

'You will live a while, son,' Antius said gruffly. 'Not for a long time, but for awhile.'

'I saved your daughter from rape,' I hissed at Segestes, looking around. There were shadows sitting in the darkness, on horses. 'From murder.'

He nodded and spoke, bored. 'I said thank you. I say it again. Thank you for that. Now, you will dwell in my house and live on until everything is peaceful in the land or until I find a use for you. I might have one, after all. To Drusus, you are dead. For me, you are a pawn. For Antius and his pain, you will not enjoy your stay. It is the best I can do for him. Ragwald?'

Ragwald rode from the darkness with a dozen men and grinned at me.

BOOK 3: THE BLACKSMITH

'You ask me about plans? The idiot who nearly died in pig shit?'
Hraban to Thusnelda

CHAPTER 12

They guided me to the edge of the Visurgis River. Segestes had spoken to them, harshly, and the result of that discussion was that I remained in one piece as we traveled. Ragwald was scowling, gnashing his teeth. Cornix was his usual mad, silent self, but they did not touch me. While waiting at the river's edge, the half-faced Roman spat in the water. His horse turned to drink from the river, and he grunted. 'It has been awhile since I first saw you on that field in the southern woods. I should have heeded Koun then and not Antius and let you slip to the afterlife. But I did not. One of my few mistakes in this life.'

'Segestes and Maroboodus, eh?' I spat sourly. 'It was always so.'

'It was always so,' Cornix grunted. 'Your father alone cannot accomplish much. He will need the help of Segestes. But your lovely Armin is making a terrible mess of things. But then, perhaps Armin is giving us an opportunity. Your Drusus hates Armin, fears him, and Armin is stopping him from taking the land and pacifying it. He will come after Armin as many times as it takes. So, we know where a famous Roman death shall take place. We will see. Then the Republic is gone for good. No more Senate and dreams of bygone ages. Mind you, I don't hate the thought of old Rome and its former honor. No. I am not political. I just collect my pay and that pay currently comes from opposing the Republic's resurgence. That simple. It's a high pay, and I'll keep at it.'

'What are you two?' I asked him. 'Antius is a soldier, and you—'

'Does not matter what we are, Hraban,' he said tiredly, his burned face twitching with that strange hint of madness always evident in the Roman. 'We have a master—'

'Or a mistress,' I interrupted him.

'Ah!' he gloated. 'Young Drusus must have guessed where all this spawns from.'

'He has not told me,' I told him sullenly. 'But he is not a fool.'

'He knows there is a plot to kill him, and he knows he must chew it up rather than avoid it,' Cornix grinned. 'He has to pacify the Germani, and he thinks he can, no matter what is arrayed against him. Unfortunately, he needs allies here, and his allies are his downfall. Sad it is. He could have been a hero like Africanus or Caesar. He would have taken the lands, then marched to Rome with a wrathful spite for Augustus and those who tried to murder him. He would have been like Juppiter himself, his face painted red, his dignitas enough to make the rabble bow before him. And you were to ride with him.' He chortled. 'Instead, here you are.'

'I will, still,' I told him rebelliously.

'No,' he stated simply. 'Segestes is keeping you alive for Thusnelda. Perhaps for his own ends. Perhaps he has thought of a use for you. For now.'

'What possible other use could I have?'

He shook his head heavily. 'You sure are no politician, either. To make sure Maroboodus does not grow too powerful? You can embarrass Maroboodus, at least? You know their plans and Segestes can, perhaps make a small threat of flaunting you before him should your father desire lands not partitioned to him after Rome rewards them both? Imagine Maroboodus waging war to wrest these lands from Segestes? He would win. So, by keeping you, he can threaten your father by setting you free to tell the truth of what took place?'

'I might not be a politician, but that sounds like an idiotic plan,' I spat.

150

'Perhaps he just wants to sell you to him? Your father would love to see you roasted over a slow fire.' He grinned.

'That sounds more plausible,' I agreed.

He looked excited for a moment and pushed me with misplaced camaraderie, his mad face twitching. 'Perhaps he wants that ring of yours? It will help him govern this hole of Hades. He has so far grown fat in the arms of Sigimer and Inguiomerus but will have to fight for himself soon. Your ring would give him Suebi mercenaries and peace, perhaps, from those terrible warriors.' Cornix looked like he was chewing on a rock for a moment, his face strange and full of wonder. Then he nodded at the crippled champion. 'But Ragwald there will not let you leave, no matter the plans of his master. You took his arm.'

I gazed at the thick warrior whose eyes never left me. I looked away. 'It is crippled? Permanently?'

Cornix hooted. 'Yes! Cannot move it. Useless. Flaps around like a bag of flesh. All he has left is an abundance of anger. And he will be looking after you. Take care Hraban. By the way. Next time you hang a man, do it yourself and wait for half an hour, at least. I had a hard time reviving him after you left, but I did manage it. All that grease in his throat must have protected him somehow.'

'I'll remember that,' I told him glumly. 'But I suppose it did not matter in the big picture as you were out here dealing with Segestes.'

'No, it did not matter,' Cornix agreed and rode to speak with Ragwald.

Segestes and Father, I thought. *Drusus must learn of Segestes. I should escape.*

But there was no chance of that. They watched me like cats would a mauled mouse.

The sun began to rise, and we waited. Then, somewhere near, there was a splashing noise.

Some birds were startled into a frenzied flight amidst the river's many reed banks, and their upset honks filled the early morning air. Then, there was a sturdy boat emerging from the semi-dark, a thick, blond-haired man on its prow. The boat was a sleek one, the man on its prow pointed at us, and the boat rocked gently as the bow aimed for the river bank. The brute waved at Ragwald, and I felt fear grasp at my innards. The rovers guided the ship to us, and the man hopped out of the boat. He had a wicked knife under his belt, one that looked well used. His thighs were thick with muscle, so were his arms and you could barely see his eyes from under thick eyebrows and a sloping, dirty skull.

Ragwald guided his horse towards me, pointed at the man and smiled. 'Meet Helmut. He is the caretaker of Segestes's estate. Helmut, meet our new slave. He is, as you see, a famous warrior, but only for the next few moments. His chain is expensive and his helmet precious. That has to be peeled off him to begin our work on shaping Hraban into a more humble man. The armor goes to our lord's armory.'

'Get down,' said Helmut with a voice that clearly desired I put on a fight.

I obliged him with the fight part.

I glowered at him, and he stepped forward. I waited until he got closer, and then I kicked him full in the nose, crushing it. It was like kicking a wall for all the effect it had, and he swatted my foot off his face and pulled me out of the saddle, painfully. I punched him in the face, this time drawing forth a sharp hissing sound, but that was all. He picked me up with one hand and punched me on the chest, and I fell to my ass in the muddy bank. I heard Woden's dance in my ears as I struggled to get up but found the long knife under my chin. The man was fast. There was a strange light burning in his eyes.

'Give up?' he asked with a barely controlled savagery.

'No,' I managed to wheeze, and he nodded, got up, kicked me in the face of the helmet and my ears rang.

'Strip him, Helmut,' Ragwald said, and men descended on me. Helmut sat on me, ripped my hands apart and then punched me so hard I doubled over. He pulled the mail over my head, savagely, and pulled off the helmet along with it.

'Ugly and angry,' he smiled wickedly.

'And coming from a man who looks like a bear's shitty ass, that is a true insult,' I gasped and got up to me knees, but he placed a knee on my chest and pushed me back down while waving the other men away. I fought him still, Woden demanding I do, but it was hopeless without a weapon. He turned me over, pulling my pants and caligae off so quickly that he dragged me on the ground after him. The men in the boat laughed at my futile struggles.

'Well, finally Hraban,' said Ragwald, as he saw my disgrace. 'I hear you were betrothed to Gunda the Chatti. She needs a man. Perhaps you are still growing?' His men laughed hugely.

'At least I can still wipe my ass,' I said with a smile, and Helmut punched me, and the world blackened.

'You called yourself a warrior, Hraban. You called me the pig of Oddglade. Now you are a pig,' Ragwald said with rage bubbling in his incoherent voice, and they pulled me up to the boat. I opened my eyes and saw Cornix receive something from Ragwald, and he waved to another boat, backpedaling near us. He was going south.

Ragwald left his horse with a man and boarded the boat.

'Let us go and see your new home,' he spat. We rowed for many hours, the men occasionally laughing at my nakedness. Ragwald was looking appraisingly at my mail, trying on my helmet. 'Segestes has your sword, eh? I would have wanted that one. The one that treacherously took my arm. I would have taken a shit on it, then given it to the gods, and they would have returned my arm. It is possible, no?' he told me while prodding me with his toe. 'I'll buy it off him.' I said nothing, aware that Helmut sat over me. Ragwald shrugged at my silence. 'Yea, best keep your trap shut. Hilmsheim is Segestes's abode. You will learn a new life, Hraban. A humble, sad life. Like I suffer from my loss, you will suffer from my ill will.' I closed my eyes and suffered the cold.

In the late morning, they woke me with a kick. I looked up, and Ragwald grabbed me by my short, dark beard. 'There, dog. See?' he said and guided my eyes to the left side of the boat. A curious estate was sprawling there. It was surrounded by cultivated fields; horse corrals full of fine steeds and countless rows of sheds, one of which was a blacksmith by the river. Others were places to butcher animals and to store food, wood, and weapons. The hall itself was like Vago's had been. It had a traditional long hall look and feel, yet it had two stories and side building with large stables. Ragwald leaned down on me. 'There was Thusnelda born and raised, and from there, Segestes holds sway over the Cherusci, raiding the northern weaklings in their hill mounds. The Chauci fear him. He is keeping the wald, the forests of Teutoburg free of the starving Bructeri. And you thought to fool him, a hero.'

'The most twisted hero in the memory of all the Germani,' I spat, for my defiance was rekindled.

He smirked at me. 'Nevertheless, you are his slave. Here you will huddle with pigs, dog,' he told me and pulled me up to a seated position. We came to a small dock, and the men pulled us close, tying the boat to a post, clambering up and out. Helmut pulled me up, and I saw the estate's occupants standing there, waiting for Ragwald. They saw my nakedness, and I tried to keep calm as they laughed and roared, women smiling shyly. One, a red headed beauty with freckles blushed furiously. Helmut took me by my beard, yanking me after him towards the estate, the people following. We walked on the road, and I cursed softly as the people laughed at me, the children pelted me with mud, and Ragwald, disconcertingly, just watched me walk. We came to the yard, and Ragwald nodded at Helmut, who took me to the side building, kicked a door open and threw me into a pigsty. Its occupants looked startled as I picked myself up.

'Here, you will live here, and eat what they eat,' Ragwald told me gleefully. The pigs in their filth looked up at me, some cold snouts experimenting with my arms. I glowered at the multitude of the people peeking at me from the door and said nothing. I felt lightheaded and hurt and noticed the wound in my neck, the one Catualda had given me was throbbing.

'I prefer their company to yours. They are more honest. Smell better and probably can finish a sentence,' I told them.

'Marry one, Hraban. This is your home.' Ragwald laughed and closed the door. There was very little light; everything was covered in pig shit and mud, and I sat down to stare up at a crack on the wall, the light casting shadows in the dark. Outside, children were laughing. I despaired and fought an urge to try to fight my way out immediately.

I fought the urge only until that very next night.

Then, I gathered all my strength, peeked under the door to see the guard very close. I got up, bashed the door open with all my strength, knocking the guard down. Then I ran for my life but soon found I was weak, and my feet were cut on stones. I ran north, but soon heard the baying of hounds as Helmut set the dogs after me. I was running in the reed thickets of the river, begging for the dogs to miss my scent, but soon large, slavering beasts spotted me, bayed with feral, hungry voices, and I escaped to the river with a splash. Helmut appeared, striding calmly for me, and I contemplated trying to swim to safety. A boat appeared, and the only escape I had was drowning. 'Come or die. I care not,' Helmut grunted as if he had read my mind. I did not wish to die by drowning and denying myself the land of Woden. I came out, shivering uncontrollably, the dogs baying and nipping at me. Helmut beat me with no apparent emotion on his thick face, using a wooden stick. Then, in the end, he pissed on me, sighing with relief. 'Ragwald's compliments.' He smiled and snapped my head with the stick. I nearly lost consciousness, and he had me dragged back by the ankles.

Next day, Ragwald crouched at the door. I managed to see his silhouette in the light and felt detached as my neck hurt, the wound slick with puss. Ragwald showed me a thick hammer. 'Outside there is a smithy, Hraban. Run again, and I shall break your fucking ankles on a wooden block. We do that to slaves who do not learn. They lose one leg and can still hop around. But you will be denied both legs. I'll not hesitate, and Segestes can still use you.'

'Is this what Segestes told you to do?' I asked him tiredly, aching all over my body. 'Kill me in pig shit?'

'Segestes told us to give you a roof over your head and work you hard. You herd pigs,' Ragwald laughed and showed me the hammer again, brandishing it with glee. I turned away.

I cannot afford to fail again, I thought.

A girl brought us food. Us, because very soon I began to think of the pigs as friends. In my ravenous hunger, I did contemplate on eating one of them during the night, but after brushing their thick skin I decided I would fail at getting to the meat. I giggled at the thought and wept, for I felt I would go mad. Locking up a Germani is a sure way to break one, for our folk lived free, enjoyed woods and open pastures and abhorred imprisonment. I survived, barely sane and finally shared the pig's food as the girl was throwing buckets of rotten vegetables in a hole on the floor. From then on, I would crawl there, on all fours and compete with my friends for the terrible dish.

Thus, I spent a month.

There was a guard outside, night and day, and while at times I felt better, by the end of the month I was growing ill again. I had been as sick when I was taken to Vago, but now my condition was rapidly growing worse. I was weak, the wound in my neck had the stench of decay that stabbed at my nostrils even through the shit and piss of the hole. The wound was rotting. It, the mud, and the room I had been given was going to kill me.

I would die, I cursed.

And yet, I did not. Not quickly, at least.

Time passed, my beard and nails grew, and I suffered. I ate leftovers and mud, drank piss sodden water. My wound festered on, and I learnt to survive as best I could, trying not to think about the pain. I was sleeping next to the pigs, and they kept me warm, even if they seemed bothered when I was coughing, which was often. I coughed so hard there was blood in the thin vomit that came out of my mouth and nose and smeared the backs of the pigs.

The fall was coming, I thought, for one day when the door was opened, the air had a sweet, bitter feel to it as if the gods had cracked the doors of Niflheim and freezing air was escaping to our Midgard. I remember seeing faces, the girl that fed us, at least, but occasionally Helmut and Ragwald would look down at me.

I hated them enough to cling to life as hard as I could, knowing I was losing the battle.

A sow had a litter of small piglets.

The happiness of the event did not extend to me, for the sow was suspicious of me and would attack if I got too close to her offspring. This was uncomfortable, for the piglets would occasionally wonder towards me, and I had to toss mud to get them to turn back. It made eating the scraps dangerous as well, for she actually bit me twice as I tried. So, I nearly starved and froze to death, sitting in a corner. Gradually, I forgot the time and the space and all about my plans of escape and gave up on Valholl. I would gingerly eat what was left after the pigs had eaten and the sow was asleep, and I crawled back to my corner and cursed Woden for letting me die there, in fever, cold and hungry in pig shit.

Then I lost the pigs.

At some point, they took most of them out. I feebly tried to stop them, but a guard pushed me away. He was prodding me with a spear, laughing to his friend who blanched as he saw me, and his eyes were drawn on my neck. I wept. Somewhere in my mind, I knew it was close to the time in the fall when livestock was culled and my friends were to be butchered. I was left with the piglets and the sows, and so I had no friends.

Then, one day, I could not crawl to the hole; I was coughing so hard, I spat thick blood.

That day I heard a horde of horses ride outside.

I gazed up at the crack in the wall and saw some snow drifting down. It was a few weeks before Yuletide, and Segestes came home. He was not alone, for I thought a Valkyrie had come to fetch me to Woden after all, but it was not a Valkyrie.

It was Thusnelda.

I remember opening my eyes, seeing a blur of her face as she looked at me in horror. I could not see well, for my eyes were failing me. She cursed, screamed, and beat a guard with her fists, and the man ran, and soon, hands were pulling me up. I heard Segestes screaming and Ragwald making excuses. 'Goodbye, dear friend,' I told the sow and the lot seemed to bid me farewell with their twitching snouts.

CHAPTER 13

I woke up, weak as a newly born kitten.

I looked around, trying to see where I was. I saw a man with an ax, standing by a door. Many straw beds were scattered around me. It was a modest place. Slave quarters, perhaps a guard's barracks. I slept again but dreamt of Thusnelda helping me eat something. Then, on the eve of the Yule celebration, Segestes came to me and sat next to me, frowning. I turned my head to him and sneered. He smiled, his fat face rather jovial. 'Have not lost your spirit, then.'

I turned my head. 'My time is nigh? You giving me to Father?' I croaked.

He shook his head at me in wonder. 'No. Where did you get that notion?'

I shook my head vigorously and rubbed my eyes. 'Cornix thought you might use me to embarrass him if he gets greedy and beats you.'

Segestes sat there, scowling at me. I saw he was about to tell me he was a warrior like Maroboodus, but he thought better of it. He waved his hand lazily. 'I doubt you would be able to smear him, Hraban. If he succeeds on what we are planning, he will be a hero indeed and few would care what his broken son has to say. We are making plans, and he does not know about you, and I doubt he will. He will have his hands full with the south.'

'So why—'

'The war is over,' he stated happily. 'For now. For this year, at least. And you shall stay here. But we did well.' I leaned back, trying to swallow my disappointment. He was looking at me with a small smile, expecting me to ask what he meant, and I refused. I stared at him mulishly, and he rewarded me. 'You are not going to ask then?' he said wearily and smiled. 'Fine. Drusus is gone home. They sacked my brother's lands and are reinforcing Castra Flamma. But the Cherusci are at peace. I made sure of it,' he said, sounding pleased with himself.

'Armin?' I asked, rewarding him that much.

A brief look of displeasure ran across his face. 'He lives. He took a wound, they say, but he lives. He is hiding in Sigimer's former lands, the woods and the hills. My brother Sigimer is lost.' He looked mildly bothered by the fact and then clapped my shoulder as if he suddenly remembered something. His fat jowls were heaving up and down, and I thought he looked very much like Antius. 'You were right. Armin is a great leader.' His eyes were calculative as he regarded me. 'Perhaps it is good he lives. His continuous harassment will make sure Drusus has to come back.'

'Is that your idea or that of Cornix and Antius?' I sneered.

He stammered, but ignored my question. 'Your father has been planning the battle to kill him, but we decided it will likely be here. Drusus cannot ignore Armin, can he? He will be back.'

'Really?' I asked, trying to get up. I managed it so that I was on my elbows, trembling, but then I felt stabbing pain in my eyes, and I moaned. I struggled to keep them open. 'Are you saying father is planning on marching the Marcomanni all the way here?'

Segestes shrugged. 'He always did plan on marching them to Luppia River. Then you made a mess of that plan. Burned his hall and all that unpleasantness. He will bring his men. At least enough to make a difference.' He looked away. 'Your sight will return, fully. But you look like shit, Hraban. The wound in your neck is healing. At least that is what Thusnelda says, and with food and rest we can get you to enjoy your short life again.' I looked at my shoulder and saw there was a herb smothered bandage covering much of my neck and shoulder. 'It will heal,' he said again. 'Though it is a miracle you pulled through. Perhaps Woden helped you, after all.' His eyes were curious, and I wondered if he had come to see if I was indeed god touched. *Perhaps he will make an idol out of my skin and hang it over his shield*, I thought and chuckled.

I smirked at him. 'Yes, Segestes. Woden came to me in the pigsty, cast spells over me, fed me juicy porridge, served godly mead and sang me to sleep each night. He kept me alive. Or perhaps I just refused to die, naked and smeared in pig shit. And on my own.'

He nodded as his face wrinkled unpleasantly. 'Be that as it may. You will live, and it has nothing to do with your father. You do not understand this, but I do what is good for my people,' he said with an irritating, priest like voice.

'You said Armin was wounded? How?' I asked him while rolling onto my back.

Segestes moved his great bulk uncertainly. 'He ambushed Drusus on his way home.'

'He did?' I laughed. 'He had no men!'

The fat man shook his head. 'The Romans were going home. They had crossed the rivers again and were marching close to the Chatti borders aiming for Castra Flamma. There are hills there, you know, and there is this old village of Arbalo. Near that there is a pass that goes between two craggy hills. Drusus's army marched right into it, thinking the war was over. Armin, Sigimer's loyal men, even some of mine attacked them there. Some thousands. They did well. Caused chaos in Drusus's columns. Killed hundreds though mostly auxilia. Lost some hundred. In the end, Drusus himself chased Armin away. He will be back. That Armin could muster three thousand men after I betrayed him and Sigimer was lost? It was a miracle.'

'They went home then?' I asked. 'Romans.'

Segestes nodded. 'They were happy to. I hear they had seen many terrifying omens before Arbalo. There were bees swarming the tent of a castra praefectus of the XIX Legion, the food was scarce, Armin kept stinging their tail,' he said, lounging in his seat. 'Of course, I made sure they are fed, but Armin stole some of that. In return of Arbalo, I seized their lands and scattered his army, Armin's as he returned from Arbalo. He would not fight, his men divided. But he is out there. Wounded, perhaps. But still free. Rome left you here.'

I nodded. 'Drusus?' I asked. 'Is he well?'

He looked surprised and then shrugged. 'I suppose. Better than you. He is home, in Lugdunum, perhaps in Rome already. He has to take care of the Tres Galliae and his building projects and make Augustus happy. Not to mention his wife! Were you supposed to take Armin to him?'

'Yes. But I was not sure I would have.'

'They are strange men,' Segestes said, mystified. 'I buy my men's loyalty, but both Armin and Drusus seem to be uncannily loved by men they take to war. If it is any consolation, Drusus did ask for you. I sent him an explanation that you have not been seen since you went to Armin,' he said, lounging in the chair. He slapped his thigh and got up. He walked around the room. 'That song bit was unfortunate, but I paid the poet to keep that latter part silent. If he should not do as I say? I will find him. I'll hold onto you for now. Ragwald nearly robbed me of a great prize. He has been admonished. You will spend the Yule and the spring here, work for Helmut, after you feel well,' he told me. 'We will see about the rest.'

'Thusnelda saved me? She must enjoy all this traitorous activity in her homelands,' I said unhappily at the thought of being anywhere near Helmut without a weapon of some sort.

'Thusnelda is a woman, and she will marry and be silent,' he said. 'I told you this before.'

'She will marry my father,' I growled. 'Now that you two are actually allied.'

'Yes, that is the plan, always was. We were ever allied, and Antius is our common link,' Segestes laughed hugely. 'She has a use with your father, after all. He will tame her, she will tell me his plans. She will because she will hate me less than him. Your time to cause trouble for our alliance is done with and gone, Hraban. Concentrate on survival now. And if Woden did help you survive in the filth, know he has helped me as well in attaining glory. I am the virtual lord of Sigimer's lands and my own, and only Inguiomerus can stand up to me. Where is your ring?'

I stared at him knowingly. 'Virtual Lord of Sigimer's lands. Sounds competent.'

'I am—' he began assuring me, but I interrupted him.

'The ring. Yes, I thought you might want that. To gain power over Inguiomerus?'

'Catualda said you do not have it,' he said irascibly, not answering my obvious question. 'Where is it?' he asked again, leaning forward.

'The vitka we spoke of? Odo has it,' I stated, deciding there was no reason to hide the fact.

'Odo? These maniacs who are after you?' he said dreamily.

'You will have to rule your lands, Segestes, without such devices. All the wars you will have to fight to the north, the Chauci and the Suebi? You have a shiny shield and bear's strength and virtual rule over rebellious lands. You don't need any rings. Eventually, you will have to fight. Just like Catualda will, should he find his place of power.'

'Catualda is a useful boy.' Segestes grinned and sobered. 'But he is no warrior like I am.'

I snorted. 'Warriors look for steel. Not rings. Get a fake one if you must,' I mocked him.

He pondered my words, slapped his knees and got up. 'Very well.' He smiled at me as he went out.

I slept, dreamt, and healed long until spring, missing the Yule feast I was likely not invited into anyway.

CHAPTER 14

The winter was unusually mild and, eventually, I began hopping around the shed. I stared out of the cracks in the walls, and for a while, I even missed the pigs. I had a fleeting bout with my conscience as I was sure I had eaten some of them during my healing spell but chased it away. The pretty, shapely red headed girl with adorable freckles brought me food; an older woman came to heal me. I did not see Thusnelda. My eyes returned to normal as Segestes had promised. I began regaining my strength though I was still weak as a kitten. I would be out of breath as I walked around, my neck was a mass of pain, and I resisted the urge to touch the formerly terrible wound. The old woman healing me would hum and cluck her tongue as she applied medicine on it, but I never saw how bad it was.

Apparently it was healed enough as I was put to work.

It was Maius when Helmut opened the door. He was thinner than he had been, for all men lost weight in the winter. He still hulked over me, and I hated him enough to consider trying to tackle him. He had crude, stained Roman made fetters with him, the kind that shackled your hands to your throat, forcing your arms to your chest. There was a mild look of disappointment on his face as he saw me standing there, still defiant.

'Here. Lazing is over,' he told me, and he was followed by a leering, greasy haired boy in a dirty tunic and there was also the pretty girl of my age who had been feeding me. The girl threw me a tunic and pants and used up shoes. I gritted my teeth, shed my blanket and pulled them on. I used rope to fasten up the pants and then I approached the scowling brute, who clipped the chains on my wrists and attached the iron collar. 'Ragwald tells me you will work in the smithy, helping the Old Saxon, but you will be doing other things as well,' he grunted and pulled me out.

It was cold outside, and I shivered. Snow was still on the ground though spring was in the air, birds were singing happily, men were enjoying the warmer wind and the sun outside, hoping to spot green grass as they kicked muddy clods of snow around. Women prepared fresh food the hunters were bringing in. On a tall, ominous tree far down the river, I noticed there was a platform where the dead were heaped to keep them away from the wolves until they could be burned and buried properly.

The boy kicked me, and I growled at him.

Helmut pulled me close to his face, his breath stinking through his rotten teeth. 'He whips you, and you say nothing about it. Nothing. Unless you thank him for reminding yourself that you are a pig. Understand? My Wulstan does not take shit from oath breakers and traitors. He is your master just like I am.' I held my peace with great difficulty, and after scowling at me for awhile, he dragged me off for the smithy, where a clanging sound was evident.

'In the morning and during the day, you will hack wood, carry coal, and do what Vulcan, the Old Saxon tells you. Vulcan takes no shit from anyone either. You would do well to remember that. In the evening, you will clean the stables by the hall. My boy here, Wulstan will look after you at that time. And yea, there are guards. My daughter will feed you,' he grumbled as we walked past the great hall of Segestes.

'Your daughter?' I asked him with surprise.

'Yes, why?' he growled.

'She has been kind and intelligent, and I was surprised, that is all,' I said with a straight face, and the brute stopped for awhile to consider if he had been insulted. I kept my face straight. While I waited for him to make up his mind to beat or to let me go, I gazed at the great hall. Warriors were coming and going, richly dressed, rings gleaming in their fingers. Horses rode out, and many men were arriving from afar, their cloaks muddy from traveling. Then I saw a Roman, a cavalryman in a ring mail exiting the hall. My heart fluttered.

Helmut snorted. 'You get no help from him. Castra Flamma is many days away, and the couriers care nothing for a bearded slave fuck like yourself.'

Castra Flamma. Woden knew how I wanted to see its walls. The great Teutoburg Wald was spreading around us, full of Germani, but Romans rode to Segestes, unchallenged. And I was there, right under their noses.

I grunted and shook away the desire to call out to the soldier. 'So the Roman army stayed in Luppia? They did not starve this winter?'

The girl smiled and nodded, her freckles glowing in the sun. 'Yes, they have only one castra near our country, this Flamma and at least one day away by Luppia River. They guard the Sigambri lands.' Alisio. Alisio remained as well. I smiled thanks at her, and she smiled back. She had an easygoing way about her, a pretty face, and evidently all the good qualities in the family of Helmut, since the boy pushed her and the father scowled at her.

'No talking with the boy, you just feed him,' he said, and the girl nodded with a meek, downcast look. Evidently, she was used to such treatment. 'Come. And stop yapping, slave, about the Romans. You'll not speak with them again. Silence is the way to brief happiness, relatively painless one. You get to keep your teeth, you see?'

We came to the smithy, and a powerful old man with a long white ponytail was hammering busily at a piece of metal and sparks were flying. His face was dry and parched. He glanced and nodded at me, his face utterly expressionless like parched bark. 'He looks weak, have you been feeding him?' the man called Vulcan asked.

Helmut grunted. 'You get what I got, I can spare none else. If it was up to me, he would not—'

The man stopped hammering and pointed the tool at Helmut. 'You do not speak to me in such a manner, Helmut. You run the estate, but I make the tools you need. I tell you, he looks starved. Weak. He has few clothes, and it is still winter. Do you wish to get punished by the Lord again?' Helmut reddened and glanced at me. So, the pigsty had had a price. I grinned at him maliciously.

Helmut pushed me, and I nearly fell. 'You clothe him. At sundown, he will be fetched for other things. For work more worthy of him. Shoveling shit, that is,' Helmut told him, yanked me around and took the fetters off. He poked me painfully and pointed at a tall man lounging near the main hall. That man was staring at me.

'Archer. One of the best. You do not want to run,' he growled. 'And I still have the dogs. And the stick. I also have trackers who would find an elf's ass in the dark.' He spat at me and left. The bastard Wulstan left after him, and the girl smiled my way apologetically, leaving me a clove of strange, hard bread. 'Breakfast. Our specialty,' she whispered, and Vulcan snorted. I wiped Helmut's spittle away, trembling with rage.

I took the bread, sniffed at it, found it delicious and began to eat ravenously, looking around with curiosity. I had been around smithies all my life, as Wandal's father was a smith. We had actually rebuilt one in Hard Hill, the capital of the Marcomanni, and I loved the heat and practicality of such places. This smithy was cozy. It was partially in open air, but the wide doorway could be shut off with an old bear pelt. It had a huge, dark anvil and well tended tools on a long table; mainly tongs and hammers of different sizes. Wood and charcoal were heaped in a room next to the main one. Yet, another room to my right had a bed. That was where Vulcan slept. He was now tapping at a horseshoe on an anvil, and next to it, in the middle of the wooden floor was a brick and stone-lined pit of burning charcoal, the forge. The heat kept the cold out, and I edged closer with my bread.

There was a door to the river and there, behind the smithy, a tree trunk had been dragged to lie on its side and an ax was leaning on it.

'Know anything of fire and iron, boy?' he asked, taking a small hammer to tap something intricate on the horseshoe.

'Euric, my friend's father was … is one,' I told him, swallowing a hard mouthful of bread.

'Euric the smith,' he mused.

I perked up. 'You know him?'

'No, I don't,' he said irascibly. 'Of course, I don't. Why would I?' He kept at it, and I stood there, glancing at the archer, whose eyes did not leave me. He was a clean shaved, tall man with powerful shoulders and an unreadable, handsome face.

After awhile I shrugged. The old man was not particularly talkative. 'Want me to do something?' I asked.

He nodded. 'Answer my question. Do you know anything about the trade?'

I grinned. 'No. But I can chop wood. Or make charcoal.'

'Useless,' he sneered. 'Any man or boy can chop wood. Moreover, slaves can make charcoal in the woods and that too is a job requiring few skills other than picking your nose and staring stupidly at your feet. But I suppose I need to warm myself in the evening, so you chop wood then, in the mornings. Afternoons, you help me with these things,' he said and gestured around him.

'Will I do hammering—'

He shook his head. 'You will learn to clean and care for the tools; you will learn how to heat the beast up and know when it is hot enough to be used. You will do things other than shaping the metal. That is how you learn; by doing the small, mean things while your mind wonders about the bigger ones. Perhaps you will, one day, touch the hammer. Take the pelt and go chop.'

I nodded, grabbed a pelt with holes for arms, pulled it on, and went outside, grabbing the ax.

Birds sang, a fox had left its paw prints near the corner of the house, and I was alive. I nearly yelled for the glory of it. The air was crisp, and beautiful, and I enjoyed the clear sky so much I laughed aloud. Vulcan snorted inside.

The archer walked up from behind the corner. He nodded at me. 'Brimwulf, at your service.' He grinned, eyeing the ax in my hand. 'Be careful.'

'I doubt I am strong enough to kill a squirrel,' I said with some shame, but he shook his head.

'No, you have been near death for half a year; you are not strong. Do not swing the ax to your leg,' he said.

'Oh! No, I try not to.' I took an experimental swing, and the icy trunk resisted me, leaving my arms trembling. Vulcan snorted again. I kept at it, my arms and back aching, feeling dizzy, but I imagined the trunk as Segestes, Odo, and Maroboodus. I imagined the blade sinking to the backbone of Catualda, crushing his face from the top of the skull to the jaw and splinters flew. Then I imagined Ragwald and Helmut shivering under the ax, and the trunk resisted arrogantly, and I renewed my attack, cursing softly. I heard Vulcan sniffle. After a few minutes of this, I collapsed next to the trunk, my pants getting wet from the snow, and the archer was smiling at me.

Vulcan dodged out, his eyes twinkling mischievously. 'They left the ax there for me to sharpen, boy. Use the keen one instead.' He handed me a proper axe, took mine and went in, cursing the idiotic Marcomanni. I stared at the blisters on my hands incredulously.

'Did he do that deliberately?' I whispered. 'He did.'

'He looks gruff as a starved old woman, but he enjoys such jokes,' Brimwulf whispered at me and then laughed with me until our eyes ran with water. It felt good to laugh. Splendid. I felt alive. I was a slave, had lost my friends and my armor and weapons. My honor. But laughter made me feel like a man again.

'Go ahead,' Brimwulf said, and I grabbed the ax. I felt an ache in my neck and thought the strain had opened up some of the wound, but I did not care. I renewed my attack on the tree and this time, it cracked with each strike.

'So, you serve Segestes? You are a mighty hero of a less than heroic lord?' I puffed as I halved pieces of the trunk.

He looked surprised at my comment. 'Just a hunter. Archer and a hunter. I have served Sigimer and my uncle is Sigimer's former warlord. I was one of his hundred men. But Sigimer is gone, and so I serve him, Segestes,' he told me.

'Why would you not serve Armin?' I asked him.

'I ... have a reason,' he told me.

'Service to Segestes is service to Rome,' I said.

'I hear you serve Rome, as well,' he answered, testily.

I shrugged. 'As far as I know, I am still signed up with the 2nd Batavorium ala. I am called the Oath Breaker, after all. The Germani hate me. But it is a mystery to me why good men serve my captor. Your master is a thief and a criminal.'

'He abandoned Armin and Sigimer for personal gain,' Brimwulf said carefully, craning his neck to see if anyone heard. 'Yes. So what?'

I went on. 'I say he is a rotten bastard, and the gods are looking,' the Old Saxon, Vulcan grumbled inside. 'He is not honorable. He seeks to enslave the whole of the north,' I added. 'He seeks to betray Rome and—'

'He has cast his die,' Brimwulf stated, bored. 'Let him enslave those who let him. At least he serves Rome now. That is nothing to be scoffed at. Their gods and ours favor him. You are called that Oath Breaker. Killer of the holy men and women, and you are your father's shame? Who are you to judge a man who has plans?'

'That is me,' I spat. 'Though the story is much juicier than that, and one might see it entirely differently.' The ax split a log so hard it spun to the river.

'You were saying? Betrayal of Rome?' he continued. 'I'm only asking since I love old myths, tales of monsters and fanciful—'

'They will slay a good man,' I huffed. 'Segestes and Maroboodus. Their liege lord. Drusus.'

He hummed. 'A good man? The Roman General? Good men are dying in our land, Hraban. Have you not noticed? Why would I be bothered by the death of a foreign lord?' he smirked, but his face betrayed grief. He saw I noticed and shrugged. 'I loved Sigimer. When he died, I cried.'

'This Roman lord,' I told him, 'is an honest one. Perhaps you should serve him. He is a lord worth crying over and will need men.'

He rubbed his face and shook his head. 'I'm an archer, not a lord,' Brimwulf told me with a unhappy scowl. 'I care little for such high men and their many schemes. And you should remain quiet now. I will not betray Segestes, no matter if Sigimer was as bright as the moon compared to Segestes and this service soils me. I'll not help you with your Drusus, either. You should get to know a man before you try to subvert him to treason. I am disappointed in you, you manipulative shit. But I suppose that is what pig shit would do to a king, even.' He looked away from me, and I cursed under my breath.

'But why Segestes?' I wondered.

'Why Segestes?' he asked incredulously. 'What business is it of yours? I think you are sticking your nose too deep in my business. I came over to take your measure, but I think you are taking mine. Chop and be quiet.'

'Fine,' I told him, cursed him again under my breath and kept on hacking. Brimwulf doggedly looked away from me and said nothing, clearly troubled.

'Get in here, boy!' Vulcan yelled after a time, and I cursed him as well. I went inside and Brimwulf followed, eyeing the ax in my hand. The old man glanced at the archer. 'If he decides to chop you in the head, you won't be able to draw your bow again. Would it not be prudent to stay further away?'

Brimwulf nodded. 'He is slow and weak still and is not faking it. I have to get to know him. He is the type to run, and I wish to know his temper if I have to hunt him.'

I snorted. 'If you think I will run, surely you should tell Ragwald or Helmut?'

He spat. 'I will not speak to Ragwald if I can help it. He is a—' His eyes settled on me. 'And here you are, again trying to get under my skin. Faugh!' He tried to calm himself but failed and shook his head and went outside.

Vulcan looked at me shrewdly, his skin pockmarked by small burns. 'Helmut's daughter Mathildis is to be married to Ragwald's son,' he said with perverse relish.

The subject confused me. 'The freckle-faced thing? Surely Ragwald's pup would marry a noble?'

'Helmut is a noble, impoverished one, but a noble. Beware of him. He takes men to the woods and some do not return,' he told me seriously.

'Sometimes they are men Segestes would like to keep alive. He says they escaped; Helmut does. They did not, and Segestes forgets, after awhile. But I do pity Brimwulf. I was young once.'

'Brimwulf?' I asked shrewdly, eyeing the man kicking at a log outside, murmuring angrily. Then it hit me. 'He is here for her? He is in love with the girl.'

Vulcan's eyes glinted with an agreement, but then he sniffled. 'He served Sigimer's warlord and met her once in a Thing. I know he is loyal and hates Segestes like a rat hates hunger, but he did not waste much time riding to Segestes after his lord died. Didn't even attend the funeral. It's none of your business, boy, of course, but I suppose you have to keep busy, trying to find holes in the impregnable wall you might escape from. Now. See here.' He showed me all his tools and explained their names and how to prepare the forge. I learned or at least tried to, and the old man was patience incarnated when it came to teaching the basics of the trade.

Wulstan came in the evening and placed a rope around my neck. Vulcan eyed him evilly, but the boy of thirteen or fourteen took no heed. 'Come, you ugly mutt,' the bastard chortled and tugged at me. I gritted my teeth, but let Wulstan guide me to the stables as he would a dog while he chortled at my dark mood. Brimwulf followed us, his face a mask of stone. 'Here, slave,' Wulstan said and pushed me inside. 'You know the pretty pigs, but here are the sturdy workhorses and fat cows. Clean the shit; new straw in place when it is moldy. Do it well, or I will have you do it on your knees.'

I considered murdering him.

He was much like Ansigar, my friend from the time we still played war in the woods of the Marcomanni, I decided. He had turned to Odo with Gernot, my brother, and I think there had always been a dark spot in his soul. Wulstan was a sturdy boy, evil and full of malice, and I did all I could to hold my patience as I regarded his ugly face. I nodded, my eyes flickering dangerously. The bastard seemed to inflate with power as I did. After I had cleaned the stalls, dirtying myself, it was dark. People were eating nearby, and I realized there was a door from the stalls to the main hall. I noticed Wulstan had disappeared, and there was Brimwulf alone guarding me.

'Good job, Hraban,' he noted tiredly. 'Seems you have cared for horses before.'

'I helped my Mother Sigilind and Grandfather Hulderic with our beasts,' I told him.

'Got to go and eat soon. Yearning for something warm,' he said with a relish.

I snorted. 'I doubt you will get anything hot, Brimwulf. I will be doing this twice every day.'

He glanced at the stall. 'Looks clean to me. What do you mean?'

'Matters not. He is a little shit,' I told him.

'Ahh!' Brimwulf began, and then Wulstan came in, and without inspecting my work, he struck me with a cane.

'Again, on your knees. Brimwulf. You can go eat.'

The archer shrugged and hesitated, evidently tempted by the offer. Then he shook his head. 'I best stay here. He can crush your skull faster than you can fart. And do not order me around, boy. I work for Segestes, not your dull father.'

The boy's eyes opened wide in shock, and he gritted his teeth in anger. Then he hit my back with the cane again. 'But this dog works for me. Do it! On your knees, dog, I said!' I went on my knees, picking up stray bits of straw and shit with my bare hands, and it took an hour before the little evil vaettir was happy. 'Lock him up for the night,' Wulstan told the archer, bored by my silence. Brimwulf walked me back to where I had slept so many months. My face was burning with shame and anger, and I did not even smile when I found the girl serving some cold porridge on a table for me, along with some sour ale. I nodded at her and sat down. Brimwulf was standing at the door, eyeing her with obvious and desperate desire, and she glanced at him, many times.

'Why Brimwulf, I can eat on my own,' I told him happily. 'Weren't you hungry? Starving?' I teased him, and he cursed me profusely.

'There will be a guard at the door, Hraban. Keep your senses,' he told me, casting one last look at the girl as he left.

'Do you need any bandages, anything for pain?' the girl asked me. 'I can ask Hilda, the old healer to bring some of her herbs.'

I shook my head. 'No, just some more ale.'

She smiled. 'Tomorrow. Only water for now.' She gave me a gourd of it.

'What is your name?' I asked her. 'Mathi—'

'Mathildis, Lord,' she said and blushed as I laughed, my mouth full of porridge.

'Lord? Not many have called me that in a long while!' I said, chewing vigorously on a piece of vegetable.

'Hraban then. You are famous,' she said. 'And perhaps you are a lord. Of pigs?' She smiled mischievously, not maliciously, and I slapped her rump like I would Cassia and realized my error. I had been too familiar with Mathildis, for her eyes opened huge as she rubbed her rear. I shook my head in apology.

'I am sorry,' I said while bowing my head. 'I'm used to pigs and thus they moved out of the way when I had to dig for food amidst them. I am a famous pig herder, a recently promoted woodcutter, and a shit collector,' I said, gruffly. 'I have no skills left with beautiful girls.'

'You took me for a pig!' she giggled.

'No!'

She caressed my face briefly. 'Grandfather said that a man has to start low to be a true lord. And perhaps you skipped such service in your previous life?' she said with renewed humor.

'I did not. And if your father Helmut was taught like that, then why is he such a—'

'He didn't listen to grandfather much,' she said patiently.

'Time to go, girl,' a tall guard said from the door. She nodded and waved at me, locking the door. I ate and lay awake, dreaming of strangling Wulstan with my hands.

I was strangely happy.

I had a routine now, and I would grow stronger.

And I had a makings of a plan. It had no form nor details, and it would be, when finished, a perilous, hopeless plan, for it depended on a woman.

Wyrd.

CHAPTER 15

Every morning, Wulstan stomped through the door, put a rough rope around my neck and pulled me back to the smithy. It was better than the fetters of Helmut, but the way Wulstan spoke to me, as if I was his dog, made the insult near insufferable, and I was glad to be rid of him for the day. The insult would resume when the evening arrived, and I picked up shit with my hands, swept and changed the hay.

The smithy was my salvation. Vulcan needed an apprentice, and he treated me like one. During the first few days, he showed me what he was doing. He worked from morning to evening, got up early to heat the forge, which took time while gathering suitable metals for his purposes. He made axes, spear points, hinges and tools, even saddle parts and bridles. In his own time, he fashioned animals out of scrap metal. He was not married.

He repeatedly explained the tools to me, showed me how to hold them, how to hammer carefully, and when not to. He was in the business of bending and shaping metal, and just like the metal, he was unyielding when I made silly mistakes. His patience was restricted to explaining the theory and the tools and did not extend to the actual business of creating a useful item. That part was a matter of pride, and he would suck in his breath, horrified at my ineptness, tearing his hair with his smudged hands as he yelled at me. 'No, boy, if the metal is white, then it is too hot! You will just make a fucking mess out of it, the result something to hide in a shit hole. No, the color of the metal has to be light orange, yellow, something in between, and only then this iron is ready to be shaped!' He showed me a dozen times how to do it on a prospective horseshoe. He showed me how to draw metal and how to bend soft metal like copper. In his hands, the metal began to take shape as if magically, and I had a renewed respect for Euric and Wandal. He was more than a smith; he was an artisan. For example, when he was making hammers, he used a chisel to make perfect holes in the handle. No matter if the handles themselves would hide them, he wanted them to be perfect. Little had I thought about the practice of making the things I so admired. He showed me how to use flux to clean a surface and how to weld items, and how the temperature was to be kept just right to accomplish this. I did not understand half of it, but it seemed to me Vulcan needed someone to talk to, and he talked constantly as if desperately trying to pass his wisdom off to someone.

I was not sure I was the perfect pupil. In fact, I was sure I was not. His patience ran out, mine did as well, and once I threw a hammer out of the shed, and he had me cut wood all day. Next day, I paid more attention, but our sessions were sometimes loud, full of curses but often peaceful and happy, as well when things were going fine. On one such occasion, I decided to ask him about his past.

'Have you had a wife?' I asked him one day when he was not entirely displeased with me.

He grunted. 'Of course, I had one! Do I look like a man who does not enjoy a soft, plump wife?'

'No, you look like you might enjoy a plump wife. Anyone might,' I told him with a grin. 'My grandfather Hulderic told us it is easier to escape a plump one when she is enraged. Which is often. Gods know if that is true.'

He looked mollified. 'She was plump. Pretty and plump. And she was kind, so I did not have to escape her. But she died. They say she stole food from Segestes during a very hard winter, and perhaps she did. She served there, in the hall. They claimed she also stole a brooch of gold and some silver rings as well.' He looked up darkly at the great house. 'That I did not believe. And then she was gone.'

175

'What?' I asked him, shocked. 'They condemned her? Surely a wergild would have—'

He poked me. 'She was condemned by a Thing headed by Segestes and yes, it was a crime that could have been made good by a cow or a horse, but Segestes did not want that, no. He wanted the gold and silver returned, and I bet Helmut stole them and blamed her. She did not have it, of course, and then the free men voted as Segestes did. I told them I ate some of that stolen food as well, and I had wondered why our table held goose and trout when we had survived on porridge, but the Thing spared me. She was not. They exiled her. Took her away,' he said, his voice choking. 'I went after her, of course. She was not very intelligent, but she was mine.'

I fiddled with some straw but asked nonetheless. 'You found her?'

He glared at me but nodded. 'A wolf.'

'Why did you stay here?'

He shook his shoulders. 'I had to pay the debts.'

'What?' I breathed. 'No, you owed them nothing!'

He shrugged. 'When it was paid, I had nothing left. Now I only work. I have nothing else. It keeps me going. Don't want to remarry, even. I feel … old. I am old.'

'You must hate Segestes,' I whispered, and he shrugged.

'Everyone does, save for his sycophants,' he agreed, eyeing me carefully. 'My, but you do work on us to find an escape. Work on the metal instead.'

I nodded and worked.

Maius was soon replaced by spring, and he let me sit outside in the mornings, eating my breakfast. The girl still brought it to me in the mornings. 'Mathildis. It is a pretty name,' I told her one day, and she beamed at me.

'Thank you. May I call you Hraban?' she said, glancing at Brimwulf, who was still my guard, though he often stayed in the hall, sitting and whittling at a block of wood.

'You may. Do you call him Brimwulf, as well?' I asked, nodding at the warrior.

She shook her head. 'No, I am not allowed to speak with him. Wulstan beats me when he sees me do it.'

'But you like the archer, no? Surely there is nothing wrong with this?' I asked her innocently.

'I like him, he eyes me, smiles at me shyly, and he is so handsome. But I am promised to Ragwald's son.' She looked about nervously.

'Have not seen him,' I told her, gulping down porridge. 'Is he as mad as his father?'

She sat next to me. 'He is serving with Rome for some months. In Castra Vet ...' she stammered and smiled. She nodded towards the west. 'Roman side of the Great River.'

'Castra Vetera,' I told her and paused to wonder at the fact I had not been there for such a long time.'

She nodded. 'He is there in Roman lands, but comes back here soon.'

'What is his name?'

She smiled. 'Turd.' She giggled, and I liked her.

I shrugged at her and told her a secret. 'Most men are turds, but sometimes, a woman's touch gives the turd a purpose and it might sprout something worthy. Perhaps he matures from manure to a likable man when he has you,' I teased her.

She looked troubled. 'Manno. His name is Manno. I know not, Lord. I do not know how to make a man happy. My father thinks I am a nuisance, my brother beats me. I will be a disappointment to the Turd as well,' she said, sullenly. 'Thusnelda speaks with him, quite often, and he seems nice enough, but he is Ragwald's son. Must be something wrong with him.'

I gave her the bowl and drank some ale. 'I am sure you are not,' I told her after emptying it. 'Ask Brimwulf. He must think highly of you.'

She shook her head shyly. 'I said I cannot speak to him. I doubt I could please him any more than any other man.' She blushed as she spoke of such matters.

I laughed raucously. 'All women know how to please a man! Just by smiling at them.'

She blushed and walked off quickly. Brimwulf wondered over, glancing in her direction. 'What did you tell her? She looked upset,' he asked angrily.

'I told her that she should be allowed to marry whom she will, even a rouge, honor plagued archer,' I winked at Brimwulf, who cursed me with a red face.

'What were you talking about?' he demanded.

'She likes you. I think very much,' I said with a straight face. 'She keeps looking at you, her eyes large as a doe's. She sighs when you grunt, shakes her head in desperation when you speak to some other wench. She is,' I said happily, 'enamored with you. She would likely utter an ecstatic cry of joy if you so much as farted.' Vulcan cackled.

'Enamored?' Brimwulf snickered. 'She never looks my way. She is tearing my heart out, and you tell me she is smitten by me? No. I would know. I'm miserable as shit, and then some liar of a man called the Oath Breaker comes along to tell me my moon is within reach.'

'But—' I began, and he grabbed my shirt.

'Hraban. I like you. I like her. Love her, yes. But I won't let you go and drag her to a lengthy escape along the rivers. I'm not the only tracker in this Hel hole. Forget this and leave me to my suffering,' he told me as he let go of me. He shook his head at me tiredly as if speaking to a child. 'I have loved her for years. Yet, I could not leave Sigimer's service to be close to her. No. It would have been dishonorable. Now I have given Segestes my oaths. How could I break them and be happy with her, without my fame? Stop tempting me.'

'But—' I started as he walked off, mumbling something about uncouth Marcomanni. I heard Vulcan snicker. I cursed, went inside and learnt about heating the iron, and why it gathered a black surface in the process.

My plan was going poorly, I decided.

Before Wulstan came to take me to my excrement gathering duties, Vulcan pulled me closer. 'He is a fool. An honest fool. But how honest are you? Not very, I think. He won't let you escape, not even for Mathildis.'

'I want no ill for him or Mathildis,' I frowned. 'Only happiness.'

He snorted. 'Right. You wish to be free. Give it time and find some other way. Be careful,' he told me slowly, and I nodded. 'Beware of Helmut.'

A month passed, then another. Drimilchi was celebrated while I was cleaning stables on my hands and knees, and the summer time, Liatha began. The celebration of Midsummer was nigh. Roman couriers came and went regularly, and I dreaded the messages they might bear. The poor bastards were visiting Segestes thinking he was their ally, yet Segestes was the enemy. For some reason that early summer was peaceful. The Roman campaign season was already partly gone, and I was sure Nero Claudius Drusus wished to finish what he had begun. But there were no sign of Roman armies. There was no news of impending invasion of the lands of the Cherusci. Segestes stayed at home.

Midsummer feast was celebrated amidst plenty, and as I was looking at the bonfires burning from midday onwards from the smithy, I cursed the vitka dancing before Segestes, all of whom were promising him favors of Tiw the Just, All-Father Woden and the Hammer Lord Donor. There was a huge feast set up before the hall and even Vulcan watched enviously at all the food that was being served. 'I'm never invited, but if I were, I would rather eat coal than see them smirk at me over the table. Eat your snot and drink your tears, Hraban. More honest food and drink you can never find,' he told me, and we grinned.

After the feast, Wulstan and Helmut arranged wrestling matches.

I saw Ragwald point at me, whispering to Wulstan, and I felt doom approaching, for I knew I was about to be involved in such sport. I was right, for two drunk guards came to fetch me from the smithy. Wulstan followed them. He was drunk and gestured at me. Vulcan growled, wiped his hands and pushed a guard. 'I'll need him tomorrow. I'm sure it won't be a fair fight, anyhow, so scramble off, toad.'

Wulstan grinned and bowed mockingly at us. 'He can finally hit back, Old Saxon,' Wulstan slurred at the old man. 'He will be the hammer, there will be an anvil, and we shall cheer his efforts and laugh at his struggles. He will work tomorrow, surely. Or the day after, surely. Come, mutt!'

'Be strong, Hraban,' Vulcan told me. Brimwulf marched after me, his face unreadable. I was pushed in the middle of the drunken Cherusci, and I found myself ringed by feast tables.

It was not hard to guess who I would wrestle with.

Helmut himself hopped over the tables to oppose me, and I could barely breathe for the rage I felt for the humiliation I was about to endure.

179

Segestes was sitting on his seat, happy and drunk, barely aware it was Hraban before him. I saw Thusnelda, her face cast down in the crowd. Helmut squared off against me, his huge, hairy chest twice the size of mine. He pushed me, grasped for me suddenly, dancing on his feet as I dodged him and the men roared encouragements at him. I whirled around the huge man, but in order to beat him I would have to grasp him and that meant I would lose. I kicked his knee, punched him in the face, and he leered at me as if I had the strength of a fly. He danced before me, mocking me and the men roared even louder. I sighed and closed in, throwing another huge punch at his meaty face and not even the Woden's song hammering ferociously in my head could help me put the bastard down. He spat blood, grinned, charged, and I could not dodge him. He pulled me up to him and then he squeezed me like I was a sack of hay, and I howled and cried in pain. I managed to put my finger in his eye, forcing him to release me. I screamed in anger, tackled him to the ground. I saw his hand coming for me, his fingers splayed as he would squeeze my face. I grabbed it with both my hands and twisted. There was a crack and Helmut screamed. One of his fingers was twisted to the side, and I spat at his face. He kicked me off him, darted after me like a spirit, and I did not manage to get out of the way and so the fight was over. He punched me hard, I tasted blood and sensed he was hovering over me. He took a spear off a guard, hesitated and turned it around and clubbed me half senseless, and Brimwulf had to stop him in his rage. Men pulled him off.

I got up unsteadily and pointed a finger at him. 'I, Hraban of the Batavi will have your guts in my hands, you shitfaced coward, and your son will show you the way to Hel. And your daughter—' I began and then I got an idea.

I did not need Brimwulf. Not really. But Mathildis was the key, indeed.

Later on in the stables, Helmut and Wulstan beat me again; both were drunk, and I did not work for a week. I healed and eventually worked again, and I asked Vulcan what was taking place, for horses were being saddled. He knew little of what was happening in the wide lands, but in that week of Junius, Segestes went to war and rumors told us Roman cohorts joined him. They were trying to find Armin, and I prayed to Woden Lif and Drusus were spared.

Time passed, the summer wore on, and I worked. I was thinking about my plan, felt terribly afraid to attempt to put it to action and decided to wait until I knew more. Then it was fall; the leaves were abandoning the trees, people spending less time outdoors. Segestes was still gone. I saw Mathildis daily though she had stopped talking of anything of consequence with me after our last awkward discussion, but she brought me meat and vegetables, always smiling prettily. I assisted Vulcan now with the actual smiting, and he rarely scolded me. We were making spear points, not for the framea, but heavy, hasta points, and he would hold the metal with thongs after being happy with the color of the heated metal. He would ask me questions and growl if I answered wrong. Then, he would show me where to hit, and I would use a sledgehammer so hard the metal began to flatten, ever so slowly, but flatten it did. He kept marking spots for me, and I hit them. I grunted and enjoyed the work, happy for the cooler air, for the summer had been hot, the crops had been partly failing, and it was as if the gods had decided to make life hard for men. It would be a harsh winter.

I wanted it to be hard.

I was steeling myself for my escape and knew I had no more time to think about it. I was frustrated with the terrible fear I felt in my gut when I thought about Helmut, afraid I had lost my valor with my weapons and vented my rage on metal each day. I swung the sledgehammer and the metal gave. Vulcan grunted appreciatively. I was strong, perhaps stronger than before, my muscles grown and my stamina was much better. Wulstan's beatings did not make me bat an eye.

'You can soon make your first ax head,' he said proudly.

I glanced at him before striking. 'I would like to try, master. Perhaps I can keep it.'

He laughed and looked bothered. 'I am but a humble smith. What do I know? But I would advice against it.'

I nodded and asked. 'Do you dislike me?'

181

He shook his head in wonder at my blunt question. 'Dislike you? No, not really. You eat too long, fart too often, and stink, but that is not your fault. They don't let you bathe often enough. You are all right. You learn quickly. I do not care about your past, and who you have killed or betrayed. They say things about you, but what is that to me? Bah. You have been here a lot longer than I thought you would be.'

I hit a particularly hard spot to flatten, and he nodded appreciatively as I kept speaking. 'They will keep me like this until they have decided what to do with me. Segestes will trade me to some high bastard, who will benefit him most. Or he will just depose of me. Either way, I wish to die fighting,' I said, bitterly.

I did not draw a positive reaction. He glanced at me and said: 'It is your wyrd, then.' I stopped the hammering. He fixed an eye on me and asked: 'What? You expect me to die for you? Why would I let you create something that could get me killed?'

I looked into his eyes. 'Because Brimwulf would not betray Segestes for the girl. Because I have a plan, and I need steel to make it work. Because you have given me these wonderful skills. They will be lost, and your legacy is gone. I know nothing, nothing at all about this work, not even after this year, but you have given me, at least, love for the craft.' It was true, I realized, but I needed a good weapon. He pointed at the spear point and stayed quiet as I worked on.

We noticed Wulstan coming for me in the evening, and Vulcan turned me around.

'Tomorrow, we make a seax. It is not easy, takes a lot of metal, but perhaps you can,' he said, and my heart swelled. I could. Both make it and keep it.

Wulstan took me to the stables and pushed me in. Brimwulf followed, bored out of his wits, rubbing his face. I stopped at the door, astonished. The stables that had been empty since Segestes rode out were now full of sweaty horses. 'Feed them, then clean, dog. Lap up the crap, sweep the hay. You know the drill, beast,' Wulstan said with an unhappy voice. He was unhappy, for there was a feast ongoing. At the other side of the stable was the wall with a door. It was by a stall, and there were cracks in the door and warmer air often carried fine fragrances of delicious food from the other side. That night, I could smell venison and sweet mead, juicy boar and steamy vegetables and all of the excruciatingly wonderful details of the fares wafted through. I felt famished. I also heard many noises. I went to my hands and knees, beginning the chore of cleaning up the few empty stalls first, but this night, Wulstan was not going away. He leaned on a stall.

'What is wrong?' I asked him. 'They don't invite pups to the feast?'

He stared at me with a shocked expression and then smiled like a rodent. 'My father says you will go soon. I will miss you, but perhaps I shall get a real dog,' the bastard told me snidely and toed my ass. I heard Segestes call for silence, and I cursed, for I was done with Wulstan. There was nothing to be done, and I got up. Wulstan blanched. 'What? Get back down this very instant, or I will fuck you in the ass with this stick!' he said, showing his cane to me. Brimwulf spat in disgust. Wulstan turned to him in fury, but when he turned his face back towards me, he saw my fist flying for his forehead. Something broke, and he flew in the air. He was not getting up. I bent over him, and I noticed to my dissatisfaction he was still alive.

Brimwulf looked at me in alarm and cocked an arrow in a heartbeat. 'What do you think you are doing, Hraban? I cannot protect—'

'I just want to clean in peace. Will you leave me to it?' I said, and he looked unsure, his eyes darting from the prone bastard to me, then to the door, and he finally nodded.

'Do not kill him, and I will go sit outside. Hot in here, stinks like vermin,' he told me, then hesitated and dragged Wulstan out. 'In fact, let's not tempt you. I'll take the vermin with me.'

I grinned at him, went to the door, and placed my eye on the crack in the planking. I saw Segestes and a Roman officer, a centurion by his haughty bearing, yet a fighter with a rough face. Rome used them for more than whipping their enemies. In his finger, there was a fine ring, a ruby set amidst gold, and I noticed Segestes admiring it every now and then. Also present were a dozen of Segestes's silver adorned chiefs. Thusnelda was standing near my wall, and Ragwald and Helmut were standing by the door. Segestes was giving a speech, his beard oiled, wearing a lavish toga, toasting.

'—and Armin, Inguiomerus, both driven away, again this year. I now hold sway over all of Sigimer's lands, and most of his men, thanks to our bravery and the cohorts of the XVII Legion, have made them retreat to Albis and Hercynian wilds. Next year, all the Cherusci are one!' Men cheered him raucously and clapped, the Roman was nodding politely. Thusnelda shuddered, evidently holding back rage and tears. Segestes called for silence, the goblet in his hand sloshing wine on the tables. He went on. 'This year, Nero Claudius Drusus, the governor of Tres Galliae, took the XVI Gallica and XIV Gemina Legions up the Moenus River, scattered the Marcomanni and the remains of the Quadi to the savage land beyond the Chatti. He built a castra near the Red and White Moenus and marched for Mattium, the Chatti capital! A splendid victory there, as well!' he told the men, and my mind was whirling. Cheers filled the room.

My Father put to flight? The Chatti scattered? I thought, leaning my forehead to the wall. *Had Drusus made sure Father would not threaten him after all? Had Drusus made a surprising move and had he won? Was Father dead?* 'If he is, Segestes is fucked,' I whispered and thought Thusnelda moved and glanced at the door. On the other hand, if Father was dead, then Segestes only had Drusus. And I would die and be buried in silence.

Judging by Segestes's happiness, Father was still alive and their plans were ongoing. Segestes's voice broke, and he nearly choked, but he went on bravely. 'The Luppia legions, on the other hand took the fight again to the Bructeri, Marsi, and Sigambri, building more fine castrum and a great route now runs from Luppia to our lands! Trade and wealth will roll in and out,' he screamed, hoisting his horn up. I heard Thusnelda curse with tears. Then Segestes sobered, his eyes glancing around apologetically, for not all faces were joyous with these victories. 'Let us honor our foes as well. The Chatti fought! They still fight. They are not defeated, but next year, Lord Drusus will finish it, and he will march here to deal with the dregs of our last enemies! The dark lands of Inguiomerus will belong to us, under a keen Roman governance. Too long have the Cherusci been reduced to fighting enemies outside, and inside. Now, we are strong!' he continued

,and some men roared their approval. 'Next year, even stronger!' So, Drusus had herded all his enemies far to the east and some of them would be in the lands of the Cherusci next year. And there Drusus would die after all, for he did not know about Segestes. Father was indeed still at large. I cursed. I should have been happy with the Roman army winning its wars. Of routing Father. Hard Hill was likely taken. Yet, my heart ached for the noble Chatti, and the thought of a man like Segestes leading the Germani nations, revolted me.

'Bastard turd,' I breathed and kept on listening as the noises abated inside.

The fat man continued. 'Drusus, our friend Drusus is gone to Lugdunum to finish his Altar of Roma and Augustus. There the Gauls gather and worship their masters. My son, Segimundus has been serving him in Lugdunum and will be a priest of the great cult, and I am honored, we are all much honored by this!' he continued, and I saw the chiefs in the room stiffen. They wanted no new gods and certainly wanted to avoid worshipping the strange Roman ones, no matter the Roman ways of Segestes's hall. *Their gods lived in the air, ours on the ground and did not get along,* I thought. Segestes did not see the scowls as he saluted the Roman officer, his jowls flapping as he spoke, in tears. The centurion was hard put to remain stoic, his eyes laughing, and his lips quivering.

The centurion got up with a horn. 'Nero Claudius Drusus! Segestes the Great! Next year we will push the savage Chatti, the stubborn Fox Armin, and Inguiomerus the Gaunt to Hades! Let them weep in the Grey Lands, and see us reap the rewards they have sown. We shall place a new border on Albis, where the Suebi will shake in terror as we flash our swords at them! It will be finished here! In your lands,' he yelled to the multitude.

'New lands for us to rule,' Segestes said loudly.

'Indeed!' the Roman centurion saluted. 'I will also have you know that Nero Claudius Drusus celebrated the birth of his son! Tiberius Claudius Nero! His third child. It is a new era!'

They saluted him for that, if not for the rest; cheering the centurion, and Drusus for his happy family, for we all loved such news. That was also the first time I heard of the future princeps Claudius.

185

A man rose up in the crowd. 'And the Marcomanni, the Quadi? What of them? How badly were they beaten?'

Segestes made a dismissive gesture with his hand. 'Hard Hill hosts a Roman castra now. The Red Hall remains are a latrine. The Matticati are recovering and allied to us. The Vangiones and Drusus took it; Hunfried the Vangione king was freed from imprisonment and the Suebic scum have fled. They did not lose many, but their lands and cows are taken. There are no longer Suebi in the Rhenus. They are gone, gone, to poverty and shame, hiding with the Chatti and fearing the Hermanduri,' he said, dramatically.

The celebration continued, and I shook my head. I had to escape and find Drusus. And Fulcher. And her. Cassia. I wondered briefly if Cassia was still waiting for me. Why would she be? I was rumored dead. And still could die. I swallowed and chased away tears, feeling alone and miserable, momentarily bereft of strength to carry on. I quit my eavesdropping and cleaned the stall, carrying the shit in my hands to a pit meant for it, and Brimwulf smiled at me from the door. 'He is coming to. Want to wait for it?'

I nodded at him and went to sit by the wall, preparing for pain.

I heard a meowing sound, then a growl outside. Then a piteous moan. Wulstan was struggling to get up, then said something to Brimwulf. Soon, I heard unsteady running steps and pained weeping. I sighed, trying to relax. Time passed.

I did not have to wait for long.

Soon, heavy feet were thumping the ground so that dust fell from the roof beams and the door opened violently. Helmut stood there, his face red. I smiled at him and raised my eyebrows in mock question, and he came to me. He grabbed me by my face and threw me roughly outside by the scruff of my neck. There I saw Wulstan holding the left side of his face, which was dreadfully swollen.

'You will pay for this,' Helmut said as he came after me and held me by the neck.

'He looks prettier now, does he not? Much better than his father,' I told him, and he swatted me with an open hand. I took it and laughed at him. 'He looks like a cow's ass!'

'Bring the dogs here,' Helmut said darkly and Brimwulf was about to protest when a guard of Helmut placed a spear on his back. Brimwulf went silent, gnashing his teeth.

He said: 'Segestes will not approve if you maim him too badly.'

'Segestes is drunk, and he tried to escape,' he said, savagely. 'It happens.'

'Just beat him, he knew it was coming,' Brimwulf told him sternly.

'Shut your mouth,' Helmut told him and looked on in glee as two large, hairy canines were brought forward from the kennel. He dragged me up and pushed me in front of the beasts, and the creatures smelled me inches away, their teeth slavering in front of my face, growling like mad things of Hel. Helmut was looking at my reactions as the hounds flattened their ears, and I am sure I went white from the face. To make the matters worse, Ragwald walked over from the hall, a lanky short man following him. The younger man's face was blank as if he was deep in his thoughts, and he showed no reaction to my dilemma. I decided that was Mathildis's Turd. Ragwald's son. *Manno.*

'What's this then?' Ragwald asked darkly, eyeing me, then Wulstan. 'He did that?'

'Lord,' Helmut said desperately. 'He did. I was going to—'

Ragwald licked his lips and glanced behind him for the door of the hall. It was clear. 'Is there any way to force the dogs to rip something like a finger off, perhaps? So that he still survives?' Ragwald mused.

'No,' Helmut frowned. 'They go for the throat. I taught them.'

Ragwald shuddered as he stared at the beasts. 'Well met, Hraban. I see you have been causing mischief.'

I spat. 'He found trouble, the little shit,' I nodded at Wulstan who was whimpering. 'A man treated like a dog will eventually bite.'

Ragwald licked his lips, looking around, his eye twitching. 'Lord,' Helmut asked, gesturing at the lanky man beside the lord. 'Your son. Imagine if this bad hearted southerner had beaten your son? Let my mutts tear him open.'

Ragwald nodded, showing his useless arm. 'I know what he is.'

'Lord!' Brimwulf protested.

Ragwald turned his face to him, pondering the issue, but then drunken savagery conquered his doubts and fears, and he nodded. 'Let them.'

'Rip?' Helmut asked carefully.

'Him apart,' Ragwald agreed maliciously. 'Make sure the mutts will leave something together, enough to call him a man.'

'Lord!' Brimwulf yelled. 'I will—'

'Be quiet,' Helmut spat and pushed me. 'Run,' he said slowly.

I did.

I pushed past Helmut and ran for Ragwald who blanched, but I aimed for his son who just looked at me, confused as the dogs shot after me. I tackled him to the ground and wrapped my hands around him, flipped him on top of me as the hounds buried us. Ragwald was screaming, Helmut was bellowing.

I held on for my dear life.

I gritted my teeth as the claws savaged my arms, teeth were tearing at us, and I shook Ragwald's son around. The dogs mostly tore at him, and I witnessed from inches away how one of them buried its teeth in his neck, shaking him. I held on with all my power as he screamed until the powerful jaws closed his windpipe. In the terrible din of the bloody canine murder, I glimpsed Segestes looking on at the sight, the centurion rushing to us with a gladius. Helmut was finally dragging one of the hounds off me. The other dog yelped as the centurion killed it. Brimwulf had an arrow cocked and ready to shoot. Ragwald was sobbing next to his son, who was flapping his lips in fathomless pain. I backpedalled from them and got up on my feet, holding my forearms, which had deep bite and claw marks.

Ragwald looked up at Segestes. 'Lord, I will pay anything for his life! Neither Drusus nor Maroboodus needs him, not really and I have gold—'

'Silence!' yelled Segestes, looking at me with an unreadable expression. 'Brimwulf, take him to his quarters.'

I took a chance. If the centurion was a man of Drusus, he could help me. If he worked for Antius, he would smile. 'Centurion, tell Chariovalda that Hraban lives!' The man opened his mouth in confusion.

'Hraban,' he said, alarmed. 'Wait, you are the man who they are looking for! What—'

Segestes shook his head in regret and nodded at Brimwulf. The archer adopted a steely expression and shot the centurion in the chest, the arrow burying itself between his ribs. The man cursed and fell on his back. He looked at me as he slowly died amidst the Germani. Black froth issued from his mouth, and I cursed myself for a damned idiot. *It is my fault,* I thought. Then Segestes had a man stab him. The warrior wrestled the ring out of the centurion's finger, admiring it before handing it over to Segestes. Segestes took the ring, placing it on his own finger, gazing at it while thinking deep. Then he moved away from the dying man. 'These are sad times when Armin's robbers still raid this far. Our future guests have to travel with guards. Hraban will be gone by then.' He took Ragwald by his useless arm. 'I need him.' Ragwald started to protest, but Segestes shook his head. 'He will go to Odo soon, Ragwald.'

I stiffened. *Odo?*

'See to your son and try to save his life. And when Hraban is sent away, he shall leave something behind. Arm, leg, his prick. I will think about it. Odo will not need all of him. Thusnelda! Go inside!' he yelled at his daughter, who stood there, looking at me. Brimwulf grabbed me and pulled me along wordlessly. He looked hard at me and shook his head, warning me to remain quiet. He dragged me to my room and left me in the dark. The last thing I saw from the door before it closed was the front of the great hall and Helmut's feverish face staring at my doorway. I saw Ragwald sobbing, his eyes pools of madness.

Wyrd, I thought, and I was sure I had ruined my chances of escape. *Odo?*

CHAPTER 16

When the morning dawned, nobody came for me. There was no food, no punishment, no Wulstan. At some point, I heard Vulcan curse at the door and a guard brusquely told him to go away. Thus, I spent two days and wondered when they would come and claim the piece Segestes had promised them. I felt a pang of guilt at using Ragwald's son as a shield to save my life, but that feeling ebbed with the hunger, and I simmered in anger, preparing for the worst. The wounds in my arms were sore and some began to get infected.

Then the next morning I got a visitor. A female voice demanded access outside the door, rather imperiously. 'Move!'

'My lady, the Lord has forbidden—' the guard began to argue.

'Yes, yes. I am here on his behest,' Thusnelda argued. 'He has wounds; I will tend to them.'

'Surely a slave …' the guard said and went quiet, trying to find an argument that left him in good steads with the formidable woman.

'No, I will do this,' she said with a voice that hinted at a rising storm. 'Stand aside man, and open it up,' she insisted with such an arrogant voice that I could imagine the man quaking in his shoes.

'Very well, but if they ask me, I shall—' he grumbled.

'Tell them,' she said imperiously. 'By all means tell my Father I came here to bind the wounds of his prized prisoner!' The door opened, and she stepped in. She wore a dark woolen dress with a voluminous cloak around her. Her eyes were red, her face drawn, but she had a nervous energy about her as she carried a sack for me.

'I need to search that,' the guard said abruptly, and Thusnelda cursed and slammed the door on his face.

'Asshole,' she hissed, in a very unladylike manner. I flinched and hoped she aimed the comment at the guard as she marched up. I sat up on my bed. Then she opened the sack and wordlessly began to ladle out a small gourd of ale, cold meats, and vegetables, and nodded at me as I looked at the abundance ravenously. Then she took my arm and started to clean and bind the claw marks, which were sore enough for me to wince. She went on with the diligent work, glancing at me every now and then. It was strange, as if we continued the discussion from the day I had been bringing her to Armin. 'He's not all well in the head,' she told me, with a mild reproof.

'Which one?' I asked, my mouth full of meat. 'I honestly do not know.'

She giggled, but sobered quickly. 'The boy you fed to the dogs.'

I nodded. 'Oh, yes! Was it—'

'Manno, he is Manno,' she said. 'Though he is known as—'

'The Turd. Yes, I know. He is alive then?' I asked, burping. 'Well, it was his wyrd. He was the best candidate for covering me. A lank faced bastard,' I said cruelly though deep inside I was again fighting with my conscience.

'He is a kind man, though Ragwald has tried to make him like he is, brutal and a foolish brute at that. Manno obeys him, but likes to sit and be quiet, and loves dogs,' she continued.

I laughed. 'Well! I think I cured him of that!' I distrusted dogs. I had once been chased across woods by a pack of them. *Twice*, I thought, *if you counted the time I tried to escape the pigsty.*

She slapped me, gently. 'He cannot speak now, and is weak. He is missing an eye, and if he survives, his throat will make him look like a monster.'

191

'So he has to grow a beard. Why are you here? To admonish me for surviving a murder attempt?' I asked, wolfing down venison strips.

She finished with my arm and sat back. 'Armin is in danger.'

I snorted. 'I have been doing nothing but thinking about Armin's problems this past year. When they beat me and nearly fed me to pigs, all I could think about was Armin's tear-filled face. Yes, yes.' She gave me a disapproving look, and I sighed.

'Sarcasm does not suit you, Hraban,' she said.

'I know,' I agreed. 'Your father is a piece of rotten gristle,' I told her blankly. 'Helmut and Ragwald? I do not know how to describe them. Are they human? And you speak to me of Armin?'

'I have no love for them. You must know this,' she told me heavily.

'We have that in common,' I laughed and finished the food, licking my fingers meticulously.

'Fine. Let's talk about you first. It seems you might be given to Odo,' she stated bluntly.

I nodded and shrugged, drinking ale. 'Perhaps,' I said. 'And I am sorry. I know your love is in danger. Your father is thinking about killing Drusus and becoming lord of the north. Armin is not part of that plan. And has Segestes not tried to hunt Armin for years? I am not sure why you are so surprised.'

She laughed bitterly. 'I merely stated a fact. Something that plagues me daily. So, you are saying my father is planning on betraying Drusus, as well?' She had a disbelieving look and was tugging at a blonde red braid uncertainly.

I rolled my eyes and leaned close to her. 'He and my father will be given lordship of Roman Germania after Drusus dies to my father's sword. Your father, an ally to Drusus, will make it possible. I should warn my lord. But now, he will give me to Odo.'

'Do you know why?' she asked me, not moving from me, and I backed off. 'Why you will be given to the Crow of the High Woods. Some call Odo that.'

'I don't care what they call him as long it is not Hraban's Bane,' I snorted. 'Why? Segestes asked me about our ring. Drapunir's Spawn.

Woden's Gift. I think he is already planning beyond the death of Drusus. He needs the ring so he can avoid the wars with the Semnones in the east. Some wars, at least, for no Germani will bow to ancient rings for a long time, I am sure, or they actually might set out to capture it? Who knows. But your father fears the lot of a warrior. It is wild, unpredictable and risky, and he loves invented heroism over scars. A poem and a song are better than a ferocious scream of an enemy shield wall. And Odo has the ring so I guess he thinks Odo would trade me. They have spoken, no? I heard him speaking, you know.'

'In the stables?' she asked, tilting her head enticingly, and I thought she looked beautiful. 'I heard you. Moaning in anger at the stalls.'

'Yes. Drusus will come here next spring with legions to finally chase your lover—'

'We have never slept together, but I do love him,' she told me with a painful poke. 'Do not speak like that or they might throw me to the swamp for being a harlot.'

'You are a harlot, lady,' I told her with a laugh. 'You are betrothed to my father, after all,' I said and hurried on as she was about to tell me what she thought about my past, 'They will come and slay Armin. They will make an end of Inguiomerus, should he still resist.'

She snorted. 'Segestes wants him dead. Inguiomerus has asked for peace, but Father does not wish to look over his shoulder for ever. How will they slay Drusus?'

I shrugged. 'Your father will betray him on the march, Father will ride in and strike hard and my lord will die. Rome won't go away, of course. Rome will conquer without Drusus well enough and finally some high and mighty bastard who wanted Republic dead will pardon Maroboodus and Segestes will be forgiven as well. But that leaves your father as the king, and he cannot fight. Rome might rule, but the Suebi are numerous. Langobardi, Saxones, Hermanduri. And the mighty Semnones.'

'Father is not much of a warrior,' she agreed. 'So, you for the ring. I thought Odo said you are not needed and that you already showed him the road to Veleda as he followed Lif?'

I grinned. 'I guess he noticed Lif got away and thinks he might benefit from having me hanging from his chains after all. He is growing impatient. Perhaps his Raven being stuck here is not something he desires, and he thinks it jeopardizes his cursed prophecy.'

She nodded. 'I know about my father and his plans with Maroboodus.'

I stopped mid chew and stared at her. 'But you had me tell you all of it at length anyway?'

'Yes.'

I shook my head. 'How did you know?'

She sat there quietly and frowned for a time until she brightened. 'Armin and Arbalo,' she said dreamily. 'You heard of it?' Her eyes glowed with pride.

'I did,' I said brusquely. 'He is the Fox.'

'The Fox thinks very highly of you,' she insisted. 'You have plans? Escaping this place?'

I looked at her dully. 'You ask me for plans? The idiot who nearly died in pig shit? Who will be mauled very soon by two halfwits? I've planned to stay alive, but—'

She nodded. 'Armin, my love will fight. He will do it alone if he must. I cannot bear it.'

I nodded. 'When your father was talking about their plans, I saw you stiffen and curse. Time to choose sides, perhaps?' I said, stretching and walking around her. 'You might help me make a plan.'

She did not move. 'I always had a side, Armin's. I'm as much a prisoner as you are. Though, of course, not without resources. I agree I might be able to help you.'

I looked at her in the eye. 'How will you get me out, and what do you want for it?'

'I want you to help Armin,' she said softly.

'I am loyal to Drusus,' I insisted, tired. 'You guessed my plans the day Catualda took us; nothing has changed. I was going to take him to Drusus. I could promise you to fight for Armin, but would you believe me? No.'

She whispered in my ear. 'Fight Armin. Fight the Cherusci. Do so. But first, you will help Armin. You will help him with something he

194

desperately needs.' She looked hard at me, her face wooden and readying for a fight. 'Segestes and Drusus will go and slay him and Inguiomerus. They will. Drusus won't fall before that, for Father would not want to fight Armin alone after. Armin is doomed. I want you to give Armin a chance,' she said plainly. 'And so, you will find Sigimer.'

I stared at her blankly and finally threw my hands in the air. 'You want me to shear Siff's golden hair as well? Or gobble up the sun for Sköll? Hunt for the world serpent? He is dead! I—'

'I want you to do your best,' she said weakly. 'Just that. I know you will fight for Drusus. I knew it when you claimed to bring me to him and change sides. You are right. Armin and you. You two have been playing with each other for ages, playing this gentle game of truths and lies. All you wanted was Lif, and as you saved me from rape and possibly death, I let you lie to him. I would have let you keep Lif and would have made sure you did not hurt Armin. But now I want more. I want you to help him survive. In any way you can. But there is a particular way to do that and yes, Sigimer is alive.'

I sat down and held my head. 'Shit.'

'Talk, you mongrel,' she said with sudden desperation. 'Hraban!'

'What shall I promise?' I asked in frustration. 'Be specific! Sigimer?'

'He is taken,' she whispered. 'Imprisoned.'

'You want me to swear that I shall free Sigimer?'

'Yes! That you free Sigimer!' she told me, grabbed my tunic and shook me. 'That is exactly what I want to hear you say!'

'What good will it do that I shall free his father?' I nearly yelled as she kept shaking me.

'Free him,' she said desperately and let me go as she noticed she had been shaking me, 'and Armin shall not be alone. Sigimer will tie Inguiomerus back to the war, for the gaunt lord hates Armin but loves his brother. It will tear my father's conquests apart; Sigimer's old warlords will return to him. They will. Most all will. They will be poor in wealth, weapons, and men, but Segestes the Traitor, my father shall find himself reduced to what he was, perhaps. It only takes Sigimer.'

My mind was whirling. 'Where—'

'Promise first!' she insisted, and I laughed desperately, held my head with two hands and nodded.

'Is he taken by Rome?' I hissed.

'No! Promise!'

'Yes, I promise,' I said thinly. 'I will do what I can. Of course, this promise is like Donor swearing to leave a giant alive, but—'

'Don't speak of Donor, oh chosen of Woden,' she said with a tremor in her voice. 'Promise in Woden's name you will try what I will ask for.'

'I … promise in All-Father's name I shall free the old, wrinkle balled bull, your lover's father, though I am not sure what I can do,' I told her and enjoyed her obvious anger as I called him her lover again. 'But now I have to escape your father and Odo.'

She smiled. 'You will have to escape my father indeed. But not Odo. You promised.'

I stared at her very intently for a moment. She looked bothered and blushed as she plucked at her sleeveless tunic, then she adjusted a bronze brooch on her shoulder. When I said nothing, she fondled her girdle and finally raised her eyebrow at me. 'Had time to figure this out yet?'

I had.

'Odo has Sigimer,' I stated blankly.

'He has Sigimer. Odo's home is somewhere to the south of the ford Sigimer fell in, and his men captured Sigimer that night when the old lord was making his escape in the dark.'

'And Odo wanted to trade me for him?' I told her, groaning.

'Sigimer riding free is not a prospect Segestes enjoys,' she told me. 'But Odo also promised Segestes your ring, after he no longer has a use of it.'

'How do you know of this? All of this?'

'Turd told me,' she said acidly. 'As I said, he was not a bad boy. Just slow.'

'Ragwald's boy told you their plans? Did you enchant the … boy?' I asked her with a raised eyebrow. 'Smiled kindly? Chirped like a bird and laughed at his jokes?'

She blushed and shrugged. 'I love Armin. I would do a lot for Armin. Even smile at Manno.'

'What else did you learn from the fool?' I grinned. 'Surely he must have told you about his dreams, what kind of children he desires—'

She slapped me painfully and hissed. 'Stop that. It's not proper. He told me much, though. His dislike for Helmut and Ragwald, for one thing. And he told me Segestes and Maroboodus are still allied, as well.'

'Fine,' I agreed. 'So, what else—'

'If you escape, you will need men, no?' she told me. 'You cannot do this alone.'

'You mean Armin will help?' I asked her hopefully. 'He will come here and spring me free?'

'No,' she said, dashing my hopes. 'Armin cannot risk leaving the southern wilds right now. He is a hunted man and traitors abound. You will have to do this. You must go to Castra Flamma and find help there.'

I stared at her incredulously. 'You think Rome would be interested in springing Sigimer from the thralldom? They would keep him a hostage if they found him!' I told her as if to a dull child. 'They don't make a habit of capturing valuable enemies only to let them run merrily back to war! Perhaps you think they will hold a feast for Sigimer before escorting him to safety?'

She stared back at me mulishly. 'I don't care how you do it, but you will find men to free Sigimer and then he will go free as a bird, feast or not. This you promised.'

'I promised to free him, but you are not reasonable.'

'There are Batavi in Castra Flamma,' she told me, and I went silent, interested. 'You are serving as a Batavi, no? You are but a smelly, lying Marcomanni, and they probably groan in shame with your appointment,' she said and winked her eye, and I cursed her, for she was very beautiful, 'but you are one of them, no?'

'I am,' I told her. 'But they are sure to have a leader. A Decurion, at least. And that leader is likely under the command of the camp prefect.'

'There is a military tribune there, um …' she thought and tried to form the words. 'Tribune laticlavius?'

197

I nodded. 'Oh, fine. I suppose they need someone like that since that castra is at the junction of Segestes and the Chatti. But that does not help me subvert a troop of Batavi to rescue their enemy.'

She smiled. 'Both Segestes and Odo have spies in the village of Castra Flamma,' she explained. 'And the Decurion of the Batavi is one. His name is Lothar.'

'How does this idiot boy of yours know such things?' I wondered.

'He is a slow speaker. Not a slow thinker. Unless with girls,' she grinned. 'He is a nice man.'

'So. You expect me to hustle over to the castra—'

She snapped my forehead with her finger. 'Yes.'

'You are very physical, you know. Does Armin enjoy this shaking, poking, and pushing routine?' I asked drolly.

'He loves it. You will go to the castra. Explain things to the military tribune. Of course, he cannot do anything about my father, not really, but he can give you aid with Odo. You tell him you know of a hole with bandits. Tell him Lothar is a cur. He is surely a man Drusus has set up there and will help him.'

'The legate of the legion commands his tribunes, and it is possible Drusus has nothing to do with his appointment to this place,' I began to argue, but she did not care.

'Then you will take the Batavi by force. And do your duty,' she fumed.

'My duty?' I snickered and waved my hand. 'It will take the time to find Odo, even if I manage to find men,' I complained. 'I don't know where Gulldrum is. And winter is nigh.'

She rubbed her forehead. 'I know. But as I said, there were more than just spies of Segestes in the village.'

'You said Odo has men there,' I noted. 'Yes, I see. Does this Lothar know this person of Odo's?'

She leaned close. 'That is how Father and Odo discuss. Through these men. Odo will send his emissaries here now that they have agreed on this deal, but Castra Flamma is where they usually deal with each other. Find out, from this Lothar, who is Odo's man in the village. Remember to do that before you do anything drastic to him to gain the Batavi. Find a way to help Armin before next campaign season. Kill Odo. Free Sigimer. And remember; if you slay Odo, your daughter will be safe. Ask the Tribune to warn Drusus of Segestes, but you will stay there and keep your promise.'

'Now,' I growled, angered by the promise I had to give. 'How do I get to Castra Flamma to perform these miracles? Shall I dig a tunnel or jump over the hills? You might as well ask me to do that as free Sigimer.'

She shook her head. 'I have little power, Hraban. Very little. I do not even have my horses anymore. I only own some slaves. Two men who own a boat. They owe me.'

'Slaves owe you? Do not make me laugh,' I told her desperately. 'You own them, they don't feel any gratitude for their mistress.'

'I helped the daughter of one when she was very, very ill,' she said sternly. 'She is alive and a mother now.'

I nodded. That I could understand. 'Boat. That would work. What about getting out of this den of thieves, murderers, and bastardy? After I mauled your boyfriend—'

'Armin is my man,' she hissed. 'Ragwald's boy is a friend.' She stammered. 'A friend who had some plans, perhaps, for me, but that is besides the point.'

'Right.'

She nodded as she cast an evil eye on me, and I fidgeted, trying to hide a smile. 'Vulcan still needs help. Winter is coming, and he has been raising Hel about raising an apprentice but then losing him to Helmut. Says he will not be able to supply the household with tools and horseshoes they will need during the winter. So Segestes has agreed you can help him, chained to the anvil. For a week. Perhaps.'

'Did Vulcan get such an idea himself?' I smiled at her.

'No, he is a pretty damned excellent smith and could manage without an inept Marcomanni slowing him down,' she said with a pretty smile. 'I helped him find this thought in his thick, fat head, but it was not very hard. It seems he has learnt to like you. I don't know why. You are insufferable. I also arranged for Mathildis to bring you food. She is grateful to you for Manno though she too thinks you are a bastard to nearly kill him.'

'You women are fucking mad. '

199

'Shh,' she told me, grabbed my lips and arched an eyebrow. I liked her. There was a fire in her, and though she had put me in an impossible situation with Armin, I wanted to help her. Women are my bane, I thought. She went on. 'Helmut is enraged she is to do this, by the way. He is not very … stable,' she said, looking nervously at the door. 'He has men watching you. Not Brimwulf.'

'Not Brimwulf? Why?'

'Brimwulf let you break Wulstan's face, so he is with Segestes now, doing something else. Wulstan is in a terrible pain and cannot sleep.'

'Should I be sorry for him as well? He is just a boy, after all?'

She grinned. 'No. But Helmut will watch you and fetch you. He will beat you if you so much as twitch the way he finds displeasing,' she said, grabbed some of my ale and grimaced as she tasted it.

I nodded, smiling at her discomfort. 'So … for me to gain my freedom, I have to escape either chains or this hall. How will I get to your boat if I am locked here or chained? Can you get the key?'

She shook her head. 'No, I cannot. Helmut has it. And after hearing about this meeting, I will be locked up as my father told me to stay away from you.' She smiled at me. 'But you will be out of here and must find a way.'

'You made me promise such preposterous, impossible things without actually having a way for me to escape?' I asked her, shaking my head in desperation. 'Is that so?'

She leaned on me. 'Find a way, Hraban. You are lucky and wily. A Fox like Armin. Or perhaps more like a lumbering, dangerous bear that smashes all the traps as it trudges on. Figure out something. I gave you a route out of here; you have to find a way to use it. You have a week. With luck. Get to Castra Flamma and then find Odo.'

'Something,' I laughed wildly. 'I must think of something?' I held my head and laughed. Then I calmed and nodded at her as she retreated. 'But I suppose it helps to get out of this room, at least. And to be fed. Thank you, and I appreciate the food!' I licked my plate and placed it in the sack.

'You already have a plan,' she said with a grin. 'Don't you?'

I nodded. 'I had one. But Brimwulf is an idiot.'

'He is a man who cannot live without his honor,' she said, understanding what my plan had been. 'Taking Mathildis away is his dream. But he cannot live a dream with dishonor on his conscience.'

'I have a plan. But Brimwulf will not like it. And it will risk Mathildis.'

She hesitated but shook her doubts away. 'I see. For Armin, I will risk both of them. The boat is near the docks, the one with a red bow. There will be someone there day and night for the next week. If you get there, you have a chance. Your plan? You had better execute it within a week. They will fetch you soon. Please save Armin. Do not let him die!'

I nodded at her; she embraced me awkwardly, gave me a kiss on the cheek and left. Your mother, Lord Thumelicus, was a fine woman. She could be a ruthless harlot, but she was a very fine woman.

CHAPTER 17

Helmut came soon after and unlocked the door. His eyes were like beady coals as he regarded me, especially after I smiled at him benevolently, my lips smeared with grease. He carried the fetters with him, and as he pulled my hands to be bound, I greeted him cheerfully. 'A beautiful day, is it not? So, no Wulstan? Is he having trouble sleeping?'

His hands grabbed my face, and he pulled me close to him. 'I see Thusnelda fed you. She will regret it, she will. Perhaps one day Segestes chokes on a bone, and I will show her how to behave like a good girl.'

I wanted to throttle him, for now I worried for Thusnelda. She had taken great risks, perhaps too great, and Helmut and Ragwald were very dangerous men. 'I'm sure Armin would understand. He would hug you in forgiving throes of love.'

His face twitched with the threat, but there was also something wild and dangerous in the look, and I knew he was the sort of a man who enjoyed being hunted. 'I've had a dozen unwilling women in this estate, boy. Perhaps I would have Armin as well, the golden-haired bastard.' *Fucking rapist*, I thought and began to insult him, but he poked me painfully. 'Shut your face, filth. Shut it, and keep it shut, or I will remove your teeth.' I grinned at him in spite, and we walked towards the smithy. There, he unshackled me and nodded at Vulcan, who wearily grabbed an iron shackle and placed it on my ankle.

'Make sure he does not escape, I will be watching,' Helmut said, leaving and walking around the general area like a hungry wolf stalking a bleeding cow.

Vulcan grinned at me. 'You managed to create some havoc, did you not boy? Did they leave you with the ability to work? Were no bones broken? You still a man?'

'I still breathe. They had some dogs try to chew on my rear, but they found Ragwald's son's throat instead,' I said and shrugged. 'Manno.'

'I heard,' he told me disapprovingly. 'He is not a bad—'

I shook my hands in desperation. 'Everyone knows he is not, and I know as well, but he was unlucky to be related to Ragwald and just standing there. What are we making?' I asked as I took up the sledgehammer, cursing the chain on my foot.

Mathildis appeared, smiling shyly, her freckles pretty as she nodded at us. 'Lentils, water.' She gave them to me, and I winked at her, making her blush. Her father was scowling at me from the corner of the house.

'You are looking beautiful today, Mathildis, very beautiful. Your suitor lost his voice?' I asked. Vulcan stared at me with suspicion.

She glanced at her father but smiled at me. 'Thank you. Also, my brother has not been beating me lately. I owe you, Lord.'

I smiled at her. 'A girl as pretty as you owes me nothing! Your very smile makes the sun pale in comparison and men forget their petty toils and aches when you approach. So I thank you, Mathildis.' Vulcan hummed and grinned briefly and looked away.

She blushed even more, her red hair spilling to cover her face. 'You mock me.'

'Bastard,' Vulcan whispered so very softly. 'You damned bastard. Sun pales—'

I ignored Vulcan. 'No, no, I do not. I thank you. Are you still to marry the dog bitten peasant?' I asked.

'He is not a peasant!' she chided me. 'I did not want to marry the dolt, but he is all right.'

Why do they all like him? I wondered and changed tactics. 'I felt sorry for him,' I said. 'Poor boy.'

She nodded thankfully. 'Helmut is thinking about some other suitors, but I want something else.'

'Brimwulf,' I smiled.

'What?' she said and looked like a frightened kitten. Vulcan looked away from me in disgust. I arched an eyebrow at her, and she grumbled. 'Yes, I am sorry,' she said apologetically. 'Is it easy to see? I mean, can everyone see this?'

I shook my head in denial, looking disappointed. 'No, it is not easy to see. Only the men who think you beautiful, the ones who are interested in you might sense you like him rather than them.'

She looked shocked. 'You mean you like me?'

'Yes, of course, dear girl,' I cooed. Vulcan went outside and began chopping wood furiously, cursing vehemently.

'I am sorry,' she said, nearly placing a hand on my arm, but wisely withdrew it in time.

I managed to sound utterly miserable. 'Ah well, I am but a slave. I know. They will kill me soon, I hear. But Brimwulf is a happy man to have such a woman.' I leaned closer to her conspiratorially and winked at her. I felt like Woden, the trickster of a god. 'He said he likes you. Very much. He is looking forward to your first night together. He thinks you will know what to do, you know?' I winked at her, and her mouth shot open.

'Do you mean—' she said, her face crimson. 'Do you men speak of such things amongst themselves?' Vulcan threw something to the wall, and we went silent for a moment, but apparently, he calmed down.

I began whispering. 'He means to take you away; he does,' I told her as I chewed happily on some lentils. She was so red, I could no longer see the freckles. 'Best not to go back yet. Your face would give you away.' She giggled shyly, and Vulcan sighed at the doorway, unable to enter. 'Alas, you are lucky. I will never again know such a fine thing. To be with a woman. I would like to, but I do not have hope,' I said, my voice full of sadness.

'What do you mean?' she asked dreamily, still thinking about Brimwulf. I felt strangely jealous of the archer, for Mathildis, despite her father, was a very sultry girl.

'They will … 'I made a cutting motion near my pants. 'For Manno. For saving you.'

'You did it for me?' she asked in awe.

'Partly,' I said, unable to lie entirely.

She nodded and felt sad for me. 'I understand, I have not, you know … I am not married. Brimwulf … talks about me?' she stammered. 'About having me? That is forbidden? Is it not? I could be condemned in a Thing for that. If they suspected we had done something.' She could not breathe for she was suddenly near panic. 'One should be married before one does such things. Or speaks of them.'

I shook my head. 'Thing. Our laws. Most men and women are already … you know. When they marry. Yes, the vitka and völva preach for us to stay chaste, but in reality? No. And Brimwulf anticipating the pleasures of your body? Your love? It is flattering. A man like him, he likes a woman who knows how to handle a man,' I added helpfully, feeling like a total idiot, like a fisherman in unknown waters filled with rocks and currents.

Some tears sprung to her eyes. 'I don't know what to do when the time comes.'

Vulcan was humming again, cursing me to Hel.

I ignored the old man and winked at her. She was more worried about her inexperience than the fact someone was going to steal her away. 'I, uh, can perhaps give you some pointers? That way he will be very satisfied.'

'Pointers?' she asked, suspicious.

'Um, we talk more in the evening? Perhaps? You will bring me food?' I asked for Helmut was approaching with suspicious fury, as I had hoped he would.

She nodded hurriedly and took my jug of water, visibly trying to compose herself as she left. I heard Helmut rage at his daughter, and Vulcan fixed an eye on me. A stern eye. I shrugged. 'You will not drag that wee thing to your escape scheme, will you? Or will you?'

'I will,' I told him. 'But with luck it will make her free as a bird. And a bit more experienced at that.'

'You bastard spawn of rats,' he hissed and then laughed, unable to contain his mirth. 'I wish I was young.'

'I will need that seax,' I told him seriously. 'Will need it, you know?'

'We are making pickaxes, axes, but I have indeed been working on a seax,' he told me softly and pulled it from under a pelt. 'Figured you would only make a mess of it.' It was the length of my forearm. The hilt already had holes in it for attaching the wooden handles, but the blade was still thick and unformed. He fixed an eye at me, and I nodded in thanks.

We worked on the axes that morning. I was hammering, saying little. In the afternoon, I hammered on the seax, ever so slowly smoothing it, Vulcan advising me brusquely. 'Gently, you dolt. It is not as strong as the blades of the Gauls. The iron is not as good, so it will have to be thicker, so do not flatten it over much! Idiot child! I just said do not flatten it, and then you immediately smack down on it like you were four years old!' he yelled at me after a particularly failed strike that made the sparks fly.

I wiped my forehead. 'If I do not know how and I want this one to be good, why don't you finish it.'

'Because it has to be made by you. You will use it. It will know you, and you will know it. A weapon made by the man who uses it will be his closest friend. You will know this weapon like you know none other,' he whispered to me, reverently. 'Including your famous swords.'

I looked at him long, hard, and nodded. All that afternoon I concentrated on the weapon. I took it out, weighted it, tapped it and hammered it and it was taking shape until it was a crude, but serviceable seax, a blade I had indeed fashioned.

'A bit longer than I usually make them, but good, good,' he appraised. 'Sloppy but serviceable.'

'It is wonderful,' I told him and meant it.

'It would be worthless if you sold it at the market because you have very few skills, but I know what you mean.' He grinned. 'I will sharpen it for you,' he told me when Helmut was seen approaching with the fetters. 'I hope you know what you are doing. Well, of course, you do not.' Helmut's hands were trembling as Vulcan released my leg iron, and he put me in fetters. He was silent as he took me to my quarters and looked at me carefully as I sat on the bed.

'Ragwald has decided,' he told me with chilling ferocity. 'On the part he will take. Want to know?'

I looked bored. 'He will take my prick,' I told him. 'I know he would love to have it in his hand.' He stared at me for a moment and then ripped the fetters off me. He left with a curse and left me shaking in terror. The guard chuckled as he shook his head at my defiance, and then Mathildis came, with soup and ale.

'I will have to bind some of his wounds,' she said while blushing. 'Will take some time.' I grinned to myself and then felt strangely nervous.

'Fine, just be careful with your father,' the guard grumbled, eyeing Helmut's back.

She came in, and I pretended disinterest. I stole glances at her and saw the red haired girl approach from the door, carefully as a doe, suspecting a wolf was close, but she did come and kneeled next to me. She laid the food next to her and took a deep breath as she placed her hand on mine. I pretended to be surprised, and she caressed it. She gulped loudly. 'I brought you food, and water, but I cannot stay for long,' she stated, but I placed my hand under her chin and pulled her closer to me.

Our faces were very close. 'It will tickle.'

She nodded carefully. 'The beard?'

'And my tongue,' I smiled, and I kissed her. She resisted, but not for long, experimenting my mouth with hers, her eyes open, then closed, and I pulled her over me. I kissed her neck, and she shuddered in pleasure. I fumbled with her brooch, a fine fibula in the shape of a leaf and took it from her cloak carefully. I pulled her tunic over the shoulder; she helped me and the tunic fell, and her magnificent breasts were bared, touching my chest. My hands caressed them; then I leaned to kiss them as she was grasping my hair. She took my hand savagely and placed it on her back, then pushed it over on her buttock and tried to move it to her intimate parts, which she did. She was warm and wild and ready.

And I was not.

207

She noticed it. She pulled away as I took my hands away from her. Her face was furious, ashamed, and she opened her arms to me. 'Am I ugly? You have been telling me how beautiful I am. And then I come here, wishing to comfort you, to learn and you ... wither!'

I put my hands on her hips, still plagued by lust, fighting the urge to take her, but I could not. For I had Cassia. She might be married to someone else, but I could not take this girl. And so, I told her. 'I've fought in a shield wall. I've defied evil gods and their priests. I've killed a king and a beast of Lok. I've wounded lords and beasts. And now I have done the hardest thing in the world. I've denied myself the lovemaking with a goddess.' And I meant it. She was superbly beautiful and desirable and had wit and fire in her. She was a girl any man could love for eternity. 'But I have a woman, and I cannot banish her from my heart. She has suffered for me; I have suffered for her, and I am sorry.'

Mathildis stared at me. She was frowning, then her face softened and suddenly, she was furious again. She moved, lightning fast and thrust her hand between my legs and grasped my very erect manhood under my pants, held it as I stared at her, my eyes agog. She tugged at it and smiled happily as I twitched in lustful agony. She did it a few times, experimentally and finally let go. 'Well. I suppose you were not lying about desiring me. And so I forgive you.'

'Brimwulf will be very happy,' I breathed, holding my face as I had a hard time breathing. 'He will be astonished at you, I promise,' I murmured. *She would be a handful for the too honorable bastard*, I thought and laughed.

'I am sorry you will be hurt and sent away,' she told me as she dressed herself. 'But you said Brimwulf—'

'He loves you. He will take you away,' I told her, looking at the rafters, avoiding looking at her body as it was slowly being covered. 'He will.'

'I will pray to Frigg for you, Raven,' she told me, and I nodded thankfully as I ate. She looked distraught as she was dressing, her sleeveless tunic covering her fine breasts, but her cloak was impossible to fasten, for her brooch was lost. She tried to find it for a time, but could not and tied it up.

I watched her as I ate and thought she was lovely. But I had Cassia. And I had her brooch. And I hoped Frigg would forgive me, for I would use it and risk Mathildis's life.

CHAPTER 18

Helmut came to me the next morning, and I again grinned insolently at him. I asked politely for Wulstan's health, but he managed not to punch me and settled into pushing me hard to the doorway, and I laughed at him.

'Stay far from her,' he told me. 'Mathildis. I saw you speaking with her yesterday. You shall make no friends in my family. Not even with the most simple of the members.'

'She was only making pleasant conversation,' I told him with a grin. 'She has noticed that with me, she can discuss things other than maiming, robbing, and clobbering and finds herself estranged from the rest of you.'

He spat on my back, and I bristled at the insult. 'Speaking of maiming and the discussion yesterday. Ragwald has decided to cut away your nose when you go. Not your prick. The price for his boy's wounds.'

'The boy lives still? A pity,' I told him and surprised how well Thusnelda, Mathildis, and Vulcan had convinced me of his simple qualities for I felt bad immediately after.

'He will take your peak, boy,' he told me as he left me with Vulcan. 'It will make you one ugly raven.'

Mathildis came with my breakfast and blushed violently when she saw me hobble towards her with the chain. 'Morning,' I said, grinning at her.

'Morning,' she told me, looking down. I munched on porridge, listening to Vulcan grumble about foolish girls and bastard Marcomanni, and I watched her squirm.

'Did you see my brooch in your hut?' she asked timidly. 'I went there just now, but I could not see it.' She looked at me suspiciously.

I adopted a hurt look. 'I am no thief, Mathildis.'

She hesitated and nodded. 'The floorboards are rotten. Perhaps it fell into a crack of one. It was expensive, you know.'

I slurped at the food hungrily, trying to forget what I was about to do. 'Things will be different for you very soon,' I said, hesitated and sighed. I leaned towards her. 'In case, just in case your father should think something happened last night, tell him I took you by force.'

Her mouth shot open. 'Lord. That would ruin your reputation! I would not! Not even to save mine!' I grinned. *A perfect match for Brimwulf*, I thought.

'I am called the Oath Breaker, no? They will forgive you,' I told her. 'Just do it.'

She nodded, scared. She had a good cause to be. 'I will think about it. Should that happen.'

'Can I ask for a favor,' I said as I finished my food. She nodded and smiled warily.

'Depends on the favor. I tried to give you one yesterday.'

I beamed at her gratefully. 'I hear your father takes men to the woods? And there he has them ripped apart in peace, no?' She shrugged and licked her lips, obviously nervous. 'Is there a specific place he takes them to?' I asked sweetly, hoping it was so.

She nodded her head for the woods south of the village. 'Yes, he takes them over there, to the thickets. Beyond these, there is a clearing with a fallen tree. It is away from the prying eyes, and nobody can witness what happens. He is not always allowed to execute those prisoners he has a great dislike for and there he can bury them in peace as well as torture them,' she stammered, and I waved her down. 'He goes to this one place. Always the same. He is a man chained to his habits.'

'Anyone ever survived it?' I asked hopefully.

'Yes, a boy who stole from him. He is cripple now,' she told me, a bit more bravely, obviously resenting the fact.

'Can you send him on an errand to bring something to the smithy, for Vulcan?'

She shrugged. 'Yes.'

'Can you do it now?' I asked her seriously, and I think she understood there was something up. She looked as if she was about to argue, and I know she wished to refuse outright, but finally she shrugged and nodded. I thanked her. 'It will do you good, I think. This deed will help you.'

She breathed a long, shuddering breath and bowed her head. 'Until evening then.' She blushed, and turned and left.

We hammered on the ax blades, and I only barely managed to keep my concentration on the work, waiting to see if Mathildis had done what I asked. I made mistakes, but Vulcan said nothing. He was also tense. Then, in the afternoon, he put away the thongs. He pulled out the long seax and gave it to me, with some hesitation. It was sharp and strong, and he had chiseled on the blade a crude raven. It had a wooden handle, with leather strapped around it and I admired it, for he had obviously also made it better.

'Are you going to shove it up your ass?' he asked curiously. 'You should for getting her involved in this.' He did not look happy.

I shrugged. 'I am sorry for it. And I did get her involved.'

'Yes, you did. I will have to defend her if he tries to kill her. I will, he said with vicious anger. 'I hate the bastard. In fact, I hate so many folks here, I think I should thank you for coming here to remind me how I am wasting my life.'

'Hopefully, she will be fine,' I glanced at the hall, saw nobody and stabbed the air with the blade. 'It is beautiful. Thank you.'

He nodded carefully. 'You made it. Sort of. You have the gift for this. Perfect it, the gift. Blades are things you know, I think. Out of smithy, and in them.'

A boy stood outside, and I saw Helmut stalking around the hall, looking at us. I hid the blade, and Vulcan strode to the boy and bent to speak with him. 'What do you want?' Vulcan asked brusquely, and the boy flinched.

Some horsemen were riding to the yard, and I saw they had spare horses with them. They were ragged and dirty and held thick spears. They were Odo's men. I apparently did not have a week, and I prayed to the gods they would wait until morning to seal the deal for me.

I turned my attention to Vulcan. 'He is here for the blade.'

'Yes, lord. I was to bring you a knife for sharpening,' he told Vulcan, eyeing me with confusion.

'Step in. Close the pelt,' Vulcan said. The boy did and stepped forward, and I pulled him over to me. He was looking at me, closely.

'Do you like Helmut?' I asked, and he nodded, smiling happily. 'No need to lie, boy,' I said and he shrugged, less enthusiastically.

'I hate him like a Saxon hates a Chauci. He did this to me for taking back a copper brooch that was mine,' he said, pointing at his twisted knee. 'I made it; I am good with my hands.'

I glanced at Vulcan. 'A new apprentice, perhaps?' Vulcan smiled and shrugged. I turned back to the boy. 'Now, we have a thing in common. Deep, burning hatred for Helmut and his weasel of a son. I hate him like shit in my shoe and wish to piss in his open skull while he is still alive. If you like, you can piss on it after. In short, I want to kill him. The problem is that I also wish to get away from here,' I informed him, and he lifted his shoulders, his eyes shrewd.

'What can I do? I am a crippled slave,' he asked. I placed the seax in his hand, and he licked his lips as he laid down a knife he had been bringing to us.

'Is it mine?' he asked in awe, but suspicion took over his features. 'I will not try to kill him! They will—'

I shook my head at him. 'No, no. However, you will tell me where one could hide this. Where would you place it in the clearing where he beat you? It is the place where he has killed others in. You know it. Tell me and then you will take it there. If you do and do not steal it, Helmut will not bother you again. Ever.'

'He saw me enter,' he hissed, twitching with fear.

'He did,' I agreed. 'And so you have to be brave and let me eviscerate him.' He glanced around, shaking in fear, and put the blade in his tunic.

'Don't cut yourself boy!' Vulcan shielded him.

He whispered. 'There is a tree. A great fallen tree. He straps the victims on the tough branches, and there is a hole on its side. Cannot miss it. It's round and deep. I groped inside it as he kicked and beat me. It was empty. I wanted to find something to hit him with, you see.'

'Perfect,' I told him. 'Now there will be something for just that purpose if you do not fail me. Here, tell Thusnelda that I have need of her slaves this night.'

He nodded, looking at me strangely and left, walking to the house, passing Helmut. He said nothing to the bastard. Vulcan gave me some ale. 'Tonight then?'

'Tonight.'

'May my Saxon gods dance with you,' he said cheerfully.

'Helmut will dance in pain,' I promised him. 'And then I shall have things to do.'

CHAPTER 19

Helmut came for me in the evening. I waited and prayed for Woden to hear my pleas. I saw Helmut walking; he wore a tunic that was white with greasy black spots of food or blood. His bushy beard and greasy hair were as repulsive as ever, his pig-like eyes glinting in many directions, his thick thighs bulging with muscles, and he had Wulstan trailing him. They both had clubs with them, Wulstan's was a dangerous one with spikes.

Vulcan glanced at me. 'Perhaps going with the strangers would be wiser?'

I shook my head. 'Trust me, that is no option. I will lose a nose before that. I thank you for your friendship, Vulcan.'

He grasped my hand. 'Gods look after you. If you fail, I will likely join you tomorrow.'

'It is possible,' I told him earnestly. He grinned and then spat as Wulstan thrust the pelt aside. The boy sneered at me, his face still swollen, and he was obviously in pain as his hand shot involuntarily for his head before he could stop it.

His father came in and grinned hugely like a boulder would. 'Well, the smith and his best and only friend the slave. Hraban the Oath Breaker, it is time to go. Say goodbye to him. He is gone tomorrow morning, and won't be as pretty,' Helmut sneered as he pushed in. Vulcan growled and pushed the big man back, and they faced off, both strong, hating each other. 'Tomorrow, I will speak to Segestes, and Ragwald. We might need a better smith,' Helmut said slowly. 'Younger one.'

Vulcan laughed. 'Tomorrow, yes. Do that.' He nodded at me, and Wulstan put the rope around my neck, yanking it savagely tight.

I was scared. If Ragwald wanted to cut my nose right then, I would not be able to stop them.

The evening was dark already, and I imagined Mathildis getting food ready for me, but I would not be there. Woden protects her if I failed, I prayed. Wulstan pulled me behind him for the barrack I had been sleeping at. I sighed a breath of relief but then sobered, for I would have to act that very moment. They would cut my nose the next day, and I could not postpone the inevitable. I gulped, prayed, and threw my dice and hoped for the best. It was hard to speak with the rope so tight around my throat, but I managed it. 'You know, it never ceases to amaze me how the men in your family are each ugly, dog vomit faced mongrels, and the women look so pretty. Of course, I never saw your wife, so the chances are that only Mathildis is beautiful, and your wife looks like the rear side of a mule.' Wulstan stopped, but his father growled, and he continued pulling me after him. I confided in Wulstan and leaned on him. 'I think, Wulstan, that your sister and you have different fathers. It's obvious as a wart on a face. I think your mother knew she would have to get mauled by that shit over there and opened her loins to a prettier man before you were born, just to have something beautiful and intelligent in her life.' I laughed at Wulstan and he turned, angrily swinging his club for me. Helmut pushed me to the ground before Wulstan could finish his swing. He placed a foot on my chest, growling.

'You wish me to break you. You hope to spare yourself a cut nose? It won't happen. Ragwald would pay me well, secretly, should I beat you to within inch of your life, but I won't.'

I interrupted him. 'They say you fuck the pigs in the pigsty. Sows. Boars. Cannot tell them apart I bet. Everyone says it is so.' I laughed and made crude hip movements while on the ground.

He snapped.

He kicked me painfully, took his smooth, but deadly club, and hit me, but I managed to get my hands to cover my face. I still laughed at him. 'Go ahead and hurt me, bastard. Right here? Perhaps Segestes will whip you, and I can laugh at least a bit as you whimper. They will tell him,' I pointed at the guards staring at us from the hall. Ragwald's bloodshot eyes showed terrible desire to keep beating me, but he hesitated. I went for the kill. 'Besides, your daughter, Mathildis might be pregnant. Would you deprive her a husband? Shall I call you Father?' I dropped the brooch of Mathildis at his feet.

He stared at it.

His hands went white as he balled them, broke the club in his hands and an indescribable grunt escaped his lips. His eyes rolled in his head, and he bellowed like a bull being hit by an ax. Wulstan was panting with anger, and Helmut licked his lips as he glanced at the guards, both of whom were staring at us intently, and one hesitated, as if going in. He grabbed me and pulled me up, throwing me over his shoulder as he stormed towards the barracks. My heart fell for he would break me inside, not in the woods. Then he ran past the hut, eyeing the guards who had relaxed. Wulstan ran behind him and the guards were out of sight as he dodged the corner, running towards the thickets. I grinned at Wulstan over his shoulder. 'I would not follow us, pup. Your ugly father is beyond reason.'

'Bastard shit walker,' Wulstan panted. 'I'll whip you raw when he is done, if you are not raw already.' I laughed and felt Woden's call fill me. His savage dance rang in my ears, and I think I saw his figure at the edges of my mind, stomping the ground savagely, dust and shadows playing around the god, and I felt the need to kill. I held the rage in check, readying myself. Helmut said nothing, but his grip on my back was such that I bled. He meant to murder me, or close to it, and I hoped he was a slave to his habits. 'Father!' Wulstan whined as we ran through a thicket of firs and then, wading in long weed field we arrived far enough away from the compound for nobody to hear my screams.

It was a meadow, and there was a fallen trunk of a tree there.

He threw me to the ground, and I rolled next to the fallen trunk.

He was tugging at his beard in rage. 'You fucked her? I will fuck you. Give me the club, Wulstan,' he told his son savagely. Wulstan was holding his head in pain, out of breath.

'Segestes will not be happy with this, you fat bastard, though the girl was very happy last night!' I told him as I struggled against the mossy trunk.

He laughed hugely, savagely, his mouth open as he licked his lips like he would before a feast. 'I do not care. I take my whipping from Segestes, and you will cry for years and years in the land of the shades, for this pain will follow you beyond death. You will join the spirits lingering here, and they, I tell you, still weep for what I did to them. Like a dozen men and women before you, you will sob your way to the afterlife, pissing yourself.' He advanced on me, and in his eyes, there was something out of this world. Perhaps he was vaettir taken, sprit claimed, and even his son followed his movements carefully. An owl watched us, wondering at the ways of men. Leaning on the trunk, I inched away from the brute who was steadily walking for me, long grass making our pants wet. I glanced at him to the trunk, seeking the hole. I saw sturdy, abraded branches, where ropes were attached and I despaired, for I did not see a hole in the trunk.

And then I did.

It was half-hidden by long reeds but it was there. It was round, moist and I edged closer to it. 'Come little raven, it will hurt, and I promise it will hurt much more than the girl will be hurt when I get back. I'll kick the baby out of her, should there be one,' he growled at me, Wulstan gingerly walking after him. 'I'll clip your wings, I will.' I reached the trunk, put my hand in the hole, groping around it, and the hilt was there. It was. I grabbed it, turned to hide the blade as I pulled myself up, staring at the approaching monster. The rope was still around my neck, still too tight. He grinned as he came, lifted the nasty cudgel with wicked points, reached out and grabbed me by my tunic, and swung.

I screamed all the anger and frustration of the past year at his face as I hacked the seax at his descending arm, Woden's song making me incredibly fast and strong.

I was faster than he was.

Dark liquid splashed on my face, the spinning hand with the cudgel hit me in the face, and I yelped as a spike tore a wound on my scalp. Then I laughed like a wicked spirit.

For Helmut was screaming in horror.

He was tottering around in front of me, holding his stump of a hand and Wulstan was trying to see what had happened. I grunted and stepped forward, the seax flashing as I whacked it on to Helmut's massive knee, making him hiss and sob as he fell on his side like a carcass of a deer. I stepped over the writhing body, leaped forward like an animal and grabbed Wulstan by the throat. He swatted at me weakly, and I laughed it off. 'Wulstan, you little bird,' I told him and held him with one hand and took the rope off my throat. 'Your dog is free.' He was whimpering as he looked at his father writhing on the ground. 'I was your dog? Don't you know me now? Do I look different? Like a bad dream? Let's play some toothy, bloody games. Helmut? How do you want to see him die?' I asked the man.

'Let him go! Bastard, just let him go!' he hissed desperately, his madness a thing of past, having been replaced by the unexpected fear for his son.

'Are you begging me? Asking nicely?' I asked Helmut and placed the seax on Wulstan's neck.

'I ask, I beg, spare him, by Woden!' he whimpered and tried to crawl towards me.

'His nose? Your master wanted to cut away my nose? If I cut him ...' I said and slashed Wulstan's nose open from the tip. 'There, pretty,' I told the boy, whose legs gave out as he fell on the ground in shock.

I stared at Wulstan in surprise and kicked him for a good measure. He really had fainted. I laughed like a fiend of Hel, kneeled next to Helmut and looked at his ugly face. 'I will let him live. Such a weak boy will not threaten me. He will live if you kill yourself with this blade.' I showed him the seax and grinned. I felt no mercy in my heart for the murdering, rapist filth and Woden was laughing in my head as I tortured the savage minion of Segestes. He cried, he spat in terror, and he shrieked for mercy, but I only remembered the terror I had felt for the man, and the terror his many victims must have felt, right there in that glade.

219

'Mercy,' he begged.

'No mercy here this evening, Helmut. Dogs, pig herders and shit pickers are short in mercy. Here,' I said and left the seax on his side, took up the spiked club and walked over to Wulstan, and rested the spiked thing on his cheek. I had done something like that with Hunfried, son of Vago the Vangione once and enjoyed the despair of Helmut as much as I had that of Vago.

He stared at me, then took the seax with a shaking hand and put it on his throat.

'It is sharp. Just think of all your evil deeds, Helmut while you do it. Wulstan will stay here in Midgard and shall meet you in the plains of cold Niflheim and Hel's rotten land one day. I doubt you are welcome in the Sessrúmnir of Freya or the golden tables of Woden. This little piece of gristle will die a coward. But you get to kill yourself fast. It s more than you deserve,' I told him bitterly.

'You will suffer at Odo's hands. Segestes will capture you again, Ragwald will mutilate your face ...' he babbled in pain and fear, and I scowled at him. He went quiet.

'Do it,' I told him. 'I know about Lothar in Castra Flamma. I won't let them take me again. And you will not see me in the afterlife, not for a long time. I'll spit on your bones, Helmut. Do it.'

He whimpered and fell on the blade, jerking it crudely across his throat. It took time for him to die, but die he did, joining his victims, and I hoped they would give him a welcome he deserved. I crouched next to him and spat in his face. Then I looked at Wulstan as I took the seax off Helmut's hands. Wulstan's nose was split and bleeding, and I could just tie him up and leave him there. Perhaps someone would find him.

Then, he would be the head of his family, and his sister would suffer his wrath, I thought.

I pressed the tip of the seax on his throat, thinking how I could have killed Gernot and Ansigar once, but had failed to do so, and how many suffered for that? Too many.

Woden's dance was fading in my head. The god was sated.

I took the seax away.

Wulstan was a fool. Perhaps a dangerous fool, but a fool still. Yet, he should not speak of the deeds of the night and perhaps that would save Mathildis as well. And I was the Oath Breaker, after all. He had humiliated me, called me his dog and beaten me. I had a reputation to upkeep. I sighed and placed my knee on his face and jaw, forcing his tongue out with my hand. He was mumbling something strange, unconscious, oddly happy. I sighed and thrust the seax to his mouth, drawing blood from his lip. I positioned it as well as I could, hoped it would suffice and sawed. I cut off his tongue crudely. His eyes shot open, he shuddered, spat blood and the fleshy bit of tongue and shrieked strangely. I had to dart after him as he was up in a second, trying to run off. I wrestled him to a tree, punched him in the belly to calm him down, took the rope they had used to hold me, and tied him up. His feet were thrashing the ground; his eyes open as two moons, and he was panting in pain, blood spurting from the cut membrane and lip. I clapped his cheek with my hand. 'I let you live, boy, but you had to pay something for the insults, no? Now you can bark like a dog, eh? None will hear you speak, and I doubt anyone cares to. So suffer like I suffered, and if you wish to find me, come to find me in the lands of Rome.' I started to walk away towards the north, holding the seax, and as I went, I saw the boy in thickets, the same who had left the seax there for me. He squinted at me from behind a tree, and I winked at him. He did not follow me, and whether he went to mock Helmut's corpse or torture Wulstan the Cruel, I do not know.

I was not sure if I should have cut Wulstan's throat after all.

I struggled through the thickets and saw light as Segestes's hall came to sight. The house was silent as I sneaked back to skirt the huts. The harbor held some men, talking calmly, and a boat that had a sleek red bow had a tall bearded man just sitting and drinking next to it, waiting around. It was Thusnelda's slave. I contemplated going that way right away. I could escape.

Then I hesitated.

The blood I had spilled made me fey. I shuddered in anger and hate as I stood there, holding the seax. I put it down and held my face. 'I promised Thusnelda. I did. I should leave and not risk dying,' I whispered. But I

221

could not leave. I picked up the blade and heard a clanging sound in Vulcan's smithy. I trotted that way, dodging from shed to shed and peeked in. The man was hammering a fine cup with a small, decorated fringe, and I sneaked in from the back door.

'Vulcan,' I hissed at him, and he jumped around, hammer at the ready, his eyes round.

'What the Hel do you think you are doing?' he asked, then calmed, his eyes examining me. I was covered in blood. 'I take it Helmut won't be talking with Segestes tomorrow about changing the smith?' he inquired.

'Nor will Wulstan,' I said, and he smirked at me, happily.

'So, you should go then?' he asked, looking around.

'Ragwald took my helmet and my mail shirt, and I want them back. And I want my sword.'

He rolled his eyes and rummaged around in his quarters. He came out with a fur tunic, new pants, and footwear, and a deep leather hood. 'Ragwald has a hall far from here. Too far for you to go there and escape after, but as it would happen, he gave the items you speak about to Segestes. I know for I took the rust out of them. He holds them in his armory. Your sword is there, as well.'

'Where is his armory, Vulcan?' I started to pull off the bloody clothes, which he threw to the forge.

'The seax worked well?' he asked as he rummaged through his gear.

'It did, but why won't you tell me where the armory is?' I asked.

'Because you get killed you fool, and I will likely go with you to die for a few pieces of metal,' he said insipidly. 'I should have kept my mouth shut.'

I shrugged. 'It is my helmet, my chainmail. I have fought with them and for them. I cannot leave them behind. Perhaps you really should come with me?'

His eyes rounded. 'Where? To Gaul?'

I nodded. 'Eventually. But before that, the armory.'

He sighed. 'It is beyond his central hall. He will be sitting in that hall, entertaining his guests and you would have to pass through it, you moronic child!' he said, shaking his head in doubt.

'He will not notice if he is drunk. He is surely content on the bounty of his table. Too much so to move. I will sneak by and—'

He nodded and waved me down, his face ashen. He went to his back room and came out with a thing I had seen before. It was the shield of Segestes, round, large enough to cover one's upper body, complete with embossed animals and a leering woman, snakes for hair. The Medusa, I learned later. It was made entirely of metal. It was the pride of Segestes, even if it looked ridiculously martial on the least martial of men.

He looked embarrassed. 'Segestes got this as a gift from Rome years past, and I have been asked to shine it every month. He holds it in the middle of his armory, topping his other trophies. He takes it out to show off. Sometimes he takes it to war with him. It is ...'

'Beautiful,' I said, running my hand across its surface.

He looked sour. 'I was going to say gaudy and fit for a Roman whore god.' I squinted at its surface. 'I doubt it has never seen a battle,' he told me.

'We should take it to the armory, then,' I said. 'Then we shall go.'

He nodded and clasped my shoulder. 'I didn't tell you this, Hraban, but I am dying. I'm old as shit. I am sick, and I spit blood. That is partially why Helmut was going to have me replaced. I will help you, and you will go after if you can. No! It is what I wish. I have no more left in me to start a life elsewhere. And I miss my wife.'

We looked each other in the eyes, and finally I nodded. 'I thank you Vulcan.'

He grunted. 'Segestes wants to call me Vulcan, after a Roman god, but I am Heimrich.'

'Heimrich, I thank you,' I said.

He nodded, grunted, and wiped a tear out of his eye. 'Now, dolt, do not touch the shield, it has to be spotless. Draw the cowl deep to cover your face.' I grinned and did as he covered the bright thing with lambskin cover. I pulled on a hood, tucked the seax on my thin belt and followed him, carrying the shield. At the door of the mansion, the guards stopped us. Vulcan rapped his fingers on the lamb skinned shield and the guards nodded. We pushed through a heavy curtain of wool into a hall drowsy with an old party, as Segestes, Ragwald, and many chiefs lounged on their seats, drunk. All were bedecked in gold and silver, lords of debauchery rather than war. Some were asleep on the tables and floors; a poet was collecting silver from the floor, his last performance over. Women were already cleaning the room. Odo's envoys were lounging far from Segestes, apparently too filthy for the high lord to stomach them closer than that. The walls held shields, banners, weapons, and many a Roman bust and silver plates adorned the tables as we ventured in.

I nearly toppled on a thick rug. A curious Roman table, half a circle, screeched as it was dragged along the wall. The fat lord frowned and gazed at us.

Segestes was sitting on one stone chair, filled with fluffy pillows, his beard wine sodden. He pointed at Vulcan who had frozen as I had stumbled. The lord was drunk and cross-eyed as he addressed Vulcan. 'What is it, old Smith? Come to carry us to bed?' Ragwald snorted, none laughed.

'The shield, Lord,' Vulcan told him softly.

Segestes smiled like he had seen the sun. 'He brings my shield, indeed! There it is. Something ailing you, old one?' Segestes asked.

'My leg, and hip, Lord. Ill, sore. It is the coming winter, and I feel the time is getting shorter for me,' Vulcan complained, and he did look sick. He had not lied.

Segestes laughed. 'Perhaps we should have kept Hraban to take over your job?'

Vulcan nodded. 'No, he is clumsy, weak as old man's piss, and couldn't stand straight after a few swings of a hammer. Drinks too much, I hear.' I grinned under my hood.

Segestes snorted. 'I have not offered him ale nor mead, so it is on you, old man. Come, show it. Who is the man?' He nodded at me, half curiously, his eyes fixed on the lambskin cover.

'He is a man who makes charcoal for me. Half simpleton. I asked him to help, my back you see, Lord,' Vulcan whined.

'Yes, yes, show it to me,' he said and I, my hands shaking, took out the round thing and turned it towards him while Vulcan ripped off the lambskin.

'There it is! No chief has owned the like in Germania. All shiny again, eh? Nothing wrong with it?' Segestes panted, clearly struggling with the desire to come and take it but too lazy to do so. I saw he had the ring of the dead centurion on his forefinger, the huge ruby prominently flashing in the firelight.

'I will take it, Lord, to the armory if it pleases you,' Vulcan said while scowling at me. He was terrified I should make a mistake. Segestes made an imperious gesture with his hand, releasing us. Vulcan pointed to the wall behind them and dragged me after him. A door was behind some wooden pillars, one with bronze handles and Vulcan pulled at them, listening to Ragwald laugh at his back over some senseless, drunken joke. We went into the dark room. Vulcan turned and fetched a torch and carried it to the room. I was astonished.

Around the small room hung the weapons Segestes had looted from his enemies. There were axes of fine make, boar spears by a dozen, framea and hasta, darts and bows, weapons of men he had gotten killed. Vulcan grunted. 'That was Sigimer's ax.' He nodded at a long hafted, double bitted ax with a wolf on the handle and the blade.

'Gift from Odo.' I whispered, knowing Odo had sent it as a proof of holding Sigimer. I rested the shield on the ground. I heard Segestes curse Armin, and a rough laughter followed it. 'So, there is your helmet, and armor,' he pointed at the far wall, where my treasure were placed on the wall. I walked over, ran my fingers over the surface of the Athenian helmet, and lifted it out gingerly.

I had missed it.

My eyes sought the weapon, and then I froze.

Nightbright, my short, slender sword was there, glittering in torchlight, resting against a wall. I rushed for it and grasped it, felt its speed and deadly balance and smiled like a man who cannot be beaten. I gulped and felt tears come and heard Vulcan snort. I nodded at myself and put the sword down. 'How many men were there out there?' I asked him as I took the chainmail off the wall as carefully as I could, starting to slip it on, the metal jingling like a stream full of silver.

'Two Chiefs half asleep, Segestes, the fucker. Ragwald I mean, even if Segestes is also a fucker.' He took the helmet and held it for me. 'Two men of this Odo.' I finished slipping into the chainmail, adjusted it and took the helmet. I pulled it on and let the metal engulf me. I felt like a god of war, like Woden or Freyr, like Donor or even Mars of the Romans. I rummaged in the shelves and pulled out a thick belt, one studded with silvery studs. I girted it around me. I took the seax and Nightbright and stuck them in the belt, Nightbright in its fine sheet.

'Give me Sigimer's ax,' I grunted as I struggled to adjust the belt now that the weapons were making it tight. He grabbed it, and I took it.

'Now, go tell him that there is a dent on the shield, and that you do not know where it came from.' I shook my head, and the helmet felt hot and heavy in my head, but so familiar.

'Dent, eh? Fine.' Vulcan grinned at me and went.

I grasped the ax handle and made some experimental swings while I went to stand by the wall and the doorway. It was the length of my arm, heavy and fine, the blade superbly sharp. I leaned on the wall, feeling like a man reborn in my helmet and mail. I had missed them. I felt Woden was watching, and I prayed to him for aid. Soon I was rewarded by a shriek and a thud as Segestes hauled his weight up and flapping footsteps resounded in the hall as he came running.

'How is it possible?' he asked Vulcan. 'How?'

'It is a shield, Lord, surely in a battle?' Vulcan told him maliciously, and I snorted.

'Armin's men ran from me; there was none to stand before me this year!' Segestes complained loudly, and then he came in, rushing for the shield leaning on a pillar and went to his knees before it.

I stepped forward and whacked him on the side of the head with the flat of the ax.

Why I used the flat side, I know not, and I did regret it later, but I remember thinking about Helmut's words over the death of Segestes. I doubted Ragwald would be any different from the man I had slaughtered,

226

and Thusnelda might suffer if Ragwald were to take over. Then I thought of slaying him for Drusus. I spat and hesitated. *Nobody would believe me. They would all think I was a murderer of the allies of Rome, and I would suffer. And Rome, it was not merciful to the friends of the traitors.*

Cassia might suffer, I thought.

So, I just left him alive.

He would be proven false later. Though I was not sure he was alive. I had hit him hard, and he had fallen like a soft ball of lard on the floor. I grunted as I looked at him lie there, his mouth kissing the lower surface of the shield, his fat lips quivering.

'So now what?' Vulcan asked.

'I'll need that ring,' I grinned at him.

'The ring?' he asked suspiciously, and his eyes enlarged in horror as he gazed at the ring of the centurion, glittering on the finger of Segestes. 'No! Hraban!'

'Yes,' I hissed and took the hand of Segestes. I laid it lovingly next to him and the finger with the Roman ring glinted. I grinned at Vulcan and took up the ax, pressing it on the finger and the fat thing came off very easily.

Vulcan made a guttural sound reminding me of a giggle.

'His first war wound!' I told him.

Vulcan laughed hard and turned, cursed, and grabbed me. The door was open, and a shadow was sprinting away. I rushed to the doorway, and I saw Ragwald running. He sprinted past the tables and stopped to stare at the main doorway. I moved after him to the hall, and he hesitated, croaked, and cursed. He abandoned the idea of sprinting for the door, took up a sturdy stairway and went upstairs fast as a spider. I sighed and went back to the armory, grabbed the fabulous shield and went to the hall, hefting the axe and the metal shield. Two drunken, but still alert chiefs of Segestes were on their feet, talking with each other, confused about Ragwald and me. I walked over to them and grinned. Both were bedecked in jewelry, silver and gold. They turned and their mouths opened in unison, confusion and drunkenness making them slow, but finally their hands were groping for weapons. Sigimer's ax came down on one's face, the shield crushed the other one's nose soon after.

I turned to Odo's men.

They got up, groping for their spears, a supremely surprised look on their faces.

A spear thrown by Vulcan took one in the back, leaving him crying in pain. The other one turned to face the danger, and I stepped forward, the ax coming down from the side. The man screamed and folded in two, dying on the floor.

Vulcan edged to the room and shrugged. 'Ragwald?'

'Upstairs. Likely climbed out of some hole already. 'Take a spear. Quickly.' I walked to the door, expecting the guards to burst through. The floorboards were creaking as I rushed, but the guards were either drunk or used to such clamor in the feasts of Segestes. I grinned at Vulcan and pushed the woolen covering to the side without further ceremony. Vulcan followed me closely. 'Guards? The Lord needs your help,' I told the two tall men brusquely.

They turned in surprise. They stepped in and stopped to look at the chaos. 'What in Donor's balls has taken place ...' one began, and then they died. Vulcan speared one with savage strength; I whacked the ax on the neck of the other and then I pulled the doorway's blood-spattered covering closed.

'I'll need the wealth,' I said and nodded at the dead men. 'Have to be fast, though.'

Vulcan came after me, and we began to loot the drunken men, pulling off rings and pouches. One man woke up to my ungentle ministrations, and I bashed him with the ax handle. I did not care what kind of men they were, to me they were just men who had humiliated and mocked me.

I noticed movement and darted and found the poet looting a man who had passed under a table. He smiled at me inanely, and I nodded with a grin. He kept looting.

Vulcan sat at the table and started to eat and drink while pulling an oil lamp near himself.

'That's it, then?' I asked him, pointed at the oil lamp, and he burped. 'You will meet your wife this night?

'Yes. Don't worry. I'll wake up the women before I do anything with the lamp. I'll eat something first, for have I not missed so many feasts in this land of misery? May gods guide you Hraban. Best leave before Ragwald gathers his courage and finds some men. Going to take the shield? Best let it gather dirt. That way fewer men go for you in battle as that is a treasure everyone wants.'

I nodded and dropped last silver rings to a pouch. It was a heavy and splendid treasure.

'Who are you?' the poet asked carefully from under the table, apparently thinking about making a song.

'Hraban, the Oath Breaker, the pig friend, and a blacksmith,' I said and grinned. I bowed to Vulcan, who toasted me. He grinned at me sadly and nodded from the doorway. Then he concentrated on destroying a leg of venison while getting up. He carried the oil lamp with him and walked for the sleeping quarters where Thusnelda and Mathildis slept. I bowed to him as I left. *I hope Ragwald is hiding on the top floor when the fires spread*, I thought gleefully but had a hunch he would survive the night. Few men were about as I walked to the harbor, and the man sitting on the boat got up uncertainly as I approached.

'Castra Flamma? I need to get there. Is this Thusnelda's boat?' I asked him with a whisper, and he nodded enthusiastically, waving at the other men lounging nearby. They rushed up, grinned at me, and climbed in. We cast off, and I heard Ragwald scream somewhere in the distance. There was smoke rising from the hall of Segestes, and I knew Vulcan had prepared his pyre. Perhaps Segestes would die.

I left to save Sigimer, Armin, and Drusus.

BOOK 4: GULLDRUM

'He thinks there is an army out there. Not a Roman one.'
Brimwulf to Hraban.

CHAPTER 20

The trip to the south was uneventful. 'Relax, Lord,' said the tall slave happily, who was likely a Chauci of the north. He enjoyed the whipping wind of the Visurgis River as he held his head high, steering the boat through eddies and unseen rocks beneath the dark surface. 'It will take this day and all of the next to row down to the Buck. We have to avoid some treacherous rocks and many strange currents. Very fast water up there, you see?' I nodded, nervous as I looked behind us, sure Segestes would send vengeful men whipping their horses up and down the river. The men grunted and cursed, for rowing was hard work. At times, Visurgis flowed far too dangerously to row, and we had to carry the boat. I was a nervous wreck when we did, but no horses nor enemy boats appeared. We ate while we rowed, and I slowly began to enjoy my freedom as the sun came up.

We kept rowing all that day, some rowers resting while others worked.

I thought of Vulcan and drank some bitter mead the slaves had with them, toasting his memory, begging Woden would find a sturdy seat for him at his table. He had fought well, he had helped me with everything and surely he deserved a smile from the great gods. I also prayed to Woden to guard Mathildis. Wulstan might or might not be alive, but I thought Segestes had other things to think about than a simple girl and a mean little mute boy. I chuckled as I patted my belt where there was a finger lodged next to a very fat pouch of Segestean treasure. A rower had been staring at me and his eyes focused on my belt and widened. I looked down to see the finger and the glittering ring, both which peeked from my belt. I picked the finger up, opened the pouch and dropped it in while I stared at the slave until he turned his eyes away. I grunted and kept my hand on Sigimer's ax. I was not safe yet. Not by far.

Night fell, and we had to rest properly. We holed up in a small, reedy bank for the rest of the night and lit no fires. I stayed up all night, hand on the ax. The next morning was unusually cold, and we got on board very reluctantly, our joints stiff.

By the afternoon, we saw many settlements. There were lots of burnt down ones, but some of these were rapidly being rebuilt as the Germani generally do not bow down to ravaging enemy or hardships. There were also men fishing from the banks. They were wearing pelts, and cattle by hundreds could be seen on the fields, fattening up for the winter. Some of the men were staring at us. Mostly, they just ignored the boat, but then one stood up, and he was staring at me intently. Then, he ran away, and I cursed. The rowers had noticed the man as well and looked resentfully at the helmet on my head. I growled back at them, but the mistake was mine. On the other hand, after the fires of Hel I had endured, I did not wish to escape like a quivering girl. At the end of the long, cold day, darkness finally fell, and we arrived at the Buck. We rowed up it, the currents much harsher than the ones in Visurgis and finally, late in the night, I saw the place where the battle had taken place. On the left side, I could see hundreds of burial mounds and even some horse skeletons amidst grass, for the moon was high and full. On the right side, there was the remains of a Roman march camp.

'Stop,' I told them and they, exhausted, lost their rhythm, nearly tipping me in. 'Put me in there,' I said, pointing to the west bank and the castra.

'You know where to go? I was supposed to show you,' the tall man holding the tiller told me.

I looked uncertain. 'I rode through here once, but it is dark. It is over those hills?'

He smiled and shook his head. 'Rode through here once? Yea, I know what happened here last year. No matter. I will guide you. You would get lost.'

I paid the men in the boat with some of my stolen silver and told them not to flaunt it. We slept the rest of the night. It was uneasy sleep, for it was cold, and we slept back-to-back, keeping up a fire. I was tired enough to doze off, at least. Next morning we ate some porridge and vegetables, drank water for all the mead was gone, and I was going to be a Roman again. It would take two or three days to walk to Castra Flamma, through the lands where the Cherusci, Bructeri, and Chatti lived and visited and hunted, and I prayed we would meet no one, if not a Roman patrol. I cursed the metal shield and covered it up with cloth, for it would attract enemies like flies.

The tall man guided me like a weasel through to the thickets of young trees, up hills and over bluffs, where an auroch looked at us majestically. I thought it was a great sign. We waded through frigid streams, avoided some fertile, crowded valleys full of people and waited many a time for young men out hunting to pass. The woods were deep and lush with small hills of sweet smelling greenery, and we resolutely made our way west, enjoying the fine sights Woden's world granted us. A strange storm hit us in the evening, and we spent another miserable night shivering under the boughs of a thick fir tree. Our food turned to mush, and we ate the disgusting mess silently. It snowed sometime in the night.

I woke up to my guide shaking my hand, hissing at me to be quiet.

I was covered in a thin sheet of snow and water was dripping morosely all around us as the meager morning warmth beat back the first onslaught of winter. The man was pointing down, looking very scared. Below us, in the woods, two men were walking, both holding tall bows. They were nearly unseen in the shadows, moving like sprits of the deep woods, vaettir.

'Svear,' whispered my guide. Terrified.

'Svaer?' I asked, mystified.

'Svear! Suebi mercenaries, from the north. They are from beyond the sea, beyond Gothonia. Hunters, working for Ragwald,' he told me, shaking in terror. 'Savage and brutal.'

'You sure they are not local?' I asked him. The Svear were crouched on their haunches, and I thought my guide was right. They had a look of very dangerous men out for very specific prey.

'I have seen them about,' he breathed. 'Savage and—'

I understood. 'I am savage and brutal. Where is the castra?' I looked towards the west, for we were on a ridge, and I saw some haze to the southwest as if smoke was rising to the sky.

'There, yes, at the end of Teutoburg Wald. It is beyond the hill and then you have to follow the road. They have a huge fort out there.'

I nodded and placed a hand on his shoulder. 'I know, I was there. Remember?'

He shook as he looked at the men stalk below. 'It has grown while you were attending pigs and hammering horseshoes.'

I saw the men below come to light for a while. They had painted their bodies gray, with dark smudges and brown lines crisscrossing. They wore gray wolf pelts and surely did not look like the Chatti or the Cherusci. They had dark hair like mine and animal-like movements of men who knew the wilds better than halls and the fields. It looked as if they were sniffing the air. I felt a brief bout of terror, just like my guide did.

'How many are there?' I asked him.

'Some ten, usually. One died last winter of snot and coughs. They hunt slaves,' he said, mumbling prayers.

'I see the two, but are there more?' I looked around but saw none, as the two below were crouched again, now eating something.

'I don't know. They are looking for you, surely. Perhaps they don't know you by looks, except for that scar.' He drew his thumb across his cheek.

'Yeah. I'm hard to miss,' I agreed.

'What shall we do?' he asked. 'Go north perhaps? Try to dodge them?'

I shook my head. 'Don't want them running after us as we go. We have the advantage now, but not later. Stay here,' I told him as I left my helmet and the shield there by the tree. 'Wish me luck!'

'Where are you going?' the slave hissed in panic. I ignored him.

I started to walk downhill briskly, prayed briefly to the gods for help and begun singing a lusty song, my fur cloak billowing around me. The two men were fifty yards away and melted into the shadows as I approached. I sang like a demented idiot and laughed to myself as I jumped over stones, the mossy ground nearly giving in under me, but I went on and pretended not to have a care in the world. The shadows of the trees were still covering my looks to the men, and I saw them whisper to each other. They were but two dangerous shadows, in the woods, I tried to assure myself, just shadows, and I forced a merry tune to escape my lips. They did not move. I took a deep breath, prepared myself, and stepped into the sunlight, looking to the right to hide my face. I was so close to them, so very close, still pretending to be oblivious to their presence. They began to move uncertainly, still wary. Apparently, they had not seen me before, for they did not react to me, and my scarred face was still hidden.

Then I pretended to stumble on a rock and dropped the pouch full of stolen silver and rings, ornaments, chains, and they spread on the ground before me like a brilliant shower of bright raindrops. I saw the shadows tense as they stared at the scattered riches. They got up slowly; one was licking his lips, and they had forgotten the fool walking for them.

And so, I yelled and ran at the leftmost Svea, with Sigimer's ax held high.

His half nocked arrow fell to the ground as the man realized I had fooled them. He raised his bow to block me, but it was of no use as I hurtled through the air for him. The ax made a satisfying, meaty sound as it thumped on his shoulder, and he fell, taking the ax with him. I searched for the other man in the thicket.

I saw him.

He had sprinted away to the right and now turned, pointing a longbow at me, and I prayed to Woden for help, then in thanks as I slipped on the wet ground and the arrow tore through the forest. The man ripped out another arrow; I pulled out the seax from the back of my belt. I streaked over the shuddering, wounded man I had whacked with the ax and screamed with primal hatred. The Svea hesitated for a second, but I knew he would get another arrow off. I gritted my teeth as the bow aimed for my chest, but that is when my guide threw a stone at him, one that did not hit the man, but distracted him as it hit a trunk. He turned his head instinctively, then cursed, and turned back to me to finish the job. He failed for I was there before him and punctured the blade crudely through his throat and fell over him. He went limp nearly immediately, and I felt his warm piss wet my armor. I was panting as the guide came down with my shield and helmet. 'You hurt?' he asked uncertainly, edging near us as I got up, pulling the blade from the man's throat.

'I am alive. Thank you,' I told him and nodded, but noticed he had lost his interest in my well-being. He was staring at the wealth scattered on the snowy grass. 'Can you collect their gear?' I asked him. The man nodded, left my gear by the silver, swallowing in fear as he approached the dead and dying men.

I cursed at the smell of blood and piss and dusted myself off. Then I walked to the scattered coins and jewelry and bent down to pick it all up. I packed it up, tied the pouch and tried to tuck it in my belt. 'Let it be,' the man said, with a terrified edge in his voice. I shot up and stared around in alarm, thinking the rest of the Svear were there. They were not.

My guide was aiming an arrow with the bow stolen from one of the Svea. At me.

'You are making a damned mistake. I would have rewarded you,' I told him with simmering anger.

He looked ashamed and utterly nervous but held the weapon steadily. 'Drop the seax, your sword, and the treasure.'

I sneered at him. 'I just spent a year as a slave to your filthy lord, the father of your mistress. You think I won't risk an arrow rather than roll over this easily? And I don't die easily, man. I once had an arrow in my throat and laughed it off.' I had not laughed it off, but it was true, otherwise.

236

He shook but took a wider stance, determined. 'Such wealth can buy my family a life elsewhere. I am a slave because I have no wealth. I could leave anytime, but go where? My boys would starve. I will take that, buy cattle, a hall, and go free. Perhaps I shall be a client to Segestes, himself.'

I smiled. 'You think Segestes might be upset when you use his rings and jewelry to buy it?'

'His?' he looked shocked.

'His, and his men's,' I told him, sneering. 'I ...' The Svea I had struck in the shoulder was shuddering and moaning, and we both gave him a quick glance, but the bow did not move away.

My guide shook his head with remorse. 'That is a fine, brave deed, Hraban. To take his treasures and escape. They would sing of it, brave men would. But I will take my chances and figure out a way to get what I need. And now I think I cannot let you go. You would hunt me if I did allow you to leave. But do not worry. I won't miss, and it will ache only for awhile.' I cursed the man. Beyond the yonder hills was my salvation, and there I was about to take an arrow for silver.

'I will give you my word you can take that worthless shit and go in peace. But I will not leave my helmet, nor my weapons. Nor the shield, and I will take the finger and the ring,' I told him, and he glanced at the pouch with the cut membrane. I began to remove it from the pouch.

He thought about it, glancing at the ruby, and I saw him lose his struggle. 'You will leave the ring.'

I cursed, he tensed, and then an arrow was jutting in his skull. He fell on his back, dead.

I charged for my shield after the initial shock. Another arrow clanged on it. I shuffled around in the dirty grass and jumped to grab the helmet. An arrow went past my face. 'Shit!' I cursed, pulled the helmet on my head, hid behind the shield and ran to the woods. I grabbed the ax with me as I stomped on the dying Svea. I thanked Woden as the trees covered me, and I pulled the shield on my back, hoping it would deflect any sagitta that might reach out to slay me. One hit a tree as I ran; another tore near my legs when I got to the edge of the valley.

I ran for an hour, then two, an arrow or two swishing past, constantly reminding me of the danger. Finally, one banged on my shield, and I fell on my face from the impact. I got up, spat moss and dirt, and ran until I went up a hill. I dodged and ran erratically while praying to Woden, scared of being captured again, cursing a rock formation I had to climb and nearly pissing myself as an arrow smacked next to my hand.

Then, I was on top of the rocks, stopping for just one second, for I saw the majestic sight of Castra Flamma below me, only some few miles away, and admired the beautiful wet land near the springs of Luppia River. It had grown indeed. The agger was now crowned by a thick wooden vallum, a palisade with towers full of siege machines and the fossa was wide and deep. The wooden barracks and lined streets ran like arrows inside the fort and the praetorium area with principia and quaestorium were partly made of stone. A small village had grown on the banks of Luppia River, around the harbor. As ever, Roman castra was attracting locals and traders, and there were clearly many cohorts occupying the area for troops were marching and training on the fields around it.

I suddenly remembered my danger and started downhill, weaving my way down the treacherous decline, the weight of my armor pulling me in a roll down the green slope. After I had stopped my roll painfully on the side of a tree, I got up, dizzy, and heard distant laughter. I did not place the voice before an arrow smacked into my buttocks, and I screamed in pain.

I cursed and sobbed as I flew on my face. The pain was intense, and when I tried to get up, the shield on my back was caught on a branch. So, I thrashed, cursed, and swore until a foot pushed my face down, a pointy thing in my neck. A voice hissed near my ear. 'Hraban. You bastard. Next time you spread lies about bedding Mathildis I will aim higher.' Brimwulf pulled me up, and Mathildis was there, giving me a warning look as she bent to pluck the arrow from my ass. I sobbed when she did, and I thought she twisted it a few times too often and on purpose. 'You run fast, though. We had a hard time keeping up with you. Like an armored rabbit!' Brimwulf smiled. 'Or a chicken.'

'You call me a rabbit and chicken? After I killed the two Svear?' I asked, bitterly.

Mathildis shook her red hair. 'The other one was still alive.' The arrow came off, and I howled. She handed it to Brimwulf and stood some steps from me, folding her hands under her breasts.

'So, Brimwulf. You took her away then,' I noted, and he went to stand next to the girl. 'So much for your honor.'

He looked unhappy. 'Yes, after you killed Helmut and Wulstan, Segestes lost his finger, and many men died in his burnt hall, I heard they blamed Thusnelda. She stood up to them, but they needed a scapegoat. Wulstan was there, incoherent and mauled, and he was trying to say her name.' He nodded at Mathildis. 'So I took her away,' he added while eyeing the girl. 'You have a terrible influence on men of honor. That arrow was warranted, but I thank you for her,' he said proudly, and the girl shook her head at me, gently and softly as I scowled at him, rubbing my rear. *Should give him pointers on what she enjoys*, I thought but decided against it.

'Why are you here? Other than pay me back for the … insult?' I asked him.

'Well, it seems I need a lord,' he said uncomfortably.

I pointed at the fort. 'You wish to join me in Roman service?'

He looked that way carefully. 'I suppose I might. I have little wealth and will need all I can get.'

'Is this honorable? To serve the enemy of Cherusci?' I squinted, mystified.

'I want her to be safe,' he explained, talking about Mathildis while looking away from me.

I thought about it for a moment and finally nodded. 'I was told to gather my men. You will be a Batavi if you like. Swear to me, and you have plenty of coins. Plenty of dangers too,' I said happily. 'But she should be safe.'

'I will have to sign something? They are always signing something in the hall of Segestes,' he asked suspiciously.

'You will get two hundred and sixty denarii and part of anything we might loot,' I agreed. 'And you will have to sign up.'

'Sure.' He grinned warily. 'And as I'm a hunter, perhaps I should get more? I will feed the lot, no?'

'They will feed us in the castra,' I told him. 'You will have a lot to learn.'

'Fine!' he said and helped me down the hill.

As we walked towards a waiting Batavi horse patrol, Mathildis leaned on me. 'Not a word.'

'We only kissed,' I whispered. 'And you twisted that arrow—'

'The guards heard you bragging, Hraban. They could have thrown me into a bog for that. Your ass hole is a minor problem in comparison.'

'Ass hole?' I asked in shock.

'Hole in the ass, you ass,' she whispered.

'You remind me of Ermendrud,' I said wistfully. 'She had a very foul mouth, as well.'

'Perhaps you have that effect on women,' she sulked.

'Just like I destroy the honor of good men,' I chuckled.

'Not a word!' she warned.

'Fair enough,' I agreed and grinned at her. She smirked back at me, happier than a young otter in a creek.

We walked to Castra Flamma and were met by a group of hard looking Batavi riders.

CHAPTER 21

The snow began to fall hard just as the Batavi guided us to the gates of the Castra. Beyond the wall, Luppia River looked gray and even stormy with white tipped waves whipping the shores and men were running after some escaped horses on its banks. Two sleek ships were tied to the sturdy docks, and a muddy military road ran away to the west on the north side of the river, where men worked under guard. A sturdy stone bridge crossed it north of the harbor.

'Bructeri and Marsi at peace with us?' I asked the grim Batavi rider who looked at me suspiciously. He had known me, but he did not speak much, his eyes staring at the woods cautiously.

'By Hercules, no,' he laughed. 'They still field troops every spring and aid the Sigambri.' Only the very river and its immediate surroundings are ours, but I would not walk the road alone. I hate that road. It is like an invitation for any young warlord to come and fetch loot and hostages. Easy to find, always there, and folks walk down it as if they were at home. Romans are too attached to such things,' he told us bitterly. 'And then we have to go find whoever did something, and sometimes the ones that were the victims.' We reached the gate. 'Wait here.' He dismounted and plunged in through the gate where a pair of XVII Legion's legionnaires wrapped in their military cloaks stood guarding it.

They stared at us for a time and then looked at each other. One noted to the other, 'a wild-looking bunch. You think they will eat us?'

'Pilum practice. Aim for the tip of the beard and you will leave them meowing like a cat,' the other instructed his friend. A centurion with his traversed helm appeared, shadowed by the Batavi. He was a young man, belligerent, full of fire as he bellowed something to immunes, evidently a hunter who had brought in some rabbits.

'You will take part in the digging duty tomorrow, brother. No man gets special treatment and extra pay for such fucking skinny rabbits. We need meat in the cauldron, for Juppiter's sakes!' he yelled at the glowering legionnaire who looked forlorn with his pair of rabbits. The centurion saw us, walked over to us, the Batavi in tow.

'Hraban?' he asked me and nodded as if he knew the answer. He used a Germani accent.

I answered in Latin. 'Yes, it is I. I rode out on a mission for Nero Claudius Drusus a year ago after the battle of the Buck.'

He nodded happily. 'And Fox, Armin took you, prisoner. Welcome to Castra Far the Fucking Away, as we call it! All the joys of home!' He glanced expectantly at the guards, one of whom had been staring at me sheepishly after learning I spoke their language.

The other one nodded. 'A broken home with shitty food, no safety, a leaking roof, wild beasts in the muddy yard, and an unhappy, pox ridden commander. But we love it!'

Evidently, this was a standing joke in the Castra for the centurion laughed. 'Want a drink, Hraban?'

'I ... no, not right now,' I told him.

He took a swig of a jar. 'All right. When we go to the praetorium, do not prance around like a whore girl in the Juventus Hill's alleys. The commander is sick and fucking tired of the place and might just send you walking back because he can.' He winked at me.

'As you say sir,' I told him, grinning.

'Lucius Hirtius Magnus, the first centurion of the fifth cohort, XVII legion,' he said, grabbing my arm. 'Pleased to meet the famous barbarian. Where did they hold you?'

'Segestes had me,' I said darkly as we walked through the wooden gate. Brimwulf was trailing after me and so was Mathildis.

'Segestes? He is an ally though? The big fat lump from the northeast? This is his land,' Lucius said, gesturing at Brimwulf and Mathildis. 'They with you?' he asked.

'Segestes, the bastard. Yea, the archer is with me, and the girl is my wife,' I said, enjoying a moment's revenge, for my ass hurt and bled. Brimwulf's face went white with fury, but the brazen girl could not hold her face straight and giggled.

Lucius snorted. 'More women. I pity you auxilia bastards for your right to marry. We are not allowed, but we can still bed them when on leave. Last week an optio bedded a woman in the village and she was a wife to a Batavi. We kept it quiet. Didn't want to lose the optio.'

I smiled at his easygoing nature. We walked for the principia through the ordered street lined with barracks, many empty. 'How many men are there?' I asked him.

'You sure you are Hraban? Perhaps you are here to take the castra?' he chortled. 'No, I suppose not. Sorry. It's so damned boring in here in winter. Now? Just two cohorts. The military tribune commands us, nominally, the camp praefectus deals with all the real matters and just month ago two legions, the whole XVII and some of the XIX were here, supporting Cherusci civil war. We also drove south to the Chatti lands. Now? Boring. Boring. Man needs a war to keep his wits. Spring was good. We have been doing a lot of Sigambri killing, in the spring,' he told me while nodding at some of the Romans lounging on the steps of the barracks. 'Now? Patrol, and patrol, keeping the peace. Long winter ahead,' he glanced at the billowing clouds. 'Soon, no going anywhere. Will need Germani trousers and socks and triple tunics.' He made silly dance steps and held his long tunic's hem like a girl. Mathildis quaffed and, the centurion bowed happily.

We reached the impressive walls of the praetorium and stopped before the immaculate guards, their chainmail shining, cingulum belts silver studded and spotless and helmets proudly hoisting the two feathers. Neither man budged as the centurion walked inside and over to the side and bent to speak to a man in tunic. The man nodded. Then he walked over a small square to a building with wooden pillars and stayed there for a good while. Then he came out, smiling timidly. 'Go on.'

I was ushered in and glanced at the principia. There were clerks and paymasters working and walking around a courtyard. There was a guard at the center of the small parade ground, and there was likely the military money chest hid under ground. I entered the praetorium and had to squint as it was very dark inside. Some officers were there, all turning to stare at us. Evidently, we were the most interesting news that day. A man snapped his fingers, and I bowed to him. 'Wait here,' I told Brimwulf, who nodded at me. The man sitting behind a desk in his tunic was young, a noble, but he was not one of the thin stripped tribunes, but a wide one, a man with battle experience and would command the legion if the Legate was indisposed. This man was in charge of keeping an eye on the Chatti and the Cherusci.

Now he eyed me with a look that seemed to equal me with an insect. He finally nodded, and I saluted him. 'Hraban? Chariovalda's man?' he asked with a thin voice and bent down to write as if waiting for me to leave.

'I am. Is he well?' I asked.

He laughed. 'I do not know. I am not his friend. I am not his father. But his Batavi are scattered from here to Castra Vetera, and he is evidently there, at the end of the string with the 2nd Batavorium and the bastards of the XVIII Legion, sleeping well in their safe fort.' He sneered at the scroll he was writing. 'We have some of the Batavi here, and I don't say they are useless.' He took a long breath and rubbed his eyes. 'And now to the ungrateful part. Lucius told me you were held by Segestes,' he said. 'This is a bit irregular, as he is our ally, and we are on his land. Technically. Land can change hands really fast, after all. I am tribune Paullus Ahenobarbus, by the way.'

I looked at his hard, squinting eyes and spoke. 'Segestes. He is a treasonous toad who is a Roman one day, Germani the next and ultimately wishes to be the lord of the northern Germania. And I would have to speak to Drusus about this problem.'

244

'You mean his highness Nero Claudius Drusus?' he asked me with resentment. 'He is high as the moon in the sky and you would speak with him?'

'He asked me to call him Drusus after I saved his life. And perhaps his army,' I told him neutrally, and he flinched.

The tribune did not react for awhile as he mulled my words over. Finally, he spoke. 'Drusus it is. But as for Segestes. The fact remains we are on his land. What was your crime towards him?'

I must have looked shocked for he smiled. 'My crime? I am a Decurion of Roman auxilia and my crime was to find out his duplicity against our lord. He did a favor to another traitor, Antius the Negotiatore,' I said and felt blood trickling to the ground from the arrow wound, which the tribune looked at with some discomfort. 'He might have betrayed his kin the Cherusci, but his loyalty is not to Drusus either. They will kill him here, as soon as he arrives. Drusus.'

He scowled at me, weighing my words against his duty to keep the castra safe. 'Armin, Armin. Arbalo was a disaster for both sides and now this. Drusus will be here the next year and you claim he is in danger,' he said, eyeing me carefully. 'Hraban. The Oath Breaker would advise me so.'

'So you know about me?' I asked him. He did not look like a warrior, even if he should be experienced in battle. His hair was immaculately cut, his chin weak, and he was obviously very well connected, but perhaps that was what a man keeping tabs on Segestes had to be like.

He nodded. 'Nero Claudius Drusus has asked me to keep an eye out for trouble. And even you, I recall. I am not over fond of our lord, though. You can see why. This hole of Hades is hardly an endorsement for one's career. But here I serve, and losing a fort would be even more disastrous to my career. Of course, we should convey your concerns to Drusus himself.' Then he turned his face back to the writing. 'Snow is coming. Soon, no man will ride or sail very far from the castra. In the spring, there will be war. We will aid Segestes, he will aid us.'

'But Drusus—'

'I shall discuss with Drusus on how we will proceed. After the winter. I do hate the snow.'

'I must leave and speak with him.'

He dipped his pen in ink and continued as if I had not uttered a word. 'As for you. You might have to leave, but not the way you thought. As I said, we should not make an enemy of Segestes. Now, out there stands a man of the same lord. A nobody, really, just a servant of Segestes claiming to be looking for a rogue who stole a fortune in silver and gold from his lord. He is requesting peaceful handover of a rogue in question. What am I to do? He demands I give you up. I could imprison you to make them happy?'

'If Nero Claudius Drusus only heard what I—'

'Drusus, remember? I see your dilemma, but I also have many men I have to keep alive this coming winter,' he said, cutting me off rather brusquely, and then he breathed deep, evidently resenting the fact that I had made him lose his patience. 'Is there anything you can tell me to give me some way of avoiding getting Segestes very upset with us? We need his food, for one. And even they don't have enough.'

I thought for a moment and then nodded. 'Was there a centurion here, not long ago who rode to his hall, on a diplomatic mission?' I asked.

He scowled. 'There was. I used Gaius many times for taking messages to the man. Armin, I hear, killed him on the road. The body was not recovered. Why?'

I smiled. 'In that case, there are men of the centurion here, men who knew him?'

He nodded. 'I knew him. He was in the same unit.'

'Then, Lord, do you know this?' I asked and tossed Segestes's dark blue finger on his desk, and it rolled on his scroll, leaving a nasty smudge. His breathing stopped, but whether it was from the smudge or from knowing the ring, I did not know. He looked at the disgusting digit, poked it with his pen to turn it over, and his eyes hardened as he saw the ring.

He nodded. 'I have seen the ring, and the finger is then my friend's? And you carry it around? Did you cut it off?' he said, silkily, smoothly.

'I did cut it off though not from your friend. The man died at Segestes's orders, for I told him my name on a muddy yard where dogs tried to eat me,' I said. 'Segestes would not want Rome to know he held a man of hers a slave.'

'Whose finger is this if you did not cut it from him?' he asked, mystified by the disgusting lump of meat.

'When you see Segestes next time, you will know,' I told him, and he smiled quickly, running his hands through his hair.

After awhile he looked up to me. 'It is an intricate situation. You can appreciate it?'

I nodded.

'Heads may fall, men could die on the roads. Worthy men,' he continued, and I said nothing.

'I will show the ring to the man next door, and thank him, then send him away. I will tell him I will write a report of a nine fingered murderer though who the man is, I do not yet know. Segestes will understand to keep his peace, perhaps,' he told me as he stared at the ring. 'It will go to the family, of course,' he murmured, and I nearly chuckled. 'Did he have anything else? He was a rich man,' he mused, and I cursed silently.

'Yes Lord, he did, let me see,' I turned and took a few very precious ornaments from the pouch and laid them on the desk.

He glanced at them, happily.

He pointed his pen at me. 'I will send the legate of the XVII a report, and hopefully it will go through to Drusus. You will stay here.'

'Sir? Can I write to Chariovalda? Or travel to him? I'd be back.' I had promised Thusnelda I would help Sigimer, but I did not trust the legate.

He leaned forward, his face full of simmering anger at my resistance. 'You will stay here in case you are a liar, and I have to do something about it. I won't send you through, and you are mad to think you can get back after the snow hits us fully. The report will indeed move, but you will not, and you will not send out alternative reports to muddy the waters. It would make me look incompetent, a fool, even. You will obey me. Come spring, we will crush the Cherusci and the Chatti, no matter who betrays whom and, of course, our commander will be kept alive.'

'Yes, sir,' I told him, eyeing him with doubt.

He eyed me back, thrumming his fingers on the desk. 'Fine then. You will rejoin the Batavi. What do you wish to do here? We have some twenty Batavi, but they have a Decurion.'

I nodded. 'I have a man of my own, and we will sort it out with the Decurion.'

'You have two, actually,' he said thinly, nodding to himself as if trying to remember a face.

'Two sir?'

'A man named Fulcher, a Batavi has been here, on and off, riding out there, trying to find you. As it happens, he is here now. You will find him in your quarters,' he said. 'He sings, very well. We would like to keep him alive this winter if you can arrange it.'

'Can I go see him,' I said, my voice trembling with anticipation.

'You can, after you take care of the wound,' he said, smiling at the pool of blood at my feet. 'Lucius! Take him to the healer. Then feed the bearded fool.'

Lucius came to fetch me. 'As it would happen, she is outside,' he told me.

'She?' I asked and then saw Cassia, beautiful Cassia talking with Mathildis.

'I introduced them. She was really keen to know your wife,' Lucius said with a nasty laugh and stepped far away as Cassia stormed for me.

'You married that harlot?' she shrieked, her beautiful face a thing of raging fire, and she struck me so hard I flew on my ass and screamed from the pain.

CHAPTER 22

She was not happy.

She was hissing like a cat while daubing something tangy on my wound, plastering a bandage on it. Eventually, I began to pick up words in the strange, unnerving, but definitely disapproving noise that drifted from between her lips. She was speaking half in Gaulish, partly in Latin and probably added some Germani words into the mix. I said nothing, for I was strangely happy. I waited until she slowed down, and I now made out the words "goat" and "a bastard snake of Bel" and also "a filthy womanizer," but I figured it was best to wait until she could breathe fully. I half wished Brimwulf and Mathildis had stayed in the room, but they had decided to give me privacy with Cassia. Finally, she slapped my other bottom with her hand, and I was sure it left a red mark and the slap could be heard all the way to the gates.

'Why?' she said, looking steadily at my eyes.

'Why did I lie about marrying her?' I asked, and her eyes went into thin slits of suspicion. She tugged at her dark braid and shook her head empathetically.

'Did you lie?' she asked me, poking a long nail at my chest.

'It's a long story, love,' I said and tried to coax her closer. 'But I am not married. Nor, in truth, have I slept with another woman.' She looked just as beautiful as she had the day I had rescued her from Varnis though her hair was longer and under her eyes there were rings of dark. She was a healer in the castra, and she wore a stained grey tunic that covered her shapely body all the way to her knees, and there was a thick, practical cloak hung over her shoulders, which had stains of blood. She had been waiting for me for well over a year, probably sure I was dead. 'I'm happy you did not marry, either,' I said and as she arched her eyebrow. I frowned. 'You did not?'

'Chariovalda kept flirting at me,' she stated maliciously.

'He is married! And old!'

'He is a all that, but also wonderful goat who would have refused if I had surprised him by saying yes,' she said with a smile. 'It is his way. But yes, many men have wanted me. Married and single men. I have been living amongst them for this past year. And why? Because you left me in fucking Castra Vetera to go and warn your Drusus, and you promised to come right back!' That was not strictly true, I thought, but nodded meekly. And then you rode off after Armin. With Thusnelda on your lap!'

'Cassia,' I sighed, cursing Fulcher for sharing the lap riding detail with her. 'I have missed you.' She raised her hand to silence me, and I wanted to touch her half-relieved, half-enraged face. She probably had no doubts about my fidelity, but she needed to whip me for something, and I was ready to let her do it. Her full bosom was heaving angrily. I had loved her the past year, the thought of her had kept me sane and nothing Segestes had done to me could take her love from me. I had seen that with Mathildis. 'I could never have dreamt of finding you here,' I told her gently. 'How come you are here, anyway?' I asked as I tried to pull the unwilling woman towards me. The barracks were empty, men on duty, some on patrol, others tending the horses, and it was uncannily silent.

She took a step forward, a tentative one. 'Fulcher told them I am his wife.' She blushed. 'But it is not the same as what you did with that girl—'

I laughed and pulled her to me, but she arched her back away from me as if I was dog's vomit. 'I claimed to have bedded her, love. That way I made her father mad, very mad, mad enough to drag me to the woods, and there I killed him. The only thing I know, Cassia, is that when I nearly died ...'

'Again,' she said softly, putting a hand on my cheek.

'Again,' I agreed, ' I only thought about you and Lif. I failed at saving her, and I failed Drusus with Armin, but right now? Right this moment? I am happier than I have been in ages.'

She nodded, blushing, still scowling. 'If you die, Hraban, I will take your skull, boil it, kick it around to rattle the last vestiges of idiocy from it and plant flowers in it, so that something useful will grow out of it. I have been so scared this past year. I nearly lost hope several times.' We held each other, and I forgot about everything that had been haunting my thoughts lately.

The door opened.

Fulcher entered, covered in snow, his spear coming first. We got up and faced each other. He smiled one of his rare smiles. 'Lord, I see you found your way home. I have been looking for you,' he said happily, but then he squared his shoulders and the smile disappeared. 'I am sorry I failed to find you. They tried to kill me out there, many times. Caught me once. But I escaped.'

'The only one who failed, Fulcher, is I. Come,' I said, got up, ran to him, and we embraced. 'You are worth a dozen men, and I have failed you more than you have me.' He grinned. 'Tell me of Drusus,' I said. 'Of Chariovalda.'

He sat down, and Cassia gave him ale as I sat on a bed across from him. 'Drusus gave me leave to search for you. He sent messengers to Segestes, even Armin. Sent that Tribune Paullus gods-know-what-his-last-name-is here with a task of finding you. After Arbalo, he visited Segestes not far from here. Segestes said he had not seen you, promised to search for you and so, eventually, Drusus had to leave. Arbalo was a mess. I hear they did very well this year with your father and the Chatti, though. What happened to you? And did you know Hard Hill is taken?'

I nodded, tired. I rubbed my face. 'I know about Hard Hill. And I know more. Segestes is an ally to my father. And both are allied to the Romans who wish Drusus dead. I still have Lif to rescue, but we have to warn

Drusus. I am not allowed to send a word out, though. That Paullus promised to, but I don't trust any man with the life of my lord.'

'Segestes is like Maroboodus?' Fulcher asked. 'I am not surprised. He is a snake. So, they will concoct a plan, and if Drusus marches with Segestes, his treason will allow your father … I see.' He was nodding sagely as he contemplated our dilemma. 'I think I know a way to send a scroll out.'

'You do?' I asked.

'Yes. I know a man,' he smiled

'Do it,' I said. 'No, I will write it.'

Cassia nodded, sitting next to me on a bed and held my hand fiercely. 'Now we can only wait, love.'

'I have something else to do first,' I said hollowly.

Cassia frowned. 'Hraban? What are you planning? And is it something we should be afraid of?' Fulcher also fixed an eye on me, his eyes goading me to speak up.

I sighed and did. 'Thusnelda helped me escape. All I should do now is to find a way to get to Chariovalda or find a man to get a message across to Drusus. I should leave and find Drusus as winter is a long time to do nothing, and he could plan on how to deal with Segestes. But it is more complicated, this situation.'

'And it's about Thusnelda?' Cassia said, sitting next to me. 'And the fact she helped you. You made her an oath.' Her voice was very accusatory, and I blanched, rubbed my neck and nodded.

'Armin. I swore to Thusnelda to help Armin.'

'Wait. You will change sides?' Fulcher asked, holding his head. 'This is very confusing.'

'No, I won't change sides, but I will do something for Armin,' I told them, knowing they would not understand. 'I promised her, and she aided me. Armin will be dead if he is alone when Drusus comes. They will hunt him down, and while that would be great for Rome, I made this promise to give him a fighting chance, to make sure he will survive. They need Inguiomerus to be able to fight. And they have to break up Segestes's army. The man who can do this is Armin's father. So, I need to free Sigimer.'

252

'His father? He has not been seen since the battle at the ford,' Cassia said in shock and breathed deep, frustrated. 'This sounds mad. Where is he held a prisoner?'

'It is,' I agreed. 'Odo has him. Tried to trade him and my ring for me,' I said with a disgusted grimace.

'Fucking Odo?' Fulcher laughed. 'This circle is small.'

I went on. 'So, I will rescue Sigimer from Odo. In doing so, I will rescue the ring and help Armin. I will spare Lif as well, maybe, if Odo falls. I want to make sure he does. I will take Sigimer to Armin or let him go, and then I will serve Drusus. We will deal with Segestes and perhaps my father, who will ride here next year.'

They stared at me as in stupefied silence.

Finally, Fulcher laughed, dryly. 'You will aid Armin and then Drusus?'

'Yes.'

He rubbed his face tiredly. 'Not much has changed then! Your oaths. You have to learn to make them and then just simply break them and don't you already have a name to match? Why not break this? It was given to an enemy.'

I pointed a finger at him. 'Didn't you teach me about honor.'

'Yes,' he agreed, 'but there are limits to upholding your honor, as well. This is dangerous and foolish.'

'You were not held my Segestes, and did not endure Ragwald's and Helmut's abuse. I owe Thusnelda.'

Cassia grabbed my hand and turned me to face her. 'Be that as it may, Fulcher is right. And how will elevating Armin help Drusus?' Cassia asked, exasperated. 'This plan will get many Romans killed. And that will take away your favor with Drusus, your new plans and any possibility for a home. If you get caught. And, of course, you will!'

I rubbed my face. 'I had to free myself, and this is the price of it. I had to be free for you, for myself, for Drusus as well. Drusus will have his legions, Segestes will be weak and exposed and in the end, the Roman army will defeat the Germani. But yes, it is a mess.' I tapped my knee nervously until Cassia grabbed it.

'Right,' Fulcher said, unconvinced, and I scowled as the two shook their heads at each other.

'How many men does Odo have?' I asked.

Fulcher frowned. 'They hide someplace to the east. I had not seen them when I looked for you. Nor heard of them. Do you know more? Or anyone who does?'

'I have an archer who knows the land,' I told him. 'He will find the way to Gulldrum.'

'He will?' Fulcher said with a raised eyebrow. 'I doubt he can find them if I can't.'

'He is a good scout,' I explained, and Fulcher went red from the face. He was proud of his skills in the wilds. 'He knows the land, I said.'

Cassia poked me painfully. 'He will have lots of men! Odo will have lots and lots of men.'

'Rabble,' I told her with a wry smile. 'But yes.'

Fulcher snorted. 'We will need men of our own, Hraban. And we serve the Roman army. We don't just come and go as we please!' Fulcher complained, but I raised my hand to calm him.

'I know,' I said. 'But there are Batavi here, no? And their job is to scout? To kill suspicious bastards they run into out there and not hunker in the castra?'

'They have a Decurion and the commander of the Castra might not let them ride around looking for strange bands of beggars!' Cassia seethed. 'Paullus is not the most active commander, but he will not let you run the castra. And there is the senior Centurion who will have needs for the cavalry and so you—'

'But this particular Decurion is not a worthy man for the job,' I stated. 'He works for Segestes.'

'He does?' Fulcher said thinly, nodding. 'Would make sense. I'm pretty sure someone has shared my plans with the local Cherusci. As I said, I was nearly killed once.'

'Thusnelda told you this as well?' Cassia said with an arched eyebrow. 'My, but you got close.'

'She is a friend! Or became one. She has tried to have me killed twice at least!'

'Right,' she said icily. 'And now she will have my man riding after a thousand mad vitka.'

'Only one mad vitka,' I corrected her.

'How in Hel's name do you know? Have you been to Gulldrum?' she hissed at me.

I gave her a begging look, which she ignored, and so I turned to Fulcher. 'What is the Decurion like? This Lothar.'

'Boisterous, lazy, unusually refined in his tastes. Has strange businesses with the merchants. There is this shack by the harbor where he stores stuff he steals and where he runs his shady businesses. He is unusually ... rich,' Fulcher said, and nodded at Cassia, reluctantly. 'And he—'

She looked embarrassed. 'He has been courting me. Unsuccessfully,' she finished, daring me to say something of the matter.

'And you call me a goat?' I stated nonetheless. 'And yes, he might be unusually rich. He has rubbed himself on Segestes. What does he look like?'

She shrugged. 'Hairy, blond ringlets, tall, muscular. Boring,' she added hastily, and I laughed at her discomfort. 'I have been avoiding him,' she told me, aggressively pushing me over the bed.

'He is my superior?' I asked as I picked myself up with Fulcher's help.

'You are both of equal rank, but the men are his, and he holds the Batavi command in the castra. I know not. His job is to scout, sometimes put down rebellions in the villages, small butchery work with bandits,' Fulcher told me tiredly. 'Few like him. He has two men who run his errands and who guard him.'

'Where does he spend his time?' I asked them, fingering my sword.

Fulcher sighed as he saw that. 'I see. I see. At the village, a tavern, full of rabble. He has a taste for the wine there. The ale is terrible. And there are the occasional women there, as well.'

'Fine husband for you, Cassia, no?' I teased her, and she fumed. 'We need to go there.'

'Why?' asked Fulcher. 'Not that I have any doubt we do, but why?'

'I will need to defend my woman,' I said with the grin. 'And I need his men.'

'Oh!' Fulcher grinned.

'And he is our enemy,' I added. 'And he knows someone who is Odo's servant in the town. They set up their deals here. I need to blind Segestes to my doings, and I will need to speak to this man of Odo's. About Gulldrum, Sigimer, Odo.'

'And you will ask Lothar who this person is?' Cassia asked. 'Gods help us. You are only two men!'

'Just don't get us into trouble,' Fulcher said carefully and shook off his gloom. 'Good to have you back,' he grinned. 'Even if I think you should forget your oaths to Thusnelda. I feel it changes things. It will get people hurt.' His eyes were glazed as he spoke, and I looked away, hating his sight.

Cassia turned me around. 'Listen to him. Is there any way we could just go west and live in peace? You and I have survived your father, though only barely. Now this Segestes is out there. You have to save Armin and Drusus? Kill Odo? And they are all coming here.'

I gazed at her beautiful face. 'Yes, they are all coming here. I cannot go anywhere.'

Cassia held my hand. 'Paullus will send this information ahead and then Drusus can deal with everything. Or your scroll will do the deed if Paellus is lazy. Just wait for Drusus, and you and he will scythe down all our opponents one by one,' she begged. 'One by one, together. You don't really need to go and free Sigimer. Armin never did anything for you. Just … wait.'

I stroked her cheek. 'I was never any good at waiting. I have ever gone out to find my enemy. Odo will not expect me. I could just end this. You see? Many problems will be solved if I only take Odo's head. And I did promise Thusnelda. I'd be dead now without her. I told you. Mutilated. You would not find me very attractive skinned and devoid of this peak.' I tapped my nose.

'I would. And I am tired, Hraban,' she whispered. 'Tired of fearing for you. You left me behind. You will leave me behind again. We found each other once, through many troubles and hardships, and we just barely ended up together in Castra Vetera. Is it my turn to get what I wish for at some point? To tell you what we should do? Or Fulcher?'

I grabbed her hands. 'I understand. But I will have to help Drusus. I will take the Head Taker and right the wrongs. There are so many men who have to fall.' I turned to Fulcher. 'I will need my sword, Fulcher. It is time it fulfills all the oaths I have given. It was Hulderic's blade, and I will gut Father with it. At least him. Others if I can.'

She slapped my hands away and leaned over. She rapped her hand on Fulcher's bed and there was a muffled metallic sound under the blankets, and I knew where the Head Taker was. 'Ever since this sword came to our life, you have been living perilously close to madness. I know your father gave you a bad deal, love, and I know Lif's loss changed you. Maroboodus gave you a scar with this blade, and you see it as some kind of a holy relic. It is a blade. Old as time, but you are a handsomer man without it. I love the Hraban who does not carry such a great, evil weight around with him. It is a cursed thing. It takes heads, they say, for the glory of Woden. I say it is the Winter Sword, a cold, bitter blade you will clutch in your hand until you die for its past.'

'Winter sword,' I said and pulled at Fulcher's bedding. There, on the bed was the Wolf's Bane, the fine spearhead of Aristovistus, an ancient relic. But there, next to the spear was also Hulderic's Head Taker, the ancient Gothoni blade of brutal, simple beauty. I had ever coveted it and when Father had fooled Burlein and me with it, giving it away and having men lie to us of his death, I had used it to carve my enemies. Father had given it away for a ruse, and I had kept it. I ran my fingers across it, ignoring my friends and thought about the blade. I had loved it when I had been a child. Hulderic had gone mad as I pestered him for it when I was growing up. Now? It was heavy. It no longer made me happy, inspired. It reminded me of Hulderic's death, of Father's betrayal. It had been there when I lost Burlein and when I lost Lif.

It was not something I loved, not anymore.

I was proud of it, yes, for it was a fine, ancient weapon, but it had changed, I realized, from an honorable weapon with a past and a proud

257

name into a demanding beast of oaths. It was the weapon I wanted to use to kill Father, Odo, Catualda, Antius, and Cornix. Even Segestes now. It wanted blood. I spoke heavily. 'Winter Sword. It is that indeed. Cold and undesirable. But it has a job to do.'

Cassia eyed it and my hand on it. 'I hate it. I love you best on those very rare moments you are not driven somewhere after vengeance. Then you are happy and foolish, handsome, and generous. That sword is a hateful thing. You never smile when you hold it. You will die with it. I feel it,' she said miserably.

'I think she might be right,' Fulcher agreed softly.

'I ...' I began and stopped stroking the blade. I nodded at Fulcher and pulled Cassia to me and kissed her neck gently. 'I'll rename it then. It is the Winter Sword. Give me some time to mull things over.' I hugged her tight. 'I have lost everything, Cassia. Their spirits are restless. My family and tribe and friends are watching me in my dreams. They gaze at me with envy and anger, and they stare at this blade and urge me on. I will try to tell them to go back to the shadows. I will be happy and foolish again. Will you bear with me for awhile yet?'

'Yes,' she told me heavily and pushed me back. 'But do not think I am happy as long as that thing is lurking in our lives. When you were ... dead, I did not have to fear. I was only very sad and lonely and hopeful one day you might come back. But you were declared dead. It helped, somehow. Now I am afraid again.'

'I am sorry I am alive,' I told her with a smile and waved down her protests. 'Fulcher, can you hold on to Wolf's Bane? Keep it safe?'

'I've kept it safe so far.' He grinned. 'Take the blade, but remember what she said.'

'I will,' I said, put Cassia down and grasped Hulderic's former battle blade. It was cold and heavy indeed. 'I will write that scroll for Chariovalda, Fulcher. And you deliver it so that Paellus will not find out.' I looked at them, and they seemed bothered. 'What?'

'He has some news,' Cassia said softly, and she nodded at Fulcher. She was eyeing the sword with a frown.

'More about the Decurion?' I asked him.

Fulcher shook his head. 'We go to the village tomorrow and deal with that. But before that, you have to do something. You came at a very opportune hour to honor someone. I doubt it is a coincidence.'

'What is it?' I asked, puzzled

'Tudrus the Older is dead. They are burying him tonight at a Sigambri village twenty miles from here,' Fulcher said softly, looking down. 'Write your scroll and then we ride.'

CHAPTER 23

'You paid too much for it,' Fulcher admonished me as I led a horse around. It was a beautiful beast, dark as night, and its mane was glistening with health. 'It's old.'

'It's beautiful. And young,' I told him with a voice that brooked no argument with my horse trading skills.

'The coat's been oiled,' Brimwulf said from the side.

Fulcher was nodding. 'I was just about to tell the fool that.'

'Of course, you were,' Brimwulf quaffed and came to stroke the beast, his hand coming off greased. 'It's older than it looks.'

'That I did say,' Fulcher complained, clearly unhappy with Brimwulf. His eyes turned mischievous as he regarded the archer. 'Who is the pretty one?' he asked me.

'This is Brimwulf,' I grunted. 'Our newest companion. He helped me along. At least he made my way to castra fleeter.' Brimwulf chuckled at that.

'No,' Fulcher said. 'I meant that one behind him.'

He meant Mathildis, who blushed, and so Brimwulf developed a serious dislike for Fulcher. 'I hear you are married?' the archer stated. 'Fulcher? Right? Perhaps I shall meet your wife one day? Surely she is here, where you take care of her?'

'She is …' Fulcher began and stammered, 'not here. I am alone.'

'Truly?' Brimwulf said with faked surprise. 'Pray your wife is as well.'

I slapped my hand on a Roman saddle. 'And that is enough, friends. I need you both, you need each other, believe me and stop annoying each other so you won't be tempted to fail all of us when the need arises.' Fulcher frowned and shook his head as Brimwulf looked away, bothered. He finally nodded and gave a small bow to Fulcher and he answered, but they did not love each other. 'Brimwulf, Cassia will show you where you are to sleep. Not with the other Batavi, not yet. And Mathildis should stay in the town …' I raise my hand to forestall his rising anger. 'But she is going to help her with her healing duties. So she stays with her. They have a house in the camp.'

'Fine. And you will go out to find more friends?' Brimwulf asked. 'Need me?'

'I know these men. They might or might not dislike us, and I don't want to risk you, Brimwulf. You will keep Cassia alive and help her find Nero Claudius Drusus next year if I don't come back. She knows what to do. But yes,' I said and mounted the horse. 'I hope I shall find some friends.' *Damn them*, I thought irascibly, *the horse is a beauty*. 'I will see if they still remember me. Keep the girls safe. And give the scroll to the man Fulcher spoke of.' I had written a clumsy scroll and prayed it would go forth. I waved at Cassia who was swathed in her cloak just beyond the gate.

'I will, no worry.' He grinned. 'Don't get lost, Suebi,' he called to Fulcher who spat and turned his horse away.

Cassia was clearly unhappy about being left behind, but she had duties in the castra, and she seemed happy as Mathildis walked to her. They were giggling, and I swear they said my name. I was happy Brimwulf was with her.

Lucius nodded at me from the vallum. 'Looking civilized again, Hraban!' he called out as Brimwulf climbed next to him. I nodded. I wore new caligae with socks. I was holding a hasta, a heavy spear, Segestes's lambskin covered shield and the Head Taker on my hip again. I had left Sigimer's ax with Cassia, but also wore Nightbright on the belt and wore a brown sagum cloak, and the smell of lanolin oil wafting from it was slightly repulsive. We rode southwest, amidst mud and battered by a chilly wind. The half-frozen ground was crunching under the hooves of the horses, and the evening was somber. Fulcher's silence was welcome.

Tudrus the Older was dead.

The great Quadi, friend of Hulderic, was gone. He had anticipated it when we met in the Thing of Drusus. I had regarded him like a father when Maroboodus had turned out to be a cold turd. I had risked my budding trust with Maroboodus to spare Tudrus my father's deadly schemes. Maroboodus had not only wanted to rule the Marcomanni, but the smaller tribe of the Quadi. He had struck a deal with the Quadi Sibratus to betray Tudrus and his family, and he had used Vannius, the deceitful Vangione prisoner Tudrus had so trusted to try to slay the old chief.

Instead, Tudrus had escaped. Thanks to me.

He had escaped with his son Tudrus the Younger, Agetan, and Bohscyld, his three sons and my one time rivals but now friends. He had led his own people, some two thousand to the north, through the lands of the Matticati to the Luppia River where they had served Sigambri lord Maelo, and there they had fought for him and then even Armin.

It was Tudrus who had brought me the deadly deal from Armin. Lif for Drusus's life.

He had been ashamed of it, but he was a fugitive, and his people were dying.

And he had asked me for a favor. Should he die, save his sons. Make them Quadi again.

I snorted. I could barely keep myself alive, I thought. But then, Tudrus the Younger was a strong, wild, and wily ally. Agetan and Bohscyld were stupid as the horses they rode, yet staunch and powerful and gods knew I could use them at my side. Then again, I had fought many of the Sigambri the Quadi were sheltered with. *Perhaps they did not consider me a friend? Had Drusus been beaten the past year when I helped foil their plan? Many a Quadi would be alive.*

With these thoughts, we passed silent homesteads, former Sigambri, now dubiously serving Rome. After an hour of navigating forest roads, we slowly came upon the settlements of the free Sigambri. A number of burned houses began to appear, and there were dirty, tired men toiling with animals. Most stopped to look at us, suspiciously, with hate burning in their eyes as they realized we served Rome. Many were tattooed men, lean, and a mean looking lot, and some held their weapons until we passed. Few trailed after us.

'Where to?' I asked Fulcher, ignoring the threatening mood.

'There is a stream to the south; then we ride west until another comes to sight. The Quadi are settled there,' he told me, and we rode that way. We found the stream, using some well-trodden forest roads leading west and then we rode under the branches of thick alder woods. The road led to halls of wet misery, villages spattered in mud and finally haphazard fields of barley and wheat, some still unharvested.

Fulcher pointed to the north where we could hear a drone of voices.

We approached a group of men standing on a bank of a small pond, hoping to ask for directions, but saw the people there were praying amidst the remains of a huge pyre. They had recently burned a corpse, and my stomach turned in agitation. Fulcher spoke to some men, who shook their heads and pointed further west. 'Not him,' Fulcher noted, and we went on. Eventually, Fulcher guided me to a shallow valley as the wind started to blow harder, promising more snow soon. A village stood there, the trunks of the halls glistening with moistness. A great number of horses were huddled in the corrals, miserable at the coming winter, their manes glistening wet. A few walked around and a man was guarding them.

'There?' I said and pointed towards some light woods. We saw a glow in there, away to the east and passed the village. Slaves came out to see us, noting our partly Roman gear, but I ignored them. An old beggar was whispering something in the dark, and I saw Fulcher was wary.

We got closer to the trees, where we saw a hundred people standing under a banner.

I saw the banner I knew; it was the bronze disk of Tudrus the Quadi.

A young vitka was praying and a cow was led there, as the priest beseeched Donor, Woden, Freyr, and all the gods to receive my friend to their halls under a somber, wet night. He sanctified the place by drawing

Donor's hammer symbols in the air and then the vitka ordered the hlaut vessels to be brought forward. Without further ceremony, he cut the cow's throat. It struggled, of course, spraying much of the blood on the mud, but the vessels were filled and the vitka began to dip an evergreen sprig on the blood, sprinkling the blood on the onlookers, blessing them. The Quadi stood around a smoldering bonfire, one that was partly burning on the side while men struggled to get it going. I saw some faces, men I had seen with Tudrus, one man at least from the day he had challenged Gernot in the Thing of the Marcomanni to spare me, and many women were crying behind the lines of men. On top of the pyre, his large body lay, wrapped in skins, and I could see a gray face and silvery hair.

He looked like the hero he was.

Fulcher nudged me and pointed to a group of men standing to the side. There stood huge Agetan, beyond him his twin Bohscyld, and also the tall Tudrus the Younger. Their faces were hard, ravaged by sorrow and hardships.

We rode in, sitting on our horses behind the Sigambri and Quadi.

Fulcher pulled my sleeve. 'It is Baetrix who owns these villages and this Sigambri gau, but Tudrus served Maelo this year. Maelo used the Quadi refugees to fight our XVII here in these woods and valleys while the Sigambri tried to foil I Germanica and XIX Legion in the west. Quadi were but few hundred by fall.' I nodded and felt sorry for the people as I pulled on the helmet Tudrus had given me. I also took off the lambskin from the shield.

Men were staring at me, at the beautiful shield and the familiar helmet.

Tudrus the Younger turned, his lean and serious face looking at me steadily, his chin tight and clean shaved. Some of the Sigambri hefted weapons, but I did not move. Tudrus the Younger nodded at me, gesturing with his hand. We rode forward and Fulcher let me go the last few feet alone, looking around at the Sigambri. He had been scouting in the area for a year. They knew him, he knew them, and there was a wary trust between them, despite their opposing allegiances. Tudrus the Younger watched me climb down from my horse. The mountainous Agetan and Bohscyld only now noted me, their beady eyes following my every move. The vitka, a dirty creature trembled in indecision and then strode forward to turn me around, apparently outraged. 'Who is this Roman mongrel?'

'He is the Oath Breaker,' Tudrus the Younger said with a ghost of a smile. 'He also broke our army last year.'

The vitka sucked in a breath and tried to swing at me with the bloody sprig. I grabbed his hand from the air and scowled at him. 'Best save such belligerence for the naughty children.'

He cackled as he tore himself free. 'Woden does not approve of you, Oath Breaker. He will put maggots in your belly. He has already taken your fame, and soon he will have your eyes. You traitor. He knows your heart. Everyone knows your heart! Leave this place and the great chief will travel in peace—' he babbled, but I pushed him away from me.

'Woden?' I laughed at him. 'Woden is my family's father, and I fight with his encouragements ringing in my ears. You know nothing of Woden, charlatan! As for him,' I said with a breaking voice, nodding at the corpse. 'He was not unlike a father to me, you foul crow. Silence!' I told him but he shook his dirty, knotted hair and turned to the assembled men and women.

'This man—' the vitka started to mock me, but I slammed the shield on the back of his head, leaving him moaning on the ground. The Sigambri and the Quadi glowered at me, fingering their weapons. I ignored them. I turned to Tudrus the Younger, glancing at the body on top of the heap of wood, some smoke rising from somewhere inside the pyre. The flames were lazily licking the standard. I went before him, to my knee. 'May I give him my respects, Lord of the Quadi?'

Tudrus nodded tiredly. 'Do so Hraban. He loved you well.'

So I prayed to Woden in the midst of the mob of hungry enemies, who all eyed me with trepidation, awe, and hate. I thanked Woden for knowing the great man, for his friendship and I prayed that the lord would find happiness in Valholl, as well as plenty of good fights, that he would hear many famous tales and have a loving woman or two. I looked up to his now smoking body, the heat starting to ignite it and then the standard burst to flame. I picked up the precious shield I had stolen from Segestes and threw it with all my might atop the pyre, which now ignited fully. The shield flew up in the air, hit a branch, and fell at the feet of the corpse with a hollow clang. 'Thus I give it to Woden, so that Tudrus the mighty shall not go undefended in the halls of the gods, and my debt is paid by a great gift!' I yelled, and I heard the Sigambri and the Quadi whisper in wonder, for it was a gift worth a king. Tudrus the Younger and his brothers stood in a circle around the bonfire, waiting for the corpse to be engulfed, and I wept, for I missed the old man terribly.

'Call me Tudrus, Hraban,' the young man said amidst his silent tears. 'For I am the Younger no longer.'

'Yes, Lord,' I said.

'I am not a lord either,' he told me with sorrow. 'Come.'

Tudrus invited me to his hall in the village. A somber feast was held, men eating the meat of the sacrificial cow and drinking sour ale. The people were dirty and tired and sat amidst tables and enjoyed the sound of a crackling fire. It was mostly a silent feast.

I leaned on Tudrus. 'How did he die?'

He snorted. 'He was wounded last year in the battle of the valley. We fought in the same war, brother.'

'I thought I saw his standard,' I agreed.

'His wound sapped his vitality. This year he led us against your Roman friends trying to take over these woods. Caught a slingshot on the ribs. Broke some. It was too much. But we saved many Sigambri from slavery and killed many Romans. And their auxilia. And Germani traitors.' He glanced at me at those words but did not press the point. After a time, he sighed and served me slabs of cow, some very dark ale, and delicious vegetables. 'I suppose we all have harsh choices to make. Romans fight well. I do envy them their discipline. Here, eat. I am sorry the fare is no better. It has been a tiresome summer. After we lost the battle last year, the legions have been raiding the fields, trying to starve the Sigambri into submission. They are succeeding in some parts of the land, but Sigambri are a large nation and can still feed us.'

'I see,' I told him, feeling bad for eating well. 'I ate shit for months, and this is like a feast of Eostere in comparison.'

He continued. 'Good. Good. The war goes on. Forever. There are still plenty of Sigambri warriors, more than eight thousand, perhaps if all would fight some ten, but they lack hope. Tencteri and Usipetes are still out there as well, supporting us as best they can. Luppia River, as Rome calls it, is falling, though. We call it the Black River now. Its beauty is waning. Many have surrendered to Saturninus, who treats them well. Some Sigambri have moved to your side of the river.' *My side,* I thought. *Yes, it was my side.*

'I know Saturninus. He is a fair man,' I said.

Tudrus slammed a mug on the table before me. 'A fair man does not war on women and children.'

I shrugged, running my hand across the foaming mug. 'A fair man rarely has control over the war in such a way as to spare men and women, but I am sorry to see the Quadi reduced so,' I told him, gravely. 'It was my warning, after all, that sent you packing from my father. Little good it did you.'

He nodded. 'Sibratus and the dog Vannius. Your father bought them somehow. We meant to return, but there was nowhere to go. Tallo, our last lord, our uncle was dead as well. The Quadi of Moenus are all Marcomanni now. So we held our wows to Maelo.'

'Maelo will put up a good fight for years still. How many are you?' I asked, and he smiled.

'We? The Quadi? Some two hundred, perhaps. Many went back, this spring, to submit to Sibratus and your father. Most did, in fact. Except Rome owns our home now, so gods know what happens to them. Perhaps they will die to Hermanduri spears? Perhaps. So now, I lead a clan, not a nation. And even the Quadi here, in our villages, my oaths men are drifting away after Father died. They think we failed. My family failed. We did, did we not? So, I have no gau, just my horse and brothers and a starving group of stragglers who are slowly leaving me.' He looked around the tables, and it was true men avoided his eyes. He poured ale to wash down the mead I had just finished. 'I never got to marry, even. Imagine that! Though I distrust women. I do. I want a noble woman, beyond reproach and doubt, a fine and high one, and here there is only mud and misery.'

'I never did marry either, though I have a child,' I said, and Agetan laughed like I imagined a mossy forest boulder would laugh.

267

Tudrus smiled. 'They know about your healer. Fulcher here told me she swore to give you a thrashing if she ever found you again.'

I gave Fulcher a withering look, and he ignored me, smiling. 'She did. I am a confused man, Tudrus,' I told him with a sigh.

'You always were, Bear Head,' he laughed, and we smiled at each other as we thought back on our childhood and the many fights the Bear Heads and the Wolves had endured. He shrugged. 'So, tell me about your daughter. And about your master Nero Claudius Drusus. And perhaps a bit about your father.' We ate, drank and I told him of my years. I told how I lost Ansbor, fell in love with Cassia and how I had chosen Drusus. I told him of Leuthard and Odo, who chased after Lif and the destruction of the world. He nodded as I told him of my attempt to capture Armin, then how I tried to trick Armin and how I failed due to Catualda and Segestes. He snorted as I told him of my imprisonment with Segestes. 'I thought I smelled pork when you showed up!' he told me, and I cursed him. I told him of the coming spring and the many plans taking place and my promise to save Armin and Drusus both, as well as Lif. I told him of Odo and Sigimer. He was nodding vigorously and after awhile, he looked at his meal, mulling over something.

'And that is what I am doing,' I told him.

He snorted. 'Yea. I see. You are doing a lot. Planning and living and leaving the past behind.'

'No. I am trying to catch up with the past. If I succeed, yes, I shall leave it behind,' I said, somewhat embarrassed, fingering the Winter Sword.

'I gave you an oath, sort of,' he said reluctantly. 'Perhaps I did. Remember?'

'The day Maroboodus, Father sent me to Hard Hill?' I asked. 'Yes. You said you might fight with me. Not for me.'

'Yes,' he nodded and smiled. 'That one.'

'I gave your father an oath,' I told him, uncomfortably.

'That day in Moganticum?' he questioned me, surprised. 'When he asked us to leave the table?'

'Yes. He wanted me to adopt you, should he die.' I grinned.

'Adopt us?' There was fury on his lean face.

'He wanted me to find you. He wanted us to help each other. He asked me to help you become Quadi again. To regain your lands.' I rapped my fingers on the mug. 'Though I am not sure any man can give the Quadi back their lives and halls. But there might be a way.'

'A way?' he asked and sneered. 'But we could give you your vengeance?' he sneered and shook his head. 'He would have Quadi nobles follow you?' he asked, and I shrugged.

I looked him in his eyes. 'I have not forgotten Maroboodus. Father. I have things to do this coming spring and summer and could use your help. Perhaps we would fight together?'

He glowered at his drink. 'I have not forgotten Maroboodus and his lies either. But you also serve Rome?' he said, and Bohscyld grunted and spat. I flexed my arms and smiled at them.

'I understand you hate them for the losses of the past years. And they are enemy to the Germani. Yes, I have friends with them. Many are Germani. The Germani serving Rome learn to fight the Roman way, and perhaps one day need not fight for Rome any more.' As Vago and Catualda had once told me, but it made sense. I continued. 'But most of all I serve Nero Claudius Drusus and obey his words and wishes. I serve their army and their state, which is glorious service for he is a just, great man. I serve my lord. He is not unlike your father. And entirely unlike mine. Drusus will be there when I meet my father again. When we deal with Catualda, Armin, and Segestes and Odo and put things right. I hope you would be there as well. Thus, at least partly would your father be revenged.'

'And after the revenge?' he asked wryly. 'What way could there be to gain us our halls back?'

I leaned towards him. 'I will do what Drusus asks me to. Perhaps we will regain what we lost. Our lands? Drusus might be the power behind Rome, one day. He will need friends in our lands. Patient, loyal friends who will bleed for him, and bleed his enemies. But who also can fight like Rome, should there be no Drusus.' *Let it not be so,* I thought. 'Father will have to fall. Others. Catualda and so many others. Odo—'

He growled. 'Vannius. You forgot Vannius the Vangione. I will want to be there when he draws his last breath,' Tudrus said. 'That dog was a prisoner to my father. He was trusted and given power. He betrayed us to your rotten father. But I said that already.' He was breathing hard and struggling to calm himself.

I squirmed for I had liked Vannius, and he had allowed me burn Maroboodus's hall. I told him of his brother Hunfried, the king of the Vangiones who was my prisoner. Vannius would have been happy to go home and become a king, but now Hunfried was freed, apparently, and Vannius was likely dead or on the run. Perhaps he was with my father and the remaining Quadi. And that meant he too, might be there in the spring. I nodded heavily. 'One day, we will corner him, as well. Perhaps this coming summer. We all get revenge or die trying,' I said forcefully, and their eyes lighted.

Tudrus put a hand on my shoulder. 'I will fetch the shield you gave Father from the pyre and bury it with my father's bones and horse and weapons. Woden appreciated your gift, and so did I. And in the morning, I will come to you, as your man. I revoke my oath to fight as equals and will follow you as long as you give us a chance to regain that which was lost. The dolts will, as well.' He nodded at the two mountainous brothers next to him, both of whom nodded stiffly. 'Next spring, the remaining Quadi will have moved to Maelos's heartlands or to Moganticum for Rome, or wherever they have room. I hear they are settling some Sigambri already south of Castra Vetera. Some will join us if we do well.' He looked at the men around the tables. 'I doubt many will follow me, but some will.'

'Your vows to Maelo?' I asked.

He shrugged. 'My father gave oaths. I have not done so. But I do to you.'

I took his hand, and we mourned his father together that night.

CHAPTER 24

We woke up to see the ashes smoldering on the fire pit. That morning, the Quadi raised a mound in that small copse of wood and covered it with stones. We buried his weapons there, his horse, and the fabulous shield though we broke it first. We prayed and added food for his trip. Then, Fulcher guided us home in the morning, and Tudrus and his brothers followed me. We arrived at Castra Flamma to meet some Batavi riders who were scowling at the Quadi suspiciously, but I growled their questions away. The man leading them pointed a finger at me. 'The Decurion wants to see you as soon as possible.'

I kept riding past them. 'I am a Decurion as well, so change your fucking tone. Where is Lothar?'

He adjusted his seat, surprised by my tone and nodded toward the village. 'You know his name? Fine. This morning he is riding to the north and scouting a village. Afternoon, eating and drinking at the village. The last ship for Castra Vetera is leaving, and he is overseeing the guards, making sure it will get on its way.'

'Robbing it, I think,' I told him woodenly.

He shrugged. 'He does what he does. But he wants to know why you are riding around, not reporting to him. He, after all, has men, and you do not have ...' The man's eyes settled on the terrible Quadi threesome, and he waved the rest of his sentence away. 'In any case, meet him.'

'I will see him,' I said with spite, and we dismounted and led the horses to the stables. We went to the barracks, and I showed the Quadi their bunks. We all had a good scare when Cassia arrived and nearly bumped into Agetan. She screamed at the sight of the wide creature, and I swear Agetan blushed at the sight of her. I nodded at the Quadi. 'Meet the Quadi.'

'I screamed once already when I saw him the last time. Or his brother, I know not,' she said sheepishly and that was true, for she had seen them once in Moganticum. She grinned and gave the huge men a fierce hug and a kiss on the cheeks. Both smiled like demented idiots. Then Cassia blushed at Tudrus, who was already waiting with open arms and a lean grin. She gave him a hug as well and shook her head at me. 'They will eat you to ruin, I think.'

'Rome pays for their food.' I grinned. 'But perhaps we should hunt to make sure we survive.'

'Spring, Hraban,' she scolded me. 'Summer at latest. Then we find something else. You find us something sane to do.'

'I will,' I told her. 'In the spring and summer, all will be made clear.'

'It is my turn to find some happiness, instead of festering warts and punctures,' she told me and poked me in the chest.

The Quadi laughed, Fulcher smirked, and I led the lot to the praetorium. The Tribune had them signed up after I explained they were Suebi looking to join the Batavi. He led them to the principia and rarely have you seen a more confused sight as Agetan and Bohscyld holding a pen that a scribe gave them with some hesitation. The Tribune was hovering near, eyeing the newcomers. 'Chariovalda told you to get your men and that is fine. We need the men,' the silky smooth Tribune noted. 'Two hundred and fifty denarii, minus the gear and the food and such,' he pointed out. 'Welcome to Castra Flamma.'

'Two hundred and fifty denarii?' Tudrus hissed. 'Is that good? Fifty, not sixty? Why won't they pay in cows?'

'Fifty or sixty, doesn't matter. And they eat the cows. That coin is what you get, minus what you pay for equipment, and expenses,' I told him, and I saw from his face he thought he was being cheated, even when he had no idea what a denarii was worth.

The Tribune was looking at my friends, one by one. 'So, they are Suebi peregrine, living in Roman areas? Or barbarians? We prefer to recruit from the ones living near our Roman controlled lands. Not that I am complaining.'

'Barbarians, raw and savage, sir,' I said. 'Chariovalda likes such men. And I have a use for them.'

He hummed and shrugged. 'Use? I have "a use" for men in the castra. Not a Decurion. My needs are your first concern. Remember that. Keep your nose clean. How was your reunion with your wife? I know she is not married to that Fulcher.'

'It was long awaited,' I said with a nod.

He eyed me with curiosity and smiled inanely. 'A soft spot for a woman. It always pleases me to see men know their priorities. Do not swim too far to the sea, Decurion,' he warned me, smoothing his hair. 'Keep far from Segestes.'

'No, sir! I will lead my men to the best interest of Rome,' I told him.

'Best interest of Rome might surprise you, remember that,' he stated. 'I have written to Nero Claudius Drusus, my friend. Given him your warnings. It will go out this afternoon with the last ship.' He thrummed his fingers on the desk. 'You can relax now for the winter.' I saluted him and bowed, and he left. *My scroll would also leave that afternoon*, I thought *though it would not be obvious.*

My Quadi friends did not glower after they got their gladius, a Roman hasta spear, good quality tunics and cloaks, with reasonably well fitting helmets. Their scutum was of fine make, and they admired the shield's thick, well-oiled leather. And when they got the fabulous lorica hamata, they beamed. I paid for them, for they had no money, and the payment of their salary should be settled with Chariovalda's officia. The best of all, they got wide, strong Roman horses, with Roman saddles and the looks on their faces destroyed the last qualms they had about Rome, the legions, and

273

the auxilia. Tudrus was patting his horse. I stared forlornly at the few pieces of gold and bracelets I had left but felt no remorse as they smiled like the sun. Brimwulf, also geared up was grinning at their looks on the side, and Fulcher was grumbling about the cost. Tudrus bowed in thanks. 'What then, Hraban? We have duties?'

'Oh, very many. You will love it. Now we go meet my fellow Decurion, the man who likes Cassia,' I said, and Tudrus's eyes narrowed in suspicion. 'He has men. I need more men.'

'Agetan and Bohscyld? They coming too?' he asked.

I shook my head. 'No. Not exactly. This Lothar is working for Segestes, so it is more than just about Cassia. Listen.'

Later, I rode to the town with Fulcher and Tudrus. We had visited the harbor and now headed for the tavern. The street was a thing of mud, dirt, and brown snow as the merchants and slaves, craftsmen and whores shared the misery of the coming winter, but it was also a place to meet and spy, and in its narrow streets you could see men from all the tribes.

We found the place where the Batavi leader holed up when relaxing. It was a mud-spattered, brown and gray hall, and the timbers and thatch made it look like it had been long abandoned. It was a tavern called the Dirty Wart. It had no real name, of course, but men knew it by that name, for the Gaul holding the filthy establishment in the sorry little village next to Castra Flamma had so many warts that his face was covered with them. His face was also ever covered in soot from the fires he ceaselessly stoked as he burnt sad meat of something that would resemble a meal.

We entered the room.

The floor creaked. It was a filthy hovel with nasty straws littering the floor, brown mice running in the rafters, and all sorts of dirty platters and mugs heaped at the ends of the raw tables, hopelessly waiting to be collected. Men were mostly drinking, and some brave ones were eating as we stalked in. The Gaul running the establishment got up from a table, wiping his hands with a dirty rag, his belly swollen under his tunic.

'What will it be, lords?' he yelled, and some men seated at the back turned their heads our way. A blond man with curly hair stared at me with very blue eyes. He gestured at us, and I nodded, walked over and slumped on a seat opposite to him, fat silver bracelets jingling on my arms. His eyes flashed with greed. I had little else left than those fine things, but they worked. He was already interested.

'You are Lothar?' I asked him timidly.

'Decurion Lothar,' he nodded. 'Speak up!'

'And I am Decurion Hraban,' I told him as I pulled my helmet off and his eyes took a calculating look.

Lothar finally nodded at me, grinning. 'Decurions here, Decurions there, and in the end only one can command a turma. And it's going to be the one who has been given the order to do so. Nice scar boy. Fancy. Rarely seen better. The one your father gave you? Yea, I know of you.'

I nodded, and the Gaul brought us ale. 'This any good?' I asked him, and the Gaul just gave me a snaggletooth smile.

'It is better than piss,' Lothar confirmed. 'But I do prefer the wine.' *Something he stole from the supplies, no doubt,* I thought, and stored with the Gaul.

I shuddered as I tasted the liquid and eyed the ugly Gaul waiting to be paid. 'I'd rather have the scar than his face. By gods, he looks like a lice ridden ass hole.'

Lothar laughed heartily and threw the man a copper coin, and the Gaul smiled in gratitude, despite the insult. He was one of those men it was impossible to insult. I gazed at Lothar. For some reason I kind of liked him. He was an easygoing, lazy man as he sprawled on the seat, but there was practicality in him that could have been useful. He was far too luxurious to be a soldier, but I thought he was honest about his many shortcomings. Of course, he was a rogue of the first degree and evil to his core. He likely could fight if pressed. He had ring mail armor with a heavy tunic of leather, a steel helmet with horsehair crest dropped on the floor, well used hand axes on his belt. His men were two louts, fawning on him, but both had a look of practical killers.

'This is Tudrus, and that is Fulcher. You know him, of course,' I said.

His eyes laughed as he toasted Fulcher. 'I do indeed. I do. The Batavi who is special, riding around as he pleases.'

'He was trying to find me, by orders of Chariovalda,' I told him, playing with the ale. 'Chariovalda, who is above a Decurion. Far above.'

He shrugged. 'It seems you found yourself, and he is out of the job, eh? So, now you are here. Chariovalda or no Chariovalda, I command the men here, so we have to have a chat.'

We said nothing for a while.

I shrugged. 'I won't fight you over the men. I am tired, tortured, and exhausted. I only want to take my men and leave, in fact.'

His eyes rounded in surprise, but only for a moment. 'My men. All the Batavi riders, and anyone riding with them, are under my command. Even Fulcher here, since you are no longer lost,' Lothar said, but I slammed the tankard on the table so hard it cracked, spilling dirt colored ale over it, dripping to the floor.

I spoke, my voice nervous. 'My men and I will go back to Castra Vetera to report to Chariovalda. I understand there is a ship? The last ship?'

He scowled at me but nodded. 'There is a ship, the navis onageria with a blue figurehead. Goes out with orders and sick men in an hour or two. But I say the men stay. And you should as well.'

I was looking around in agitation and saw Lothar lose all respect for me. I whispered to him. 'I have to go. I can pay some. I know you know the ships and their captains. I have a hoard of coins from … well. I cannot say. I found them in my captivity.' His eyes narrowed as he played with a splinter of the tankard in the table. I went on. 'I have important news, as well. On Segestes. He is a traitor!'

'Really?' Lothar said with an angry scowl. 'That is surprising news indeed.' His face did not twitch, and I hoped Manno had been right when he had told Thusnelda such news.

I opened my hands to him in supplication. 'I have to go.'

'You are a nervous one, are you not?' he breathed and was nodding at himself as he thought about the dilemma. 'And this treasure? That goes to Castra Vetera as well?' he inquired, languidly.

'I wish to be away from here,' I said, nervously. I clapped at a bulging pouch on my side and it clinked. There were but few coins there, of course, and many rocks but it worked. Lothar licked his lips. 'I'll give you some gold for this service. Well worth a trip down river.'

'You are not what I thought you would be, Hraban. Did they hurt you much in the lands of Segestes?' he asked, smiling arrogantly.

I shook my head in denial, my eye twitching. 'Nero Claudius Drusus wants me on that ship; Chariovalda wants me on that ship. So I will go. The tribune does not, I am sure, but I will not tell him. I am asking you, as a fellow cavalryman to help me out. And you will be rid of me at the same time,' I told him as the Gaul brought me another mug, scowling with a warning. *He does not like Lothar,* I thought.

'The tribune does not know?' he asked, nervously.

'No, he thinks I should stay, but I am sure you see it differently. I'll just go. I'll go and the treasure goes and the news of Segestes as well and you will be the sole Decurion in the castra,' I told him, pretending desperation.

'You seem a wreck, Hraban. A wreck,' he told me with amusement. His men laughed obediently.

'I am tired, Lord,' I told him. Fulcher and Tudrus were glowering at the two men with Lothar, unhappy with my dishonorable act. 'We shall sail.'

'I see,' he mulled it over in his head, glancing at me. He was a proud man. I could see it. His chest heaved as he decided the matter, and he forced a laugh from his chest. 'No,' he said simply.

'No?' I said weakly, my hand shaking.

'No,' he repeated, smirking at the shake in my hand, and my nervousness.

'But—'

He cut me off. 'I command the Batavi and your men stay here if they signed up. You take your prizes to Chariovalda alone if I let you.'

'I cannot leave my men and my woman!' I told him, and he shrugged.

'Your men belong to my command. Who is your woman?' he asked, curious.

'Cassia, the healer. We just reunited, and she cannot keep her hands off me,' I told him, smiling blissfully, if nervously.

That did it. His face took a grey hue as he regarded me, his eyes rolled in his head, and he looked away, spat on the floor, and thought deep. Then he nodded. 'I will escort you to the ship and keep your horse here. I will also send men to fetch Cassia. The ship leaves soon. The men stay here as well,' he said, pointing at Fulcher and Tudrus.

I got up, and Tudrus and Fulcher nodded at me as I clasped hands with them. 'I will see you later then.'

Lothar smirked as he adjusted his armor. 'It is too bad Cassia must come with you, Hraban. But she will keep you hale and help you overcome your ... timidity,' Lothar said mirthfully. 'You will come back, and bring her with you. She is a great one with herbs. She once healed my ... well, down there.'

I swallowed and nodded, and his men laughed at my discomfort and the insult. Fulcher was about to open his mouth, but I shook my head. 'She is a great healer. She is,' I agreed.

Lothar sneered at me in disgust but nodded towards the door. He picked up his helmet. 'Shall we?' He threw a copper on the table. We went outside, and Fulcher and Tudrus mounted their horses.

Lothar faced my friends. 'You two, ride to the barracks, and wait for me there. I will assign you your orders when I come back,' he told them and gestured for the ship as Fulcher and Tudrus rode away. He leaned to speak to a small boy, servant of the Gaul, and he scattered off, mud flying. 'He will get Cassia. Shall we?' I nodded, and we rode to the ship in silence and dismounted. The ship was new, obviously, with fresh paint on its sides, and a happy crew, for they were keen on leaving. There were some sick men covered with blankets, a few wounded legionnaires and an optio with orders and reports, likely the one the tribune was sending to Drusus. The trierarch, a short, stocky man was on the deck, and Lothar climbed a gangplank to him, gesturing at me to stay back. He spoke with the man, a grizzly sailor with a surprisingly clean tunic and gestured at a shoddy structure on the side of the pier. They argued, and Lothar pulled a coin out of his pouch, evidently cursing the man's greed. The trierarch nodded happily and all was made well, apparently.

Lothar clambered back down the gangplank and gestured at me to go inside the building. I turned to walk that way. The two men followed me.

278

'Come! It cost me, but nothing is too good for dear Cassia. You have all your treasure with you? None left behind? I forgot to ask,' he said, and I noticed some panic on his face.

I patted a bulging pouch. 'All here. Gold. So much of it. I'll pay you. Over there?' I said, gesturing to a door in the wooden structure.

'Indeed,' he said, guiding me that way. 'Best you pay me where few see it. It's not a safe place to flaunt gold at, this harbor. And they are not ready to depart. Soon. Hide here so nobody can see you. I know this place very well.' He opened the door for me, smiling at some sailors looking on, and pushed me in. An oil lamp was sputtering on a desk, and I walked over to it as Lothar came in. The room was a dark one, its corners unseen.

But then, I knew the room already.

'You like it?' Lothar asked. 'Homely and dry.'

I nodded as the two men came in with him, their armor jingling. They stood to face me.

Lothar smiled at me as the door closed. 'The pouch, please,' he said, his hand out.

'What do you mean?' I squeaked like a girl.

'I'm robbing you, you damned fool,' he explained.

I looked around, playing scared. 'You did not send anyone for Cassia?'

He shook his head. 'The boy ran on some other errand. I will have Cassia. You will not. She is a proper woman for a man like me. I tried to hump her once, you know? I grabbed her and pulled her over me, but she had a pugio on my throat! Imagine that! But if you are gone, she will need a man to console her. A real man, not a nerveless turd like you. Besides, I will have to deliver you back to whence you came from.'

'To Segestes?' I mouthed, tired with the game. 'You ... you do not work for him?'

'He pays well,' Lothar grinned. 'I was mulling about how to do this, but you solved my problem. You will stay here, cuffed and bound until the night. So you'll live awhile. Be happy!'

I nodded in faked terror, dropped the pouch on the ground. Lothar scowled at me and nodded one of his men to fetch it. The man came forward, leering at my weakness, pulled a sword, and leveled it at me while reaching for the pouch.

'Your helmet, armor—' Lothar began, but was interrupted.

An arrow flew from the dark corner and hit the man with the sword. It shuddered in his eye, and the man fell like a sack. Lothar's mouth was open, his friend cursed and pulled a cudgel and a dagger and charged. They were Batavi. They would not die easily, but I did not care. I pulled my seax and ran for Lothar, ignoring the man coming for me. Agetan emerged from the shadows, grinning like a terrible monster from the dark mountains as he tackled the man with the cudgel to the darkness, and I saw Bohscyld receive him, and together the brothers broke his arms while keeping him silent. Lothar had in the meantime drawn his axes, but his eyes were darting in the darkness, full of fear. He turned, pulled at the door, which opened up as Tudrus pushed in, and Lothar retreated for me. He looked like a cornered, pretty doe as Brimwulf appeared with a cocked arrow from the corner.

'All good?' I asked them all.

'Fulcher is outside, and nobody of importance saw us,' Tudrus said. 'Have to pay the captain to keep him silent. But I suppose this curly fool has coin on him to cover what I promised him, no? What shall we do?' he gestured for Lothar, whose axes were shaking as he looked at Agetan and Bohscyld emerge from the dark, leaving behind a corpse, a man they had killed barehanded.

'I will fight you Lothar,' I said. 'Just you and me. You see, I am not really a gutless turd. And you have made a mistake.'

'I cannot just disappear!' Lothar said, dropping his axes.

'Men disappear all the time. We looked for you. Waiting for you in the tavern. You never showed up,' I said. 'Who is to claim otherwise? I'm sure the Wart won't. And you did try to hump Cassia, right? Pulled her over you? And she healed your cock? Did she?'

He sneered, nervously. 'She did not, and I did not, do not be a fool. I am a Decurion of the turma, and you should consider how my disappearance will look like.'

'You are a lazy thief. Few like you. But you are also a clever one. I might spare you,' I told him coldly, and Tudrus pushed him forward, and I punched him. He flew to the floor, and I placed a seax on his throat as he held his nose, eyes full of terror. 'You know much about Segestes, and his misfortunes at my hands, do you not?' I said, prodding him. 'And mine at his. So, tell me all you know. '

He shook his head. 'I'll not survive if I speak of him!'

I leered at him. 'You have to trust the word of an Oath Breaker right this very moment, cur and not fear rage of Segestes in the future. And I promise you will howl like a dog if you do not speak out. What do you know of Segestes and this village?'

'You wish to know of his men in the village?' he ventured and looked confused. 'But you caught his man in the village.'

I laughed. 'You work for Antius. He pulls the strings of Segestes.'

'I know nothing of that,' he frowned and then nodded vigorously as the seax broke skin. 'Yes. But I am alone here! Nobody else gets paid like I do!'

'Yes?' I asked and pushed the blade on his throat. 'Perhaps I shall believe you. And I hear you dealt for Segestes in the case of Odo. No?'

'Yes,' he whispered. 'He has a man here, as well. I guess you know that, as well.'

'Speak,' I spat, and he did.

The ship sailed with Lothar, for he was ill. He had broken ribs, a dislocated jaw that prevented verbal communication, but he lived. I was made a Decurion of the turma, and I had to save Sigimer. And there was a man who might help me. Reluctantly, but he could.

CHAPTER 25

The winter had blanketed the land with snow. It was near Yuletide and the cohorts had settled in to a comfortable, dull life, getting fat and keeping a lazy eye out for trouble. The tribune had put me in charge of the turma of Batavi, and so I found myself leading twenty-one men, suspicious men at first, but soon happy enough as I put them through much more rigorous duties than Lothar had. Apparently, Lothar had not been very popular, except with the men who were corrupt and evil, and we had dealt with both. I quickly found out that one of the two men we had killed had been the duplicarius, a double pay man and what in turma was the same as an optio in a century of legionnaires. A sesquiplicarius, a one and a half pay man, had been the other one. In effect, we had killed the under officers of the turma. So, I had only a signifier, a standard-bearer with the unit standard to help me out, and he was a young, brave man, with an easy grin, white teeth and no beard. His name was Hund. I chose two of the brightest men to take the under officers' places, and they were happy with taking some of my duties for the extra pay, and it was so easy for Lothar's legacy to be forgotten.

Our routine was simple. Half the men would ride patrols, half would train and fix gear, and I got to learn how much time leading a group of men took. It took me a week to settle into the duty and to plan my next steps. In a week's time, I found Tudrus and sat him down. 'Friend. How do you like a Roman castra?'

'It is … organized, I suppose,' he allowed and saw my face. 'I hate the morning wake up and the meager breakfast. But I guess you really wanted to ask me something else? What is it?'

'Do you like the town?' I asked him with some intensity.

'No Germani likes the town.' He frowned. 'It's filthy and full of mongrels. Wait. You are going after this man of Odo next? Right?'

'He is the key to Odo.' I grinned.

'What did he tell you about the man?' Tudrus said with a frown. 'He was whispering and you never told us.'

'Well, his name is Oril. Have you heard of Oril when you have visited the filth of the town?' He shook his head though I detected there was a brief frown of worry on his face. 'You sure?' He smirked weakly.

'I have seen one Oril,' he told me very reluctantly. 'And I doubt there are many. And you know where I have seen him.'

'Yes,' I agreed. 'I know.'

He blushed. 'I was curious.'

'A whorehouse can be a curious affair. There was one in Castra Vetera, as well. But I merely drank in there.'

'I also only drink in there,' he said fiercely. 'That a woman would subject herself to such a–'

'They all terrible creatures, eh?' I inquired with a sweet voice.

'Well, yes!' he huffed, his lean face clouded. He was trying to rip his newly grown beard, but noticed I smiled at that and gave up on it. 'No. There are some that are. Most are just, women.'

'Sad victims of the war, no?' I asked him.

'But …' he breathed. 'Their honor.'

'They are people. And Oril, the owner is Odo's man.'

He blinked. 'I wish you had told me Oril is Odo's man,' he growled. 'I would have been visiting some other tavern.'

'I was planning,' I answered. 'And it is a good thing you have been curious. He knows you.'

'Barely,' he frowned. 'I have visited the place and enjoyed the wine they offer.'

'If there were trouble, someone might help clean the house?' I asked him. 'We will need to get close to Oril.'

'Oh!' he nodded. 'I see. I'll be sitting there and toss out some scum you pay to make trouble. I assume you pay them to take a beating?'

'That would work, no? Especially if one drew blade on Oril? And perhaps punched him. He would be scared and grateful. Such things bond men.'

'It might,' he agreed. 'But I don't want to be bound with Oril.'

I grinned and whistled. Hund, the signifier entered the room. He was a sturdy lad and had jumped to help us out. I leaned on Tudrus. 'Hund will make friends with Oril. You take the punch. They know you, no? They will know you rode in with me.'

He scowled. 'Oh?'

'I thought you hated the place?' I said, surprised.

He grimaced. 'Why don't we just take Oril to the woods and find out what we want?'

'He might not be alone in the village,' I told him. 'Cannot risk going after Odo if the bastard is waiting for us. We have to know Oril. His friends, if he has any. And it is winter, and we have time.'

'I see,' he growled. 'I suppose that makes sense.'

'So, will you make trouble there?' I asked him with a small grin.

'Will I be able to spend time there after?' he asked so softly I could not hear him.

'What?' I asked, smiling.

He hit the table so hard our armor and weapons fell off it. Hund smiled again, wider. He had the strangest grin, wide and full of white teeth. 'You bastard, Hraban. You know I want to go there.'

I pushed him with a mischievous grin. 'You fake.'

'My soul is burning with the shame, Hraban,' he said with a thin smile and slumped. 'What else do you know?'

'Agetan spoke to Cassia,' I told him with a roaring laugh. 'You seem to be getting on with the girl preparing the food. Pretty thing, no?'

'Agetan?' he asked me with confusion. 'He doesn't speak. Neither does Bohscyld. What are you talking about?'

'They speak to Cassia,' I told him and clapped a hand on his shoulders. 'This evening, Hund there will get too friendly with her. You will be unhappy about that and make trouble. She is still your girl, Tudrus, but Hund will toss you out. You will see the girl later, yes, but at Wart's. And Hund will be loved by Oril.'

'Donor's balls,' he breathed, his face red. 'Hund had better not touch her improperly!'

Hund laughed. 'I'll sit her on my lap. And you throw me down, then attack Oril, and I will kick you in the ass. Make it look good. Gerhild is a fine girl and all yours.'

'She is just a friend,' Tudrus said with a blush.

'For now.' I laughed.

'Shut up. I'll suffer this duty for the girl. When, and let it be soon, we will confront Oril, what shall we wish to know?' he asked me. 'Of this Gulldrum?'

I nodded. 'It's not a hall. It's a cave. We have to know what is in there. And if Odo is in there as well. And Sigimer. That way we will have one thing less to worry about in the spring. And I have kept my word to Thusnelda.'

'I'm not sure I like this new Hraban, the one keeping oaths,' Tudrus complained.

'I hate him,' I told him.

So, Hund made friends and Tudrus took a beating.

Oril, who turned out to be of the Chauci tribe and the seedy man, had indeed been grateful for brave Hund, who saved him from Tudrus, who had pulled a pugio at the whore master. And soon, Oril paid Hund to keep the place in order during the evenings, but Tudrus met his girl at the Wart's place after hours. During the winter, Cassia listened to Hund speaking of the girls. 'One is fat and quite smart, very smart, in fact,' the merry Batavi said in wonderment. 'Never thought they might be smart. I mean, you know? Most are thin and only get fed if they bring in enough silver. I hope we deal with this Oril soon. Or you? I don't know how I figure in your plans.'

'You've earned a place to die for Hraban's mad plans,' Tudrus laughed from the side. 'Gerhild safe?'

'She is,' Hund said. 'Oril barely notices her. She cleans and none bother her.'

'Not even ...' Tudrus began.

'Not even I,' Hund grinned. 'But I hate that man. Hate him. I'd like to rinse my signum in his anus but that would dishonor it, would it not?' he wondered. 'The signum, I mean,' he added.

Fulcher grunted. 'There will be other Orils, soon enough. Men want girls. Girls need copper and silver and so they will need someone to make it all happen and someone who protects them.'

'How much copper do you give them?' Brimwulf asked Fulcher irascibly.

'I don't visit the place,' Fulcher told the archer woodenly, glowering at him.

'I give them food, not silver,' Hund sniffled. 'It's enough Decurion Hraban asks me to frequent the place, but I cannot bear to see what is happening to them. There are Batavi and Romans visiting them, and while most treat the girls fine, it is dishonorable. I miss home.'

I snapped my finger at Hund. 'Start telling him how much you hate me. I am a bully, slave driving thief and the men hate me. Loath even. You would love nothing more than to stab me in the ass. Or gut.'

Hund raised his eyebrow and nodded reluctantly. 'You want me to lie?'

'You can pretend to clobber Tudrus, but you cannot lie?' I asked him with incredulity. 'What if Oril asks you if you are in league with me?'

'He won't, Hund said sullenly. 'And we are doing this to free your daughter? This Odo is out to hurt her?' *I had not told him enough*, I realized.

The others glanced at me murderously. 'Yes, that is one reason,' I told him.

'There is something else, right?' he asked, his face confused. 'But that's fine. The boys like you, and I'm happy you trust me. So, I'll lie for you. I will. And if he bites?'

'Odo wants me,' I grinned. 'Let us see if he still does.'

'Try to keep Gerhild out of it,' Tudrus grunted at us.

'What would your father say about this Gerhild?' I chided him.

He sighed and held his head. 'Father and Mother. They would whip me.'

'Is she noble and … how did you put it? High?' I teased him, and he pelted me with a log.

'Good for you,' Cassia grinned, and Tudrus smiled tentatively.

'Brimwulf?' I said and nodded him closer. I leaned over him.

'You want me to find his place? Odo's?' Brimwulf stated. 'Near the Buck? Yes?'

'I hope Oril will eventually spill his guts on what is waiting for us inside. But we will have to find it,' I told him. 'You and Fulcher should go and see what is going on there when the snows allow. I need you to find their haunt.'

Brimwulf sniffled. 'I will find Odo's place. Easy enough. Keep Fulcher here. He would make a mess of it. Stumbling over branches and his spear.'

'I can stay. Mathildis likes my company,' Fulcher said viciously from the side, and the two eyed each other angrily.

'Can you both go, please? And both come back?' I bashed my hand on the desk, and they agreed with reluctant nods.

So, during that winter Hund visited the brothel, complained like a drunk, made sure everyone knew he hated me. I had robbed him, humiliated him, he had no future in the riders, and he had once been a lord of the Batavi. So he drank to my death, for many an evening.

And slowly, Oril began to believe him.

In the meantime, Brimwulf and Fulcher rode the lands to the east.

We waited. Yuletide came, and we celebrated it, thanking Hercules, Woden and quite a few gods, for not all of the men were native Batavi. Some were Gauls, and things could get confusing when men toasted their divines. We celebrated, drank, ate, and patrolled, and enjoyed life as best we could. The Romans celebrated Divalia in honor of the goddess Angerona, a festival for happiness and mirth, and the two celebrations mixed just fine.

Brimwulf and Fulcher rode out when the weather was mild and always came back together.

Then, one day Fulcher pulled at me. 'We found it.'

'Where?' I asked, excited.

'It's an hour away from the ford of Buck River. We rode past it many times, but then we spotted a hunter of theirs and followed him. It's a low hill, very hard to see.'

'Show me, soon. Now, there is something else I need.'

Fulcher listened to me and nodded, smiling.

I rode out with Cassia one month after Yuletide, for we had had precious little time together. I pulled her to my horse and buried my face in her hair, and we did not speak as I guided the Moon to a wooded hill above the castra. A serene fir wood hid the hill, thick and evergreen as I took the horse deeper and higher and there, in the middle of the wood was a snow covered well, and beyond the well a sturdy, small hall. I guided the horse to the front of the hall and jumped off. I smiled up at her.

'Inside? I smell meat roasting!' she said with wonder, but I shook my head as I sat down on a boulder. Fulcher stepped out from the house, smiling at me. He took the bridle from Cassia and nodded at me.

'What is going on? Are you going to murder me?' Cassia asked, smiling.

'Not today, love,' I told her and took off my caligae, and the snow began to sting my feet, even through the socks. I took them off, as well. 'This is how you Celts do it?' I asked her as I indicated my feet.

She looked at me as if I was mad as a hare. 'Do what? Get sick? You are standing in the snow, you damned fool.'

I laughed at her and stood up calf deep in snow. 'I asked the Wart Face. He is a Gaul. He said he has never been captured like this, but he also told me it should be done in the woods, barefooted. That is the way a man and a woman make ties to each other.'

Cassia's eyes were large as eggs.

I grunted as the cold started to get uncomfortable. 'He told me that there are several ways to marry. Some make a deal, where property is exchanged, and I have no property. Another way to marry is to agree you are a husband and wife when children are born. Gods know I don't want to wait that long to call you wife. There is the simpler ritual of hand fasting that can be performed before the actual marriage, and I say we do this, then I shall take you in and by morning, we are married. Fulcher?' Fulcher tied the horse to a bough and came forth with a linen wrap, carefully eying us.

Cassia was taking deep breaths and then calmed herself after a visible struggle. She shook her head. 'The Wart Face knows precious little about marriages, it seems. But it matters not. You are, essentially, proposing to me?'

I shrugged. 'Yes, of course. I love you. You are the stone in my life that I cling to.'

'I sound harsh and uncomfortable, cold and abrasive,' she chided me with a scowl.

I waved my hands at her in denial. 'You know what I mean. Now I don't know if this is a proper Celtic wedding or not, but a wedding it is. It could be a Germani wedding where I just ride off with you, but I have things to do here in the spring and summer so would you just say yes.' I grinned and shivered, and I noticed the cold was making my feet blue.

'Will I be happy with you?' she asked with mock concern, ticking her finger on her tooth. 'So far I have been running away from tribes of angered Germani and mad vitka and then worried myself to death as you learnt of honor and love. And then last year you were idiotic enough to disappear. Hmm.'

'I hope I manage to make you smile once a day, at least,' I said, rubbing my feet together. 'I will try to build you a life worth living. Unless I die in the year.'

'Die,' she breathed. 'Or I.'

'Never,' I told her.

I pulled the Winter Sword and thrust it in the snow. 'In Woden, All-Father's name I make an oath to you. If, this year I shall not kill Father—'

'Hold,' she said softly, and I stammered. 'Say rather "deal" with Father. Perhaps, after all, you will not kill him.'

'What? He must die!'

'Is your father, Hraban,' she said sadly.

289

'I ...' I began and shook my head in simmering anger but defeated the vaettir shrieking in my mind to deny her words. I calmed myself and did as she asked. 'Deal with Father and his men, deal with Odo, deal with Antius and Cornix and Catualda. I shall, this summer deal with any man who stood against me, even lord of the land, Segestes. Let them all be here, and let gods guide my sword, this sword, and I shall pledge over it I will abandon all my oaths that are unfulfilled by the summer's end. We shall follow Drusus and this ... Winter Sword shall not come with us. My family is gone, this sword was theirs, but you are my family now and so pledge I will serve you over me. I'll abandon this thing.'

'And shall you serve me over Drusus? Never again wage war?' she asked sadly.

'I cannot,' I said softly and shook my head. My feet were near white, but I shrugged. 'He is a good man.'

'He is a Roman patrician, a high lord in war and politics of Rome, and he will use you like your father did,' she pointed out. 'But I agree he is a good man. Sometimes that man rises over the mean and dirty needs of his world and those times we can be happy.' She was tense, obviously thinking hard, but finally she giggled and shrugged. 'You know, one's feet are indeed supposed to touch the ground while doing this, but I think even Celts have shoes in the winter, if they marry then. Most marry in the summer for this reason. But I shall let that pass.'

'It is not ill luck there is snow on the ground, is it?' Fulcher asked with a frown. 'Should we dig until there is mud?'

I nodded, grimacing. 'I cannot walk, so can you dig?'

She shook her head and pulled off her shoes, jumped down to me, and we held each other's hands. She snapped her finger at Fulcher, who chuckled in pity for me and came forward and wrapped our hands together with a linen strip of cloth, smiled and walked off to his horse. We stood there until the bitter cold started to get too painful for Cassia. 'You ready to give up?' she said giggling.

'I can't feel them, so it's no problem if you want to stand here a moment longer,' I told her with chattering teeth.

290

'Best go in then, so you won't lose the feeling in anything else,' she told me and laughed as we grabbed our footwear and ran inside. I fell a few times, cursing the tingling feeling in my toes and then we were under the low, overhanging roof when she turned my head to her. She kissed me. She did so for a long time, and when she was done, her silvery eyes regarded me. She said: 'My blood is yours, yours is mine.'

I nodded. 'Mine is yours; yours mine.'

We were married.

'There had better be food and drink in here,' she told me as she pushed in. There was, Fulcher had arranged it well and had kept Bohscyld and Agetan far from the ale. We spent a night there, and in the morning returned to Castra Flamma, our hand fasting turned to marriage by what we did in the darkness of the night. I was oath bound again and touched the sword on my side. I would let it go and felt both pain and relief at the thought of it.

When I rode to the gate, saluting the guards, Hund grinned and came to me.

'Where have you been?' he hissed, eyeing the guards.

'Sir,' I said, and he glowered at me. I leaned down and whispered. 'You are supposed to hate me, and so you can call me sir. None of the others do.'

'Where the hell have you been sir,' he said loudly and leaned closer. 'Oril is making plans for you, Lord. And a man or two arrived today. They had an extra horse. With a saddle. Looked strange.'

'The horse?' I asked him.

'The men! Joyless and dour both of them,' he told me. 'Look, I don't want to be seen talking to you. But Oril spoke to them. I overheard them.' There was an excited note in his voice, and as Hund glanced around, I saw he was evidently enjoying his double-faced operation.

'Anyone from the castra or the village giving him special attention?' I asked him. 'Anyone he speaks with?'

'No. Plenty of men speak with him, but he does not give any special attention,' he told me. 'There two did, however, get rooms. Look out, some of the Batavi.' I noticed two men walk around the corner and wave at me.

I ignored them, spat at Hund's feet and harassed him like a Decurion would the most useless man in his command. He glowered back, and then I spoke to him again. 'They got rooms?'

'They did,' he said. 'And I think there are more than just two. They mentioned names and this castra.'

I cursed. 'That will complicate things.'

'If you don't want to have Odo prepared for you, sir, then you had better know all your foes,' he said.

'So what did you hear?' I asked.

'Oril told the men he would produce the package this spring, and they should sit tight,' he whispered. 'They are to lead the package away. Guides, they are.'

'How did you learn of this? Surely he did not speak like this in front of the customers?'

He looked bothered. 'I know the whores. They have holes in every wall, and they gossip. They keep the holes secret because they look out for each other.'

'And they told you?' I asked, incredulously.

'They told me; they trust me,' he said, strangely proud. 'They are like cats. They hate Oril, but even if I get paid by the man, they have a hunch I don't like him.'

I walked to the side with him and continued our discussion in the shadows. 'You sure you have not told the girls anything? Oril trusts you?'

He huffed. 'The girls are noble. Many are. There are so many nobles here in the east, I don't know how they manage to command their armies. And such girls are very smart. They smell treason, and some have a hunch Oril is in trouble. Or perhaps I just glower at the man's back so much. I know the girls very well.' He blushed.

'They probably hope you will take over the establishment.' I sighed.

He shook his head. 'I've said nothing. And yes, Oril trusts me because he is an idiot, but only to a degree. Later, after he spoke with the two men, he told me he has a job for me, one with silver involved. I drooled,' he said. 'Then I nodded. He told me I would enjoy the job.'

I laughed, looking around and making sure none saw us. 'Make sure you remember I'm your friend.'

Hund snorted. 'He told me it would be months, early spring, but I should be ready. They will act the day the armies of Drusus are near.'

I paused. 'Why then? That will make it very hard for us to take on Odo. They will expect us to soldier for Drusus.'

Hund looked bothered. 'The Batavi are twenty men. Who will miss them? We might very well ride out, and who knows what orders you have received, eh?'

'I can lie to the Tribune, but I would not like to lie to the men,' I told him morosely.

He leaned forward. 'Chariovalda trusts you. The Batavi do as well. They will fight for a good cause.' I nodded at him, cursing Thusnelda's request. *The men would not take kindly to freeing Sigimer.* I clapped his shoulder, unsure what to do.

In the spring, late spring or early summer we would settle it all. I stroked the Winter Sword and tried to learn patience. Oril had taken the bait. But we had to wait.

CHAPTER 26

It was end of Martius and the snows had partly melted. We had sent scouts around to the south, but I had taken some men to the east. We sat on our horses, Fulcher and I, in the wooded hills near the Buck River. Up to the south in the low mountains of the Chatti, a smoke pillar rose up to the sky, and it was the same all over the land. People were out and about. The snow had been replaced by mud of drab brown and grey color though grass was starting to push up in many places.

But we were looking for a specific pillar of smoke.

'There, up there,' Fulcher said and pointed his spear to a craggy patch of a hillside, high up on a hill, with the river winding its way around it. An eagle was flying around it, and there was a track leading up. He looked sour as he continued. 'That is what Brimwulf calls a bear hole. It looks almost like that of an animal's abode, but it's not. He managed to get close enough to glimpse inside. There is a stone laden hall, right inside the doorway, and sort of a stable, at least a temporary place they hold horses at,' he said, and I spied Brimwulf sneaking around in the woods. Mathildis was pregnant and happy. And Cassia had been feeling sick that past month. Gods help Brimwulf and me, though I had been through pregnancy with Ishild once. Unlike Ishild, Cassia was happy as a sparrow in the spring.

'Why do you dislike him so much?' I asked him.

'I don't trust him,' he said simply. 'I have a hunch he is not honest. He is hiding something.'

'But you cannot prove anything?' I asked him. 'He could have killed me.'

'I am not saying he is not loyal,' he explained, brushing his long hair aside. 'But I am not sure he is loyal to us. He is mysterious. Silent and secretive.'

'You used to be silent and condescending. You still are condescending, in fact,' I grunted. 'And you are jealous of his skills.'

'My son died. Briscius's head cured me,' he explained and then looked bothered. 'Granted, Brimwulf is a great scout. But it is more than being jealous, Hraban. Listen. At the end of the hallway, there is a doorway, leading down. How far down, none knows. If they have him still, they will hold Sigimer down there, but it is a blind shuffle in the dark though there are likely holes to bring in light, and they use torches, of course. Brimwulf says he spied some light on the bottom the other night.'

'Odo wanted me for Sigimer,' I told him. 'Sigimer is there. Too valuable to waste, even if I ended Lothar and Segestes's plans. Oril has been given the order to fetch me, but I doubt he would throw Sigimer in a hole to rot,' I said with confidence I hardly felt and nodded. 'We must return. Oril will know more. And he is making his move soon.' Hund had told me they had been speaking a lot more lately, the bastard and the two men of Odo's.

'The Tribune must worry,' Fulcher agreed. 'We have been out here in the snow for a week.'

I shook my head. 'I told the Tribune that there was a rumor of a brewing rebellion in this area, and we would scout it out, but yes, we will go home. Did Brimwulf see through any of the holes in the hill?' I asked.

Fulcher shook his head. 'No. The light was too high, and he was afraid they had guards in the woods. Below, he might have spied a door. Poor Sigimer. Gods know if Odo is casting spells on him.'

I shuddered. 'My brother? Gernot. Any sign of him?'

He said nothing.

'Fulcher?'

He nodded, sighing. 'Not sure. No man with one hand. He might be dead. He never was truly useful to Odo after he no longer spied on you.'

'Ishild?' I asked, feeling strangely upset if Odo had killed Gernot.

'No sign of a pretty blonde woman either. Nor of Odo's small boy,' he told me risibly, shaking his head. I had asked every day we had been out there. 'If Ishild only wanted to keep her son safe and left us for him, then how will you deal with it if we get Lif and Ishild both back? Keeping a daughter from her mother is not kind.'

'You will fetch your family, Fulcher, soon. That way you need not worry about mine,' I said brusquely. He went quiet, and I shook my head in apology. A weak apology, but one nonetheless. He clapped my shoulder.

'I will. After the spring.' He grinned weakly. 'I miss them. And yes, you will have to deal with your family issues.'

Brimwulf walked to us from the left side. 'They have patrols and guards up there. Fairly relaxed lot.'

I grunted. 'We will take Oril prisoner and find out all we can. The two men of Oril's must fall as well, and we have to make sure all Odo's men are slain in the town. Then I shall steal the turma of Batavi and send these sons of whores to Hel. But I will want to know ways out of there and what is in. Can't afford to have them escape.'

We returned to Castra Flamma to find a ship in the harbor.

That was like a wakeup call for the castra and the legionnaires. The Tribune was on his horse, soldiers parading and training, for spring was truly coming, and war was nigh again. I guided my horse there, and the Tribune nodded at me. Lucius was standing by the Tribune, grinning at the fat merchant vessel as it moored. Sailors jumped to the planking and pulled the ship closer. A dirty, strong man was carrying a gangplank and oars were being pulled in. A horde of amphora could be seen in the hold.

'Wine, by Mars,' Lucius was saying.

'News, by Woden,' I smiled at him.

'Wine and news, my friends,' Paellus agreed.

'Any news, sir,' I asked the Tribune. 'Of Nero Claudius Drusus?'

'I am here to get news, Decurion,' he said irascibly and then shrugged. 'I am sure he will be warring soon,' the Tribune said languidly. 'I Germanica and XIX will again be burning the Sigambri and Tencteri settlements and our XVII cohorts of Castra Alisio will be in action against the Sigambri soon enough. Did you see anything out there?'

'No,' I said. 'They are asleep and docile. False alarm.'

He smiled at me like a ghost would, and I was not sure he had listened to me. His eyes were staring at the ship, and then he rose up on his horse. We saw there was an official looking man carrying a bag of scrolls. 'Orders. Here we are. Excuse me, Decurion.' He rode forward.

I leaned on Lucius. 'Doesn't he have a scribe to fetch these things?'

Lucius leaned on me and whispered. 'Probably begs to find a scroll ordering him home.'

I grinned and raised my voice so Paellus could hear me. 'Any from Drusus?' I asked him, anxious to see the orders.

He smiled as he received them in a bag, eyeing the lot. 'I will call you if there is. Do not worry. I sent him a warning last year. Does not mean he would send something back immediately.' He nodded at the courier. 'I'll send my reports with you before the ship leaves in the afternoon,' he told the clean shaved man. Fulcher sat next to me as we eyed the unloading of the ship.

Lucius stepped up. 'Is there a scroll for me, sir?'

'For you?' the Tribune asked, confused. 'You write, Centurion?'

'A girl, sir,' Lucius smiled.

'I will leave them in the hands of the officia, Centurion, after I pick out mine,' he scowled, 'but fine.' He rifled through the scrolls and glanced at the Centurion. 'I am sorry, Lucius. She probably has someone to warm her bed.'

'That is fine,' Lucius said evenly. 'She was too expensive anyway.' The Tribune snorted and left.

Fulcher shook his head and stared at the ship as it was a center of mad bustle. A man was windmilling in the prow and fell to the river. They set up to save the fool and men were wagering on their success. I glanced at Lucius, who was scratching his neck, and I saw he was hesitant. 'Yes, Centurion?' I said.

'I like you boys,' he said.

'I'm married,' I told him drolly. 'But ask Fulcher.'

'You are too hairy for me, Hraban, and he has no hips,' he said grinning. 'But I did send your scroll last year.'

'I thank you for that,' I answered. 'And you have been writing with this girl before?'

'All of the past year,' he agreed. 'She always answered before. She is a Gaul noble, a Roman citizen, and we have gotten along very well. I put your scroll in mine, asked her to take it to this Chariovalda and now? She does not answer.' Lucius looked very glum.

'Someone searches the scrolls,' I told him. 'There is a plot against Nero Claudius Drusus and so, I think, there is a fat bastard in Castra Vetera who somehow gets hold of all the orders. This man is called Antius.'

Lucius looked unhappy. 'It could be she used it to wipe her rear. But I think she loves me and does not wipe her rear very often anyway. You have put me in a bit of a danger, Hraban.' He scowled briefly and smiled. 'I'll settle them should they come for me, I've been in trouble before. I think you should be worried, Hraban. This Antius is keeping an eye on the castra and will know you are here, so you are probably in danger.'

My eyes went to slits, and I nodded gravely, staring at the official looking man, who was fetching his gear. 'Perhaps he has taken the Tribune's scroll, as well. Or perhaps ...' I was thinking hard and felt shivers of doubt as I considered our plight. I turned to Fulcher. 'You think you could ask that man if he would see me? Just ask him to visit me before he sails. Make sure it is after he has received the reports from the Tribune.'

'Yes, I can,' Fulcher said happily, his eye glinting. 'I'll take Agetan with me.'

'That should do it.' I grinned and moved away, clapping Lucius on the shoulder.

Later that day, the man came to me. I was sitting in Wart's tavern, drinking, and he popped his face in. He was carrying a sack, and the ship was about to leave. 'Hello?' he asked from the doorway. He was a Gaul by the accent and sniffled as he spoke. I saw Agetan's wide shadow behind him. 'You asked for me?'

'Yes, I did,' I told him and nodded at the bench before me. 'Sit.'

'The ship is leaving, Decurion, and I—'

'Sit,' I growled, Agetan grunted, and the man was seated in no time. His blond hair was quivering as he apparently held misgivings about Wart Face, who served him ale from a relatively clean horn. It was a great favor to me, for the Wart rarely washed the plates and the mugs. 'So,' I stated and leaned closer to him.

'Lord?' he said, not touching the ale.

'You brought the Tribune scrolls today?' I stated.

'Yes, of course. That is my function,' he nodded.

'What, pray tell me, did you bring him?'

He thought about denying my request and telling me to go to Hel, but then I saw he considered the sanctity of his bones and joints, for he saw a hard man who likely would not back down. And I would not. He looked around, and Wart Face had cleared the tavern, and we were alone. The man noticed it as well and went white as snow. 'Reports. Orders,' he whispered.

'Reports of the happenings of the wide, wonderful world?'

'Yes. I can tell you some if you like?' he suggested helpfully.

'Please,' I whispered.

'Nero Claudius Drusus is a Consul,' he said happily.

'I suppose that is a great thing,' I nodded.

He blinked his eyes for a bit. 'It is a great honor. And the Consul Nero Claudius Drusus and the Legions of Moganticum, far to the south are cutting a bloody path through Chatti lands for us. They aim to burn Mattium, the Chatti oppidum, and then they will come here to finish with the Cherusci.'

'The XIII Gemina and XIV Gallica Legions? I see,' I told him. 'Was there anything from Chariovalda? Or even a simple scroll for Lucius? To anyone?'

'No, nothing from this man, and nothing to this Lucius,' he told me carefully. 'The Batavi won't be here anyway. Most of them will fight the Sigambri this year.'

'Any personal note from the Consul to one Hraban or the Tribune?' I asked.

'None,' he said, looking puzzled. 'The Consul would write you?'

I ignored his puzzlement. 'Was one sent from the Tribune to Drusus, the legates of the legions, or Chariovalda last fall?' I snarled.

He began to sweat. 'I cannot remember there was one for the Consul or Chariovalda,' he said, sorry to disappoint me, and afraid to, as well. 'Only supply requests to Castra Vetera. That last ship last fall brought simple reports on manpower.'

I nodded as I had been afraid of that answer. 'And you work in Castra Vetera and take all the orders and go over the lot?' Fulcher asked from the side, having sneaked in.

'Yes, I am sure I would have seen all of them. We take copies of most before they are sent forward.'

I sat still, and he absentmindedly tasted the ale and went white of face. He smiled and shrugged at the terrible brew, looking ready to heave his innards. With a nod, I indicated he was spared from the ordeal, and so he unhappily sat there, the ale in his trembling hands. I mulled over our issues and then my eyes settled on his sack. His eyes followed mine.

'What did he send?' I asked the man.

'Pardon me?'

'The Tribune. What did he send? Now. To whom?' I asked slowly. The man licked his lips nervously.

'Same as before. Reports on the activity here. Supply requests, mostly wine, and wheat, I think.'

'Supply requests?' I asked sweetly. 'Who is dealing with the supplies?'

'The negotiatores?' he said softly. 'There is always one for the negotiatores.'

'What is in that scroll? Exactly? What was in it last year?' I asked with a tilted head, my patience wearing thin.

'Ah, let me correct my earlier statement,' he said with some embarrassment. 'Those we do not open up. They say these are too minor requests to bother taking copies of. I find that strange, since supply issues are always topics for debate, later as they count the budgets and ...'

I made an animal-like grunt, and he flinched. 'Unless you wish to drink down every last drop of that rat piss, you will tell me this. Is there a scroll there now for one Antius the Negotiotare?'

'Antius?' he told me. 'This fat man? Someone hung him, did you know?'

'Yes,' I grinned

'There is,' he said dejectedly, staring at the dark ale to remind himself that duty was not above all. 'You wish to see it, then? I am sure it is nothing but requests for garum, wine, more wheat and a list of supplies that are needed now after the winter is over.'

'Here,' I told him and ripped the sack towards me. 'Show me.'

He pointed out a scroll and looked mildly hopeful. 'Can you read Latin?'

'I can,' I told him as I tore out the scroll bound around wooden rollers. I rolled it open in front of me and read it.

"From Paellus to Antius, greetings.

As you feared, he has spent the winter settling to the leadership of the Batavi. He had ousted my man before I knew what was happening.

I have been working with Segestes and trying to explain to him it is not possible to just send Hraban back. He has been seen, and it would be very risky to kill him. He will have to be dealt with discreetly, here with his men. I, of course, understand his concern that Hraban will reveal the part of Segestes being allied with Maroboodus on our great goal. There is, however, a way to control Hraban and it will serve Segestes well. This Odo will get his due, and Segestes will get Sigimer and this ridiculous ring, after all, and our shifty Cherusci ally can relax. The plan is moving.

As for Nero Claudius Drusus, and with Hraban silent and brooding, we will proceed with the plans of slaying the Consul. And again, do not worry. I know this Decurion is a slippery fuck, but he will be soft as an egg very soon.

Your servant and friend, tribune, Paullus Ahenobarbus."

I snorted at the scribe and played with the scroll. Then I rolled it up and placed it on the table. I snapped my fingers at him, and he got up, lightning fast. 'Drusus is coming here then, unaware of all that is taking place. Take your leave, and if you mention this meeting to anyone, I shall have my boys drown you in such ale as this.' I tapped his abandoned horn. 'The scroll stays with me. There is no request for supplies here, anyway. Just a very personal note.'

'No, Lord, I shall be quiet. And I have no cock in any fight you might be having with the Tribune and fat traders.'

'You will go back to the Tribune, and then you will ask for a new one. You lost this scroll; it fell to the river,' I instructed him.

'I see,' he said, a calculating look on his face.

I growled at him and the look dissappeared. 'Know there are men watching you. Fail to keep you mouth shut, and I will tell people you know of treason against the Consul. Against Drusus, who is my friend. I will tell the Batavi to find you if some unhappy event takes place.' He blanched and opened his mouth, but left in a hurry.

I watched Fulcher carefully. 'They will make a move for me just before Drusus is here. We will be ready. Oril will invite me over, and then we will fight it out. Paellus was Lothar's commander. A treason at the highest level. I want you to ride to the Consul when we go and kill Odo. You are to warn him and take this scroll to him. It is a proof of treason. Something he always desired. A cause for war.'

'I was away from your side when you rode east,' he grumbled. 'And now again, you ask me to go.'

'I ask you, for you are like a brother to me. And Drusus knows you.'

He hesitated and nodded, taking the scroll. 'As you will, Hraban. Let it be so. But I no longer see myself dying old in my bed.'

I rubbed my face to dismiss his fears. 'We wait a while longer. They will move soon,' I said and thought of the lost winter. Paellus was with Antius. Antius had bottled up Luppia River. *How many other were traitors as well?*

CHAPTER 27

Spring turned to summer, and Hund reported nothing.

I seethed, for Oril was laying low, apparently waiting for Drusus, who was a Consul that year and Tudrus, I think, was entirely in love with his Gerhild. Cassia was heavy with a baby and worked far too hard though Mathildis helped her. Brimwulf was also happy, for Mathildis and Cassia found support in each other in their pregnant state, and he did not have to bear the whole burden.

I was nervous.

The Batavi scouted south, and we had many small skirmishes with the Sigambri. We lost a man and buried him, and the Sigambri lost many as the Luppia legions were making life hard for them to the east. There were rumors of a great battle in the south and the Chatti capital of Mattium having been burned. Some said Oldaric and Adgandestrius, father and son, the great Chatti had been slain, others claimed they had escaped with most of their army. Some said Father had died in the wars in the south. There were rumors of the Consul on his way to us, but as Junius arrived, I began to wonder if I could keep my promise to Cassia after all.

I despaired and hated the rumors.

Maroboodus, Catualda, Segestes, Antius, and Cornix. All alive. Odo. Not to mention Odo. I began to make plans for a raid to Odo's hold in any case and decided I would soon torture Oril for any information he might have.

Then, on the first week of Junius, the Batavi spotted smoke pillars to the south. I gathered the turma and riding that way, we ran across Thracian and Noricum cavalry that was screening the XIII Gemina and XIV Gallia. A burly, dusty man got down from his saddle as he noticed our Roman gear. He was a clean-shaven Thracian and scowled.

'Batavi? Or shall we spear you?'

'Batavi,' I answered brusquely. I raised my hand at him. 'A turma of 2nd Batavorium, from Castra Flamma. You are half a day from the castra.'

He was nodding and speaking with his men, some of whom turned back. He then eyed us.

'Thank you. We have been trekking through the forests, chasing an army of Chatti we routed a month ago. They are truly scattered. They are heading for the higher lands to the northeast, some thousands of families. Have you seen any?' he asked.

'No, not seen them. Where is Drusus going?' I asked. 'Castra Flamma?'

He pointed a finger at me. 'Consul Nero Claudius Drusus. Remember that if he passes you. He was made a consul for this year, and will end the war this year.'

'I remember,' I told him. 'So he is coming?'

'Will meet Segestes near Bhugnos River. Then we shall go and hunt Armin and Inguiomerus together. Come back and burn anything the Chatti still have.'

'The Marcomanni?' I asked him.

He shrugged, confused. 'Routed some of them early spring. Haven't seen any since. Now, lead us there.'

Fulcher leaned on me. 'Should I go?' he clapped the bag on his side.

I hesitated and looked at the Thracians. They were a somber lot, irascible, and I did not trust them. 'Go. But take your own route. We will see you soon again, Fulcher. Very soon, my friend.'

'Yes, Hraban,' he said, embraced me, and so I nodded as he waved his hand, riding to the woods. We guided the Thracians to Castra Flamma.

Cassia came out of the castra, her hands bloody. She had been dealing with a spear wound. 'Is he coming?'

'Drusus? Yes.' I gazed at her with love and nodded. 'I've asked two Batavi to stay close to you.' I nodded at two young men who seemed very eager to do so. Their long blond beards shuddered as they nodded at her fiercely, and both smiled. She nodded at them wryly.

'I've seen them,' she said. 'Handsome boys,' she teased me, but her voice was serious. 'Paullus will know the Consul is coming and so …' She stopped speaking and stared at me.

'Yes,' I said. 'They will move now. It is time for the summer's oaths. Stay far from the Tribune.'

She nodded. 'I won't be fooled. I hope never to see your sword again.' She smiled sadly. 'Be careful, love.' I nodded at her as she left, shadowed by two young Batavi.

Paullus walked idly to the gate, glancing at her go. 'Decurion?'

'Sir,' I said woodenly. 'The Consul is coming.' I nodded at the Thracians, who were sending men back to guide the leading elements of the legions.

His eyes grew large, and he licked his lips. 'Thank you Decurion. The camp prefect will kick the men into shape in no time. I am missing some of the centurions. I know where they are. In the taverns. I will get them. But you have to get your men ready.' He cocked his head at me.

'Yes, of course, Tribune,' I told him. 'I will get the turma ready.'

'You have been lax in your duty,' he told me crossly. 'Your men hang around in whorehouses.'

Here we go, I thought. 'Yes, sir,' I told him, eying him. He was hesitant and whispered something to a man, who nodded and ran off. He raised one finger on his thin lip and nodded thoughtfully. 'It is evening, sir, and they are with the girls, no doubt, but I shall get them,' I told him innocently.

'Your signifier is reputedly drunk in Oril's hall,' he said with deep loathing. 'A signifier is supposed to be beyond reproach.'

'He has balls like any other man, sir,' I said woodenly.

'Get the signifier here and make sure he is sober,' he said very evenly. 'Understood? Right this minute.'

305

'I'll go immediately, sir,' I answered.

'Good man,' he agreed and turned to treat with the castra.

I turned to the Batavi who had been scouting with me. 'Tell the turma to gather outside the gate. Full gear, full speed. Be ready to ride. Get the vexillum for Hund and his horse ready,' I told them, and they rushed to obey. I spotted Brimwulf looking down from the vallum of the castra, and I nodded at him. 'It is time,' I mouthed at him.

The archer nodded and disappeared. I turned to look south, and in the distance the foremost men of the legions could be seen marching in perfect lines, their gear on their furcas over their shoulders. They were far still, but looked impressive like an army of heavily laden, single-minded ants. There were some ten thousand legionnaires and auxilia streaming for war, and many men from the surrounding areas flocked to the area, lining the lanes to see the spectacle they both dreaded and admired. The first Batavi came out along with some of the Legionnaires of the XVII Legion's cohorts and many if not all were shining their helmets furiously.

I decided I had waited for long enough and rode to the town. I made my way to Oril's ramshackle hall. I dismounted and got down and entered. I pushed the door open and found Hund lounging on a bench, a pretty elfin girl on his lap. Tudrus's Gerhild was stoking the fires. I saw Oril, a man of a bulbous nose and small eyes and a long, dark beard glance up at me from a table he had been cleaning at. I stepped in the middle of the room, cocking my helmet at Hund. 'You. I should have guessed. Here bitching to women about your duties, you gutless piece of shit?'

Hund spat and snorted, pushing the girl away. 'Decurion of dogs. Come here to lick my sandals?' *For someone who hated lying, he acted pretty well,* I decided.

'Pay your dues to the whore master, you rot nosed fool. You, man.' I nodded at Oril. 'He has to pay. What does he owe you?'

'Lord?' he said amicably.

'He is leaving,' I stated and nodded at Hund. 'The Consul is here and the legions need to begin soldiering again. Not fucking and disobeying orders. Take his money, and we can leave.'

Oril nodded. 'Unfortunately, Hraban, he will stay. And you will also stay here for a time until it is done.'

Until it is done? I thought, confused.

From the side rooms burst out not two, but six men. Hund's eyes went wide from surprise, and I guessed he had not been paying attention to the happenings of the house for awhile. They were large, sober, and their eyes glinted in the semi-dark. They had huge shields, spears, and they nodded at each other as two stood before Oril, four behind me. I spat at Hund's feet. 'Hund has been very useful, Hraban,' Oril said happily. 'By just sitting here, he delivered you to our hands.'

Hund grinned at me and spat. 'I'm so happy to see you, Decurion.'

'What is this, then?' I asked them, grasping the hilt of the Winter Sword.

'Nothing, boy. We will keep you safe for awhile,' Oril chortled, putting his fingers under his thick belt. 'Then we shall leave. You will stay. Drink this, and we don't have to hurt you.' He nodded at a mug of ale in his hand, and he placed it before Hund.

'Will make you sleepy, is all,' one of the men behind me grunted.

'You will leave?' I asked them, bewildered. Didn't Odo want me after all?

'You will understand in due time,' Oril agreed. 'We will go, you will stay. And you won't bother anyone anymore.'

'You are with Odo?' I stated, done with the lies. 'And he wanted to buy me from Segestes? And I am to stay?'

Oril looked strange for a moment, fidgeting. 'Yes. That is right. But Odo is happy now. You are free.'

'Free? What the fuck do you mean?' I asked, entirely mystified.

He smiled a wide, rotten smile. 'Fine then. An explanation. He was worried about the greater events. You know which. He had not found Veleda and Lif and saw the Raven was imprisoned. He wanted to trade Sigimer for your freedom to ensure you are going to finish your part in Lok's curse.' He nodded around. 'And then there is Segestes, who is very worried about you. So is—'

'Paullus,' I hissed.

He looked shocked for a moment. 'Yes, of course. And Odo is worried since you have been scouting his stronghold. We are no fools, Hraban. So, we will take actions to ensure you will not speak of Segestes to the Consul, and you will play your part in Lok's game. Drink.'

I took some steps forward and reached for the mug. I saw Hund nod ever so slowly. 'No, I'm not really thirsty,' I said, and the Winter Sword came out at the same time as I rushed forward. Woden's call rang in my ears as the blade swished into the air and came down, cutting the man who had been reaching for me. He fell like a lump of stone as the man next to him thrust his spear hard at my legs. He could have skewered one, but Hund pummeled into him, stabbing with a pugio. Oril's eyes opened up wide, and he turned to run, but Tudrus's girl was there, grinning impishly as she swung a broom's handle on his face. Blood flew, Oril's nose flattened, and he fell over the man I had killed.

Behind me, yells.

The four men were charging, holding their shields high, spear points flashing in the dark. Hund was getting up next to me, ready to face the enemy, but there was no need for that.

The door burst open, and Tudrus, Agetan, and Bohscyld charged in. They held wicked axes and shields and Brimwulf's arrow tore into the back of one of Odo's men. He fell screaming, and Agetan and Bohscyld tore into the enemy's ranks. The axes flashed, and fist-sized bits of flesh and clothing fell to the floor. The huge, wide men kept at it, grunting, and soon the three men of Odo were nothing more than quivering corpses on the floor. 'Enough,' Tudrus told the twins, both of whose bristling hair was caked with blood. 'Anymore, and the girls will never get it all off.'

I glanced at him and grinned, and he shrugged sheepishly as Gerhild came to peck him a kiss. She was blonde and short and had a beguiling face, and I bowed at her in thanks. She dimpled in gratitude. 'No other customers here?' I asked her.

'No, Oril drove them out,' she told me shyly. 'We were careful.'

'And those men?' I asked Hund. 'Where did they come from, eh?'

'I forgot,' he said with a frown. 'I did tell you they hinted at having more men in the town, no? And nobody told me things were happening. Didn't matter anyway. We took them.'

I toed Oril savagely. 'Brimwulf, can you wake him up.'

Agetan grunted, pushed the archer out of the way and picked up the Chauci by the hair. He lifted him high and slammed the man on the table so hard it broke and Oril's eyes flew open in shock and pain. He squealed like a whipped dog and stared around in stupefaction. Bohscyld appeared at his side and slapped him to get his full attention, and we had to wait until Oril spat a bloody molar to the floor from between his lips. He glared at us balefully.

I stepped in front of him. 'Now, Oril. I see into your future.'

He snorted. 'Do you see Odo using your skull as a shitter?'

I slapped him, and his attitude was immediately changed to a more humble, very attentive one. 'I see you living far away, far in the lands to the west. You will be a discontent house slave, one beaten, perhaps fucked by your master. I will find you a master like that, Chauci. There are some Romans who have a taste for such as you, even ugly and old. Or perhaps I will find a man of trade? You look strong. Perhaps an ore mine where you break your back? I know not. Your future line of work does not really concern me. That is for the buyer to decide. But I will find one that breaks you, one way or other. I see this in your future. Tears and shame and death.' There were girls looking out of some rooms, frowning at Oril. I grinned at them. 'You should be glad. These options are a far better future than leaving you at the mercy of the girls here. You did not hear it just now, but the new owner of the establishment ...' I looked up at Hund, and he nodded at an older woman, standing with a happy glow on her feral face. 'That one there, the eldest of your freshly freed slaves, just decided they will eat your balls.' It was not true, of course, but scary enough by the terrified look on his face.

He went ashen gray as he strained his neck to look at that woman. She flashed him a sweet smile that sent him sputtering. 'I was going to leave. And would like to, still.'

'Let us speak then,' I said with a growl that made him flinch. 'I wish to know what you meant to do with me? And I wish to know of Gulldrum.'

He held his hands over his face and sighed. 'I see. And you want to know about Gulldrum? The hole?' he mused, sweat pouring and mixing with the blood on his beard.

'Gulldrum? Yes, we wish to know about it. What is it like, how many ways are there in and out and where do they hold Sigimer?'

He snorted again. 'And the girl?'

'The girl?'

'Your woman? His sister? The one he gave to your brother. Yes, he did. He punished her for letting you go last year,' he giggled, and so I beat him. I did it with little passion. I broke his fingers until he howled like an animal, and even the whores were silent as I worked.

'I have a woman, man,' I hissed at him. 'And if Gernot has hurt my friend Ishild, I will add him to the pile of corpses this summer.'

'Yes, you have a woman,' he chortled in his pain. 'Fine. There are three halls in Gulldrum. It is ancient and holy; the whole place as old as your family. The trees and mountains were young when Lok spawned his men there in challenge to Woden's and there they live still.'

Tudrus toed him. 'The specifics, not poems, cur.'

He nodded. 'Three halls. There are ways between the three, and the bottom one holds rooms for the prisoners. Sigimer is there, likely unless Odo wishes to keep him in the middle one out of the goodness of his heart.' He chortled. 'So he is likely at the bottom. There is a way out there, yes, at the bottom.'

'Go on, you dog-faced bastard,' Brimwulf told him, squatting by the door, looking out. 'There are some men looking in.'

'Keep them out,' I said and kicked Oril. 'More.'

'The middle room is where they live,' he panted in pain. 'There are beds and bunks and a holy altar.'

'Reeking of blood, no doubt,' I spat.

'Odo lives there with his men. Some --'

'Hundred,' I told him.

'Yes, you have been scouting.' He grinned. 'Tribune told us it was so.'

'The Tribune has a lot to answer for,' I said bitterly. 'And the top chamber? The one beyond the door?'

'Ah, that one,' he said. 'Nothing.'

'I will give you over to the ladies now,' I told him and began dragging him to one of the rooms.

'It's trapped,' he blurted. 'The roof? It can be collapsed if you hew down some pillars. I would not be standing in the room if they go down. No.'

'Really? And who are there to hew them down?'

He shrugged. 'He has fanatical men who are just waiting to do his bidding.'

'Not quite as fanatical, are you?' I told him. 'Where is the doorway out? Exactly? And are there more than one?'

He squirmed. 'I do not know. I don't know that! Never used that door!'

'That door? Only one door?' I asked him coldly. 'Any ideas? At all? I would have some if I were you. Right now.'

'I don't know!'

My face hardened. 'Fine. And what were you to do with me? Keep me here? Until?'

'Yes,' he whispered. 'If you will let me go, I will tell you.'

'Speak,' I told him and grasped his broken finger, and he was trying to breath in throes of pain. I let go, and he banged the floor with his legs until the pain abated. I lifted my eyebrow at him, and he made no more demands.

'The Tribune,' he whispered. 'Segestes could not kill you. You couldn't easily disappear. You might have managed to send your messages to Chariovalda, after all, and they might have be asking for you one day. No, you had to be alive, and that is what Odo wanted anyway. He needs you and so we needed a Raven that would not croak. We wanted you to simmer and suffer and be quiet. So both Segestes and Odo wanted something to keep you calm and docile.'

'What is that, you nasty cur?' Tudrus asked.

'There was a way to keep you silent until everything is finished and done with. Eventually, Odo would see you find Veleda, and Segestes would have Sigimer and do whatever he is to do and ...'

'Maroboodus would slay Drusus. And why would I sit still?'

'Paullus,' he hesitated.

'What about the bastard?' Tudrus asked him, his patience wearing thin. 'He failed. He sent Hraban here and failed. As we planned.'

I slammed my fist in his face and grabbed his beard. 'Speak.'

'Lothar is back,' the man whispered.

'We mangled Lothar!' Tudrus demanded.

'No, he is a hard man to mangle,' Oril told us with pity, but then stuttered as he looked at his own condition. 'Lothar has been back a few months. Bleeding and hurt he was but the negotiatore Antius had him fixed up and sent back after Maius. He barely made it in the snows. They will send Odo something to keep you on track. Something very precious to you.'

Hund was looking at the corpses. 'These are not the men who lived here this spring. The ones with the extra horse.'

I grabbed my head and my thoughts were whirling. Oril nodded. 'There is a way to keep even the Raven from being too much trouble in troubling times.'

'He is after Cassia?' I asked Oril thickly. 'She is guarded. No!'

He shook his head, almost sadly. 'Nobody is guarded enough if one is determined enough. And they know Lothar, don't they. They won't be very alarmed.'

I got up in panic and saw him smiling at me, trying to inch away. Tudrus saw it as well and crouched over him. 'Hraban is not much of a seer,' the Quadi told Oril savagely and twisted his head with simple brutality, the neck making a vicious grating sound.

'I wanted to do that!' Hund complained, but Tudrus cut him off as I rushed outside and jumped on the surprised horse.

The others followed after us, and I was cursing myself for being an idiot. 'Woden, let my wyrd be kind. Let her be unharmed. May Fenfir swallow Paullus and that bastard Lothar.'

'Go!' Tudrus screamed.

We raced for the castra.

312

Far away, we could hear the legion's buccina as they wound their way closer. We reached the gate and there, a cohort was getting ready to receive the Consul and the Batavi were readying their horses. 'Look!' Brimwulf screamed and pointed towards the east. I made a desperate sound of a wounded beast, for there, not far, I saw many men riding, and with them, I saw Cassia's long hair. Mathildis was riding behind them, one man leading her horse.

'Who are they?' I screamed at Lucius, the centurion marching his men back and forth, trying to make the rogues look respectable. His face snapped to me, then at the men riding away.

'It is Cassia; they were bringing her to you! They said you were hurt,' Lucius said, alerting the Batavi, who all turned their helmeted faces towards the riding men and Cassia. There, amongst the riding were the two Batavi guarding Cassia. One turned to look at me, and then I saw a blond man throwing back his cape, and I witnessed Lothar's pale face. He flicked his fist and the Batavi were stabbed from all sides. Cassia's face was one of shock as the men fell from the horses. Mathildis was struggling with her beast, the man pulling it along.

'Lothar!' I screamed. He did not turn. Cassia was pulling at her horse, her face a mask of terror, but she was hopelessly outmatched as the four men around her hefted their bloody weapons and grabbed her horse, riding on each side of her.

'Hraban!' Tudrus screamed at me. 'Cassia!'

'Follow me,' I yelled and I spurred my horse as the Batavi contingent looked on in confusion. The Tribune was screaming something after me, but I rode after Lothar, scared to death for Cassia.

'What are you doing?' Tudrus screamed at me, his brothers barreling after us. 'They will kill her if we attack!'

'They shall not take her there! I'll die with her!' I screamed back. 'You can stay here if you fear the dark!'

He hissed at me. 'Of course I won't! But we must catch them before the night falls.'

'We have a day and a half to catch the fuckers!' I panted and whipped the poor horse.

Brimwulf grunted near me. 'If they hurt Mathildis, I'll rip their hearts out.'

Tudrus panted. 'At least we won't be alone.'

I glanced behind us and saw the entire turma of Batavi take after us, following Hund's vexillum. They looked fey and dangerous, their shields banging on their back, spears hefted, and I nodded at Hund who made a throat cutting motion at the fleeing enemy. For Cassia? For me? Or for the men that had died? I did not care. They were there for us. Paellus was staring after us, his face horrified.

There are moments, Lord Thumelicus, when everything falls apart.

All your plans and hopes taste like dust and dirt, and all you can do is to beg to recover that one precious thing that truly matters. I saw Cassia trying to break free, glancing back at me, and then I saw Lothar hit her gleefully and she went limp on the saddle. The man with Mathildis was struggling with the woman, who jumped down from the horse, landing heavily and got up to rush back. The man turned to her and pulled a framea. 'No!' Brimwulf screamed.

I grabbed my heavy spear and spurred the horse to a near impossible speed. The man stalking Mathildis was clearly mad, uncaring of his own fate as he licked his lips in anticipation of a kill. The arm went up, the framea quivered as he prepared to throw it at the running woman, and I begged to the gods as I threw the heavy spear. It spun in the air, hung low and came down. It hit the horse of the man on the side and it whinnied wildly, throwing its rear up, spilling the rider over its neck. I saw Agetan pull Sigimer's ax and ride for the man, who was getting up. The ax went up, and then I saw no more as I spurred after the enemy holding Cassia.

We were not gaining on them.

Their horses were good, excellent even, the best available, and they knew the land and plunged into the wooded valleys and hills with cool familiarity. Happily, Brimwulf knew the land very well, and the enemy did not escape entirely, even if they were out of sight occasionally. I feared the night, I feared the thought of losing them and what they would do to her. I wept and raged and hit my horse on the flanks, not gaining on them at all. 'Don't give up!' a burly Batavi screamed at me from behind, and I was nodding, hoping against all hope not to lose my mind. The sun trekked the sky, lower and lower. The color of the faraway clouds hinted at the approaching night. We slunk through the forests and rocky hill sides, through tight game trails. We passed small trails leading past high crags and had to slow down, but so did Lothar. In the wild lands before the valleys next to the Buck, we managed to catch up some and his preference to luxury did him ill justice for when we broke free of the woods to a lush valley, he was again closer, and I saw his face was ashen with fatigue. His guides were urging him on, and he yelled at them.

Their horses gave a mighty push, and they sped along.

Thus we rode, whipping the beasts. Right when the night fell, a horse of one of the men ahead stepped on a hole, and he fell heavily under the screaming beast, not getting up. We steered past him, and I met Lothar's eyes as he looked behind. He was cursing, I could see it, and he must have cursed Oril for failing. And then the night fell, a sliver of the sun casting some final light on the land as the wolf Sköll chased the horses Arvakr and Alsovior, dragging the sun after it. Up came Mani, the moon, which the wolf Hati chased across the sky, and we despaired, for there was a cast of clouds filling the sky.

We lost sight of our quarry.

'That way. That is the best road!' Brimwulf yelled, pointing at some elevated ground and indeed, a hint of a trail could be seen. We rode forward at a pace which seemed very slow to me. We rode listening to the sounds of the night, saw villages pass by, our men riding through them with alert eyes. There was a scream up ahead. Cassia. We spurred the horses to a greater speed.

Thus, we played that night. We lit torches we stole from halls and houses, rode and herded the enemy. We found one of his men who had fallen behind and left him on the ground, dead and hacked open. Many times, we were close to losing them. But always, thanks to Woden and Brimwulf, a sight or sign of them or their passing was found, and suddenly there were no clouds to hamper us as the moon lit the sky.

It was the longest, scariest night of my life.

Then, in the morning, the divine horses pulled the sun back up to the sky, and we saw Lothar and his last man spurring ahead, Cassia still slung over a saddle. Our horses protested, but we caught glimpses of the glistening Buck River, and so we were close. I still had seventeen men and my friends with me as one man had fallen behind in the night. All of the ones riding after me were exhausted but determined. We followed our enemy and finally reached the river, and there Lothar splashed into the ford where some Suebi traders were crossing, screaming for them to get out of his way. Some men fell into the river, animals scattered. Then they saw our troop with our spear points glinting, charging for them, and the merchants all went in, swimming for their lives.

Lothar turned south, to the woods and small hills, and in the distance, I thought I saw the ridge holding Gulldrum.

'Don't let them get in!' I screamed. 'All you got, boys!'

But Lothar kept his distance.

An hour later, the hill was reaching up before us, and I despaired. The curly haired Lothar tugged at his last man, and cursed. That man was shaking his head, but finally relented, prayed visibly and turned to face us. He was shaking in fear but lifted his club and rode at us. I welcomed him with a scream of hate, hewing mightily with the Winter Sword. The blade cut through his arm into the horse that rolled away. The man fell under the Batavi hooves. 'Lothar! Come! Your turn!' I yelled at him.

Hund was riding next to me. 'We will not make it!'

'We will ride through Hel if we must, and if any man wants to stay out of it, let him!' I yelled, but the Batavi grinned grimly. The road narrowed as we went up. A man perked up from a stone he had been sitting at, one of Odo's men. Brimwulf skillfully stopped his horse and shot him through his chest, and the enemy fell out of sight. Lothar's horse shied and trembled ahead, and we gained on him. Brimwulf was aiming his bow. 'Shoot the fucker!' I screamed.

'I might hit her!' Brimwulf answered desperately, for Cassia was now between him and us.

I cursed and turned to the men behind us. 'After them. Inside, and put the bastards to the sword and spear. Steel to the belly of all the men in there and don't let them hack her down!' They yelled hoarsely and spurred their horses and not one shied away. Ahead of us, we saw Lothar's horse surge forward with its last vestiges of strength, and we saw the open maw of Gulldrum. He went in, his face jubilant. We saw two men emerge from each side of the gate, staring after him, and then they turned to look at us. Their eyes were open in shock. 'Haiaah!' I screamed and whipped Moon so hard it whinnied in pain and in I went, riding over one of the guards.

The hall was dark though there were torches fluttering around, and up ahead I saw Lothar turning his horse, screaming at a dozen men approaching him carefully. The Batavi entered with their lathered horses, helmets and chainmail glinting in the torchlight, the unit signum a shadowy, tall finger of death. The enemy looked at us in confusion, and they likely did not know Lothar either; Odo's guides were dead. He was just one man, and most of the enemy turned to stare at us, wondering whether we were with the bastard or just intruders. Lothar was screaming at them to make sure they understood the latter was the case. The enemy began to turn to face us, their faces shocked, and we saw spears and axes come up hesitantly.

The pale faced Lothar dismounted and turned to Cassia, whose horse was being held by a bald man. I hit my horse, forcing it forward. My men followed me, and I shivered in savage delight at the screams of Agetan and Bohscyld, feral and bloodthirsty. The groups of men and horses mingled in a savage battle in a stony hall. My horse bit at a man, I hacked down with the Winter Sword at another and hissed as I guided Moon forth. He gleefully rammed Lothar's animal, which bolted, pulling the bald man to the floor. Finally, my horse bit Cassia's horse, throwing her out of the saddle to a shadow of a pillar. The bald man got up dizzily and thrust at me with a broken spear, tugging at my chainmail, and I hacked at his face, taking off his lip and jaw. I turned the horse around and around and noted all the Batavi were engaged in a wild, wicked melee.

Then hands grabbed me.

Lothar tried to pull me out of the saddle and some men around him were following his example. 'Marcomanni shit. Pretender Roman,' he hissed as he heaved and managed to rip me from my seat. I twisted and fell

317

with Lothar, trying to strangle him. He tried to put my eyes out, but my helmet stopped him, and we rolled on the floor. I groped for the seax, but he held an ax and struck me on the helmet with it. I reeled with the blow and the next swing glanced again off my helmet and drew sparks from the rock. I grasped his beard and butted his face with mine. He hollered, his nose flattened by the steel. He rolled aside as I rose up, Woden's savage dance filling my mind. I laughed wildly and spitefully as I grabbed the Head Taker in two hands. Two men of Odo came forward to guard Lothar. 'Come and then go eat at Lok's tables if he will have you!' They were young, very young and brave. They raised their clubs and charged. I impaled one so hard I felt his spine crack, and then I pushed him to his friend who fell on his back. I sawed the butcher's blade off the corpse and stepped on the young man struggling to get up. I crushed his knee, and then kicked his mouth with my hobnailed caligae. Teeth scattered around the floor. Lothar was reeling up, and I gave him no time to grasp his ax. I charged, nearly slipping in blood and the Winter Sword came down in a huge overhead arch that would have cleaved a god in half.

It certainly did Lothar.

His corpse jerked as the blade buried itself on his side, and I laughed at the shocked look on his face as he nearly folded over the blade. I pulled the blade out, and it made a grating sound in his broken armor and spine. I poked him with the sword, enjoying the dimming horror in his eyes and missed a burly enemy coming for me. I saw him from the corner of my eye and whirled to block the spear thrust, but the man was quick and about to stab.

Then he shrieked and fell at my feet and fey, fierce Cassia with her bulging belly pulled a bloody spear from his back.

The man still tried to lift his arm, but the spear impaled him in the neck. Cassia stood over him, her hair half hiding her face, her chin up. She nodded at me in thanks and love, and I grinned at her, relief bursting out with a huge shuddering breath. 'You, all right? The baby?'

'I'm alive. The baby is as well. Fight them, love,' she nodded at the fight.

Around us, spears danced, and the death ruled.

Men and horses were scattered on the floor, and in the light of some sputtering torches, I saw many were dead. A Batavi was slain under a horse, but the efficient auxilia killers were butchering many of Odo's badly trained and armed men. The Batavi had formed a wall of shields in the middle of the room, and their spears flashed and dispatched many an enemy venturing too close. Agetan and Bohscyld were on the side, butchering some of Odo's better-armed men in an orgy of torn limbs and broken bones. Tudrus was commanding the shield wall, his eyes meeting Cassia's in relief, and Brimwulf was there as well. They pushed forward, Odo's men dying in pairs and singles, but then in the far wall, a hole gorged confused enemies to the hall by a dozen. A horn blared down below mournfully, then with great intensity. More men charged up.

'The wall! Towards the hole!' I screamed, and Hund nodded, Tudrus pointed at the doorway, and the shield wall turned that way, the bearded Batavi stepping forward together, slamming shields together, thrusting spears overhead at the enemy. Men on the second rank made sure none who passed the spears lived to kill the first rankers, and gladius and ax grew red. I pulled Cassia after us, and Bohscyld and Agetan joined us, the wide men guarding her fiercely. 'Take care of her,' I told them, and they nodded with unholy glee.

'Swarm them!' I heard a man rumble and turned to see a man with a dark shield and a bear tunic by the tunnel's entrance. He wore a leather helmet and apparently commanded the dozens of warlike men around him. 'Break them! Don't think!' he screamed and pushed men forward. Round eyed, the men obeyed. The group of men rushed the middle of the advancing Batavi and a man of mine fell, screaming as his arm was broken. The animal-like enemy pushed hard at the line, and I joined the shield wall with the brothers, slashed open one of them in the chest, then another, but the whole Batavi line was stopped by the swarming enemy. We struck over our first line, pushing spear and sword at bearded, ugly faces and the smell of piss, shit and blood filled the air as men fell. More and more of the enemy charged, directed by the bear tunic. By me, Agetan and Bohscyld were grunting at men to hold firm, and Brimwulf was rushing to the flanks of the enemy, killing some men trying to flank us. Now even some scraggly women were lifting weapons against us. Brimwulf's arrows killed a lanky man in the middle, and the enemy line buckled.

The bear tunic was staring at his dying troops and then lifted a horn.

He blew a high blast on it.

I heard slapping footsteps. From behind.

I turned to see a pair of large men emerge from a small tunnel and run towards a pillar in the middle of the room, holding hammers. They were grim, thick men, grimacing as they stepped on a wounded Batavi, killing him. They began to strike the fragile thing. 'Hraban!' Cassia yelled as dust fell to the floor.

I aimed my sword at the bear tunica man. 'Push them! Push them! Quickly! Over that bastard and to the hole. If you can't make it, run to the sides of the hall!' I screamed, and men turned to me, not comprehending. More enemies poured from the hole, and Brimwulf shot one of the men holding the hammers on the back, and he fell on the pillar.

The floor shook.

'Charge that man!' Tudrus screamed, and the Batavi roused themselves, abandoning the shield wall, dropping spears in favor of axes and swords. As we went forward, pieces of roof began to fall. There were hunks of mud, fist sized pieces of rock, and rotten wood. Some five Batavi were still in the fringes of the battle, not heeding my calls. Horses ran around in panic as I slapped one away from me. I pulled at Cassia and hacked with the blade. I saw the Batavi swarmed over the enemy, losing some but killing many, and the bear tunic tried to push us from the doorway in vain as Brimwulf stabbed him with a gladius, his arrows useless in the press.

The roof fell, and I pushed and pulled Cassia away from under the cascade of rubble.

I saw shadows in the dust as we fell on our bellies.

Rocks came down to the middle of the room with ear shattering noise as if a god was screaming, rubble avalanching to the sides. Dust and piteous whinnies of the horses filled our ears as we all prayed. A man near us turned to red gristle as a jagged rock rolled on him and then, suddenly, it was silent.

Cassia was coughing under me, and I rubbed dust from my face. Men were picking themselves up, awestruck. A few torches were still burning fiercely in the hall. I saw a Batavi get up and stab a man of Odo's in the face, and little by little, most of the turma gathered themselves. There were some twelve left. I saw Brimwulf get up on shaky feet and move to the open door leading downstairs. He cursed, took out an arrow, and began to shoot down where men were screaming.

I looked around. Only the edges of the room were relatively free of debris, but the way back was blocked. 'Tudrus!'

'Here,' the Quadi said, on his knees. 'I'm all right. So are the brothers.' I saw what I had taken to be boulders get up on their feet, with only eyes showing from under a layer of dust. Agetan and Bohscyld grinned at me. Hund was cursing and tugging at a Batavi half-buried by stone and mud. He was alive though obviously dying.

'Finish him,' I said, and to ease the comment, I continued, 'Give him honorable death.'

Hund nodded and stabbed down with his gladius. My men were picking their way over stone and root and were shuffling towards the doorway. An arrow shot back up from the tunnel, and an ominous chanting could be heard. I grabbed some of the torches as Cassia; her face bruised, picked up a small shield and a fallen gladius.

'Men!' I yelled, and they turned. 'We are superior to them. We have shields, swords, and most of all, we wish to kill the bastards who tried to capture her.' Cassia grinned at them, and the men answered her smile. 'They would have used her as a ransom, dangling her before my eyes to betray Nero Claudius Drusus. For there is a treason on the works against our Lord.' They growled, the smile replaced by fury. I pointed at Cassia, gnashing my teeth. 'They would have raped her. Let us rape them with our swords.' They roared their assent, a group of dust-covered fighters ready to take on a Jotun. A man yelped down in the tunnel as Brimwulf shot another shaft. He was running low on arrows.

Agetan, Bohscyld, and Tudrus linked their shields as we grouped up. The rest of the men were following suit as we turned the corner for downstairs. There were dead and wounded on the rocky slope, and we

321

marched over them, brutally slaying any who were alive. I counted eleven Batavi and then my friends. It would have to do. The way wound around a corner, then another, and water dripped around us, roots touched our faces as we walked towards the den of Odo.

'How far down does this take us?' Tudrus grumbled.

Hund was next to me, behind the brothers. 'All the way to Hel. It is evil what they are doing down there. I smell it.'

It did smell odd.

It could have been the smell of turf, of the rocks and roots, but there was definitely something more foul down there, the smell of corpses, perhaps, or something unnatural. The Batavi prayed as they went down, and I did not wish to remind the wary men around me that it was said Lok made his men in that terrible hole. We turned another corner and a door was barring the way. It was a heavy door with a slit on top and an arrow flew out of it, hitting Tudrus's shield.

'Kick it in,' I growled.

We rushed forward and hammered on the door. Agetan was kicking it, and it shuddered. There was a crack of wood. Brimwulf was waiting to see shadows on the slit, and then he released his arrow. Someone screamed. Bohscyld began kicking as well, and a plank spun off. The door gave but slammed back in as men pushed back on it. 'Give me an ax!' I growled and Agetan handed me Sigimer's and I grasped it. I grunted, and the others took steps back. I heaved the door so hard a plank split. Then again, and the ax went through it and a man whimpered and cried. I kept at it until the door resembled something lightning had shattered. I could see light beyond and shadows running.

I cursed and kicked the door.

It flew open.

I retreated as spears flew by and arrows flew in the air. One Batavi cursed as a shaft pierced his side, but Brimwulf shot a shadowy man through the hole. I rushed to be covered by the shields and saw Cassia behind all of us, face ashen gray, yet braving it all with the rest. I did love her. Gods, but I did, and now she was in danger. 'Shields out when we go in,' Tudrus yelled. 'Go!'

322

And we did.

We shuffled forward, our shields out, and we formed a small semi-circle facing outwards and stayed by the doorway.

'Welcome, Hraban,' a voice said dryly. 'I didn't quite imagine meeting like this, but you are here, and that is wyrd.'

Torches flared in the room, and I saw Odo by the far wall. He was the same red headed, scrawny, rotten faced skeleton he had always been. He looked evil and was, and if Lok made his men to compete with those of Woden, then surely he made them perfect opposites to what my family was like. He was standing in a doorway in a dark robe. The way next to his led down to the third hall, no doubt. His men, some fifty stood in the hall, facing us in groups. Some had been pulled to the side, where they bled.

The Batavi shuddered and took a step back. On the floor, there was painted a horned shadow, a creature of power. It was old, and yet it reeked of blood. Above it there were remains of men and women hung from thick ropes. Their throats were cut, and they had obviously been bled on the figure. They had been old and young, men and women, even a child or two, and we saw flesh had been cut from them.

'You don't know how to hunt?' I asked Odo, hiding my terror with callous attitude.

'We have hunters, but we don't hunt for deer.' He giggled. 'Sometimes such flesh is easiest to capture. And one of us only eats this meat.'

'So,' I spat. 'You wanted to see me?'

He shook his head, his eyes flickering in the torchlight. There was a feverish look on his face as if he was troubled. 'I did not. I, like Segestes, wanted to make sure you behaved.' His eyes regarded Cassia feverishly.

'It's nearly two years, Odo, when I was at your mercy. You claimed I had fulfilled the prophecy and set you on the path of finding Veleda. What changed that?'

He grinned. He flicked something golden in his hand.

It was Woden's Gift.

The splendid ring of the family, holy to the Suebi. And the one Veleda was to be bled on. Except I had laughed at him when he took it from me, for I had learned from my dying, god cursed great uncle Bero that Woden's Ringlet is not golden. I said nothing.

Odo's eyes flashed. 'Indeed. You mocked me that day I took it from you. Since then, two years have passed. Lif went on to Godsmount. We lost her the day after taking after her. I searched for ways up the hills and could not find one. They chased us off, the Cherusci. Did I not say you might still have a part to play on this? I was right. And I think, judging by the way you mocked me when I took the ring, you knew I had erred.'

'I know nothing of that, you skeletal corpse, but soon I shall know what your innards look like,' I told him. 'Stick the ringer up your ass.'

He spat and pointed a finger at me. 'The ring is worthless to Lok. It is not Woden's Ringlet of the prophecy. No. When we returned here, as time passed, and nothing happened, I began to wonder what I had missed. I asked the god. Lok. I asked his wife Sigyn for guidance. Do you remember what I did to Bero, your great uncle to find out the full prophecy of Lok?`

'You tortured him with spells and gave away his life in return for answers. Not that I believe in it, mind you.' I laughed.

He giggled. 'You saw Leuthard, scion of wolf Hati and still you do not believe.'

'He was a madman, not a divine thing,' I argued though I was very unsure of it.

'He was more than mad, Hraban. Gods answer, they meddle in our affairs. Leuthard was Lok's wolf. Hati's legacy. One of the many. I asked Lok for advice. I sacrificed lifeforce for the answers that seemed to plague me. Where was Hraban? Why had he laughed at me when I took his ring? I was stuck here. Lif and Veleda were not to be found. I had Sigimer though and he would be useful.'

'You tortured Sigimer for the answers?' I spat. 'And what did you find?'

'No, I did not,' he said with a mad smile. 'I could have, for he has royal blood in his veins. Like Bero had. Northern blood. Your blood. But he was hurt and weak, and so I only had one other with such blood at hand. A useless man, but more obedient now. It was an easy decision to use his life after he failed to capture you and Lif.'

I stared at a figure being guided up from the tunnel. There were two, in fact. The last one was twisted to the side, and I saw the thin face and braided brown beard of Ansigar, our former friend. The first one lacked a hand, and he was my brother Gernot. His face had a scar like mine, and he was thin, so thin he could have fallen by a strong gust of wind. He was shaking and obviously in pain as if he had suffered great horrors.

'Brother,' I said darkly.

Odo put a hand on Gernot's shoulders, and he shirked. Odo kept a grasp on his arm though and Gernot, my poor brother could not move. 'He surprised me. Much more resilient than I thought. He is still sane though a bit rocked by the torture I had to use. I broke him, gods ate on his force, but he is healing, do not worry, Hraban. Your Bero got much worse. But then, you do not worry, do you? You never cared for him.'

'I did not,' I said, feeling some distant shame for the fact. 'He betrayed me, killed Hagano at your orders and has followed you around since. And Ansigar. You fuck. Greetings. Good you are here. Everyone will fight, and this is done with.'

'Hraban,' Gernot said, his face resentful. Ansigar stared at me with resentment. I had whipped him when I took Gernot's hand; that day Father had tried to give me to Odo. He hated me, but I was not sure if Gernot did. His face was blank, scared and perhaps even ... sorry?

Odo waved his hands and brought us back to the matter at hand. 'Now. The goddess that apparently spoke to you spoke to me as well. She is Sigyn, as you no doubt guessed. Lok's unhappy wife. She resents her husband, caring for the trapped lord until times end. And they will end. Soon. As soon as I have the real Woden's Ringlet.'

'It is not golden, is it?' I said spitefully.

'I did not understand it until she told me. The very same fact that made Maroboodus resent you, the thing that sets many in your family apart and gave you your name, Raven, Hraban. That is Woden's Ringlet. Tear, mother, told you this once, but I doubt even she understood it then.'

My hand shot to the locks of curled hair running down from under my helmet.

'Yes, your black hair. The one thing that marks your family is related to Woden, dark, different. Your father thought your mother had betrayed him, but no. Woden's hair it is,' he smiled. 'And so I will have it. While Draupnir's Spawn, the fucking ring there is called Woden's Gift, your hair is the right gift. I will bleed Veleda's heart over it on your god's holiest place and defile his creations. Cocks shall crow, Hraban, and the Jotuns and the dead shall march.'

'I think not,' I spat. 'How will you take it? And where is Ishild?'

'Ishild? And my son? By the way,' he leaned forward as if giving me a great compliment. 'My son is eagerly awaiting Lif; the two will populate the world after I am done ripping it apart. Ishild is below. She is married to Gernot now though he is unable … to enjoy her. Right now. Perhaps if he heals? If not, faithful Ansigar will marry her.' Ansigar grinned at me. The very thing that had driven us apart still made me hate him. He had tried to take Ishild once. I did not love Ishild, perhaps never had, but he had set out to have her, and a small part of me told me perhaps he should have been allowed to try.

Wyrd.

Odo flicked the ring out of sight. 'I'll keep this. Useful bargaining piece with the Cherusci. As was Sigimer. Now. Nothing has changed. The Raven will lead us to Veleda. I learned from Sigyn you were held by Segestes. So, I set out to free you. I did not desire you, never did. You will go free, and we will find her together. But this is unfortunate. That you came here. Oril failed badly, then. I could have used another woman of yours to keep you calm.'

'I was aware of Oril and have been looking at him all winter,' I sneered.

'But you missed Lothar and Cassia's peril,' he sneered back.

I spat. 'And what now? You will shave me?'

'I doubt you will shave easily,' he laughed. 'No. We will leave. It is unfortunate your woman is not under the blade, and things would be bloodless when we reach Godsmount, as we will, but this is the way of it.'

'No, I doubt you will leave,' I spat and my men thrummed their swords and axes on their shields. 'Half of your scum are dead. Will you fight? Cast spells at me, oh vitka? Where is your wand? We will not let you go.'

He smiled, but there was a nervous tick in his eye. He was worried for we had surprised him. 'It has not been controlled very well, Hraban,' he allowed. 'But we still have useful tools.'

He snapped his fingers.

The fur clad men shuffled together. They were better armed than what we had fought above but still not up to the standards of the Batavi. I pointed the Head Taker at them. 'Remember what Adgandestrius and his Chatti did to your last army? When he came to help me? These men are better.' The Batavi took up a chant, again banging their shields with their weapons.

Odo bowed. 'I will never forget. Your friend Koun crippled half my hand that day.' He lifted his fingers, and indeed, some were bent and broken. 'But I forgive you for not thinking about my health. Do you remember the day when your father began fooling us as well as you? We had a case of getting a hold of you. We demanded you, for you had slept with my sister. It would have been just, and I wanted to possess you, to lead you here. He wanted to ...'

'I was there, dog face,' I growled. 'He wanted to use me against the southern Marcomanni and denied you your request. What of it?'

'He asked us if we had a champion to fight you for the truth. He knew my men had no chance against you, and I told him I had one, but far, far away,' he said.

'I remember,' I answered and felt an ominous rake of cold claws of fear across my back.

'Well,' he spat. 'That man is no longer far away.' Odo nodded in the shadows. The creatures of Odo shuffled carefully away from the shadows as a large, darker shadow moved there, a huge man was apparently getting up. Odo chanted and cooed at the shadow, which stepped forward to the light.

We were quiet.

It was a man, perhaps, but a legend would be sung about the Brute of the Gulldrum, the giant, Jotun of the hill. He moved to the light, carefully, holding a smith's hammer in his gnarled fist. He wore a loincloth, had muscles the size of boulders, shoulders so wide he would not be able to leave the room easily, and perhaps he never did. Perhaps he lived there in the dark, shunning torchlight and ate corpses. He had eaten many, for he had human skin stretched over his shoulders, yellowed with age, and a human skin helmet, with eye slots. Feral eyes glinted at the dark. Our men took an involuntary step backward, and like wolves smelling a skittish animal, Odo's men around us smelled our fear and closed in. 'He will kill them, all of them, save for you and Cassia there,' Odo told me as if there were none else present. 'He will drag your face on the skin of Lok and leave you senseless. Then he will take Cassia. He will bring her to me, and we shall carry on. I desire to see your pain, but we shall be elsewhere until we know how things turn out. I've learned you have an uncanny luck. Wyrd is fickle. And no matter if he succeeds or not, you are free, and I am sure we will meet at the end.'

'I will come for you, so will they,' I said and nodded at my men, who cheered though everyone eyed the huge thing before them.

Odo shrugged. 'One way or another, we shall meet at Godsmount,' Odo said and nodded. Ansigar pulled a horn. He grinned, and we tensed. Then he brought it to his lips and blew in it.

The horn blared. Thirty men and women of Lok turned to Odo, who gestured at downstairs, and they followed him. Twenty of the enemy before us hesitated, and then attacked. The giant raised his hammer, eying their attack, gauging their success.

They had none.

We held our own grimly, stepping briefly forward to take the edge off of their ragged charge, ramming the shields in their faces, and they mostly fell back or died. Yet, they were many and we were few, the stone was slippery as we fought under the hanging corpses in Gulldrum. We fought like maniacs. We slammed our shields together, Tudrus guarding my flank; I was guarding Hund's. The enemy weaponry was that of hunters or poor Germani peasants. They were mostly thin iron-tipped framea, some daggers, a seax or two, hammers, mauls and axes. The corpses piled up before our armored rank, but we eyed the giant, who was looking at us, grinning, waiting for the men to do some damage.

And they did not give up at all.

They laughed, drooled, and climbed over the dead and dying, pulled one Batavi on his face and they dragged him with them, hitting and biting him. Then another fell to a thrown framea and Cassia was pulling him to the rear. The giant saw his allies thinning. It was breathing heavily; the horn blared again.

It growled and charged.

We gritted our teeth as the maneater plowed to our line, flattening two of the fur clad men fighting us. He aimed for Agetan and Bohscyld who grimly hacked their axes for the body of the monstrosity, but the thing growled and slammed them aside, stepping on Bohscyld who howled like a rock would howl, a gritty and dark sound echoing in the hall. 'Stop him!' I screamed while stabbing down at a dying woman. Brimwulf shot an arrow at the thing's face. It jutted crazily in its skull, and the thing did not seem to notice. Agetan was pulling Bohscyld aside and the men around the monster hesitated.

They should not have.

The beast roared and charged to the right of the hole he had created in the line and slaughtered two Batavi, hammering one to the wall, smashing the other one from behind, and he bit the dying man in the neck, tearing off a chunk of meat and hair. It happened so fast he was turning for more before we realized it. 'Step back!' I hollered and cursed the thing. I raged as the Batavi retreated towards the door, blanching at the unleashed ferocity of the creature, who swiped the legs from under one of my men, ripping to his skull with his hand and long nails.

'God, great father,' I begged Woden and knew I would have to kill it.

Woden had been dancing with me the whole time. Now I felt the god approved as I filled my heart with bravery, laughed with little care for my life. I pulled Sigimer's ax and charged the thing as it was chasing after one last Batavi, who was hoping to escape to the door after having killed two men of Odo. He was reaching for the man, and I jumped on its back. The ax came down.

It thunked to the flesh and parted it and the beast shirked like a child. I held onto the ax and was pulled into the air as the thing roared. It shook me, turning around wildly, slashing an enemy of ours down; Odo's man who was trying to stab me. Tudrus and Agetan came forward to stab and hack at the thing, and it heaved its hammer at them, dislodging the ax in the process. I rolled and saw it kick Tudrus to the Batavi rank, and I roared, slamming the ax head on a madwoman rushing for me. I flitted forward like a vaettir and again hacked down with the ax, splitting the skin helmet, drawing blood. It roared but it still lived, the massive shoulders shuddering with pain.

It reached back, and its filthy claws found my arm. I swung again, awkwardly with one hand to the side, this time at a skinny man trying to reach me, hitting him on the cheek, leaving him senseless and bleeding on the stone. I noticed the Batavi charging the remaining enemy, killing many and scattering the rest. The recovered Bohscyld and raging Agetan charged to my help and were hanging onto the beast's legs, trying to topple it. The beast was windmilling and then before it fell forward it grasped and embraced me.

Then it fell over me.

I hissed in pain as I grasped my seax, my hand on its nose, trying to keep it from biting me dead. I had a feeling the beast had no recollection of the instruction given and would slay us all; Cassia included. I hacked the seax on its head as I would hack down a carcass of mutton. I saw white as skull glinted under the skin blood, and then it rammed me with its full weight, and I lost my seax, the steel broken in two.

The beast kicked Bohscyld away and beat back at Agetan so hard the man swooned and rolled away. It turned to stare down at me, climbed on its feet, grabbed me by my chainmail and threw me across to the room. I landed on the dire shadow on the floor, grunting as my face hit the stone. The beast ran after me unsteadily, placed its foot on my throat and began to press. An arrow appeared in its cheek, it did not care.

Agetan sawed at its other foot with his gladius, and Tudrus impaled it from behind.

It did not notice.

It grinned and pushed harder as I choked and bit my tongue, my blood flowing from my mouth. I looked at the creature as I was dying, its inhuman eyes regarding me with glee.

I would die there.

That would break the fucking prophecy, I thought and laughed hysterically inside my head. Unless, of course, they only needed my hair; I added in my already blurry thoughts. Then, my head will suffice.

Things started to black out for me.

Then I saw Cassia dart under its arm, trembling in fear and punching the gladius she held through its throat.

It shrieked, stood up gurgling and fell, his arms wheelmilling, hitting Cassia on the head with brutal force. She fell over me as the beast went to its knees, holding its throat desperately. Hund and another Batavi fell on its back, stabbing and stabbing until it fell forward. I sobbed and pushed at Cassia. I cursed as I tried to make her respond to me, but there was nothing; her eyes were closed. Around us, the Batavi slaughtered the few wounded enemy mercilessly, no matter their gender, and Brimwulf and Tudrus came to help me with Cassia.

'She will not die!' I screamed, and the men around me gave me space, searching the room, guarding the door down. There were some thirty dead men and women scattered around us. The rest had fled.

'She breathes, but ...' Tudrus said, carefully examining her head. 'Bleeding, her nose bleeds, she has to be still,' he continued, and I watched as a small pool of her blood spread on the stone.

Hund came to me. He kneeled and shook his head. 'Six of the men left, and the brothers and the archer. I am sorry.'

I nodded and clapped his arm. 'You followed me to Hel. I thank you.'

'We did it for her,' Hund grinned and shook his head to indicate he was jesting. 'They will be missed.'

'They will indeed. And Odo will be paid back in full,' I acknowledged with a hollow voice, Cassia's fate haunting me.

He got up to arrange the men, and Hund nudged me. I turned my eyes on him. He indicated the wreckage. 'We failed. Utterly.'

I nodded. 'She is not his prisoner, though.'

'We failed,' Hund said miserably as Agetan and Bohscyld kneeled next to her, their harsh faces streaked with tears.

331

'I'll face the vaettir spawned Hel dog after I find Veleda,' I grimaced. 'If she dies, I will make sure Paellus hangs from his intestines at the vallum of Castra Flamma. I will do so anyway.'

Tudrus nodded heavily. 'Paellus will have to pay.'

'He will,' I told him. 'I made an oath to Cassia. Over my sword. Winter Sword.' I ran my hands over the Head Taker. 'It will all be settled now. But if she dies ...' I gasped and nodded at Tudrus. 'Then I shall hunt them all across the lands as long as it takes. You are released.'

'So be it, Hraban, but I will not be released,' he told me and nodded at his brothers and then at Cassia. Agetan and Bohscyld lifted her onto the shoulders of Tudrus. Brimwulf shook his head at me with a questioning look. I got up, groaning from pain but nodded at him. He loped downhill, and we went after him.

I prayed for Cassia. And was determined to murder Odo.

Should she die, I would indeed carry the sword across the realms and seek death by giving it.

CHAPTER 28

We probed down the tunnel.

The walls were moist, clear water was running down them in rivulets, and we had a hard time keeping our balance. There was no sight of the enemy. I wanted nothing more than to run down to find Odo and torture him to death, but I could not leave Cassia. She breathed, but her color was not good, and I steadied her on the shoulders of Tudrus, guiding them gently down the tunnel as Batavi went before and after us, holding torches.

Brimwulf appeared and shook his shoulders. He nodded down and there was a strange look of relief on his face. 'There is a man there. Wounded and bereft of a leg. But they are gone. This man, down there? You get to keep your oath to Thusnelda.'

Sigimer.

But Odo was gone and so was Ishild and his son. And Gernot as well. I sighed at the thought of him. Tortured. Used by Odo. Only Ansigar seemed to enjoy truly their chosen allegiance.

Wyrd.

We got to the bottom, and there was no door. There was a strange, torch-lit chamber with roots, bare stones and a large hole in the ground, draining water even deeper. The men touched their weapons in fear, praying to Woden and Donor, to Hercules and the Gaulish gods Sequana and Damona for deliverance, for the sight was uncanny and oddly dangerous. There were cages scattered around the area, small stall for horses and little more. On the side, there was a door of roots and wood, and it was ajar. Brimwulf was out there, smelling the air. He waved us through, and Tudrus gently set Cassia down on a mossy bed of grass. Brimwulf nodded to the side. There sat a man of silvery white hair, thin and fragile.

It was Sigimer indeed.

Why Odo had not killed him, I knew not. Perhaps it served no purpose to him, and perhaps he had forgotten. There were some wounded and dead around us, men we had fought earlier, but only Sigimer was alert. I nodded my head at Hund, who set about finishing the ones with life in them. I thanked him with a nod and went to sit near Sigimer. I tilted my helmet off and stared at him. 'Lord Sigimer.'

His eyes rounded. 'You are—'

'Hraban,' I said simply.

'The one who hurt Rochas,' he said and pushed me weakly. 'You traitor. You were to kill Drusus.'

'I had a pang of conscience,' I told him. 'Brimwulf, his ax?'

'Here,' my friend said, grabbed it from Agetan and tossed it to me. I was so fatigued I nearly cut myself with it as I grasped it from the air. I grinned at him, despite my sorrow over Cassia.

'Nearly got your revenge. It's a great ax. I used it to cut the finger of Segestes.'

'You what?' he asked, confused.

And so, I told him much of what had been taking place with Armin and the Cherusci. He listened and didn't say much. That he had endured his hardships so well, spoke much of his spirit and noble blood. When I was done, he only nodded.

'Lord?' I asked.

'What should I say?' He grinned. 'So, they are lining up against my boy. And Rochas is a traitor. Segestes a Roman? I feared it was so, but I did not

334

understand his full ambition. Lord of the North! Hah! And now, I am a prisoner to Rome.'

I sighed. 'Armin needs a fighting chance. You have to show up.' Brimwulf was nodding his head at my words, listening in.

'What?' he asked, confused.

'You will go to your boy, unite your men with Inguiomerus, summon your lords from under the banner of Segestes and then you will fight Rome,' I told him while rubbing my face.

'And your Nero Claudius Drusus will allow this?' he asked, incredulously. 'War is no game, Hraban. You take your advantages and use them ruthlessly.'

I hesitated. 'I gave my word.' I handed him the ax, and he took it. His eyes were full of wonder at the weapon and then filled with tears.

'To whom?' he asked.

'Thusnelda. I was a prisoner to Segestes. She set me free and told me to do everything in my power to save Armin. So he will at least have a fighting chance, eh?'

'He might,' Sigimer said gruffly. 'They will feed me, strap me to a horse, and I will fight and die for him. It will be interesting. Segestes and Drusus, Maroboodus skulking around. Then there will be our men if we can pull them together. Chaos.'

'Chaos,' I agreed. *But Drusus will be ready, and he will cut through the chaos,* I thought.

'Segestes was ever the weak link in the family,' Sigimer whispered, admiring his ax. 'Cut his finger?'

'Yes.' I smiled.

He laughed softly. 'Too bad you didn't cut his balls, but I doubt he has any use of them anyways. I will summon my lords. Their warbands will join us. Inguiomerus as well, with what he can spare. We will have eight thousand men, at least, unless many have died. With all our warriors, it would be tens of thousands, but it would take time. So much time. We will do our best.'

'Thank you, Sigimer,' I said grinning. 'May the best army win. I will tell Drusus of your brother and it might be he will find an ax in his neck.'

'I do not love him but make it an easy death,' he said gently. 'Is the woman all right?'

'That is my wife,' I sighed. 'And I do not know.'

'Frigg will heal her. My wife always prayed to Frigg and cured Rochas once or twice,' he said reverently. 'I will pray for her.'

'I will ask the men to find some water, as well,' I said gratefully and got up.

I gave no orders, but Hund set guards. We sat in the sun and breathed deep, trying to fathom our losses while two men scouted the land with Brimwulf. Eventually, Hund came to me while I stroked Cassia's hair. He fidgeted with the pole holding the vexillum of the 2st Batavorium until I waved my hand at him. 'Sir, there is a war going on. Are we going to go back to it? We do not want to be thought of as deserters,' he said while carefully eyeing me. 'And that man? He is Sigimer?'

I nodded at him. 'Cassia needs healing, and she was the healer in the castra.'

'There are medicus in Castra Flamma. Granted, they are not as skilled as our Cassia, but we are stationed there,' Hund said with a frown. 'That man. I have seen him before. In a battle. I am sure it is Sigimer.'

'We will go and find Nero Claudius Drusus,' I told him savagely, and he flinched. I calmed myself and rubbed my eyes. The fingers came off gritty and bloody. 'We will find him and get her healed, and our Consul will be grateful. Fulcher should have reached him already. If the army is in Castra Flamma, then fine. We will go there. If not, we will not. I will take the blame.'

'I did not mean ... ' he began and nodded. 'Very well. And I suppose that is not Sigimer?'

'No, that is not Sigimer,' I told him and he shook his head, grinning. I went on. 'If he should go home to the Cherusci, Hund, it will be for an oath or honor. And who knows, it might not hurt Rome at all.'

'Yes,' he said and stared at Sigimer. 'Chaos in the enemy ranks is always a good thing. More chiefs, more easy the victory.' I nodded. *He was right*, I thought, as Hund left. *Sigimer's freedom would break Segestes but might make leading very hard for Armin.*

Brimwulf came back a bit later with another man. He nodded to the north. 'There are again some merchants down at the ford. They have horses. Odo and some twenty of his creatures went there, over the woods and hills. That way,' Brimwulf said, nodding towards the north. The other Batavi looked uncertain as he fidgeted on his haunches. Brimwulf nodded at him and scratched his beard. 'He has some other news.'

'Yes?' I asked, dreading the mounting problems stopping me from getting Cassia to a legion's doctor.

'There are signs around the Buck River,' he told me. 'Not made by simple merchants.'

Brimwulf sneered. 'He thinks there is an army out there. Not a Roman one.'

The Batavi shook his head. 'There were footprints, horse turds.'

'You read horse turds?' I smiled, despite my anguish over Cassia.

'And this,' he said darkly.

He gave me an arrow with white and grey quills. 'They come from a Chatti quiver. The feather is theirs. I know them. They forage as they go, this one was stuck on a root. The Chatti are shadowing Drusus.'

'How many?' I asked, eyeing the arrow, thinking about Oldaric and Adgandestrius. They were coming there with their Chatti to avenge their losses and Ebbe. And perhaps also to support Maroboodus. Father.

'Few, but an army would go through the woods, far from the Roman exploratores. Few men raise no suspicion,' he said.

Brimwulf shook his head. 'The Chatti hunt here anyway. I see no reason—'

Then, a Batavi guard ran downhill to us. 'You should see this!' I got up, and Tudrus nodded at my imploring look. He would stay with Cassia. Agetan and Bohscyld just scowled, and I thanked them with a nod as I placed Cassia's head on the lap of Bohscyld. I got up and ran uphill until the guard made warning gestures, and we went to our knees. We crawled in a field of blueberries, sneaked through rocks and settled down on a small ridge. 'They should be right there.'

'Chatti?'

'Chatti? How did you guess? Yes, Chatti,' he chuckled, his blond beard in tangles and full of thorns.

We raised our heads.

To the north and downhill, one could see an occasional gleam amidst the woods, and we soon saw a sneaking column of men, stretching to the south, women walking next to them. They were men with their hair cut from their foreheads, marks of Chatti, who had killed. They were a line of lean and mean warriors, men hunting for Drusus.

'Chatti exploratores have passed. That is the army,' hissed the Batavi. 'But look, there. Beyond them. Another army.'

'I see him,' I said heavily.

The Chatti were marching in a valley. Beyond them on a hillside rode a column of a thousand men with elaborate hair knots. That was the mark of a Suebi, and these were Suebi indeed. They were from the south. They were men who followed the figure in a gleaming chainmail, wearing what had been Hulderic's beast masked, silvery helmet with red hair spilling over the brim. He was a large man, and his shield was black with a red, rampant bear. He held a long spear with a red banner fluttering in the wind and wore a red tunic. Brimwulf grunted. 'Your father is here, then. Maroboodus?'

I nodded. 'Yes. Last time we saw him he was burning our home. He is here to deal with Drusus. He is in league with Segestes and Woden knows what their plan is. Likely, they will let Drusus and Segestes kill Armin first. I hope Fulcher has reached Drusus and revealed Segestes so these bastards will march to their doom,' I said, and the grip on my sword was that of a desperate man seeking his salvation. *If I could slay my father, Drusus would be safe*, I thought.

'We go and help Sigimer reach Armin, then?' Brimwulf asked. 'Or you still go after Odo?'

I shook my head. 'Odo is right, it is of no use to struggle against the prophecy. I will see him later. A bear is slain, a raven finds the way.'

'What?' Brimwulf asked.

'Gods piss on us. They piss on us all the damned time, and all we can do is stand still and smile,' I cursed. 'That there,' I said, pointing my quivering

338

hand towards my father, 'is the Bear, I am the Raven and when a bear is slain, the lines say, then Raven will find the way. We will not worry about Odo now. I will, later. We just have to find Armin and Drusus now, and the rest will fall into place sooner or later,' I whispered. Father was looking around, speaking to some of his men, and I saw Nihta there with the Marcomanni. The lithe, small man was clean shaven, wore a great, gray cloak and looked tired and drawn. I had miraculously wounded him the night Father dashed our dreams by burning Burlein's village. I wondered what had become of my Aunt Gunhild who had been heavy with Burlein's child, despite being still married to Father. She was Balderich's blood, that of great Suebi Aristovistus like I was, but perhaps Father no longer needed such high blood to keep the Marcomanni fighting for him. There they were, some thousand of them. *Surely more,* I thought, and the remains of the Quadi must be with them. I nodded and spotted a man under a crow's wing banner. He was Sibratus, Lord of the Quadi. 'Thousand?' I asked the Batavi.

Brimwulf grunted. 'Some three thousand total. See. The Chatti have an army and a train of supplies coming as well.' True enough, many horses were being pulled by women. 'They always prepare well for a campaign.'

I nodded and shrugged. 'They are not very many. But we have to leave quickly.'

'They have scouts all around us,' the Batavi guard said bitterly. 'We have to hide for now.'

'How long?' I asked.

'It will be a day. More?' Brimwulf told me unhappily.

'Cassia—'

'Will not survive a meeting with your father. Or the Chatti,' the Batavi said softly. 'I agree with Brimwulf.'

We hid for two long days.

We ate berries, drank water from the cliffside and dared not go search for munitions inside Gulldrum. It rained, and it was humid, and we kept Cassia and Sigimer covered from the elements as best we could. We had no idea where Drusus was, nor Segestes, but the Marcomanni and the Chatti army trailed east, crossing rivers high in the woods around us, foraging, and Brimwulf would sneak out at night to check on their progress and find us food. We ate rabbit, fat birds, fairly delicious mushrooms and a lame horse Brimwulf had found during the night. Cassia had opened up her eyes a few times, though briefly, but long enough for Agetan to give her some food and water. She took it but curled up, not heeding the world.

Then, on the night of the third day, Brimwulf came to me. 'Nobody in the woods. Last of them are gone, all the stragglers, as well. There were some tardy war chiefs but seems they have gone east along the Hercynian, as the Romans call them, woods. The Buck ford is clear as well.' I nodded and rubbed my face. He continued. 'The Roman army passed the ford yesterday morning. They are making good time.'

'Best move on, then,' I breathed. 'Freya's luck, we need it if they have already gone too far.'

Brimwulf nodded and rubbed his stubble. 'I—'

I sat back down to look at him. He was blushing, and I sighed. 'You were sent to me by Thusnelda? That day I escaped Segestes.'

His eyes popped out, and he found himself nodding. 'Why. Yes.'

'And you did not feel your honor was much stained, as you pretended to serve me over her.' I grinned. 'She begged you to take Mathildis away?'

'She hid Mathildis that night Segestes's hall burned,' he said with some shame. 'She told me I owed her and that her father would slay Mathildis, for Wulstan would make sure he knew who was to be blamed for the finger. I swallowed my honor, Hraban and told her I would serve her if she helped us.'

'She told you to help me?' I asked him with a lopsided grin.

He grunted. 'Come now. She told me to make sure you did not fuck up or betray her wishes. But you did not. And you saved Mathildis. And freed him,' he said, nodding at Sigimer, who was joking with Tudrus. 'You are freeing him, right? You said you would.'

'I am,' I said. 'And I like Mathildis. She fed me, helped me, kept me going.' I blushed as I thought of her without her clothes, but Brimwulf did not seem to notice.

He stared at Cassia. 'They can make all the difference in our lives. Has your Fulcher sight? Saw I lied? That why he did not like me?'

340

'I think you are just a hard man to like,' I said with a grin. 'Too hard headed. Like me.'

He smiled and rubbed his face. 'Will you have me?'

'I thought I already had you,' I laughed. 'But yes, if Thusnelda did not ensnare you hopelessly in oaths.'

'She said I should make sure Sigimer is free. After that, I could choose my lord. And I owe you now. For her.'

'I welcome you,' I told him. 'And I think I have a request for you. It might or might not sit well with you.'

'Oh?' he asked, worried. 'I'll pay a heavy price for my lies, I think.'

I thought about what I was going to ask until he began to fidget. 'Armin will have to fight a war. And Thusnelda would like to see him live through it.'

'Yes,' he agreed. 'Of course.'

'But we will need Drusus for our path later,' I told him.

'Why not just let them fight it out, and we join who is left?' he stated.

'If Drusus dies, Brimwulf, Armin will die anyway. Rome won't stop at the death of Drusus. One way or other, they will send tens of thousands of men here, and Armin will eventually fall. Eventually. And we have failed Thusnelda. So, I will ask you for something. Not now, but perhaps later. We will see what takes place out there, but I have an idea. You served Sigimer?'

'His warlord,' he said suspiciously. 'But he knows me. Sigimer.'

'Good,' I told him and smiled.

'Your ideas usually deplete my arrows,' he stated morosely. 'But as I asked to serve you, I suppose I have to obey your orders, no?'

'Yes, that is the idea,' I agreed. 'It will be hard, but yes. Let us leave now.' I roused the camp, prepared the men for the trip, and they agreed enthusiastically, speaking excitedly. We put Cassia and Sigimer on a litter made from cloaks and wood. We made our cumbersome way through game trails, scouting and carefully seeking danger, but there was none. We hiked the harsh forests trails for the fords of the Angry One, struggled through heavy woods and blueberry patches, carefully checking around for an enemy presence and found nothing but some bloated corpses swollen on a field. The Batavi looked entirely unhappy for the lack of their famed horses as we struggled on, but there was nothing to do about that, and so we went on. Far in the east, there were again smoke pillars, and we were making terrible time with the wounded.

'Hard to miss a Roman army,' Tudrus said with a grin while carrying Cassia and Sigimer with me and two other men. 'But they are far. Been keeping busy.'

'They can march very fast,' I agreed, despairing.

'Should there not be a castra in sight?' Hund wondered as we passed huge, abandoned march camps. Nothing permanent was apparently being constructed.

'Drusus is cocky,' Brimwulf agreed. 'They should fortify the way.'

'I'm not sure what he is doing,' I growled. 'Let's march after them.' They all groaned at that, for the litter was making us very, very slow. The Roman army was drawing far from us.

Next day, Tudrus was grunting next to me as we hiked for the Holy One, and it's ford. He nodded at the smoke. 'Sigambri send their children and elders away from the burning halls, the men and their women towards the smoke. Sometimes Rome burns a large settlement and just waits while your Batavi … our Batavi … us Batavi ride around to capture the women.' I chuckled at his confusion and nodded at him, cursing and sweating as I was dragging the litter. Tudrus was sweating next to me. 'She has gained weight in the winter. You should make sure she does not get too fat.'

Sigimer pelted him with a piece of wood from the litter. 'She is a mother. Have some respect, whelp.' Tudrus grinned at me, and I grinned back.

'She is pregnant.' I winced as I stabbed my toe on a rock.

'Some stay fat after giving birth,' Tudrus expertly informed me. 'Mother did.'

'Just take care of your little woman, and I will try to care for this one,' I retorted, and Sigimer hummed in agreement as he lathered Cassia's face with water.

'Have to start thinking about hiding our alliances,' he grunted. I nodded. We had begun to see Cherusci. Most were refugees with no weapons, most were allied to Segestes, but they did stare at the odd troop

342

of men, and some disappeared in a hurry. They would not be in a merciful mood if they happened to be with Armin, and perhaps, if Fulcher had warned Drusus of Segestes, there was no lord in the land. All across the eastern horizon the Cherusci were suffering as Consul Nero Claudius Drusus was determined to burn until the Cherusci gave in. We did not know it, but he had let his cavalry loose and the legions were marching double time for Inguiomerus's lands. But the smoke told a story, and I think we all thought it was too late for Sigimer to help Armin and Inguiomerus. I looked at him, and he nodded, his eyes moist. Should I take him to Drusus, after all, I wondered.

'There should be some farms around, no?' I asked, shaking the misery away. 'Brimwulf?'

'Hraban?' he asked from ahead.

'Hall, find us stables and a hall,' I told him. 'Something that has not been entirely robbed. Horse. We need a horse. Or anything to make us faster.'

'Hall? Already did,' he hollered back at me. Far ahead, we could see the ford, and there would be half a day before Sigimer's lands and the last river. There, to the left stood a brown and green hall. There was a dog in the yard, looking at us suspiciously, but it put it's tail between its legs and slunk away as we approached. Brimwulf ran to the stable end of the hall and stared around the doors. He flashed a smile at us and disappeared inside. Then he cumbersomely pulled something out.

It was a benna. A wagon. It was a rickety thing, but useful.

'Horse?' Tudrus yelled.

'None,' I snorted. 'But it will be better than carrying and dragging this thing.' All the Batavi grunted in agreement. The litter was killing us. We placed Cassia and Sigimer in the benna.

'Hide the signum inside,' I told Hund, and he nodded. 'Shields and helmets as well.' We heaped the Roman gear next to Cassia and began pushing the cart. It was fast, much faster than carrying the litter, but we had to use the roads.

That night I was sitting with Cassia when Brimwulf came to me, his mouth open.

'I have no food to put there, man. Close it back up,' I joked but saw him staring up into the sky. There, in the sky, streaks of silver were coming down from the heavens. Some quick, others slower like tears of gods flowing on the edges of the sky. We stared at them for a long time, wondering if they were a good or a bad omen, each in our thoughts.

In the morning, we pushed forward while eating a meager meal of berries, and really, anything we could find. One Batavi had bark in his mouth while chewing it thoughtfully. Brimwulf had been hunting, and some men enjoyed something I thought was a squirrel, but I was unwilling to ask him. Thus, we traveled a day, slept a night and then, that next day we reached the last river, the Holy One.

That was when the disaster struck.

We pushed the benna to the Holy One and struggled in mud to guide it gracefully to the water. We were midway, nearly over the worst places, and then Hund whistled. 'Over there!' he yelled and pointed to the north, where some twenty men were riding for us. They held Germani shields, oval and square, painted with moons and stars and animals and were tall and well armored.

'Trouble,' Tudrus said.

'The man in front, the armored bastard, he has a limp arm,' a Batavi said. 'Ragwald?'

'Get the shields and helmets,' I cursed, and the men did. The Batavi took up the shields and hefted their spent weapons. They surrounded me, and Hund lifted the unit standard high above us, proudly.

It was Ragwald.

They were technically allied to Rome, but it was Ragwald, and he was not allied to me. He had twenty men, men I knew from Segestes's household, and they rode under Ragwald's banner, which was apparently a dead man's skin. He pointed at us, and they spread out. My men prayed, and shields slammed to cover the man next to them. The wall of horses approached slowly, raising dust and grit to the air. They stopped at the edge of the water.

Ragwald's eyes went to slits as he regarded us. Then those eyes opened as large as eggs, and he stammered. He pointed a finger at us. I saw

Brimwulf look up to the sky with no hope as he cocked an arrow. He would suffer like I would for his treachery. Ragwald smiled like a wolf with a fat, lost lamb in the woods. His men stopped and stared at us from the river bank. They were well armed with heavy, long hasta spears, axes and cudgels and some bows. They glared at Brimwulf, whom they all knew. Ragwald guided the horse to the water, cursing the mud. He fixed a glare my way, and I spat on the current. I called out. 'How's your son? And that whore's boy. Helmut's whelp? Lost his tongue?'

'You bastard.' He laughed. 'Here you are. All the silver in the world would not tempt me to let you go. I'll drown you. But first, we will pull your guts out through your ass. Is that your woman?' he asked, trying to see into the benna. 'She will warm my bed tonight. Pregnant? Oh, my. How careless, Hraban. A new slave for me. Perhaps it shall be a girl?' Agetan grunted and grabbed me as I had walked forward. Ragwald was cackling on the river bank. The big Quadi stared at my eyes and fingered a long pugio. His pig-like eyes went to Cassia, and I nearly sobbed. Then I nodded. He would make sure none of Ragwald's promises would come true.

'Come and fight, crippled piss pants,' Tudrus yelled, and my men rattled their weapons on their shields.

Ragwald was in no hurry, though. 'And I thought you were looters,' he sneered at us. 'Batavi pushing a fool in a cart. Oh, and Brimwulf. All the eggs in the same basket. About to fall from a fence.' Sigimer was rousing himself, but I shook my head at him. He nodded, holding his ax. I said nothing to Ragwald as I squeezed the hilt of my blade, cursing the gods for this misfortune. Ragwald pointed a finger at us. 'You are all on Segestes's land. You are trespassing. But we will let you make the land richer with your decomposing corpses.'

'You will rot in hell, getting humped by a filthy dwarf, Ragwald,' I told him cheerfully, bored of it all.

'No, you will watch me hump the woman. My boy died. His wound swelled, and he died. I will cut you to ribbons. Nothing else matters, really.' He gestured towards us, and his men dismounted.

'So, come and take us, Ragwald, I tire of arguments with a one armed dimwit,' I told him. He nodded, raised his arm and then our luck changed.

Out of the eastern woods, an army emerged.

They bore a strange standard of a two-headed serpent, and Armin was at their head. I saw the golden hair flash as he gave orders, and I thanked Woden for his mercy. Apparently, the great god was not done with us yet. There were many hundreds of the Cherusci as they walked towards us. Ragwald went white from the face and started to turn his horse west to rush over the river. His eyes gauged Brimwulf's cocked arrow. The archer looked him squarely in his eye, but Ragwald took the risk and whipped the horse as Brimwulf released an arrow. It hit Ragwald in the shoulder, glancing off, and he shrieked with fear as his horse splashed by us and through the ford and the river. He whipped his horse past us as he raced away. The rest of the men stood in a sullen group as Armin approached. The Cherusci approached and in their faces, one could see the torn looks of men who had fought for two years against their own and Rome. They were dirty, spent, and fey, their weapons used and well mended, but ready to fight again. Armin stopped to stare at the men of Segestes. They were Roman and would likely die. He spat and looked at the tallest man. 'Was that Ragwald?'

'Lord, he was,' the man said fearfully. 'He probably thought you were Roman auxilia.'

What in Hel's name? I thought.

Armin grunted and cut the man off. Armin might have been young, but his displeasure was deadly, no matter how high a man. Silence reigned as Armin sat there on his horse, staring at me. Finally, he roused himself. 'His lord Segestes waits for him in the camp,' Armin told them sullenly. 'Return there and fetch the coward.'

I stared at Armin in shock. *Was Segestes in his camp? Had Fulcher succeeded and Segestes had switched sides?*

They turned their mounts, and Armin's men scowled at them. There was no love lost between them. Some rode past us and took after Ragwald and others returned to the camp. Armin came where Ragwald had stood and stared balefully at the Batavi. I stepped forward, and he nodded

346

reluctantly. He waved his men off, and they rode a way back, staying there to stare at their enemies; us. The young chief was in a fey mood. One could understand it by looking at the ragged band of men, who used to be wealthy, respected and feared by their neighbors. Armin's armor was used, his shield scratched and his hair dirty. *Now,* I thought, *Armin finally looked like a real thiuda, a War King.* I stopped short of the bank and tilted my head at him. 'Armin.'

He nodded at me. 'Greetings Hraban. Care to come over here?'

I smiled and nodded at him. I walked his way until I got out of the water. He looked down at me from his powerful horse and got down. He sat on the grass, pushing his horse further away and squinted up at me. 'Sit down. My ass is killing me. I have been living on a saddle for two years.'

'I herded pigs,' I told him as I sat next to him.

'I am sorry I failed you,' he said sadly but rubbed his face, and I realized he was giggling.

'You ...' I began and went silent. I opened my mouth again, but he waved me down.

'I am sorry. But pigs? I never thought the brutes Segestes employs have such a keen eye for creatures of the same temperament,' he blurted, wiping his eyes. 'And I mean it in a good way. Like god Freyr, you fight like a mad boar.'

'I'm beholden to Woden, and these were not wild boars, but regular pigs,' I fumed. 'But I thank you for your help.'

'I was unable to help, Hraban.' He smiled sadly. 'I have lost all my land once and twice, only to creep back in the deep winter to take it back. I hear Segestes tried to get the ring from your foe Odo to pacify Inguiomerus? And my father to pacify me?'

He had not seen Sigimer.

'Yes. But Odo only wanted to see me go free. He does not care about our struggles.'

He hesitated and shook his head. 'I will have to go and try to free Father, one day. Your Odo made an enemy of me, as well.'

I bit my tongue, as I saw Sigimer rousing himself in the benna. 'Why is Ragwald going to your camp? And more specifically, Segestes?'

347

Armin snorted and rubbed his face. 'Because Segestes suddenly asked to join. Thusnelda told me Segestes was in league with your father. He was more than a traitor to the Cherusci, but also to Drusus. King of the North!' I snorted, for his father had said the very same thing. He went on. 'And now he is to fight Drusus with the rest of us because he has been exposed.'

I spat. 'He was going to march with Drusus until you lot were dead and only then was he to betray Drusus. But I made sure Drusus found out about his betrayal.'

Armin laughed. 'I thank you for the army, then!'

'Yes,' I said, thinking how Sigimer had not been needed after all. 'Thusnelda sends her slaves to tell you?'

'Yes,' he agreed. 'Well, Drusus is here now, burning my lands. And the lands of Inguiomerus. Or was. I had no men to give him battle two days ago so I take what I can. Segestes and your father are going to fight him here as he returns. Drusus is the greatest threat to the Cherusci. I hate Segestes and Maroboodus, but we will have an army. And I don't care if they serve enemies of Drusus or not, in the end, it is about our lands and people and Drusus has to fall first and soon. I only have to survive the battle, your lord has to fall, and then I will challenge Segestes, but later. I have no choice, Hraban. I have to join with them for this one great cause.'

'I've seen Maroboodus,' I said bitterly.

'There are some Chatti as well. If Drusus dies—'

'Segestes won't kill Romans after Drusus falls,' I said sadly. 'He will abandon you and Rome will win, without my lord.'

'If Drusus dies, we have a chance to beat anyone that replaces him,' he said stubbornly. 'Now, I have to endure your father's Warlords, Inguiomerus, Segestes himself though Woden be thanked his shield was stolen, and we no longer have to endure that travesty.' He grinned at me and winked. 'And Catualda. The bastard mocks me at the side of Segestes. But together we have a plan.'

'What plan?' I asked him.

He snorted and clapped my back. 'You will find out. I began this war with no hope, but I have some now. What are you doing here, behind the Roman army?'

'Because I promised Thusnelda I would help you,' I said bitterly. 'She released me so I would help you. And so, now we have done so.'

'How did you help me?' he said with curiosity. 'She hinted at you trying to do something for me but did not tell me anything specific. Was probably afraid I would ride to help you and die in the process. But you did, didn't you, if it is your doing Segestes joined me.'

'I visited Odo's hole,' I said happily and pointed at the benna. 'Sigimer is there, on that wagon. She thought he would be able to summon his old lords and Inguiomerus to the war for you. But it all went to Hel.' His eyes turned that way, and he shivered. He tried to get up, but I pulled him down. His face turned to angry red, his hand groping for a sword, and I heard his troop rumble. 'What of us?' I asked him.

'You?' he said with a throaty voice, his eyes creeping to his father. 'What of you?'

I cursed. 'Us. Shall we go in peace? Or shall you keep us as we know your plans.'

He shook his head. 'You don't know their ... our plan. And I won't tell, no matter if you kill him or not.'

'I will not slay your father.' I sighed. 'Not even if you slay us. Just spare my wife,' I stated bitterly. 'She needs help. She is with a baby. And she is hurt.' My voice shattered, and I held my head briefly at the sorrow of it all.

'Cassia?' he asked. 'This is that Cassia Thusnelda mentioned. She is pregnant?' He had great eyes.

'She is,' I said desperately. 'If you will kill me here, at least—'

'You can go to Drusus,' Armin laughed. 'It won't matter. There will be a great battle, and I don't care if your lord finds out about our allies.'

'You realize,' I said in wonder, 'that Segestes will likely give Thusnelda to Maroboodus after the battle. To cement their alliance. They will likely sit on your corpse as they agree on it.'

He went very silent as he sat there and then shook his head. 'This will be a grand battle, Hraban. It will be fought very soon. Segestes will not survive it. I have made sure of it. But I need his men and those of your father so it will be all about timing. Or it will end as you described, and I will go to Woden or Freya, and she will also die.'

'Thusnelda?' I asked him. 'Will die?'

'She will follow me,' he breathed. 'No matter where. She promised me this.'

'I see.'

He waved his hand around. 'But now, with my father free? I will have a much better chance challenging Segestes. So, this is my gift to you. Go free and tell your Drusus there will be some thousand Marcomanni Suebi men breaking to his flank. Go and tell him this, Hraban. In the end, the Cherusci will fight, and that is the way to end battles.'

'You prefer to assassinate your enemies,' I said suspiciously.

He smiled at me and clapped my back. 'Sometimes I too, prefer a fight. Perhaps this time.'

'Perhaps not,' I cursed. 'Is Inguiomerus with you?' I asked him.

'He bowed to Drusus not days ago,' Armin said carelessly as if he was describing a boring fishing event.

'They are finished?'I asked him in stupefaction.

'Not really,' he said smiling. 'Only partially. One surrenders. One changes one's mind. We will see.'

'And he has changed his mind?'

He shook his head. 'Some might come, but not all. The Suebi attacked him after Drusus forced him to submit. I thank you for Thusnelda. For her life. And for my father. We found you a day ago, and I suppose I did save your hide just now.'

'You did, and I thank you for Cassia. She will need care,' I told him squeezing his shoulder. I did not trust him, but I was grateful. 'And Lif?'

He smiled at me. 'We can escort you to Drusus. We are going to meet them in battle soon, after all.'

I thanked him but did not budge. 'Where is Lif?' I asked again.

He nodded towards the east. 'Lif is safe, I am sure. She is hidden in the Godsmount. And your Veleda is alive, and well. In fact, it was she, who made the great Consul turn around from Albis and Inguiomerus.'

'She ... what?' I asked in confusion. 'She was just a wee little thing!'

He shook his head in wonderment. 'Veleda met Drusus on the banks of the tributary of Albis, some days that way. At the borders of Inguiomerus,' he gestured to the forests and hills over the smoke pillars. 'He met her and she cast spells for him and asked him why he comes so far. She told him that to go further would kill him. To go back, might as well. She spoke at length with him. And now he is coming back.'

'How do you know this?' I asked him.

'Your family. Our family. I know Veleda. We have guarded Godsmount for ages,' he told me.

'Odo told me you were related to our family,' I stated. 'Is it true?'

'It is true. You are Gothoni, but some say Woden set our family here to keep an eye on the Godsmount. I know the way up there. Few do, but I do. And I did ask Veleda to stop Drusus and turn him around. She did miraculously.'

'Thusnelda saved me,' I told him. 'Women can work wonders in our world.'

'We can but drift in their wake,' Armin agreed. 'When all is over, and if you survive, I shall send a man up there with you.'

'What man is this?' I asked him.

'A reluctant man. A man of conflicting emotions. I have a need of him for now. But after the battle? He might wish to lead you up there. I have told him about it, anyway,' he told me as he massaged his neck. 'Yes, I think he should be the one. I'll give him the instructions.'

'Thank you,` I said as I got up.

He laughed. 'Come. Let us ride to end all the quarrels,' he said cheerfully and got up. He mounted and rode to his father. I saw him nod at the older man, who laughed audibly over the water, and they embraced. I envied Armin his father, your grandfather, Thumelicus, my Lord.

We got the horses, and the Cherusci rode with us for the east. I mulled over the situation and decided Armin would die, no matter what took place. Sigimer as well, likely. So, I gave Brimwulf some instruction as we rode, and he listened to me very carefully. At the end of my speech, he finally nodded, though reluctantly, and I clasped arms with him.

BOOK 5: THE BEAR AND THE RAVEN

*'Am I not your son, Father? See? How casually I slay. Very much like you,
no?'*
Hraban to Maroboodus

CHAPTER 29

I watched Armin's silhouette against the rising sun. His hair was a golden halo, and he lifted his sword high into the air as his horse reared and struggled against his wishes. He grinned like a young god and rode away. The signifier, Hund shook his head at me. 'That man and that nobody we saved will cause us much hardship yet. But it will all be put to rest soon.'

'Soon,' I agreed, and we waited as some Thracian and Gaulish exploratores approached. I hailed them, and we showed them our standard and shields, and the men nodded towards the east. We rode over heavy woods and some glittering streams of water and made it across a few low hills and ridges. Tudrus rode after me, Agetan and Bohscyld with the Batavi and so we reached a tall ridge. I looked at the lightly wooded plains and rich fields to the east and nudged Tudrus. 'So many fields.'

He nodded and looked over the fertile land. 'Not exactly like Moenus River, eh? Rich folks here. But now it will all burn and churn produce for the Romans. Err ... us that is.'

I shook my head. 'The Cherusci have not lost all that much. They will survive. They have been growing rich here for decades, and now they have to toughen up. And men like Segestes? They are unlikely to last, no matter how many fools bow down to them. When the Romans go home, it will be like Luppia. Only the roads are Roman; the rest will continue thanking high Woden and sooner or later even Segestes will find himself ruling only his hall, if that.'

Hund stopped next to us and grinned foolishly. 'I think that is how Rome wants it. Subdue people. Set some fool to govern it, and they are sure to have a reason to come back with the legions. They will burn, enslave, and steal. Their armies get training, fools lose their heads, and then they rebuild. Rome goes home. Some chiefs get power-hungry, men weep over their past fame and honor and rebel again only to be butchered again. Rome will slowly bleed the land out like they have been doing with so many nations. In the end, no man remembers their past, their history, their fathers and the deeds that made them proud and only Rome remains. Just look at the Sigambri, Bructeri, and Marsi. Most warriors are young. Soon, they will be gone. But not the Batavi. We just keep being Batavi.'

Tudrus snorted. 'If the Cherusci fall, the Suebi will move west from the unknown lands and take up the spear. Rome will never truly take these fields and woods. There are many nations in that way who know how to fight. And they will get better at it.'

I guided my horse forward, holding Cassia tight. 'Rome will try to take this land anyway. And I have a hunch we will see how it goes. Starting tomorrow or the day after, they will fight here.'

Tudrus yawned. 'Then, let us hope they make a martyr out of Armin soon, and they get peace here for a moment at least.'

'They will try,' I said with a troubled voice, looking at sleeping Cassia, whimpering with pain and nightmares, 'but Armin is not an easy Fox to catch. He has a plan again. Or my father does. Segestes is with them.'

Hund turned to look at the way we came. 'The bastard found out you beat Odo and knew he would be exposed as a traitor to Drusus. Turned tail and ran to Armin. They have the Chatti and your father, true, but what more surprises can he spring? There are ten thousand legionnaires, and Thracian, Noricum auxilia with many Alpine men. Gaulish? More? Five thousand more? Armin has lost.'

'He does not know the meaning of the word,' I mused as Thracian riders came to us from a game trail and saw our standard. We were escorted over a large wooded ridge dotted with abandoned halls, then down it, across a bright, beautiful stream and there, in that valley stood a Roman castra. A huge one.

We rode up to it, dismounted and walked in via Porta Praetoria, escorted by some Aquitani auxilia, Gauls with tall mustaches and bracae pants under the Roman lorica hamata. We found a squat tent after the fifth street and demanded a medicus to attend us and the Aquitani to wait. After a while, a medical orderly arrived, blanched at seeing a female patient, and we had to explain the dire nature of our need nearly at a sword point. He agreed it was an urgent issue, left, and a medical optio arrived, wiping his hands clean of blood. The man was unsure about what he should do, and Tudrus had to explain to him that she was also a medicus, and a chirurgii was summoned. Tudrus was dirty and growing fiercely angry and amidst his growls the chirurgii fully understood our need for haste. He began to care for Cassia, gently feeling her skull, and the Quadi brothers stayed with her until I returned, for the Gaul auxilia escorting us were at the end of their patience.

We were escorted to the praetorium.

The command tent was large, its white sides flapping in the wind as the XIII Gemina and XVI Gallica were busily perfecting the camp. The army had marched there that past night, and the agger and fossa were being reinforced in haste and vallum and towers were nearly ready. Apparently, Drusus knew Armin was to give battle soon, and there was no reason to tear down the marching camp. I stared at the dusty, fierce legionnaires at work and the bustle of auxilia everywhere. Arrows and armor were being fitted and fixed, and there was a hopeful smile on the faces of the southern soldiers. They had been marching for months and apparently, their battles had been few. I stood in front of the tent, trying to glimpse inside but only saw the occasional foot, some with a sturdy boot on, others with the usual caligae. It was evening, and the Consul Nero Claudius Drusus was sending men out with orders for the next day, and as some of these men left, I saw him.

There stood my lord, and he glimpsed me.

His movement stopped, and a wide smile spread on his lips. He was obviously exhausted and perhaps ill, for his color was pale, but he was happy. I bowed to him and then the wind closed the tent.

I waited.

'Nervous bunch,' Hund whispered, and I looked at the faces of the men working around us. Though they were smiling, happily anticipating action, they did seem nervous, anxious. A man was whispering about wolves to another, the other one was nodding, speaking about gods riding in the camp two days prior, two strange, glowing boys, and they both seemed assured they would not see their homes again. I snorted. *Veleda and Armin,* I thought, *had done well.* They feared their own shadow. Their skills were not diminished by the gossip, visions, and superstition. Everyone I saw was working or training hard. There was a lot of noise from the men, more from the mules carrying the gear of the troops. I saw an auxilia group marching by and saw their standard. It was 1st Vangiorum. I smiled at that. Vangiones. The age old enemies of the Marcomanni. The tribe father had duped to attacking our village only to fail by his saving spear. That bit of double-dealing had spiraled Maroboodus to glory. *That attack orchestrated by Father had killed Mother and Grandfather,* I thought and hated him for his callousness. The marching men reminded me of that faraway day. The Vangiones were armed like the Romans, and I thought of Vago, their king I had killed in his hall. I again wondered what became of Vannius, the third of the brothers, who had betrayed Tudrus and joined my father. He had, perhaps, tried to take Hunfried's place as the king of the Vangiones after I captured Hunfried, the ax tattooed bastard for Burlein. Hunfried had fallen into Father's hands after Burlein fell. Had he been rescued by Rome from Maroboodus? Yes. I remember it was so.

There they marched. Our old enemies, now allies.

Then lictors filed out of the tent, and I turned to stare at them. They carried the fasces, the rods and axes and most were old soldiers. You could see it by looking into their eyes and the way they stopped to stare at me. I was filthy, stained in crusted blood and armed to the teeth. I flipped the helmet off my head and set it down before me. They relaxed, but not by much. I realized most were different men from those I had known two

356

years ago, and there were more of them. *A Consul*, I thought, *would be allowed a more extensive following.*

And then the Consul stepped out.

He was a father, a noble, a builder, and a soldier, but for some reason he loved men like me, young and old, crude peasant-like warriors. He could have been a poet, but he wrote orders. He could have been an intellectual, but he preferred the farts of armored men to the drone of philosophers and so, to the chagrin of his bodyguards, he rushed and embraced me, tears flowing from his eyes. I embraced him back and felt like falling on my knees before him. 'Congratulations on your new child,' I told him, and he roared with laughter, pushing me to arms length.

'You failed in finding Armin for me! But I am so happy you are here!' he told me. He pulled me to the tent acting as a praetorium and stopped his lictors from entering. He ordered any remaining men to exit. They filed out, wonder in their eyes when Drusus seated me down on a sturdy seat with a yellow pillow, poured me sweet wine and handed it to me. Then he dragged his chair before me. 'They told me you were dead. Chariovalda searched for you, and we sent men to find you, but they did not. Fulcher failed, even. The Tribune in Castra Flamma could not find your body. Where were you?' he asked. 'I was sure you were killed after time passed.'

'Who told you I was dead, Lord?' I asked. *Had Fulcher not told him everything?*

'Segestes did, he showed my men your helmet and mail shirt,' he said. 'He said that Armin had killed you when you were going to join me for Arbalo.'

I nodded carefully. 'Segestes held me, Lord.'

'Drusus, remember?' he told me and did not look surprised, only disappointed. He mulled his wine after a time and nodded to himself. 'I see. And now Segestes is a traitor. He was to join us at the borders of the contested land, and he joined our enemies, suddenly. The exploratores told me he rode off while marching his men to us. Just like that. I have never been more generous with a so undeserving lord. And why did he join Armin, and why did he hold you?'

'Where is Fulcher?' I asked him.

He looked at me strangely. 'I have not seen him. Why?'

I rubbed my face and worry twisted my belly like a clamp. I leaned forward in anguish. 'I sent him to find you. He had a scroll, and he was to explain to you what has taken place.'

'I see,' Drusus said sadly. 'Perhaps he got lost?' I shook my head. *No, he failed. He is dead,* I thought.

Drusus waited patiently and after some time, I managed to speak up. 'Segestes is with Armin,' I said, tasting the wonderful wine, sorrow making me ill, 'but only until you die. He has a plan, you see. He is with my father. Always was. Antius is his friend, in more ways than business. He will rule the north and Father the south after you have died and Rome has forgiven everything. And he held me because I knew. But I escaped, you see, and he dared not march to you. Likely, Segestes would have helped you kill Armin and then they would have helped the Marcomanni slay you in some surprise. Now? They are improvising. They are all here. With the Chatti.'

'Your father?' he asked in wonder. 'Maroboodus? I routed him and the Quadi in the south last year and some lord of his early spring. This year we burned Mattium of the Chatti. Oldaric ran, and they are fugitives in the east. You mean to say they are plotting to kill me here? Even now?'

I nodded, my hands trembling. *I had sent Fulcher to his death.* He had had sight, and he had been right. 'Paullus, the commander of Castra Flamma, works for Antius as well. He, Segestes, and Maroboodus are all in a league, and the latter two are ready to claim their prize. I had a scroll as proof and sent it with Fulcher.'

Drusus frowned. 'I believe you. So. The time has come for Drusus to fall, eh? Your father is truly out there?'

'And Oldaric with some Chatti. And the Quadi,' I said. 'I've seen them.'

'You've seen them?' he wondered. 'Thousands?'

'Three thousand,' I agreed. 'Estimate only, of course. Segestes is there now, with the enemy. They will have some twelve thousand men, at most? If Inguiomerus joins them.'

He stared at me in stupefaction. 'He won't.' He leaned back, looking at the ceiling. 'So, had you not escaped, my camp would have thousands of traitors and at some point, Segestes would have handed me to your father to kill. A fine plan. Now they have to fight for my head, no? Too bad about the scroll. It would have been rarely written proof that I am so hated by those who would strip Rome of its dignity and past. Can you guess Armin's plan, now that they cannot slay me with betrayal?'

I waved the goblet of wine towards the west. 'Armin did not tell me.'

'Armin saw you?' he asked incredulously. 'He spoke to you? When?'

'He escorted us here,' I said sheepishly. 'I did save Thusnelda for him once,' I told him with a defensive sniffle. 'And Thusnelda made me promise her something. But I would not trust him, and he probably has a plan beyond a simple battle. And Father is sure to have one as well.'

Drusus slapped my knee. 'Yes. That bastard is planning more than just fighting a battle. After Arbalo and the debacle in Bructeri lands, I have grown very tired of him. And what is to become of him if they should destroy us?' Drusus wondered. 'They are in a forced alliance, but Maroboodus and Segestes will not bow down to a whelp should they win by Fortuna's treachery. And I am friends with Fortuna so that it won't happen.'

I laughed hollowly. 'He is planning on doing all he can to destroy you. Then he will kill Segestes,' I told him with a tired grin. 'He will likely attack Father after. For Thusnelda. Segestes is still planning on giving the woman to him to cement their alliance. Father does not have many men, but Segestes is Armin's first enemy after they have destroyed us.'

'Destroying two Roman legions is no small feat, though, Well,' Drusus grinned. 'We will beat them in battle, and we shall spare them the need to worry about such matters. We will find the Chatti and your father, root out anything they have planned and just deploy enough men to beat them.'

'Yes, Lord,' I told him. 'The Chatti. You burned Mattium?'

He waved his hand. 'Well, no. Did you know Ebbe died?'

'No, Lord,' I said and felt sorry for Adgandestrius. I had liked his father; the one Drusus had imprisoned to keep the Chatti peaceful. His eyes flashed, and he waved his hand.

'I know. You were right. They went to war with us when I took to attacking Maroboodus in the south. Ebbe did not take to the imprisonment well. He withered away. I burned Oldaric's people out of Melocavus and built castrum there. This year, we marched past Mattium, but it was empty, and I only burnt the outlying villages. I left it standing, so we know where to find them next year. They have new lords after Ebbe died. Oldaric, Ebbe's son Adgandestrius and some fool called Esgaroth,' He glanced at me. 'About the Marcomanni.'

'Of the Marcomanni? I hear they fled, and Hard Hill has a castra as well,' I said, mulling the rest of the wine in the cup.

He shrugged. 'Your father led most of his people away. There are still some thousands of very well armed men under his service. And now he has led the best of them here. I fought them not three months ago, Suebi remnants, rich in cattle, but lacking in will to fight. Wise of them. So, the Vangiones tell me. Hunfried ...'

I stopped mulling the wine. 'Hunfried?'

'Hunfried, their king tells me most of the Marcomanni went towards the lands of the Boii. Your people are not dead. Just dislocated. I wanted to tell you, so you would not worry too much.'

'They are not my people anymore, but I thank you,' I said glumly. *And yet*, I thought, *why do I keep hoping they would survive?*

Drusus grinned and nodded at me. 'Right. We might have to deal with your father eventually, if not here,' he told me, clapping my shoulder. 'We will try very hard to finish it here, Hraban, so the people you no longer care about will be spared further wars. And perhaps, one day, they can return to Moenus River?' he said, twiddling his fingers.

'Thank you, Drusus,' I said and smiled. He read me well.

'I have a need of you,' he shook his head heavily, 'in Rome. One day? When you are old and wise and less inclined to swing a sword, you might return to these lands to rule there,' he went on, and my heart cried for joy, for that way I might be able to keep my word to the Quadi as well. He nodded and went on. 'But that is a matter for the future, and now we have to deal with our enemies here and later, in Rome. That will mean a long, long war.' His face looked drawn as he said that, for had not Rome fought decades worth of civil wars previously? 'We will see. For your services, Hraban, you will be well rewarded.' He got up and stalked around, back and forth, trying to control his anger. He stopped in front of me, bent over me, and looked into my eyes. 'Your daughter?'

'I hear you saw an apparition? A ghost?' I asked, carefully.

He looked confused, squirmed and fell back to his seat, and I saw him struggling with his thoughts. Then he nodded. 'A young Germani ghost, a girl, told me I should turn back. She glowed. She had an elfin face, and she was not of this world.'

'Glowing, Lord? Drusus?' I asked with a small smile.

'She stood on the other side of this tributary of Albis River, amidst Inguiomerus's tribesmen. They did not appear to see her, but she yelled at me, across the river,' he said, wonder in his eyes. He got up and brushed at his sword. 'I met with Inguiomerus later. Inguiomerus said it was a vaettir, a thing of the gods, a messenger. Men were afraid.' He glanced at me. 'Yes, I was too. So, we erected a monument to celebrate the trek, for few Romans have been there, so far from home. I carved the names of the Marcomanni, Chatti, and Cherusci in it, and gave it to Juppiter. I made a deal with Inguiomerus and came back to look for Armin.'

I laughed. 'I hope the Germani have not made it shorter, Lord.'

He looked offended. 'Inguiomerus will protect it. No matter if he fights us again one day. There is no honor in defying the gods. Why did you ask about this spirit? Your daughter? Is she alive?'

'She is, I hear, holed up with this glowing ghost. Veleda is her name, by the way.' I grinned. 'She is, I think, very much alive.'

'Where?' He frowned.

I waved my hand east. 'There is a mountain near here. Godsmount. I hear my daughter is hidden there. I will find her,' I said. 'After I have killed the Bear.'

'The Bear?' Armin looked shocked. 'Your father?'

'Yes,' I said. 'I will, if you give me leave, lead my men up there and finish the matter once and for all when the battle is over.'

He nodded and grinned. 'Do so. We will hunt your father, and then you go and tell the glowing ghost girl I will not be fooled again.'

'I will. She seemed like a serious type when I last saw her,' I told him and put the empty wine cup away. 'But I suppose she did smile after Armin asked her to turn you back.'

Drusus glowered at the thought of having been duped by Armin and a slip of a girl, but soon nodded peacefully and put a hand on mine. 'You will go after all this is settled. And then, we shall plan for many great things. We will get you married, perhaps?'

'I am married,' I told him. 'She was hurt in Odo's den, but she is with the medicus.'

'Is she pregnant, as well?' he smiled and hooted as he saw my face. 'She is! Gods, you shall never sleep again!' He cackled for awhile, and I thought of Lif and how she had been a baby when I last saw her. I had not minded being a father and not sleeping at all, but I humored him with a wry smile and a shake of my head. He finally relaxed and nodded. 'Well, they have us here then. And now we will have to kill the lot. We will be patient. Armin will come.'

'He wants a fight, Lord,' I agreed. 'He and his father ...'

'Sigimer?' he breathed. 'He died. Years ago.'

'No, he is with Armin again,' I said. 'I ... uh.'

He turned to me. 'You found and returned Sigimer to them?' he asked with a wry smile. 'Was there a good reason for it?'

I nodded, reserved. 'There was and I did, Drusus.'

He laughed and embraced me. 'Thank you. If Sigimer leads the enemy, this will be easy. More high nobles to their camp, I say, and they will fight badly and forget Armin's plans.'

'But not the plans of Maroboodus,' I warned him.

'Wait,' he said and took me out of the tent. He pointed his finger to the east. There, far, a low range of hills or even a mountain rose. I thought I could make out low, wooded slopes, crags and twin peaks, but I was not sure. 'In case I die, that is where your Lif is. That is the place they call Godsmount. I asked as we passed it.'

I stared at that far away place and felt a flutter in my heart, impatience pulling at me, and I longed to find a horse and make my way there. 'Thank you, Drusus.'

362

He stopped to look at me strangely. 'You are welcome. You know. My father used to call me his bear. It is amusing to have something in common with your father. And I am sorry for Fulcher. He was a worthy man. Is. I ... hope he is still alive.'

I bowed to him and swallowed my sorrow. *Was Drusus called the bear?* I cursed the elusive prophecy and felt like a leaf in the wind as I walked out, pulling my helmet on.

CHAPTER 30

My friends and the Batavi took the news of Fulcher's loss heavily. I honed the Winter Sword, thinking about his family and how we would miss his practical wisdom and skills. He had set out to avenge his son, and he had, but now I did not even know what had happened to him.

In the meantime, wolves prowled around the camp. Night and day, they howled in the fields and woods around us and then, in a few days time, they went silent. That was disquieting. We would see all across the horizon great flocks of birds flying in scared droves before scattering to the four winds. Deer and moose were seen running wildly past the castra. After being issued new orders by Drusus, the auxiliary commanders had begun to set exploratores on high alert to find the enemy.

Soon, they did.

One day, I saw Thracian cavalry pummeling for the castra, and soon an exploratore was pointing his spear to the north and west. A military tribune was listening and then ran, his helmet spilling from his head. 'Armin's army is here,' Tudrus said as we looked on at the porch of the barracks reserved for the Batavi. He was braiding his hair and shook his head. 'Last bit ahead, Hraban.'

'Perilous bit,' I breathed. 'But yes. Armin's alliance is here. Or Father's, rather.'

'At least the Luppia tribes are busy,' Tudrus grumbled. I nodded and turned to look east. There, the clear weather made it possible to see a mountain's outlines. It was, I decided, rather more like a series of very tall hills, superbly wooded and full of ravines and crags. It looked deceitfully low, but I was sure it was painful to climb. Somewhere out there, Lif awaited. I gazed at its slopes, the hills around it, the two hazy tops and the woods scattered around it. A bear was to die. Then I would go there.

Later, I watched with the Batavi as Drusus gave a speech to the gathered legions. He exhorted them, reminding them of home and a road to victory would lead to riches, loot, slaves, and glory. They listened willingly, sturdy and tough soldiers and prepared for battle, and the somber, frightened mood was dissipating from the ranks. Looking up to the ridges surrounding the valley, we could see fires already burning in the woods, and men were making jokes about the foe.

The next day, the exploratores rode busily along the woods and ridges. Some did not return but most did. I tended Cassia and Agetan, or Bohscyld was always there to guard her. Tudrus entered and looked at her breathe peacefully and nodded. 'She will be fine. The chirurgii claimed there is no fracture on her skull.'

'Any news?'

Tudrus nodded. 'The ridge is full of Cherusci. Segestes is in the middle, his army best armed currently. Armin's and Sigimer's men are to the left of Segestes, and then there is the army of the Chatti to their right.'

'Chatti?' I asked him, surprised. 'They did not keep them hidden to make things interesting in the flank?'

'No,' Hund said. 'They are up there, and they will be in a huge shield wall the day we march up the hill and ridge. Oldaric's standard is there. But the exploratores have seen the Marcomanni to the woods to our south. They are laying low. Some thousand of them.'

'The best men Maroboodus has,' I agreed. 'Likely those he trained to fight as Romans.'

'It seems like a futile battle,' Tudrus grunted. 'There is nothing else out there. Nothing. This time Drusus has had his men ride far around the land. Nothing, nothing beyond the enemy army. Inguiomerus is in the east, driving Semnones back. The enemy is numerous. Some ten thousand. Nine on the ridge. But that is it. After Segestes was exposed, it seems like they have nothing but spears to set against our Consul.'

Hund nodded. 'They are not even on the top of the ridge. They are down the hill and the ridge, halfway there.'

I shrugged. 'We will let them grow bored for a day or two more as we scout.'

And we did.

The Batavi joined the activity and Marcus Lollius Paulinus, the young tribune who had been with Drusus since Luppia River gave us our orders. He sent us on errands, mostly on bold excursions to scout behind the enemy lines. Drusus took no risks this time. Exploratores were out, wide and far. I sat on my horse with my Batavi from morning to evening.

When not riding, I enjoyed Cassia's gradual recovery. She was weak, but she smiled, though she did not speak yet. The chirurgii again deemed her skull to be intact and a capsari, a low ranking medical assistant was charged with keeping her healing process going. The young man enjoyed the role so much, I had Agetan growl at the man to keep him on the right track.

Then, after five days of scouting, the army had been told to get ready for the morning.

That last night, we were sitting around Cassia, discussing softly with each other. We had spent the evening counting fires on the hills, and the ridge and soldiers grew restless. Tudrus sighed. 'Tomorrow? Drusus had better fight it out soon. They think he has lost his balls somewhere,' he growled. 'And optio was brought in today, complaining as he had a huge laceration on his knee. Some Marcus was apparently going to take his place. Said it would not have happened if they had fought and gone home already with their loot and slaves.'

'Drusus will fight,' I said gloomily. 'He will get his men up tomorrow and march them up the hill.' I was glowering at the oil lamp, deep in my

366

thoughts. My plan had failed. *Or, they did wish to have a bloody battle, with no devious plans involved*, I thought.

'But ...' Hund argued, and then a legionnaire popped his head into the tent.

'There an uncouth bastard by the jawbreaker name of Hraban here?' he asked brusquely.

'I am Hraban,' I said, getting up.

'Big bastard, aren't you?' he cooed. 'Yet, afraid of the toilets as are all the Germani. You lot shit around in the woods and our horses shy away from the stink. I remember—'

'Can you get to the point, you motherless hen herder,' I grunted and the man grinned, not insulted at all.

'Well, that is more like it. There is a man on the Porta Decumana. The back gate, in case you wondered.'

'Really?'

'Yes. Doesn't know the passphrase. We thought him a spy and planned of jailing the big bastard, but he seems to ride from the Fox himself and claims to be there on a mission. So, before we truss him up and clobber him, you want to have a word with the man?'

'Is it Brimwulf?' I asked, brightening.

'I don't fucking know if it is Brimwulf. He said that is his name, but it could be Clodius for all I know. Get there and find out,' he spat and laughed and left.

'Brimwulf?' Tudrus asked, horrified. 'I had forgotten him. I have not seen him since we left the Cherusci.'

Hund grinned. 'Where did you send him?'

I strapped on my weapons. 'Agetan? You mind ...' The boulder-like Quadi nodded and pulled his wicked ax. He sat by Cassia. 'The rest. Strap on your weapons and come on.' The Batavi did, Hund telling them to gear up.

'Where was he?' Tudrus echoed Hund as he pulled on a helmet. Bohscyld followed suit and filed after me as I rushed out. 'Hraban?' Tudrus demanded.

'He has served his uncle who is close to Sigimer,' I told them. 'I gave him two things to do. One was to bring news if he found out something. After I had heard Segestes was there with Armin, I wanted him to spy.'

'The other?' Tudrus asked.

'To keep him alive,' I whispered.

'Who?' Tudrus demanded. 'Armin?'

'Yes, Armin, for I promised Thusnelda I'd do everything in my power to do so,' I grimaced. 'This is the best I can do.' I did not tell them how Brimwulf was to keep Armin alive.

'He is but one man,' Tudrus admonished me.

'I had none else.'

'Well, he is still alive,' Hund said as we approached the gate. 'Hares are jumping!' he called out to the guard.

A Legionnaire turned on the wall. 'But we still starve!' he answered the other half of the passphrase and nodded below. We walked under the gatehouse that smelled of fresh wood, were admitted through the gate, jumped across muddy pools and walked outside past some grimy guards who had apparently been building the gatehouse before their guard duty. I stepped out and saw Brimwulf eating an apple, sitting on a trunk. He grinned at me, and I grinned back.

'So, you missed my skills?' he asked me.

'I've missed you, friend,' I told him and embraced him. I pushed him to arms length, and he shrugged. 'You have gained weight,' I admonished him.

'They have plenty of food. That much Armin has prepared. And Segestes, of course,' he said and looked around as if there were spies listening. 'Something came up,' he whispered, swallowing a huge bite of the apple.

'You going to kill me with suspense?'

He nodded and then shook his head. 'They held a Thing. That father of yours is one grizzled bastard. They hate each other more than I hated Helmut. And that is saying a lot. He is giving the orders and has no respect for lords of this land.'

368

'The lords of this land have no respect for each other. And did you hear what they spoke about?' I asked, excited.

'Nope,' he told me, and there was a glint in his eye. I put a hand over Tudrus's chest as he nearly barreled over the archer.

'But?' I asked him.

He grinned at Tudrus and nodded at me. 'They had a heated discussion on a grove dedicated to Tiw and made oaths. Armin looked like a dead man walking as he left the ring. Maroboodus, a Quadi named Sibratus, and Segestes stayed a while longer, with a man.'

'A man?' I asked with a premonition of doom.

'This man had a melted face. A melted one. Looked like a hideous, skinned bear. He was to ride to the castra.'

I stared at him, holding my fist so tight I noticed nothing until Tudrus budged me.

'Cornix,' I hissed. 'And he was to ride to our camp?'

'He is,' Brimwulf said. 'I heard your father tell him to convey the orders.'

'So, they have a plan beyond dying in a shield wall,' I said to myself. 'When was this?'

'Cornix ate. He took wine and venison and ate, and I rode here as fast as I could. What now?' he asked.

'We have to see who he meets with,' I told him. 'You will go back to Armin after you help us out.'

'Fine,' he said. 'He …' Brimwulf said softly and shook his head.

'He what?' I asked him.

'He has that fancy old spear of yours. This Cornix does,' he told me seriously. 'Didn't Fulcher look after it?' he asked.

I leaned on a tree. *Cornix had killed him before he had reached Drusus.* 'Yes. And Fulcher is dead.'

Brimwulf nodded and looked away. 'That incompetent idiot. We will avenge him.'

CHAPTER 31

We waited near the gate. We lounged in the shadows of a wooden, hastily built barracks, ignoring the legionnaires looking at us curiously. I had sent Hund and the Batavi to all the other gates, but we went to the Porta Praetoria, the main gate facing the ridge, and there we hunkered down. 'What,' Tudrus whispered, 'if he uses the other gates? The Batavi might very well miss him if his face is covered.'

'He will use this one,' I said stubbornly, praying for Woden's help. 'Why go anywhere else? He is a Roman. A respected one, no doubt planted here by Antius's many allies.'

'Best hope this will work,' Tudrus growled.

'It will,' I said and nodded at Brimwulf lounging near the gate. He was gesturing at me madly. 'Draw your cowls over your heads.'

They did, masking themselves. We waited a while longer and then I saw a small altercation at the gates, then a man in a high helm of a Tribune was marching imperiously past the quivering guards. The plume was white, he had a ribbon under his chest and over a silvery sculpted armor. His leathery petruges skirt was studded with silvery studs, and the sword on his side was long and expensive. Tudrus looked at him incredulously. 'Like a cock. If he wanted to stay undetected, perhaps something less jubilant would have been appropriate.'

'He walks in like he owns the place, the fat knee cripple,' I cursed. Cornix's other knee was a bit strange, and the powerful man had a hint of a limp. I noticed Brimwulf also watched the dangerous man, fiddling with an arrow. I shook my head at him. Brimwulf looked hard at me, but I shook my head again.

Tudrus hissed at me. 'Are you or are you not trying to kill him, Hraban? Ansbor's blood is in his hands. Fulcher's. Kill him. It is easier with a bow. Then just disappear. I could hardly miss his ugly face from here, and Brimwulf there has his tail up.'

'We will wait. I said we have to find out their plans,' I said, and Bohscyld agreed with a simple grunt. 'Men die easily enough later. And this one shall indeed.'

'So, we just keep him alive?' Tudrus said with distaste.

'His death is but postponed,' I said darkly. 'Come. He is moving.'

Cornix took the Via Principia towards the praetorium. He passed tents and some hastily erected barracks. He walked arrogantly as a younger Tribune, but the real power radiated from the expensive gear. Men nodded at him, some distastefully, others with respect, but none could miss him. 'Is he going to the damned praetorium?' Tudrus asked, bewildered. 'We cannot follow him there.'

'I will expose him if he is. He is an enemy to Drusus,' I whispered as we dodged tents and ropes and legionnaires sharpening weapons and adjusting kit. Cornix ambled along. Then a man crossed before him, coming from the tents and bumped into him. I half drew my blade, but the man apologized to him and walked away.

Cornix stopped.

Then he turned to follow the man between the tents. He went quickly, dodging through men and even beasts being prepared, and I nearly lost sight of him. 'Come,' I hissed at them and went on. My enemy was easy to spot, thankfully, and soon we picked up his trail. He made his way forward resolutely and aimed for a rough building where a shadowy figure had just disappeared. He followed the man inside.

Tudrus snorted. 'Why would they build something that permanent in a camp like this? Waste of time.'

'Wait.' I looked around and crouched in the shadows near the building. I saw two pairs of legs on the side and went forward to the corner. I peeked around it. There were men working on bellows, arguing over some past love affair. I came back and smiled at my friends. 'It's a bathhouse.'

'Bath?' Tudrus asked suspiciously. 'Some Roman torture method?'

'They put you in a cold bath, then scalding hot, and someone beats your back so that you groan and shriek,' I told him conspiratorially. 'They always build one if they plan to stay for a longer time. It's as important as the latrine.'

'I don't get it,' Tudrus said.

'We wait a moment,' I told them.

'Why? We can wait inside for anyone coming to meet him. If he is not there already. He did follow that one man, no?' Brimwulf hissed from the side.

'It's best Cornix is nude,' I said with a grin. 'Will make him less likely to resort to violence when we beat him blue.'

'What makes you think he would go to a bath?' Tudrus asked.

'He is Roman. We bathe. They do it in hot water.' I grinned and leaned on the wall. 'He won't be able to resist it.'

'Grows them lazy,' Brimwulf agreed. 'I will go around.'

'Do so,' I told him. We squatted on the side of the building for a time until Tudrus began to pull at his braid. I stared at him, and he nodded. We stood up and walked to the door. A man with a pug nose poked his face out of the door. 'Private meeting. Go away.'

'Bohscyld,' I stated, and the rock-like man reached out, pulled the man out of the building so hard a part of the door came with him and tossed him into the dark. We walked in.

In the tub, there was Cornix.

He had been leaning his head on a stone bench as he lay in the tub and his hand was a pugio. His cold, mad eyes grew very large as he regarded us entering the room. I wanted to murder him then and there for Fulcher, but before him, in the same tub sat another man. He stiffened. And did not turn. He looked familiar, and I walked around the tub. I saw his face rise from his chest, and his long, blond hair was wet. His eyes were huge and scared, and I nearly dropped Nightbright.

It was Vannius.

'Hraban!' he breathed. 'Look! I can explain!'

The Vangione, the third wastrel brother and son of Vago. He was an ally of Maroboodus, yet a greedy one, and I had enticed him once to let me burn Father's hall by telling him his brother Hunfried, the king of the Vangiones was our prisoner, leaving him the king apparent. His face went white as a Roman sheet as he regarded the men stalking to sight around him. My friends were Quadi. Vannius had helped Father take over their tribe, leaving my friends vagabonds and exiles. Tudrus saw him. Bohscyld saw him.

And they forgot our mission.

For that boy was partly to blame for the downfall of the Quadi.

They roared like animals and tore the poor fool out of the tub. In fact, the tub broke apart as they ripped through it to rip the man apart, and that gave Cornix his opening. He rolled free of the tumultuous fight on the floor, if you can call it a fight, for Tudrus was pummeling the fool in the face, Bohscyld was tearing at his leg, which snapped and Vannius howled. Cornix, however, threw his whole weight against the far wall, falling through it in a heap of planks and flesh, taking the two Legionnaires working on the bellows down with him. They cursed and grappled, and I jumped through the hole.

Outside, I saw Brimwulf slinking to the shadows.

Then I saw a dozen pila pointed my way as a dozen Legionnaires faced me. The man who had been guarding the door was hunkered behind them, holding his lacerated face. Behind me, men thudded through the door as well, and I could hear Tudrus cursing profusely at the men. Vannius was hollering and still alive. Men ran from the shadows, more Legionnaires, spears and swords in hand. A bare headed centurion with a sword stalked forth and kicked one of the sprawling Legionnaires out of the way. He stared at Cornix resentfully, bile in his throat. 'Your doing, dog?'

Cornix rose up, hairy and strong like an animal. 'I am Tribune Gaius Ahenobarbus. A special envoy from Rome. My brother is Paellus Ahenobarbus, commanding Castrum Flamma. I am here seeking the legate—'

'Lies! He is a traitor!' I yelled.

The centurion snapped his fingers at my fuming face and spied the tribune's gear inside. He raised his eyebrow at Cornix. 'You can, of course, prove this?'

'Yes, I have the orders in there,' Cornix said with a grin. 'This bastard tried to rob me. They hurt that poor soul I was sharing the bath with. I suggest you imprison him.'

'I demand to speak to Nero Claudius Drusus,' I gasped, clenching Nightbright. 'This man is in league with Armin, Maroboodus, and Segestes and was here plotting with the Vangione Vannius there.'

Cornix smiled inanely, indicating his nude condition. 'Centurion. Dear man. I am a Tribune. He is filth. Let us deal with this in the morning. Put

373

that animal in the jail for the night, and we shall confront the Consul first thing in the morning. That is reasonable, no? He is preparing for battle and has little time for drunks and murderers. '

The centurion hesitated, then he pointed his finger at me and shrugged. 'Take that one and make sure he is guarded and pacified until the battle is done. Then we will deal with him. Or rather; see he is given proper army justice.' I did not give Cornix satisfaction of hearing me scream and kept quiet. 'The rest,' he grinned and nodded at me. 'Put them with the Thracian unit and prepare them for battle.'

I cursed but knew it made no difference to fight them there. I shook my head at Tudrus, who was flexing his fists, but he nodded at me. My eyes caught a shadow in the dark as Brimwulf disappeared. Then, before the Legionnaires herded me away, I saw Vannius getting carried out of the ruined bath house and Cornix rifling his gear. He smiled at me with his humorless eyes and picked up Wolf's Bane. He showed it to me, and I turned away, rage making my strides jerky. They pushed me on, and I shook my head, breathing hard. *Fulcher. I would not forget him.* I rubbed my head and tried to think about Armin and Maroboodus. Father was sending Vannius a message. Why? And why was Vannius in the camp? He had contemplated on going home to Vangiones to challenge nobles for the Vangione kingship while his brother was Burlein's prisoner. Then, Hunfried had been Father's prisoner.

And now Hunfried was the king of the Vangiones.

He was with the army, was he not? The Vangione auxilia was marching along with Rome.

And that meant Vannius was with Hunfried for Father. And that meant Hunfried was also with Maroboodus?

No.

Yes, I thought.

Armin's war was not Armin's at all. All he hoped was to come on top, see Drusus killed, escape, and then challenge Segestes. This was all Father's plan. He had a thousand men, the best and most agile. He would try to reach his goal, no matter the opposition. He had had Segestes with Drusus, but he also had Hunfried and had not left anything to chance. Perhaps

Segestes had never had a part in Father's plans at all? And his goal was to kill Drusus. For his future kingdom, for his rewards. For the son, he had in Rome? *Yes, for that as well*, I spat. The guards looked at each other, and I glanced at them. The young one carrying my weapons looked sheepish as my eyes took in the weapons, but the older ones just tightened their grip on the pila and shields. Finally, we reached a silent part of the camp, near the eastern walls. They whispered to an optio who looked thin and sick, and he nodded back. 'Optio. I ...' I began, but he refused to listen.

'The Tribune said you are one with wild stories. Fever? Broke a bathhouse and tried to rape the Tribune?'

'What? No!' I yelled and then calmed myself with a struggle. 'Whatever. I need you to take a word to the Consul.'

He shook his head and laughed. 'Take a word to the Consul? What will I tell him? That a trout is good eating? That you know how to sing? What possible interest would he have to you and anything you might say? You will stay and send no words anywhere. Into the tent with you, and don't make us shackle you to the tent post.' I dodged to the tent and begged Agetan was guarding Cassia. I begged and prayed and hoped Cornix stayed far from her.

Drusus was going to battle.

And there was an enemy in his army. *Not Segestes, but Hunfried.*

CHAPTER 32

I waited in the tent. Outside, the optio had left with his century, leaving my gear with a guard, an eight man contubernium and a freckle-faced immunes in charge. He was strict enough, for he had pushed my face back inside as I tried to see what the fuss was about. I seethed, walking back and forward in the tent, kicking at bedrolls. Outside, I heard men march from the camp. Drusus was putting his men into position when it was still dark, sending more and more exploratores everywhere around the enemy, making final plans. He had much to prove, and the fool did not understand the enemy was in his ranks. I tried to lift the tent's far side to see how good my chances would be to dash to the sea of tents, but a burly foot nearly slapped down on my face. It was the immunes. I cursed him impolitely and seethed, and he thanked me by placing two guards in the tent itself. The men also had shackles with them and left them prominently in sight.

The rest of the night passed, and I contemplated on my options.

There were none.

I would have to fight the men, but no matter the hour, the legionnaires stood there, not tired in the least, their eyes were not leaving me. I wondered if they were asleep on their feet, but when I tried to move around, their eyes followed me.

The dawn broke, the rays of the sun breaking the misty vapors of the night, the valley filling with fresh winds. I could smell smoke as the wind buffeted the tents, and the camp outside was strangely silent, save for a distant tramp of feet and wild whinnying of horses. Then, the tubicens rang the trumpets, and I knew the Army was deploying for battle.

And so I charged.

I ran like a wraith in between the two men, rolling to avoid their grasp and burst through the tent flap. On the left, far, I thought I saw the two Aquila of the legions march after the men from the praetorium where they were kept, following the last of the army.

There were two guards outside the tent.

And they were as alert as the two running after me.

I flew back to the tent and found myself staring into the eyes of the immunes. His young face was grave, and he was fondling the shackles. 'They say you are a famous man. That you are friends to the Consul? Perhaps that is so, but even friends to consuls have to obey the military laws, and you are putting me in a damned hard position. You have to calm down. He will see you after the battle. I am sorry you will miss it. We are. Most of us are.'

I rubbed my lobes. 'You do not understand. There is something afoot! I would not make such claims just to escape some punishment.'

He shook his head, nervously licking his lips. 'I cannot do anything. I am here with orders. What the fuck do you think I should do? Let my prisoner go, and I'll then tell the high and mighty in my charge had a charming voice and was surely not up to anything evil? By Juppiter and Cronos! Yes! And then you slit the Consul's gut and people begin to wonder how it is possible I forgot to guard you.'

I pushed my finger on his chest, and he went silent. 'Or, you might be asked why you did not tell the Consul his army is about to be betrayed. They might think that is a problem, as well,' I spat, frustrated.

He licked his lips uncertainly but shook his head. 'I am just doing my job. I would lie down if I were you and listen to the music of the trumpets, the cornu, and the buccina as they attack.'

I decided to grab him and hold him hostage, a scenario that would likely end badly. Then a horse was approaching, it was clear. It neighed outside, and a man was guiding it with clicks of his tongue. 'What in the name of Achilles now?' the immunes breathed and turned to go. 'Watch the bastard,' he breathed and stormed out. The horse stopped before the tent. Its shadow could be seen, and the Legionnaires stood around it. They seemed excited.

'Get that woman down from the horse!' the freckle-faced immunes screamed. 'There is no riding in the camp. It's forbidden!'

'Sir, she is no soldier!' said a guard.

'I don't care if it is the harlot of Mars, she will get down, now!' The guards in the tent hesitated, tempted to see the woman and shuffled back to try to glimpse what was going on outside.

'It's a woman all right,' said one of the guards to the other as he carefully opened up the tent flap to gawk at the sight. I nearly shouted with joy as I glimpsed Cassia with a large bag, sitting on a dark horse. Agetan was leading the beast.

'Get down!' yelled another man. 'You bring ill fortune on the day of the battle! Come!' a burly legionnaire was reaching for her waist.

She looked drawn, in pain but determined as she let the man lift her down.

'Who are you?' asked the immunes leading the guards, looking down at her imperiously. 'A pregnant woman riding around with an idiot. What is that?'

'I was looking for the centurion Magnus of the fifth cohort of I Gallica. Am I lost? He bought these honey cakes, and I need a payment for them,' Cassia complained about a nervous tremble in her voice, as if she was being cheated.

Men laughed as the immunes gestured around him. One was gesturing around him. 'Girl, they are all out to have a small fight. He has no use of your honey nor the cakes.'

'Oh!' she said, pretending to be a fool. 'What am I to do with them?'

The immunes chortled. 'Why, he asked me to take them for safe keeping. You will be paid later, yes, later.'

'Truly?' she was batting her eyes alluringly as she hesitated. The men nudged each other, the guards coming from behind the tent to hover by their comrades.

'Truly!' the immunes said happily and took the sack, opened it, and put his hand inside.

Agetan and Cassia charged at the tent and pushed my two guards further inside. Agetan's foolish grin turned to savagery as he punched one of the guards so hard I saw chips of teeth fly several feet in the air. I grasped the other one and pulled him down, spun on top of him and crushed my elbow on his face. We kept at it as Cassia pulled the tent closed, her face pale. Agetan turned to rope down the guards, and I grasped Cassia to me. 'What in Frigg's smile are you doing?'

Outside, screams.

She giggled. 'A hornet's nest. You see, there is a tree they left standing when they built this camp. They think the bees and hornets are messengers from the gods, and so they are holy. Well, Agetan fetched the nest, and now the gods are upset, I think.' I nodded, pale for the pain I heard being inflicted outside. The men screamed on. The leader had plunged his hand directly inside the nest, and his piteous yell was such that it was likely heard out on the battlefield. The savage drone of the winged, enraged beasts was audible as the hornets surged out of the sack. The homeless, terrifyingly mad creatures plunged their swords at the hapless legionnaires, crawling on their arms, legs, and neck, even under their armor. This we saw as their shadows ran back and forth outside our tent, spilling helmets and weapons and even armor in the mud. They ran around, screamed, rolled in the dust, cursed like haunted spirits, and finally cried for mercy as more and more of the cloud descended on them with a vengeance. A man dodged inside the tent and ran to Agetan's fist, falling back out. A hornet stung me, and I cursed at the pain as Agetan struggled with the tent cover.

The men ran away.

I dodged to the side and glanced outside from under the tent. The legionnaires were running through tents as if they were on a racetrack, pulling up tent pegs. Only the leader was left behind, shuddering on the ground with the painful stings. His face was like a hilly mountainside, his hand and arm featureless as he shivered. 'Wait!' I said as Cassia went forward. 'Plenty of the bastards around still.'

'The hornets?' she asked.

'Yes, the hornets,' I laughed. 'Ymir's frozen blood that was splendid! Thank you, both. How are you?'

Cassia shrugged. 'The baby is fine.'

'How are you?' I repeated.

'I'm dizzy, terribly nauseous, but I will live. Thank you, love,' she said tenderly.

'Thank you for saving my life,' I said affectionally. Agetan grunted, rolling his eyes and nodded outside.

'We have to speak later,' Cassia breathed. 'Brimwulf said you found out something and left us to deal with you. He had some mission you gave him?'

'Yes,' I agreed, grateful to the archer.

Cassia smiled and stroked my cheek. 'So, I guess this is the summer all your oaths will be held.' She looked sad and played with my hair. 'I survived my pain by being stupidly brave. Go and survive yours.'

I held her tight and nodded. 'This is the last time, Cassia. Last time I put myself in front of you.'

'I believe you, perhaps,' she told me playfully. 'Agetan will guard me.'

'He had better,' I growled and dodged outside.

Cassia came out as well and leaned down on the mutilated immunes. 'Fennel. I'll need fennel. I'll treat him. Sometimes men die from such stings; even a few are enough. I hope he does not die.'

I smiled at her. 'He is a thieving jackass. But at least he did not murder me. Save him if you can. Where are the others?'

'Is it true?' she asked, and I knew what she was asking.

'Fulcher is likely dead,' I told her.

She nodded, tears gathering in her eyes. 'Agetan told me. Find the man who did it. We will mourn our friend.' She nodded in the direction of the battle to be. 'Brimwulf said they gathered all the Batavi for the battle. A Roman praefectus commands them in a Thracian ala,' she said, having

Agetan pull the immunes aside. Some hornets were still stuck in his flesh, and she frowned as she tried to clear them off. I ran around the tents until I found the weapons. I wrapped the Winter Blade on my side and stuck Nightbright to my belt. I grabbed my helmet and pulled it on. Then I took a legionary shield from the tent and went out to see Agetan slapping at some stubborn hornets.

I waved at her and nodded at Agetan. 'Until we meet again.'

'Until then,' Cassia agreed and did not look up at me, but glanced at the Winter Sword.

'You won't see it again,' I promised her and ran away to the maze of tents.

CHAPTER 33

'There are horses held at the gate. There are many medicus and chirurgii, and they have men ready to pick up the wounded and bring them here,' a slave told me by a tent, after I had accosted him for the location of some beasts. 'Juppiter, we love and adore, that is the passphrase,' he added, and I thanked him as I ran to the main gate, where the guards challenged me.

'Juppiter!'

'I fucking love and adore!' I yelled at them as they stared at me incredulously. I brazenly grabbed a horse, a fine white beast and pulled it past the men at the gate.

'Slept late, lad?' one of them asked. I saw there was at least a cohort guarding the walls though the tent city was quiet.

'They forgot to wake me up,' I told them and their grins faded as I vaulted on the horse just outside the gate. A centurion appeared, hoisting a vine stick and stopped to stare at me in utter confusion. 'Hold! That's mine!'

'I'll but loan it, sir!' I yelled at him and whipped it so hard the centurion winced. 'If it dies, you'll have to walk!' I laughed, and the horse took off.

'Stay! It's not yours, I said! Thief!' they yelled after me, but I was whipping the horse for the west.

I rode along a muddy track crossing the valley. Ahead in the mists, cornu, and buccina rang harshly, and I knew Drusus had commanded the attack to begin. I could see the ridge and flashes of color along it as the Germani tribesmen stood their ground. I heard a distant barritus yell as thousands of determined men screamed harshly from behind their shields at their hated enemy. Soon, I begun to see flashes in the morning mist and knew I would soon see the heaving mass of metal clad killers in the triple axis formations, the deadly cohorts set up in three lines of bulky columns, getting ready to march up, slit the throats of the Cherusci thwarting them.

I passed pickets, screaming the passphrase. I crossed a destroyed wheatfield where fat dogs slunk away from me, having sniffed at a dead horse. Medici and suppliers were riding towards me and soon around me, I saw men whipping mules full of pila and water gourds for the battle. The Roman army was in action.

Then I saw the army.

I reigned in my horse, and it was neighing and fighting my commands as I tried to make sense of the scene.

Down before the ridge an army was making war.

A dozen evil looking ballistae and catapults were firing, the squat constructions jumping with each shot of stone and spear. Two legions spread around them, metal helmets gleaming like a stream in sunlight as the evil missiles jumped into the air and reached cumbersomely for the enemy ranks. Perhaps seven to eight thousand legionnaires stood in lethal ranks under their Aquila and cohort and century standards. On the flanks were the cavalry. There were hundreds of Noricum riders to the right, and Thracian cavalry to the left, and there would be my friends, as well.

In the middle was Drusus's consular standard, very near the catapults, and I saw his lictors standing around his purple cloak and the red ones of the many tribunes. He was seated on a white horse like mine and seemed to be staring up the hill. Behind him, he had a reserve, and that mass of men made me cringe. There were Vangiones infantry with Alpine ones standing behind him in serried ranks, spear points flashing. They were several thousand strong. My throat tightened.

Above them on the hillside stood the Germani, who were watching as slingers and archers sprang forth from the legions to make their life miserable. There were many of the enemies, perhaps as many as there were of the Romans. Their wondrous standards waved in the morning air, boasting skulls, banners of beasts, moons and stars, bones and skins. They were tall and proud and there to stand together against the enemy. Their barritus yell echoed bloodthirstily as it drifted across the land. It would be a brutal pushing match, and thousands of men would die. Beyond the enemy, the women encouraged the men, ready to lob rocks at the Romans and to care for the wounded.

They would not be able to run far, for I learned later Drusus had sent half his cavalry, all of the Gauls and the Legion cavalry to circle around Armin's troops.

They did not mean to run. They were there to fight. To win. *If Drusus fell,* I thought, *they might. Just might.*

I gazed at the army of Segestes on the hill. I prayed Brimwulf would be able to keep Armin alive and asked Donor the Avenger to grant Armin luck in whatever he had planned for Segestes. I turned in the saddle and gazed to the south. There, Roman exploratores were riding lazily, and I was sure that was where Father would spring to try to slay Drusus in a savage sally. Drusus knew where Maroboodus was, no doubt, and he would deploy the auxilia there to stop him.

Except Hunfried would obey Father and let him through. Why? *To be rewarded like Father was? Was his family held at sword point?* I wondered. It mattered not.

As if summoned, I saw movement in the southern woods. There was cavalry out there, flitting under the thinning boughs, and the exploratores rode for the army, their horns blaring. I saw Drusus move his hands languidly. His standard dipped, buccina blared forlornly, and the Vangione and Alpine standards waved. The savage Alpine tribes cheered hoarsely and with Hunfried's Vangione army streamed to the southern flank. The king himself led his men on a run and began forming a thick line of shields and spears, three to four lines deep. The Thracian cavalry formed at the junction of the legions and the Vangiones, ready to stop the Marcomanni from savaging the legions in the flank.

The flags waved and horns blared again, and the legions began to march forward, apparently unconcerned about Maroboodus, the ballistae and catapults ceasing their bombardment. The elevation was such that they had done very little damage anyway, and their power lay in terror. A dozen ripped and mangled corpses, limbs missing were scattered in the Cherusci and the Chatti ranks. The legions kept marching like metallic insects. They splashed into the stream below the ridge, and the water turned to mud. The Germani roared and their champions danced in front of the lines, coaxing their enemy on, but many of the men in the Legion were glancing to their left as a milling mass of Marcomanni came in sight.

That sight stopped me.

They were my people.

Had been, that is before Father had disgraced me. Before I had listened to his lies. There they were, their hair knots elaborate and fine as the Suebi liked them, their backs straight and the armor Father had looted from Castra Luppia adorned many a proud chest. They were not unruly like the average Germani army, but rode in strict ranks, flitting skillfully down the hill to sight. With them came Sibratus and his Quadi. The Quadi and Marcomanni were outmanned by three to one as the Vangiones, Thracian cavalry, and Alpine infantry thrummed their spear on shield, yelling insults.

I roused myself from the scrutiny as arrows and stones began to rain up the hill for the Cherusci. The enemy mocked the Roman auxilia, laughing in derision as the shots and arrows found shields and flesh and soon, some javelins rained down on the archers. Many fell, for few rivaled Germani in javelin throwing. The legions faltered for a moment as they began to climb for the not so distant line of the enemy.

I cursed Maroboodus and Segestes, and I spurred my horse for Drusus, who was readying the Noricum cavalry on his right to move behind where the Vangiones had stood.

I passed men carrying the wounded, mules bringing gear forward and nearly missed a man who was riding for the fort. He had detached himself from the army of the Vangiones, and he was riding hard. I saw he was dressed in auxilia gear, with bright chainmail and simple helmet. He evidently saw me coming, for he reined his horse so hard it nearly fell, and its forelegs struck air. The man pulled out a long spatha as his horse trotted for me.

I aimed for Drusus, but the man was angling his horse to cut me off.

He got closer and closer until I saw it was Cornix.

He resolutely guided his horse between the army and me. I stopped and turned to face him. 'Leaving the battle, Cornix?'

He snorted and pulled his spatha. 'The muscle is in place. There is no need to risk the brains. You are too late boy. Very much too late,' he told me, testing his grip on his sword by swinging it in a lazy circle.

'Fulcher,' I said and pulled the Winter Sword.

He laughed, tiredly. 'It has been a long few years traveling in Germania, Hraban. I am bored with your smelly halls and tedious, irascible nature. I'm tired of even Antius. Now, your high friend will finally die in a war as he should have died years past, and we will go home. It will end today. And you will not stop it. I should have put you down long ago. As I did put down your Fulcher. Paellus had us watch you and your friends. That bit with Oril was surprising as Lothar did not admit to having said anything, but I never lose sight of the most important part of the mission. And that was keeping the Consul in the dark.'

'Segestes left Drusus anyway,' I sneered.

'He is a coward. But this will be enough.' Cornix grinned. 'The Vangiones is enough though Segestes could have made this much easier.'

'Fulcher, I asked you,' I spat at him.

He smiled. He lifted the hem of his sagum, and there was a pouch with the scroll and Wolf's Bane on his belt. 'He is gone boy. Just get over him.'

A huge barritus yell could be heard around us as Cherusci troops cheered their allies, and I saw many hundred javelins start to drop onto the two resolutely climbing legions. Cornix glanced towards the huge, thunderous sound of Germani nations reveling in the war and coming death. 'Noisy lot.'

'Brave lot,' I said, my sword on my side as the legions hunkered down under their shields, enduring the steel tipped rain of death. 'Well. Since it will end now, will you not tell me who is to be blamed for all of this shit?'

'Will I?' he snorted.

'Just speak, you murdering fuck,' I spat at him, guiding my horse around him, but he moved his to mirror my movement.

'It is a woman in Rome,' he sneered.

'I know it is,' I laughed. 'Drusus knows.'

'He knows.' Cornix smiled. 'But you don't. Perhaps it's the daughter of the princeps? The only child of Augustus? Julia? Gens Julia, gens Claudia, one of the highest women in the land?'

'Perhaps?' I smiled. 'You are not sure.'

'I know who hired us.' He grinned. 'Why not the daughter of the mighty man, out to make sure her sons inherit the land? That the dream of yon Drusus there, the restoration of weak Republic after Augustus dies will not come to haunt her and her loved ones?'

'And my father serves her?' I stated, trying to find room to dart past him, our horses making their way slowly to the standard of Drusus.

'He guarded her,' he nodded. 'He bedded her. And his son? Not all the children of late Agrippa and Julia are of Roman origin. When the baby was presented to Agrippa, the fool picked up this one like he had the others, thinking for awhile it was his indeed.'

'You are saying my father's son; the precious son is in line to inherit Augustus?' I sneered. 'Lies.'

'I said perhaps,' he snorted. 'And your Drusus there? He hates Julia. For Tiberius, who had to marry the cunt. For many things. And so, perhaps it was Julia who is outwardly a silly, simpering thing but also very, very astute, and wealthy?'

'Perhaps,' I hissed.

Up on the hill, a horn blew. The Germani launched all their remaining javelins downhill, a veritable rain of steel and wood and it rained down on the legions who again braced themselves. A curious sound of sharp raps filled the air and so many glinting; bright legionnaires went down. Rocks began to come down, for all armies employ rocks as the javelins and

387

arrows run out. Then the Roman war machine closed ranks, forgot about the dead, ignored the rocks, and the moans of the wounded and went on. The Suebi on the left waited, thrumming their shields with their spears while sitting on their horses.

'Or perhaps it was not Julia,' Cornix spat and turned his horse and charged.

I turned my horse to dodge his charge, sprinting to his left side, and he cursed as he tried to swing at me from a very disadvantageous position, over his horse. I dodged and turned the fine beast and saw the Suebi had stopped thrumming their shields. Their horses knew what was to come before the riders did as I saw some take steps forth. Then Father, wearing a red tunic over his armor raised himself in the saddle, thrust his heavy spear into the air and yelled.

The Suebi charged.

They charged at their ancestral enemy, the Vangiones.

At the same time and above us, the Germani were heartened by the attack of the Marcomanni. I saw Oldaric's Chatti scream, launch the last of the javelins, grasp their framae and run downhill in a series of clannish cunus formations, many arrow-like masses of bristling spears and streaming down for the legions. They were fast and skillful, rushing in with unsurpassed savagery, and they surprised the Romans preparing to launch their pilum. A mad melee began amongst the first two rows of columns as the enemy pushed and pulled at the silvery legionnaires. The first cohort, the most elite held, but the third cohort fell apart, giving the Chatti a central position in the Roman envelopment to fight from. The Romans were not fazed at all, but pila flew at point blank range, the disarrayed Chatti army suffered and then the further columns charged them, their gladius out. The Chatti were brave, but the death toll for the unarmored warriors was horrid. In but moments there were heaps and heaps of men on the slopes. The Chatti and Cherusci women were coaxing their men to fight to the end. The legions were losing many men, but the gladius, armor, and discipline were tearing Germani rage to ribbons, and especially the Chatti were getting the sharp end of the gladius in their frenzied attack.

I turned back to Cornix, cursing the Suebi cantering for the Vangiones. 'We have to be quick about this, candle face!' Cornix laughed and hit his horse's flank. He swung his blade wickedly at me, and I guided my beast at him, clumsily bringing the shield up as I did. The blade bit into the leather and wood and got stopped, but his horse staggered, and then I stabbed the beast. It reared in pain, and when the horse came back down, I was there. I stabbed at his face, hoping to puncture his eye but opened up his chin instead. Blood spurted over my face, and he howled at his wound.

He swung again, slicing into my saddle, but I stubbornly stabbed again, now puncturing his armor at the shoulder. He cursed and tried to guide his horse away from me, but I hacked at the horse's face and it reared again as a bit of its lip was carved and flapped crazily, revealing the teeth. I maneuvered the horse behind the enemy beast, cursing my enemy, hearing Woden call for his life blood. I slashed him across his back and then stabbed. The chainmail made a jingling, jarring sound and he stiffened, his mouth open in agony. His eyes whipped to look at me over his shoulder, and he awkwardly swung his heavy spatha at me. It flashed in the air, but I let it hit the helmet, for the strike had little force in it, and I punched the Winter Sword at his leg so hard it went through it to hit the horse. He cursed, bled and cried, and I looked him in the eye as the beast faltered under him.

'Ansbor. Mother and Grandfather. Fulcher. All the people you have helped kill.'

'What of them?' he spat spitefully, the horse tottering.

'Greet them, if you see them mocking you across the dark river,' I spat and punched the heavy sword through his throat. His eyeballs rolled back, and he fell so fast I barely had time to understand it. I jumped down and tottered to him. I tore out the spear and the sack with the scroll and clambered on the horse.

The damage was done.

I turned to see the horses of the Marcomanni bearing down on the Vangiones. No normal force of men would charge a bristling wall of spears, but Maroboodus was a cavalryman of Rome, a guardsman of the highest mark, a warrior since he could walk, and he had trained his men well. In a wall of leather, hooves, and steel, the Marcomanni and the Quadi stampeded against the Vangiones. The Thracian cavalry and Alpine infantry started to gravitate against the horsemen that were sure to be stopped by the many ranks of spears of the Vangiones.

Hunfried's flag fluttered.

The Vangiones raised their heads in surprise and two hundred men, the personal warband of Hunfried ran.

They ran away.

They scattered, leaving some braver champions standing alone to fight the horses and men bearing down on them. The king ran, his fleeing men pushed and pulled the ranks apart as they did and took the weaker men with them. Then, another band of men ran. I was betting it was that of Vannius, for there was a man on a horse, his leg bandaged.

There was a gaping hole in the line.

Officers and signifiers turned to gawk at Drusus, looking for orders, and I think I saw my lord's shoulders sag at the terrible sight of betrayal. The Marcomanni rolled over the few Vangione defenders, stabbed at the edges of the hole and scattered the rest of the enemy easily. Over a thousand panicked Vangiones threw away their shields and spears and ran after their king. Hundreds of gleeful Marcomanni turned to fight the Thracian cavalry, some hundreds faced the Alpine infantry but most milled in the hole left by the Vangiones as Father was gazing at the sieges machines, and then he spotted Drusus.

Drusus tore his gaze off Father. He pulled his sword, screaming orders. Buccina and trumpets blared, Drusus was riding around, yelling at his men, and they reacted slowly, utterly shocked by the events.

The Noricum cavalry that had been deploying was in confusion. They had three hundred men, and slowly they turned to the Marcomanni, the ranks in chaos. I saw over five hundred Marcomanni break free, make a dangerous, spear bristling column and start to ride for Drusus's standards. I saw the Consul turn in his saddle and stare at the disaster, yelling orders and the Noricum ala finally got their orders and the praefectus commanding them waved his sword. They charged forward at the same time I did.

Up above the Cherusci and Chatti shield wall, now some seven thousand long, a ragged line of tired men went to the attack. They had to engage the legions, to keep them fighting, sacrificing blood and were trying to push the Romans downhill. I saw, while whipping the horse, some hundreds crash to the steely legions, killing brave centurions and taking a cohort standard, which a bearded, armored champion held aloft, his glory eternal. They were mad with fury. Armin's horn rang thinly, rising, ululating, and blood flowed downhill.

My father guided his horsemen mercilessly for the young Consul.

There was a fierce fight going on with the Thracian cavalry, some of whom went around to tear at the charging enemy on its sides and a desperate one was taking place with the tough Alpine infantry, as Maroboodus did not have men to rout the thousand strong, solid unit. Some Marcomanni even harassed the running Vangiones, but there was no need. They had seen their king run and had no appetite for the fight.

Maroboodus just needed time. And he had it.

The Noricum cavalry thundered before Drusus. I desperately whipped my horse and guided the horse for the Consul.

The five hundred elite Quadi and Marcomanni tore towards the Noricum cavalry, and there was a slight tremble on the ground as the horses went at full gallop. Where normal cavalry usually dismounted to fight in a proper shield wall, these men would have none of that, for they had no time for such finery. I felt the strange power of death on hooves rocking the grass around me, and Woden sang in my head, his dance thrumming in my ears. I saw the rearmost cohorts on the hill turn in stupefaction and the rearmost centuries of men began to run downhill. A hundred men had rallied around Drusus, for everyone knew what Maroboodus was trying to do. There were legionnaires, scouts, archers, and slingers, artillerymen and standard-bearers with the tuhicens lifting swords. There were tribunes and Immunes, and they all were ready to die for the Consul.

The Noricum cavalry hit the center of the Marcomanni and Quadi column.

Men fell, horses died, and so many were wounded. Flesh rolled in mud and blood flew so high it seemed it was raining. The Noricum were brave, but soon surrounded, and Maroboodus's men rolled around them. I saw, I think, Tudrus and Bohscyld on their horses with the few Thracians circumventing the Marcomanni. My friends were slashing wildly at the Marcomanni, even at their fellow Quadi. Hund was riding gleefully after Tudrus to topple men from the saddle. Then I saw a Batavi hiss as a blade wounded his side, and then I was in the middle of the battle, trying to reach my lord.

Before me were bearded faces. I could tell the Suebi apart from my allies by their head knots, and that day I made my final break with my tribe.

I shrieked Woden's hate at the men before me. I felt my shield shuddering with hits, my helmet, and chainmail getting tugged at by spears, and I did not care. For I was stabbing and hacking in the battle rage. I stabbed my blade up, I stabbed it down at the flesh of men and horses and waded through the milling battle of the Noricum cavalry and the Suebi. Somewhere ahead, I heard the Suebi reach the hundred men guarding Drusus, for there were Roman curses in the air. I killed a youngster with barely a beard, stabbing him in the side. My blade was sticky with blood, oily with guts, and I was covered in sweat and the tangy lifeblood of my enemies. Around me were now pockets of Noricum men in Roman armor, and I accidentally stabbed one in the throat as I had not seen him coming from the side. The press of horses and men was terrible, and there was a coppery smell of blood in the air, mixing with that of human piss and excrement. My ears rang, the chaos made me dizzy, and Woden's song made me deadly fast.

Up ahead, I saw some more centuries detach from the battle on the hill as they raced down to help. Archers and slingers on the left flank had drawn pugiones and gladius to charge the enemy, but Maroboodus was relentless. I pressed on in the chaos. Suddenly I saw a dead lictor, another spitting blood as the knot haired savage men pushed on. Then, up ahead I saw what they tried to reach. I saw Nero Claudius Drusus, the purple-cloaked man in bright armor, on his wild horse. His gladius was flashing in the air, and his men died around him. There was a Roman shield wall around him, manned by sturdy legionnaires, and the horses found it hard to push through them. There were men dismounting and tearing into the press and pull. Drusus's horse had a framae sticking from its flanks, but the horse was as brave as its master.

A tall Marcomanni rode through the shield wall, literally over a man, and he managed to grab the hair on Drusus's helmet, pulling the young lord half from his saddle. I screamed and killed a Marcomanni from behind, another hit me with an ax, but the armor deflected it, stealing my breath away. I ignored the man, and a Noricum man was his next victim. I rode forward amidst corpses, but then my horse stumbled. I fell, heavily, dodged stamping horse feet and got up. Up ahead, Drusus was again fully in his saddle, minus the helmet, and his assailant was dead on a horse, dead by an arrow. The shield wall still held, lictors picking up shields to join it. Drusus had men wave the standard and blow cornu to summon more help, but the Marcomanni still had over three hundred men, and fifty were especially trying to reach the young lord.

Then I saw Father and Nihta.

He had his bear standard behind him, his face and Hulderic's helmet caked with blood. He was howling, bawling at his men to push, then he speared a Roman archer, after that a brave man of Noricum, grinning like a demon under his helmet, about to become a Germani legend. He was within reach of his plans; one step away, and he had the tools to achieve his goal. Father hollered and pointed his spear at the shield wall. Men struggled in the press and dismounted, some ten hefted axes and spears. Some fell to arrows and spears, but seven remained, and they made a small cunus. The lead man was a brute with a huge hammer, his face marked by scars and a tattoo covering his forehead. He screamed and ran forward, climbing horses and wounded, and the legionnaires in the shield wall braced themselves at the specter of death. The man jumped onto the wall, his belly split by a gladius but brought the hammer down on his slayer, caving in a helmet. The rest of the Marcomanni swarmed after and a bitter fight ensued in the gap. I struggled to get there, swatting away horses, opening a belly of one whose rider sought to stab at me. He fell, and I went forward, getting hit, pushed, and constantly stabbed in the thick fight. I wounded and killed and prayed I would get to Drusus in time. Miraculously, I was barely hurt.

The Marcomanni assaulting the legionnaires were finally put down. The wall was rebuilt. But it was thin, in places not a wall at all.

And then Maroboodus nodded at Nihta. The deadly warrior prayed, visibly gathered himself and pulled his thin, long sword.

The slender man guided his horse to the wall and spurred forward, splitting the face of a young tribune on his way, kicked a wounded legionnaire to the mud and crashed through the wall. Drusus turned his horse for the oncoming horseman, and I despaired as I put away Nightbright and picked an ax from the mud and ran after him.

Father saw me, his jaw hanging open. I spat at him as I ran past.

Nihta was closing in on Drusus, who was guiding his horse sideways to fight the deadly man. Nihta said something to Drusus, who laughed at him, and then they slammed together.

Nihta was fast.

He was deadly.

He delivered a swing that made Drusus flinch, but the swing turned to the familiar, snake fast stab, which wounded the young lord in his arm. Drusus held his grip on his blade, his horse dancing away. Nihta laughed and came at him again, blocking Drusus's strike and this time, his blade was going to come for the throat of the Consul.

I screamed, I screamed for Woden and Hel and ran at the lithe man whose face flickered towards me, buying Drusus time to dodge away.

Nihta saw me, his face a thing of disbelieving hate.

He had once told me I would never best him in single combat. Only in the thick of battle would I have a chance, he had said. I had once wounded him by wounding his pride first, but I had no wish to test my skills in swordplay. This was the thick of battle, and he was there, unprepared, sitting on a skittish horse. I came to him, the ax high and all his finery with blade, all his fighting styles and deceptions did not matter in the least as I, in a berserker rage swung the large thing at him, smashing through his blade to bury itself in his belly, ripping his armor apart. I saw his face turn to a mask of a dead man, his mouth open, and beard dripping with blood as I pulled him down from the saddle. 'Man whore, shit fucked half beast, die!' I spat at him as I tore the blade out. Behind us, Maroboodus howled, and his men charged again, and again and I stepped before Drusus, which many men saw and flocked to me. Some out of breath legionnaires were now splashing through the muddied stream.

We held, I swung the ax, killing men and horses and the Marcomanni despaired. The standard of Drusus fell in the mud as one of my father's riders from Rome killed the bear pelted staff holder, a veteran of many wars, but the man came close to me and the ax ripped off his shoulder. My weapon was now dull, nicked and flattened as more enemies came at me. Drusus cheered behind us as the centuries from above started to lob pilum at the Marcomanni, and many men were now hacking at the milling horsemen from all sides. The Alpine troops were routing the last, stubborn Marcomanni. The Thracian cavalry were filtering more and more men to us as they engaged some two hundred Suebi still.

Maroboodus was failing.

Their surprise was spent.

Maroboodus's face was ashen gray with hate, I saw it in his cursing mouth, the only thing showing under Hulderic's old beast helmet. He pulled at a large man, who nodded. The great Quadi chief, Sibratus, clad in a barbaric chain and leather armor spurred his horse across my vision, and Drusus spurred his horse at the man. They met, both breathless and tired, and the Germani swung a black cudgel with spikes at Drusus. The lord dodged it and stabbed Sibratus in the face. Sibratus's horse guided him away, the master of Quadi spilling blood, his men moaning in horror as the chief spilled from the saddle, and Drusus laughed. 'Keep his armor! I wish to dedicate it to the gods in Rome!' he yelled, having achieved what few Roman generals had; killing an enemy chief in single combat.

Marcomanni energy was starting to wane.

The enemy was despairing as the few remaining men of Noricum, fresh legionnaires, savage Thracians, legionnaires, and archers cut and stabbed at them amidst piles of dead. I was fighting a large, fat man, breaking his shield with the now hammer-like axe when I saw my father curse, raise his eyes to the gods like Nihta had, take up his spear, and then he threw it.

It was a splendid throw. The gods approved of it.

I turned to look at Drusus. He was holding his sword up, exhorting the newly arriving legionnaires, in glee at his recent feat, his face a shining sun. Despite the deadly surprise, his men were winning. He was a young hero at the peak of his glory. He would conquer. He would beat his enemies to the dust and crags of Hades. The gods would reward him richly, and he would, by Juppiter, save Rome from Augustus and tyranny.

Father's spear flew over my head, and I could not stop it. I killed the stubborn Marcomanni and turned to look at the deadly throw.

I breathed in relief.

Drusus's horse was hit, the hasta deep in its chest.

Then the horse fell, taking Nero Claudius Drusus with it.

He fell and howled. It was a brief howl, but speaking of terrible hurt. His leg was stuck weirdly under the horse, and as the horse thrashed an audible crack was heard. Drusus's eyeballs turned white from pain, and he fell back to the mud.

I saw my father grin.

I screamed defiance to the gods as I charged him. He sneered at me and turned his horse, commanding his men to turn. I saw Vannius amongst the fleeing men, but I ignored him.

I threw the ax with all my might.

The blade spun in the air, and I thanked Woden with all my heart as I saw it slam into Maroboodus's back. The ax was dull, it would not kill him, but his mail split, a red wound briefly in sight, blood flowing as he slammed his face on his horse's neck. A Marcomanni grabbed his reins, guiding him away. Arrows flew in the air, some pulling down Marcomanni, a few men of Noricum. A few hit Father, and he howled as he whipped his horse.

The battle was won. The price had been great.

I did not look about to see Armin's snake standard fall as victorious legionnaires hacked it down, nor did I see Segestes's troops run en mass, much reduced. Segestes was unharmed, Armin's plan failed, but I would not have cared had I known. I missed Armin getting captured, Brimwulf's arrow in his leg, for I had told the archer to save Armin's life by capturing him for Rome. I did not witness the flight of the Germani, the many who got captured and the heaps of slain on the red hillside. I dimly heard Armin's horn being blown by jubilant legionnaires, drunk on joy for their trophy.

I only saw Maroboodus flee.

My father's men turned their horses and fled south, skirting the enemy auxilia, the Alpine troops trying to block their way. Arrows and slingshot punished them, Thracians, and Noricum men cutting off many of them. I grabbed the reins of Nihta's horse and pulled myself up. The horse was slick with blood, and I spat at my former tutor's corpse. Then I spurred the horse after the fleeing enemy, the dregs of my people being torn apart. Had they managed to kill Drusus? I did not know.

Men joined me.

The enemy dodged the pursuit by riding east through the gaps of the Alpine cohort, aiming for the distant castra, trampling some medicus who were in the way, then getting hit by volleys of arrows again. There were, but fifty men left, most of the Marcomanni with expensive Roman armor had fallen in the charge. Father's standard still flew proudly, marking his position.

If Drusus were dead, it would make my father a hero.

He would succeed after all, and my oath would have failed, if he fled. True, Cornix and Nihta were dead, so was Sibratus, but that was not enough. I wanted Father. The Bear had to die. And then I would head for Lif and Odo. I cursed and whipped the horse harder, and blood flowed from its flanks. I saw some of the Batavi and my friends were alive though I noticed Bohscyld was hurt, hobbling with a bloody foot for a horse. Tudrus looked like spirit taken, covered in blood and mud, Hund was badly hurt, his beard torn, and he spat out a bloody mess I thought was a tooth.

Then I forgot them.

The bear standard was up ahead; carried by a bronze helmeted man, and he rode with my father, who was leaning forward in the saddle. The Marcomanni around us were scattering, fleeing, some dropping from their horses, suing for mercy.

But not my father, who was now guiding his horse back south, for the woods and hills of the Chatti. We hammered along a muddy field, Father, his standard bearer, and another Marcomanni, all eager to get away. They kept glancing back at me.

'Father! Halt! Die with dignity! Tell your dogs to heel! Let us keep this in the fucking family!' I screamed at him, and I knew he disagreed for I saw him gesture at one of his men who nodded. We rode further and further south, the woods and hills coming closer and then the man turned his horse. I screamed at him and rode on. The man was hurt and slow, and I dodged under his spear. I slammed the hilt of the Winter Sword at his face, tipping him from his horse. I glanced at where the battle was still raging. There was nobody there, and I saw in the distance my men were fighting a determined Marcomanni group.

I was alone.

Father and his last man spurred their horses on. We entered a lightly wooded depression before the Hercynian wilds, and they guided their mounts towards the far woods edge, desperate to get to safety. There was a stream running across the depression, glimmering with pure water from the high grounds, and a deer raised its head from its depths, staring at us, the bloody, tired monsters entering the pure, sacred place, defiling it.

Then, I howled.

For Father's horse had stumbled, throwing him to the water. His sword fell from his fingers; the helmet slipped off his head as he hit the rocks. I shrieked in happiness, panted with joy for my soon to be retribution. The standard bearer cursed me, slammed his standard on the ground by Father, on the other bank, pulled an ax from his belt, and spurred his horse for me, water flying high.

I spat at him and rode my horse for him. He was an old man, one of the Roman guards, a brave man who screamed defiance at me as his horse bore on mine, and we fell in a tangle of horsemeat and arms and legs. He got up first, pulling his helmet off to see better. I was breathless, my sword out of my reach as he came for me. He was favoring one leg, had a smear of mud on his face, and reached over me, grabbed me by my mail as he started to swing his blade.

I took hold of his beard, yanked him off balance, and we rolled together to the water, where I landed on top of him. He struggled, he fought, but he did not say anything, for I kept his face underwater for a minute, and then another, and he died. I killed him slowly, watching my father drag himself onto the dry land by his standard; panting, hurt. His handsome face kept looking at me, in terror, a terror that fed me. He grasped his standard weakly and tried to stand up, unsuccessfully. I stared at him while I killed his last man, and I knew to my delight Father finally feared me, for he licked his lips nervously. 'Am I not your son, Father? See? How casually I slay. Very much like you, no?'

He left his helmet in the stream, and he was dragging his standard after him as he tried to stand. The man went still and I, panting, went to the Winter Sword, hissing at Father. 'Your father's blade. As you killed him, it is just you die by it.'

He snorted. 'I've known that blade since I was but a boy, Hraban. It will be like meeting an old friend.'

'You were not reluctant to let go of this friend to fool Burlein and the lot of us that you truly were dead, were you? Some old friend this sword is to you. But then, you always left your friends easily enough to drive your cause,' I mocked him. 'Men, women, and swords.'

'Yes,' he agreed, sitting back, cursing at an arrow in his back. 'I let it go. I wounded you with it, carved your face, and I should have killed you with it, but I did not. Perhaps I just wanted you to have it, after all.'

'Why would you give such a blade to a boy you thought was illegitimate? Eh?' I sneered. 'Would it not have been better to give it to the son of Julia? Your lover's highborn bastard?'

His face went slack as he stared at me. He shook his tired face and wiped his hand across it. 'You know nothing of Julia.'

'I know she was not Sigilind, my mother. Your wife,' I spat.

'No, she was not. Where I barely knew your mother, I guarded Julia with my life,' he said softly.

'With your body, yea,' I agreed. 'You fucked her, got her pregnant, and she used you to make sure her sons, yours included, will take the reins from Augustus when he dies. She has plotted to kill Drusus; her idea was to make you a lord in Germania, and that fat shit Segestes, as well. I dare you to deny it.'

He laughed softly, pulling at an arrow, which came off. He hissed in pain. 'Not wise to pull them off like that, Hraban. Might bleed to death.'

'Do you deny it?' I yelled at him.

He sighed. 'Julia. I shall not speak of Julia. I shall not speak of the plans we made and with whom I made them. Yes, all the Republican nobles have to fall before Augustus dies. That is true. And the poor broken Drusus out there? He is a bright star in the sky. Everyone loves him. And he hates Augustus. For the humiliation of his own father? You know Augustus took Livia, his mother when she was heavy with Drusus? Livia's husband had to attend their wedding. Augustus is a fucking goat. But you do not understand Julia.'

'Please explain Julia to me, Father? After all, my family is dead for your decision to throw your lot in with these strange, Roman ideas,' I sneered and walked to the water. He flinched and raised his hand imploringly, and I shook my head. 'Don't worry. I have some time now.'

He grinned and nodded, grabbing his sword from the wet mud. 'Yea. Just some time. So, the Bear will be slain. Finally. Is Odo near?'

I nodded. 'He is. That is my last trip this summer.' I nodded towards the Godsmount.

He looked at it, and his eyes lit up in understanding. 'So that is the place they were all so excited about. Why my father exiled me.'

'Yes, I'll ride there after you begin to rot. Up to the Godsmount. To save your grandchild Lif. Another soul you spat on for a whore of Rome. And for a bastard. And to think you had the nerve to call me one! You claimed you had no love for a bastard, but you fight for one!'

'Julia,' he told me, struggling to sit. 'Julia is not what you think she is. She is weak at times, strong only when the sun shines. She hates her father—'

'Kindred souls we are,' I breathed.

He lifted his hand to silence me. 'She is weak, Hraban. Very, very weak. And beautiful as the sun. I was her protector, the one who listened to her when she was married to Marcellus when she was but fourteen. Then, to old bastard Agrippa, who was an ancient man, with hair growing in his ears. That old, rancid pedophile Maecenas advised Augustus to marry her to the mightiest general in the land to avoid another civil war. She obeyed.'

'And you saw this?'

'I was your age when I served them. I guarded her and in the darkness, she had nobody to speak with. She had had plenty of sycophants, but not an honest Germani, who will only tell her the truth. She loved the truth, and I gave it to her. She was a noble sacrifice.'

'And you loved her. And forgot your wife,' I said spitefully.

He rolled his eyes. 'Please, Hraban. How many men forget their wives when they travel far, with little hope of returning. My father, your fucker of a grandfather, fled from Gothonia fearing the prophecy and then feared it even more when war followed in the form of Bero. He sent me away. Is that my fault?'

'I ...' I began and went sullen, unable to deny there was some truth to his words.

He nodded sagely. 'It is hard to judge a man, Hraban when you have not walked with him. As for you?' He shook his shoulders. 'You have not seen Rome. Not its glory, its splendor. I forgot about home. When I was offered a crown of the South Germania for the death of one Drusus, I hesitated. I had Julia. I had Rome. I had its sweet flowers and rancid smells and a purpose in my life. But ...'

'You also had a son,' I sneered. 'A son that everyone thinks belongs to Agrippa.'

'Yes,' he smiled. 'I have not seen him. She was pregnant when I agreed to this plan. For I have also seen the evil of Rome and knew the fifth child of Julia would be different from the others. He would look like me. And to keep him safe, I had to have a kingdom. And allies. Allies who are high and powerful.'

'And just like that, you devised a plan to make yourself the Marcomanni thiuda, killed your father in the process, your wife as well and disowned me and Gernot.'

He pointed a finger at me. 'You saw me crying for Sigilind. Those sobs and screams, Hraban, were not false. I lost my soul then, boy, for I had loved her once. As for Father? I had a grudge against him. For that, I will not be sorry. No matter if he was like a father to you.'

'And are you sorry for us?' I snickered. 'Your true sons?'

'I am …' he began and stammered. 'In some ways, yes. But you go and live in Rome, Hraban, and come home to find shepherds and villains and force yourself to love near adult bastards you have never seen. And I had lost your mother, Hraban. No. I was not sorry for my sons. I did risk you all. That I cannot deny. I did it for Julia, for my son and the glory. I could not have Hulderic compete with me for power, and I needed to be seen as the victim by the Marcomanni. People had to die. But I did not wish to see your mother go to Hades. As for you, Gernot? I suppose you are my son, despite your hair, but I am also a very suspicious man. I will never know for sure, and that doubt will never go away.'

I looked down, hurt by his words, despite the fact I knew his thoughts already. I felt tears in my eyes, astonished by the fact he could still hurt me. 'Bastard.'

He grinned. 'I admit, when I saw you presenting Vago's head to me, defying me in my hall, then burning it around me? I admired you. You even survived Nihta later. And I hear, the Beast.'

'I killed your Lok spawned Hel Hound,' I agreed. 'Leuthard killed friends of mine.'

He pointed a finger at me. 'Yes, that is so. So what? And Julia agreed to this plan. She convinced me. But did she devise it? Or someone else close to her? No, not Augustus. Augustus would love to see Drusus dead, but he would also grieve him, for he loves the boy of Livia though not Tiberius. Julia is guilty if you seek someone to blame, but she is not brave or powerful enough to plan this. So, if you ever see her, do not touch her. She but obeyed.'

'No?' I asked, and he growled at me and then grimaced at his pain. 'Perhaps I will find your son?`

He stared at me, not willing to show how my words upset him. Finally, he wiped his red, sweaty hair off his face. 'Here we are,' he breathed. 'Threaten me, not him.'

'Finally, we are here,' I agreed and walked closer. 'I made a promise to my wife all my issues would be settled this summer, so I won't walk away now.'

We said nothing for a time but looked carefully at each other. He spat blood and smiled, his handsome face and red hair dirty with mud. He grunted as he sat up, trying to stand, failing.

'Where is Gunhild?' I asked him, trying to find the resolve and hatred to kill him. 'You fooled her like you did me, made her betray her father Balderich and then you married her, cheated her, used her high blood to force the south to rebellion and finally, when you lost her to Burlein, you took her back in burning of Grinrock, and you beat her.'

'She was my wife and betrayed me, Hraban. Gods frown on women who do not know their place,' he said with spite. 'But she is alive. I have her baby. She is the royal blood of Aristovistus, after all.'

'She?'

'Yes, she. Burlein had a daughter. A final failure of the bastard,' he hawked. 'But they are well treated.'

'You shit,' I told him wearily. 'Utter, cold hearted piece of shit.'

'Yes, Son, the one who serves Rome as I do.'

'Where is Marcus Romanus?' I asked him. 'He still setting up your new kingdom?' I asked, interested to know about my former tutor and Maroboodus's friend as I tried to decide what to do with him.

'Amber, Hraban,' he grinned painfully. 'That is the lifeblood of a great empire. It will flow from the Mare Gothoni through the lands of Segestes to the Rhenus River. I might get myself a piece of fine land in the south, but that land needs an income. That is what Marcus is to do. He will set it up. It can make Segestes rich. Or it will flow through the lands of Albis River and our kindred Suebi to the south into my lap, and I shall trade it for the rest. That is why I wanted to keep the ring. To give me easy access to such a trade route with the Semnones. But Marcus is dealing with it. He is with the Semnones right now. We only have to drive the Boii of Danubius River away, build our land and trade amber.' He looked at my cold eyes and hesitated. 'But I guess we won't now. Poor Marcus. He has been working tirelessly with the Semnones and the Langobardi.'

403

I smiled and stepped next to him. He gazed up at me and tried to get up. 'You are going to die, Father. I am loath to kill you, though. I would not want you to soil Mother's presence in the next world,' I told him. 'And what for? A kingdom, a whore of Rome, a bastard son you have never seen, and riches in amber. You are a fool. You could have been a great man and respected. And loved by your family, Father.'

He laughed sadly and leaned back, in pain. 'You will understand one day, Hraban, how one has to make harsh choices if one is to achieve anything. Now. I will fight you, boy. Even riddled with arrows and wounds, I am no easy prey. I am hurt, but will slay you son. You killed many a good man of mine.' I toed him and laughed at his foolish boasts. He grunted and swung the sword as he sat in the grass, but I blocked the blade, hacked it down and placed the Winter Sword on his throat. He spat. 'I say you do me ill when you have not seen what I endured in Rome. You will regret it when you do.'

I looked at him with discomfort. 'Your men are dead, slain. They are waiting for you, a fool who led them to their deaths. They curse you; they followed this device to their demise.' I nodded at his standard.

A bird landed on the standard and croaked angrily on it.

It was a raven. A huge, large raven, silky black, its eye a pool of darkness as it regarded me mysteriously from atop the red bear standard.

I stared at the thing, feeling trepidation in my heart, my hands shaking slightly.

Father looked at it in stupefaction. 'How did the prophecy go?'

'A bear is slain; a raven will find the way.'

'Not the ...?' he grinned. 'Think that is a raven?' he asked sarcastically.

'Yes. But the bear is ...'

'A bear. I might not be the Bear that has to die,' he said with some amusement. 'The prophecy is a mess. Nothing is in order. It is impossible to understand. But there are so many signs now that perhaps there is some truth in the matter after all?'

'It is just a raven,' I hissed.

'Well, he seems to think it has relevance,' Father said with glinting eyes and nodded up to the bank.

We were not alone.

There, up on the bank of the shallow depression was a gray horse and on the horse sat the dirty red haired creature called Odo. Behind him were men, Ansigar, Gernot and many men, regarding us.

But in that, I was wrong.

They regarded the bird.

It croaked thrice and took to its wings, circling above me, croaking a few more times. Then it caught the wind and flew away, heading for the east, toward the Godsmount. Odo looked down at me, and to my father, deeming us inconsequential for he smiled and rode after the bird. He called out. 'Ride after us, Hraban. If you can!' he yelled. 'Here, a gift! He was separated from some men you do not wish to find!' he laughed, and I saw they left a man behind. It was Catualda, bound, entirely bruised.

I stared at the prize Odo had left me and then forgot about him and forgot about Father. I thought about Lif and the raven and knew it was no coincidence. It was indeed a raven that would find Veleda. But the bear had not fallen. Unless Drusus had died.

Odo's troop rode off, ignoring us, trying to keep up with the lazily careening bird. I watched him go and sensed Father was crawling away. He was going, and I hesitated for a long time until he was nearly in the shade of the woods. *Had Drusus died, the Bear to his father? Was Father to die before the raven found Veleda? Perhaps not.* I hesitated and felt tears roll down my cheeks.

I had beaten Father.

But I did not desire his life.

He was a damned soul, and I hated him, but he was my father. *Had he said I did not understand him? It was true. Had I not changed greatly the past few years?* I sighed and felt I could breathe and think about the past, for once. The sword in my hand felt weightless as I gazed after the man who was my father. He would go and lead my people, he would go and grow rich and that bothered me, but he was my father and had not Hulderic once told me to respect him?

In truth, I did not know what he had endured in Rome. I should follow his path to judge him.

He stopped at the edge of the wood and half wondered and mocked me. 'Like Hulderic. Letting that prophecy deny you what is yours. He left the north and the legacy of the family. You leave me alive, and I shall be triumphant. If your Drusus dies? I shall be a king.'

I nodded at him. 'I did not let you go for the prophecy, Father. I left you go for I pity you. And I shall go to Rome, Father, for in Rome are kings made. I will find Julia, I will find your son and I will, perhaps, be more savage and decisive that day? Perhaps they let me serve in the Germani Custodes Corporis and set me guarding your bastard?' His face went white as he regarded me. I pulled out his standard and broke it on my knee. I threw them into the stream and watched him crawl away. I rubbed my forehead, thinking of my oaths to Cassia. I yelled after him. 'I will go to Rome, Father! I will see what you saw, do what you did and we shall see if I will hate my family after like you do!'

Had I failed? Perhaps. I would indeed go to Rome and see what he had struggled with. I would see Julia, I would see his son, and while I would not slay them, I would learn of him. I had time. I felt weight leave my chest and then I turned to Catualda. But I did not have to leave Father to reign supreme, did I?

Catualda began to shake his head.

I walked over to him and kneeled next to him, staring into his eyes. He was ragged and bloody, his fat, full lips cracked with thirst. I stared at him like a beast would at a carcass. He had schemed with Father and helped him kill my family. He had fooled me more times than I could count, and he had killed Koun. I poked him, and he shrieked in terror. 'What men were you riding with?'

'Segestes sent some to find you,' he said. 'Before the battle, he asked me and Ragwald to ride around the Roman army to find you and bring you to him. He lost a finger, you see? Ragwald took men, but he hamstrung my horse in the valley not far. He is planning something else than bringing you to Segestes. Then those vultures found me. Please, Hraban. You spared your father. We both hate him. Spare me.'

'Silence,' I said, thinking. 'Do you know what Father planned?' I asked while holding the Head Taker loosely.

'He ...' he said and looked confused. 'He wished to build a kingdom in the south. Segestes told me about this. Your father enticed us with it when we were still allied.'

'And you wanted the ring and to build one in the north?' I grinned. 'You vermin.'

'With Armin, then perhaps one day for myself,' he agreed sullenly.

'But you betrayed Armin, did you not?' I grinned.

'Segestes will have me.'

'Segestes? He will not love you. He will never share power with anyone. No. More. I will tell him you helped me escape him.'

'I did not!'

'Silence,' I spat. 'And so, you have few options as I do.'

'I can go home to the north,' he whispered with clear unhappiness.

'They don't like our family in Gothonia. Or our strain of family, remember? Our relatives fled it. And now Father is making a new kingdom. He might succeed.'

'You let him go!' Catualda spat.

'I did. I won't explain it to you. But that does not mean he should be allowed to play in peace. You have no land. But why not take his? His kingdom?' I asked him.

'What?' he retorted. 'I'm going to die. You are playing with me.'

'No, but you will bleed, dog,' I told him and sawed the Winter Sword across his face. He howled and wept and cried, and I held him in place until he was simply sobbing, holding his face. 'That way you will look kingly, Catualda. Like I do. Father is weak now. He will, perhaps, lead the Marcomanni and the Quadi remnants to the south to challenge the Boii, but he lacks, perhaps, the Roman support he thought he was promised after I am done with him. And he needs the Suebi of the east for amber. He is building an Amber Road.'

'Yes, he plans to set up a trade route,' Catualda said with sobs.

I grabbed his slashed face. 'Go to the Semnones, Catualda. Go to them and tell them you took my father's sword in battle. Tell them you have the ring and tell them he is a lying bastard who is after amber and he will cheat them. There will be Marcus Romanus there, his ally. Tell them he is a cheater's apprentice, a liar, a horse thief and a cur. Be like Father. Be a hero, let men flock to you. Grow strong in the east, and then take war against your cousin.'

'I have neither his sword nor the ring!' he sobbed, holding his face. I took some mud and slapped it on his wound. He grimaced.

'Take any ring and claim it is Draupnir. And take this.' I gave him the Winter Sword, even if my heart broke. 'Take his standard and his helmet and pretend. You are good at it. Take his amber, his land, for are you not Bero's son and the true heir to Draupnir and all its glory?'

'I am,' he sobbed. 'Wait, you are letting me go?'

'I am letting you go, you filth. And should you not do these things, bastard, dodging this charge I gave you, I shall bring the true Draupnir wherever you are and summon an army to hunt you down. I will find you. I will make sure no hole in Midgard is going to be welcome for you. I can be stubborn. You know it.'

'You don't have Draupnir's Spawn,' he told me as I took my foot away from him and stepped back.

'I will,' I said and gazed at Godsmount. 'Go, dog-faced, double-dealing piece of offal.'

I left him, left the Winter Sword on his lap and went to look for a horse.

Father and Catualda. Dealt with, as Cassia suggested. Wyrd.

BOOK 6: THE PLATE OF WODEN

'For some reason, you think it is your duty to thwart Odo.'
Veleda to Hraban

CHAPTER 34

I heard Catualda running down to the water to fish out Father's banner. He had ever moped after his land. He had worked against his father Bero for my father though he hated both equally. He wanted Draupnir for its legacy and power but got Father's armor and gear and weapons instead, and he would have to fight, for once, to get power. I was sure he would procure a golden ring and pretend it was Draupnir's Spawn just fine. I hoped he would travel to the Suebi lands and raise an army to fight Father, at least eventually. Perhaps he would. Perhaps Catualda would end up the richest bastard in the land, lord of amber and a god of war and it was all my doing.

Or the Winter Sword would kill him or make him miserable, at least, I chuckled.

But I knew what he was. I knew him; he knew me, and he would ever fear me.

Germania. Honor. Fame.

I was going to leave it all behind. As soon as Odo was sorted.

I went down to the stream and kneeled next to the tangle of horses. One was dead, and Nihta's was dying. I killed it with Nightbright and climbed back up and looked around. Further away, I saw the man I had struck from the saddle. He was struggling on the ground, pulling himself along, his knee painfully bent. He was going for his horse that was calmly and happily taking an advantage of the situation by eating green grass, and then checking his master's progress with an appraising eye.

I ran for the horse.

The man saw me coming, cursed, spat, and struggled harder, managing to drag his hurt leg along so that he was on his hands and knees, but he had no chance to escape, even if he managed to get to his horse. He looked at me with pleading eyes.

'Please,' he said miserably on his hands and knees. I ignored his words, picked up his spear and shield and used his conveniently arched back to mount the horse. He cursed and groped after me, but I shook my head at him.

'Its name?' I asked.

'Star God,' he said, miserably.

I threw a Roman silver denarius at him. 'Thanks,' I said, guiding the beast away from the man. I stopped to consider the distant battle scene but knew if I rode there, there was no guarantee I would be able to ride for Godsmount. I had to hurry, and so I turned away and followed the tracks. I did not see Odo's men, but the summer had been wet, the grass was churned up, and I guided the horse after them and for the mountain. The man had water on the horse, a gourd that I drowned greedily, suddenly exhausted. The sun was getting lower in the sky, and I flew with the horse.

It was perhaps my imagination, but I thought I saw the bird, a spec in the sky, flying in circles.

Towards the evening, I began to despair. I spent time riding around, staring at the ground, for much cavalry had been passing there during the previous weeks, and I cursed I did not have Brimwulf there with me. *Or Fulcher*, I thought and spat in anger and swallowed in sorrow. Finally, I decided that some of the tracks were fresher, and I rode after them. In some hours time, it was dark.

I knew the way to Godsmount, and I kept the horse going that way, terrified of the beast breaking its leg on an unseen hole. The fresh tracks could still barely be seen in the moonlight. Then, up ahead, a fire was burning. I approached it, carefully, hefting my spear. I pushed to the

411

woods, begging for the horse to be silent. There were pinecones and twigs on the ground, and I made relatively easy time as I went on. The fire was burning in a clearing of a forest and a man sat by it, looking harmless enough. He was roasting a rabbit over a fire, singeing its meat badly, and cursing occasionally. He drank ale and sniffled, talking to himself. He did not look like any man of Odo's.

But he did look like Ragwald. The man's right arm was useless.

I cursed softly and looked around and saw nothing moving in the forest. I sat there, thinking. I spurred the horse to turn it carefully.

An arrow stuck in its neck, and the beast collapsed. Another hit it in the flank, near my leg.

I sat on the dead horse, in the sight of the man on the fire, and I saw him look back at me, being very unsurprised by my bizarre entrance to his camp. I looked around at the night and felt my skin crawl. Ragwald was nodding happily. 'My lord Segestes asked me to find you. He has a bone to pick with you, and I'd wager the damned ring is with you? You visited this Gulldrum, after all.'

'Is Armin alive?' I asked him, feeling foolish as I sat on the dead beast but did not dare to move.

He grunted with a very unhappy voice. 'I left before the battle. But I hear he is. A prisoner to Rome. And Segestes is now the lord of the north. Did you kill your father?'

'No,' I said, my belly cold from anticipation. Ragwald's eyes probed me with amusement. He was much calmer than usual, taking his time. He nodded.

'I also heard your Drusus is not dead yet. But he is hurt. Hurt enough to die? Perhaps. Hurt enough that his time in Germania is over? Likely. And as I said, he might die yet. Your father did well. You failed,' he smiled. 'And so Segestes would have that fucking ring. And you, of course. You left quite rudely.'

'Odo has the fucking ring,' I spat.

'He escaped? You failed with him, as well?'

'Yes,' I said.

'Damned to Hel, you are,' Ragwald complained. 'Fail here, fail there. Now. If you don't have that ring, then I suppose we have to take you alone back there.'

'Didn't Catualda lead you?' I asked him carefully.

'Oh!' he exclaimed. 'You saw him, as well? I bet he is also alive.'

'I've done nothing but fail this day,' I agreed, sitting on the dead animal. 'But he did tell me you might have other plans than taking me to Segestes.'

'He was damned right, boy,' Ragwald mumbled. 'Damned right. Too bad he spoiled the surprise. I hoped to give you hope of survival, at least a brief one, and then snatch it away, but hopeless or not, Hraban, I shall enjoy this.' He was nodding to himself, and I knew he was not sane. 'Shame about the ring. Expensive, precious. But I suppose that matters little. Around you, Hraban, are men. We saw you coming hours ago and set this place up. Some even followed you. They are good men. Some are my old men; some died in the battle, and few are new. And I do have some boys who do not like you much. They usually follow the whim of Segestes dutifully enough, but on this matter they are willing to help me out and not get paid. They despise you.'

'Gods know that could be anyone in this land,' I said and smiled. 'I saw nobody following me.'

'Yes,' he hawked. 'But these men are experts in tracking, and you would not see them until it is too late.' He chuckled. 'They are trackers, Hraban. Very, very good at tracking beast and man.'

Oh, gods, I thought. *Woden spare me.*

Ragwald waved his hand and men emerged from under the boughs. Most were armored in leather, some in helmets, all armed with framea and axes, daggers, and heavy spears. One had a full face helmet of dull iron, and I thought he had helped Armin when I had tried to capture him for Drusus. One was Ketill from Oddglade, and one was the young Hugo. But there were also five painted men, men with gray and black faces, wearing furs, armed with arrows and bows.

The Svear.

'They lost some brothers,' Ragwald said, nodding at the dangerous men. 'They are not happy.'

'Their brothers wept as they died,' I said with a bright smile, hoping for a quick death.

Ragwald laughed, turning the spit. 'All men weep when they die, and you will find this is so for you as well, very soon. Segestes told me to keep you alive. You recall I was reluctant to do so before Armin interrupted us. And I still am. I shall pursue my earlier inclinations and skin you. I will make a pretty purse out of your ball hide,' he told me, poking experimentally at the meat.

I pointed my spear at him. 'I already suffered enough at your hands, Ragwald. At yours and Helmut's. I'll fight to the end, and I will take you before anyone can twitch.' A hollow threat, I knew.

'He brags a lot,' Ragwald told his following with a bored voice. 'He brags and causes mischief and now it shall end.'

I sneered at him. 'You are a sick man, Ragwald. It was inevitable you would lose your family and service. Slaying me will not bring you joy.'

'Indeed, Hraban, I am a sick man. In need of medicine,' he said suddenly. He looked at me with a thoughtful scowl. 'Too often have you escaped me.' His eyes grew suspicious, and he rubbed his belly as if the idea of Hraban escaping him again was indeed making him ill. He was nodding vigorously. 'I have my medicine at hand. I will heal when I have seen the small animals of the forests devour your intestines. I shall laugh. Laugh, Hraban. Happily. Then I shall make a new family, and find a new lord,' he told me, seriously.

I spat. 'You left Segestes?'

He nodded absentmindedly. 'I did. I left Segestes. I am disobeying him and the Svear will go back, and tell what happened and blame me, as I agreed with them. They will still be in his favor, I shall not. I care not. I have no home with him, no. I left him. While sitting here I decided I would. I won't take you to him. I will serve Inguiomerus, perhaps, and see if you were right or wrong about ever finding joy again.' He grinned at me and yelled. 'Now!' I braced my feet, turning around, expecting an attack. My spear darted from man to man, but none of them moved. Ragwald laughed at my confusion. 'Not yet! Let none say I don't know how to have fun. The Svear are like dogs of Gymir, Hraban. They guard their lord. But Gymir's dogs were bound. I shall set them free in a bit. Now, off with you.' He waved me off, and I stared at him. 'There is the mountain. Go!'

'And you will hunt me?' I asked with spite.

He nodded. 'We will hunt you. I want you to fear, Hraban.'

I started to walk towards the mountain. 'Come after me and never leave this mountain,' I told him spitefully.

'A few moments is all you get then,' he laughed, and I ran, waiting to be hit by an arrow or spear. But I was not. The Svear made a strange, gurgling sound at my back, one that intensified as I ran, and if Ragwald had wanted me to fear, then I did.

The mountain's hilly sides rose around before me in the night. The air was crispy, a bit wet, and I despaired as I ran to the woods. There were game tracks that I took, but I wondered if I should take to the lush valleys full of blueberries instead and hide under moss. They would find me, no matter what.

A horn rang behind me.

Woden was laughing, I was sure of it as I ran on. The chainmail was heavy, and I played with the idea of abandoning it but decided against it. I'd need it more than speed, for I did not know the land and they would. *They would overtake me at some point*, I thought and cursed myself for letting Father go. At least he should be there, in the afterworld pointing a quivering, raging finger at me as I came that way.

Then, I heard birds calling.

There were many, the song was excited, then soft and forlorn, and I realized they were the Svear trackers communicating by whistles. I fidgeted and ran off. My enemy were still whistling, but now also eerily snapping their fingers as they silently came on. They were like a ghostly elf pack or deadly vaettir of the dark groves, and I knew they would soon spot me. I would die slowly, an arrow in my leg, tortured and forgotten.

I put on more speed and heard whistles and snaps nearby. Perhaps they had heard me?

Before me were old alder trees in a cluster of dark woods, and I stopped under a low hanging bough. I hesitated and swallowed my fear. I thrust my spear into the trunk above, pushed the shield at a precarious angle up to a thicker concentration of boughs and leaves. Then I pulled myself up to the tree, climbing like a squirrel on fire, trying not to drop too many twigs and pieces of bough to the ground. I barely managed it with my armor.

I pulled the spear from the trunk, turned to stare down and tried to calm my breath. I pressed myself against the trunk, my cheek caressing a rough surface of the tree. Should they miraculously miss me during the night, I knew daylight would bring doom. But in the dark, perhaps even the Svear would not see me. I prayed goddess Freya for luck, for Woden would surely be busy soon as I needed his battle rage. I hoped she would see fit to aid me.

And so, I stood still on the bough, hid by the heart-shaped leaves.

I heard a strange shuffle.

A moment later, one of the Svear walked by, bent down to examine the ground and he was there for a while, looking ahead, hesitating. I prepared to jump on him, but he whistled softly, snapped his fingers a few times and ran on. I held my breath. He stopped to listen again and to sniff at the air. Then he finally moved off. Horses rode up in the dark. I could see Ragwald and his men spread out in the thick foliage, confident their trackers knew what they were doing. Hugo was speaking softly with Ketill, and I grinned as they passed under me. The forest was quiet, some birds began an eerie song in the foliage and some bugs crawled under my armor, but I refused to swat at them. I was about to move when another Svea walked up, his short stabbing spear at the ready, his shadowed eyes staring around, his dark face smeared with green and grey ashes, looking around and smelling the air. He walked under my tree, bent on going ahead when he stepped on some fresh bough, fallen from my climb.

Then he stopped.

He bent down and took some of the boughs in his hand, rubbing it.

I jumped down behind him.

He turned, and I threw a spear at his chest, easily impaling his fox fur tunic, and he flew back to the foliage, gurgling, and spitting blood as I bent down and stabbed Nightbright at the mass of thrashing legs until it did not move. I listened carefully, sweating in the darkness, and all was quiet, save for some clicks ahead. I knew I had to run, for they would understand that things had changed when this one did not answer. I grabbed the spear and my shield and moved away.

I had run east up the hills for the mountain, but now I careened a bit to the north. I ran with my shield and my spear, holding onto my helmet. I tore off to the night, my heart jumping at every sound in the awakening forest. My armor weighed a ton, and I felt like throwing up. All the Germani run in the woods, our men lasting for long stretches on winding, tiny hunt trails, hours on hours, for few can afford a horse, and the prey in the woods or in war can only be had if you have the stamina of a beast and lots of god-given luck. And gods and luck are fickle friends at best.

I took after an auroch and it was bounding and running before me, a large female, hoping its tracks would hide mine. I was begging it would confuse the trail, but it was faster than I was and turned to the east, bellowing in anger and I kept on. There were no whistles to be heard.

Soon, the forests grew thicker and my spear would catch on thickets and branches as I weaned my way forward. I was now leaving plenty of bent and broken branches and twigs behind me. I stopped to drink from a small stream as the dawn came. It was a sad and gray dawn, banks of heavy clouds thickly filling the sky. I went on until I had gone ten Roman miles and broke out on a field. I found I was on the lower hills of the Godsmount, the rocks and woods on its slopes rising up before me like a sitting Jotun, high, so high an eagle would find it hard to reach them. The two strange peaks were visible high above me, and I hesitated as I wondered how I was to find Veleda and Lif. I ran through the field, and then a brightly beautiful forest, scaring a drowsy fox feasting on a rabbit, and the beast didn't run, it just bared its teeth at me. I laughed, wondering if that one too, would take after me.

I nearly froze.

Behind me, I could hear whistles and the neighing of horses, for my enemy were close. I cursed and went on, scared out of my mind, and Ragwald had been right. He had wanted me to fear, and I did.

Where to go? I wondered.

In front of me, rising high to the sky, the peaks beckoned for me. I despaired as I looked at the vast woods and crags and steep sides hidden by vegetation. I had no exact idea where to go. I looked up to the green slopes, and my heart stopped.

The huge raven was high up there, I was sure, circling a rocky crevice that split the two tops in the middle.

I surged forward.

A large man got up from a copse of tall grass in front of me, holding a bow.

He was painted in green and gray; another moved behind him, and I screamed defiance at them, charging with my spear held low as the arrow flew.

I put my head down, felt the arrow crash against my shield as I jabbed at the man, who had been drawing another arrow. He rolled away with perfect balance, coming down to aim his bow at me again. Fight them, my god screamed at me, and my body obeyed as I flipped my spear into the air, grabbing it so that it was ready to be thrown. And throw it I did. It flew from my hand with a force unmatched as the second man was moving to support his brother. He realized he was the target. He dropped his weapon, trying to roll down, but he caught the spear in his chest, yelping, and the archer released his last arrow, hissing in hate and fear. I screamed and shield bashed him straight in his face, falling over him. I tried to get up, but he held onto my shield and then he struck a weak blow with a club, clipping my shoulder.

I laughed in battle madness, I swatted his arm aside, and hit him in the face with my helmet repeatedly until he shuddered and went still. His face was a thing of blood, his skull caved in, his tongue lolling out of a misshapen mouth, and I got up, gore dripping to my chin from my helmet as I turned to face the seven men chasing after me.

They were there, five on horse, the two Svear on foot. They were staring at me in the dark wood. To them, I must have looked like an escaped spirit from some dark realm of the elves, for they talked to each other with hushed voiced. Woden gave me strength. He whispered to me, prodded me to mock the enemy, and so I did. I laughed at them, danced before them, my short dark beard dripping blood. I took up my shield, bent down to the dead man, and with Nightbright, I slashed his throat.

418

Ragwald was whispering to a tall man at the helm, a man with a wolf pelt on his shoulders, but he did not move. I walked over to my spear and saw the man I had speared was still alive, hissing in pain as the huge blade was embedded in his chest, but I cared not and took it out, deliberately making him howl.

'Come, hem holders of Frigg, you girly bastards.' I laughed.

The two remaining Svear ran for me, and I retreated, running to the woods. I noticed I had an arrow in my side, and while I ran, I just kept looking at it as it was sticking through my lower right side. Curiously, I felt no agony. I heard Ragwald get his men moving forward. As I ran, I saw a man up on the hills, riding far above and even this far, flitting through the woods I saw it was Odo, looking down at me and up to the raven. I cursed and ran after Odo but then pursuing men on horses got close, and an arrow thudded into the rim of my shield, and I saw I would never catch him.

The raven circled high above me, still flying around the crevasse splitting the mountain's top, lazily riding the currents, and I could almost hear Odo yelling at his men to ride faster..

I cursed and weaved as the horses behind me were finding some hardships with the rocks. Ragwald was screaming at the men, and they obeyed, and I would soon be caught. I burst into a small wood, then out of it. An arrow hit the rock next to me, and I nearly roared in anger. My goal was so close, and there was Ragwald, Ketill, and the rest of the bastards robbing me of justice.

Then, ahead, I saw a patch of rock and a rugged cave.

I had no choice.

I sprinted ahead with the last vestiges of my strength. A horseman crashed through a thicket before me, and I slashed the beast with the spear, making it throw its rider downhill. I ran over the rock for the opening of the narrow cave and turned.

There they were, Ragwald, the two Svear, the man in the helmet, Hugo, Ketill and one other. I could no longer see Odo, but he was going up, no doubt. Ragwald was cursing me, his men were dismounting, and the Svear ran to whisper something to Ragwald, pointing towards Odo. Ragwald blanched as he regarded Odo's troop. He shook his head and pointed his finger at me. I fully entered the cave, cursing. I looked at it, despairing. There was no sign of life. I was trapped. I was surrounded. The raven croaked somewhere far, and the echo mocked me.

CHAPTER 35

I sat in the cave, watching my enemy.

The cave was dark, as caves are, chilly and wet, and I was so hungry I could have eaten my helmet. I glanced outside and held the arrow in my side, gently tugging at it. It hurt. It bled very little, and I decided it had not touched anything vital. Some links of my mail were in the flesh, but it would not kill me unless it got infected.

Outside, Ketill was gesturing towards the cave, evidently trying to cajole his leader into coming in. Ragwald shook his head and walked back and forth. Eventually, he stalked towards me. 'Come boy. I will geld you, but I will make it easy for you. I could skin and then geld you, but I will take your nuts alone. There is no route out of there.' He goaded me with obscene movements, and the Svear took out bows and arrows, and I retreated deeper into the dark cave.

I yelled back. 'Why do you not go back to your village and retire, cripple. Perhaps they will let you herd cows?' I dodged as the Svear shot some arrows at the sound of my voice.

I waited and looked out again and cursed, for the Svear had vanished. I began to listen to the sounds around me. When you are in such a predicament, of course, even the most innocuous sounds will make you jump with terror, and so I decided to concentrate on guarding the entrance.

They were no doubt looking for a way in and no matter the sounds and taps and falling small rocks, the entrance was where they would have to come in from.

Unless there was another way in.

I prayed there was none. Around, I could see rocks and shadows, but nothing else, and so I stayed put and prayed to Woden. They let me pray for hours. The men outside made camp. They seemed content on sitting and waiting, one of them always on guard. They took out meat, and vegetables, and drank wine and mead, and my belly growled, and I cursed them. Finally, I moved around in the cave, as far as I could, trying not to make a single sound, but I could not help setting boulders rolling, and I noticed when they began to roll, they went downhill. And they would only stop far down in the darkness. I thought about going to investigate, but in the dark, I would fall, break my leg and die to Ragwald, helpless, and I was so afraid. I feared such holes in the ground. *Would it not lead to the lands of the dead, and the vaettir were sure to travel these halls*, I thought.

I stayed put.

I strained not to stare behind, fought not to make a sound, and I went on with my guardianship. Lif and Veleda. Odo was out there. I cursed and waited for the darkness. They would either come in, and I would kill the lot. Or I would go out and escape in the dark.

But the night was far.

I tried to calm myself again and stared across the land. The sight from the hill was spectacular. While Godsmount had looked like a rather low mount, it seemed I was high above the woods and fields even at the bottom of the actual mountain. The hills spread out under me, birds were flying level with me, and far, far away, I thought I saw the ridge where the battle had taken place. The castra was, perhaps, in sight; a brown smudge surrounded by a gray haze. Snakes of glittering rivers and streams were a calming sight, and vast stretches of hills and fertile valleys gave me some peace.

Then the men around the fires got up and pointed downhill, to the valleys beyond, and they quickly smothered their fire.

I got up and stretched my neck to see better.

Far down there was a stream of horses riding. Friends to whom, I did not know. At least Ragwald would eat raw meat, I chuckled. I smacked my dry lips and drank droplets of smelly water dripping down the side of the cliff. I spat it out for it was bitter, and my mouth felt raw after. I chuckled and cursed. There I was stuck in a hole, following a damn bird and thirsty and bleeding. Did the gods truly wish to kill me like this? I cursed in my head.

The day wore on.

It turned into an evening. The divine horses of the gods were fleeing Sköll and dragging down the sun, the moon would take its place, the celestial horses fleeing Hati, brother of Sköll. I searched the faces of my enemy and saw nothing but boredom. I did not see the Svear and felt tired. I slapped myself, then thought of the past day, the terrible battle, my hunger.

Then I fell to sleep.

Falling asleep on guard duty is a deadly offence, both for the Germani and the Romans. In the Roman army, it violates the fides, the trust of fellow soldiers, and the punishment, especially in wartime, is death, or fustuarium, being beaten to death by one's mates, all armed with cudgels. That was the first thing I thought about when I woke up and my eyes trained on the five men I had been looking at before I fell asleep.

It was very dark.

But I saw them still.

They were close, very close, advancing on the cave. Torches flared, and the stabbing light hurt my eyes. They ran with shields and spears at the ready. I panicked, hissed at the pain in my side and retreated hastily, rolling to my feet. The men charged into the cave, throwing spears and stones at shadows, and I fled back, thinking to run down to the darkness.

I ran into a wall of muscle. My helmet crunched my nose as I fell to my ass.

Usually, bears range outside during the short summer days and nights, hunting deer, eating berries, making new bears and whatever it is bears like to do. They rarely return to their winter hideouts. The bear I had run into did not follow these sensible ursine habits, and when I looked up,

423

there was an angry set of sharp, jagged teeth bared at my face from ten feet height, for the bear was on its hind feet, and obviously upset by our trespassing. It was easily the largest bear I had ever seen and must have weighted near two thousand pounds. The slap it gave me threw me amidst the hunters, and I lost both my shield and my spear as I fell over Ragwald, cursing because the bear had ripped my chainmail apart at the shoulder.

Smelling piss and fear, the bear bellowed hard enough to shake one out of his feet, and then it charged us.

I would see many of these bears fighting animals and men in the future, but there, in the crowded cave, there was no room to dodge. The bear ran like the fastest dog in the middle of our suddenly single-minded group and swatted the man with the iron helmet to the wall, where he moaned and crumbled. Then the beast fell on Hugo, clamping his claws on the boy's head. What was left after he took his claws away was a screaming mass of skinless meat, and Hugo went rolling to the side, hollering and sobbing. The bear roared and charged one other man, who was backing off in horror, fell over him and we saw red meat fly in the air as he died. I got up with Ketill and Ragwald. We glanced at each other and charged.

Outside, the horses tore their holdings and ran away as the beast let us know the charge was not to its liking, or perhaps just in mockery of us.

We stabbed the raging bear from the front, Ragwald swatting it awkwardly with his left hand, an ax swing that just seemed to infuriate the furious beast even more. Ketill, his one remaining man was courageously punching a spear into the tough, messy fur, making it yelp and roar loud enough to make us all soil our pants. I took up a spear dropped by the man with the helmet and thrust at the bear's throat and missed, ripping fur and skin. One would think such a cumbersome thing would not be so fast, but this one was very fast indeed, and it fell over me, its claws ripping at my helmet with enough force to pull bronze furrows across it. I crawled away from under it, felt its back paws crash down on me as it was banking and jumping in rage, and I was crushed to the stone. I cursed and kicked myself free, out of breath. I backed off as the bear concentrated on Ketill, who was now white with fear as he backed off.

The bear shuffled like a Greek boxer towards the man, screaming in anger and pain as the spear came for its gut once more. This time it went deeper and the growling ball of death fell on Ketill, biting savagely and tearing at his chest, arms and face, and my foe just went limp, spurting blood all over the floor, which the bear promptly licked while yowling curiously. Ragwald threw up at the sight, gathering bravery.

This was when the bear turned its eyes to me, and then it simply charged.

I cried in terror and ran for it.

I punched my spear up hard, very hard, as hard as I could at its face, hoping to hit the gory mouth. It was just about to roar and bite at me when the blade pierced its tongue, entered the soft meat of its mouth, sliced to the bone and entered its brain. Like the beast of Maroboodus had, Leuthard, this one died surprisingly quickly. The ferocious mound of muscles turned to decaying meat, the furry thing fell to the stone like a huge wet rug, burying me, snapping my spear and all I could do was to try to breathe. I tried to push it off me, but could not. Ragwald was there, and the two Svear entered, apparently having been scouting the column of the men below. I struggled as I saw their gleeful faces, and I chuckled in a panic, as I thought my nuts were safe under the dead animal. I knew I would be lucky to join the bear soon, but likely, I would do so later, and I thought of Lif and cursed wyrd and its fickle masters and the three spinners of misery.

The men saw I was helpless and checked the dreadfully mauled men. The one in the helmet shook his head and climbed and leaned on the wall while Ragwald stood above me like a conqueror. 'So. I thank you for my life, Hraban. But that does not bring back my arm and my son,' he hissed at me, and as he got closer, I slapped him with my left hand, and he went into a rage, tearing my helmet off with his good hand, throwing it out of the cave. The Svear snickered and took off their tunics. 'Tie his arms!' he told the men, and I saw the helmeted man lean back, looking at the ceiling. The hunters did it efficiently, not saying much, even if I had killed their brothers. One of them was old and grizzled. He saw me look at him, and he shrugged.

He spoke with a strange, yet strangely familiar accent. 'No, they were no relatives. Just men I hired. You fought well,' he whispered to me. 'You are of the Gothoni? We used to fight your kin in the north. Lost a king once to your father. And the Star of the Snow.' He giggled. 'She was a beauty. I was young, but I remember.'

I shook my head, trying to clear away the fear. 'My father?'

'Ask him one day. There was war and—'

'Shut it,' Ragwald said disdainfully. 'He is meat, not a friend. You don't speak to your meal.'

I fixed an eye on the Svear, and he nodded, almost apologetically. 'We have this habit, you need not fear. You will be dead. Your heart. We will have it.' They dragged me out from under the bear and stood me up. The arrow had broken in my flesh, and the younger Svear tore the rest out, making me swoon.

'Hold him,' Ragwald said as he walked back and forth, and the Svear did as they were told, grabbing my hair as Ragwald took out a knife. He lifted my chainmail and placed it to rest at my genitalia.

'Now. This will go,' he lifted the knife higher, nearly making a wound, and I tried not to flinch. 'But first, I will skin off your face. Then your arms. I will piss on your raw flesh, boy, and thus is my medicine taken.'

He pressed the knife behind my ear, drawing blood. 'I will rip it off, and know, boy, that sometimes eyes come off at the same time. They will flow on your raw cheeks, Hraban. Then we are both crippled.' He laughed and was tensing for a slow cut when the man in a helmet got up. I saw him swoon as if a man who has lost his soul, shaking his head in denial. I heard him sigh.

Then he hacked an ax into Ragwald's spine so hard that the wolf pelt flew off his shoulders.

The Svear looked up in alarm and stared at their dying lord, who was now kissing the bloody floor. 'What the fuck are you doing?' asked the older Svea. 'You betrayed your lord!'

The helmeted man laughed. 'I am saving my former lord!' He shook off his helmet and his long, blond, sweaty hair came spilling out. The helmet fell on Ragwald's side.

It was Wandal.

His face was leaner than it had been, his blond beard shorter, but the strong bones, the lion-like face was as stubborn and feral as I had seen it the last time. In battle.

I made an audible croak at the wonder of my friend. Wandal, my companion from childhood, the boy who had followed me as I had tried to reverse my fortunes with Father. And he had saved my life before, and now again. The boy who had fallen in Castra Luppia when father made himself a hero of all the free Germani, and the one I had sworn to find.

Wyrd!

It was indeed the summer to deal with all the hardships of our lives. The bad and the good.

Wandal was taller than I was, stronger than a mule, for his father was Euric, a blacksmith and so was Wandal, and now he was enraged. He stalked the Svear with his shield held high, and the two men turned on him, lithely running to each side of the young champion. He backed to the wall, but not before the younger Svear slashed his broad-bladed spear at his arm, and this was when I jumped after that enemy, slipping the cords in my hands over his head and pulling him back, hurting from the wounds and scratches, and my head throbbed with pain, but I didn't let go. Wandal blocked the attacks of the older man, who was cursing, glancing at our struggle, and he then decided he would not be able to break Wandal. He dodged my friend's savage ax strike and ran out into the dark. The man on my chokehold was panting and gurgling, and my muscles were aching, and he tried to gouge my eyes, but his strength was failing, and I felt warm liquid spread on my legs as he pissed himself and slowly died.

All that time I stared at my friend.

Wandal had taken up a bow and was aiming at the distant shadow running down the hill and he let loose, the arrow sprung to the night. I was panting and hurt and let go of the man. 'Did you hit him?'

He shrugged. 'I don't know. I am terrible with bows. But who cares, eh?' He looked at me long and hard and grunted as he dragged the body off me, and I thanked him with a nod as he pulled me up to a sitting position. 'So. I have heard a great deal about you, my friend,' he said, and I laughed,

laughed until tears poured from my eyes, and he chuckled but went serious.

'From whom?' I asked him.

'Armin,' he said.

'Armin?' I asked, incredulously. 'Yes, you were with Armin! When I tried to capture him. What happened to you when I lost you?'

He snorted. 'After I fell from the wall, I was taken a prisoner by the Vangiones. There were many others, and when your father wrecked their army and that of the Matticati, we escaped. Yet, as you recall, your father was no friend of mine.'

'Thanks to me,' I allowed.

'Thanks to you, eh?' he agreed. 'I ran north. There were others, and the Matticati hunted us down, one by one. They were a bit furious, eh? Very furious after the losses of their lands and lord. Some made it across the hills to the lands of the Tencteri and Sigambri. The Matticati sacrificed many to Donor. I made it.'

'I have something to tell you,' I said, thinking about my failure with Ermendrud.

He raised his hands. 'A warlord of Varnis found me, starving and robbing a winter cellar.'

'Wandal—'

He slapped me. Then again. 'You lied to me, eh?'

I spat blood and nodded.

'I gave you my oaths, my friendship, and you gave me a woman. You told me I was her savior; she needed me and yet, you were but abandoning a girl that was not high enough for you. You shit! You had slept with her, she was pregnant, she lost the baby for fear of being alone, and then she died to Leuthard when you did not look after her. And you told me she was not yours. You wanted a princess, Gunda.'

'All of this is true, Wandal,' I said, and he slapped me again.

Then he looked at his hand and shook his shoulders. 'It did not feel as good as I thought it might, eh?'

I agreed. 'I wanted to kill my father and had him under my sword. I know what you mean.'

He laughed roughly. 'All the shit I hear you went through to kill him, losing my Ermendrud to Leuthard and then when you had him? Eh? You let him live?' He raised his hand again, this time in a fist, but let it fall. He rubbed his forehead. 'Armin bought me from the Sigambri. He was visiting the Sigambri before the great battle, making plans, and he remembered my face. He was going to give me to you after Drusus died at your hands, but then I heard of Ermendrud, and you joined Drusus. And so I joined Armin. With all my heart. To oppose you.'

'Were you with him? In the battle?' I asked him in wonder.

'I blew his horn, Hraban.' He grinned. 'When he was leading his troops, I carried his standard. I loved his dream, and you had killed mine. I wanted to slay you that day Thusnelda put you down, but he told me to be patient, eh?'

'I vowed to search for you,' I said miserably. 'I loved you and love you. And I have failed.'

He nodded. 'I saw you nearly kill Rochas. I saw you trying to take Armin's life. Then I saw you bring Thusnelda to Armin, and I hated you. I knew you wanted him and Lif, both.'

'I see,' I said and lay back. 'Yes, all of that is true.'

'I smiled when I heard Catualda had taken you to Segestes,' he admitted, looking away. 'And hated me. You were so mad. Mad with your fame, your precious honor, your position and never stopped to think what your friends had, eh?'

'I know, Wandal,' I said with anger, but not at him, but at myself.

'Ansigar had nothing. They had two cows, and a rotten hall, no fields, and his uncle was a drunk,' he spat. 'Ansbor lost his father the same day your mother and Hulderic fell. And I? We had the smithy. Sometimes we had no food. I ate with Hulderic and your mother, very often. Remember? Euric would send me to your hall in the mornings so I could get some porridge. We visited your grandfather's grand hall, your friends and followed you for we loved you and the thought of you. A grand lord? One day? A friend and a lord, Hraban. These were the things we saw.'

'I failed,' I told him plainly.

'Yes, you failed. When you lost it all, you failed to rise above your father. Had you asked, we would have left with you. But you fought to get yours back. At any cost. It has been a very fucking high cost, Hraban. Very high, eh? I think we all have lost much more than we had to.'

We stared at each other, and after a while he sat down. I shook my head, holding it for a moment, hurting. 'So, how come you are here?'

'Armin sent me to serve with Ragwald. They had never seen me, and I was useful to Ragwald. I was to keep an eye on Segestes,' he told me. 'And ...'

'And you were to slay him during battle?' I asked with a laugh. 'I asked a man of mine to make sure Armin survives the battle. To become a prisoner.'

'You what?' he asked, incredulous.

'I decided Drusus should hold him before he dies in this war,' I stated. 'Thusnelda asked me to keep him alive. I did. Though not entirely as she asked.'

'Oh? Well,' he scowled at me and finally laughed, rubbing his face. 'I suppose it might save him. I failed Armin. I was hovering near Segestes when I saw him giving Catualda commands. To find you. I hesitated, knew I had a duty with Armin, but for some reason I could not keep my oath. I begged Ragwald to let me come with him. He agreed.'

'Why?'

'I don't know; I told you! Because they were after you? I was undecided if I wanted to see you die or to kill you myself.'

'How do you feel about it now?'

He took a deep breath and sighed deep. 'I heard you spared your fucker of a father and that I cannot understand, eh? But I hear you have a new, better life, and you have a daughter.' His voice cracked as he said that.

'It was mine, Wandal. Ermendrud's child was mine,' I said softly. 'And I am sorry I duped you with her.'

He snorted. 'I knew it, I just told you. I look and sound like a mule, Hraban, but I am not so stupid as to think a child is mine without bedding the woman, eh?' He grunted and pushed me. 'But you told Ermendrud I was a good man, and I found she was a girl worth knowing, despite the lies. No. She saw you like we did; an escape. And then she loved you, for a moment. Until you betrayed her. But she loved me after and that is no lie. And then you let her die.'

'She wanted to show us she was brave,' I said, tears running down my cheeks. 'She went to the woods crawling with the enemy. She went after Ishild, who left Lif with me as she went to care for her son, Odo's and hers. Leuthard found her in the woods.'

'Was it an easy death? Eh?' he asked, desperate for the right answer, and I gave it to him.

'Yes,' I said, and he knew I lied. He nodded and looked away.

'Odo up there on the mountain?' he asked.

'Yes. He went up the ridge. He is following a raven,' I said and looked at the bear. 'And I guess the Bear was only a bear. Lok's prophecy is taking place and all I wish to do is to get Lif.'

'An unselfish act may yet the doom postpone,' Wandal recited. 'Right?'

'I left Father alive.' I grinned. 'But I guess that does not count. I'm not sure what the damned act might be, but I will go up there and give away my life for them if I have to. I care not to recite the lines anymore. The raven is going up there, and I shall go there as well, and I think it has been destined to be so since I met Father. Tear warned me not to fight it.'

Wandal nodded. 'Armin told me the route goes up the left peak.'

'He told me he had a man who would know the way,' I said. 'He didn't tell me it was you.'

'I think he hoped to reconcile us.' Wandal smiled. 'His mother was a vitka,' Wandal said. 'And took Armin there when he was a child.'

I rubbed my face and thanked Woden for his great gift. I picked up the spear, a shield and went out for my helmet and placed it on my head. 'I will go to Rome after this. I married Cassia, and I have a troop of Batavi. And some others. I will serve Nero Claudius Drusus ...' I faltered and hoped he was alive and would survive. 'He is a good man.'

Wandal shrugged. 'As long as they are not your selfish goals and those of a ... good man, I will join. But goddess Siff save you under her skirt if you should lie to me again.'

'I will need you to keep me on track,' I said with a deep bow. 'I will go with Drusus too, and I will see why Father left us, betrayed us. I wish to understand him and fight for fine causes. If Father survives and builds his kingdom, I will follow Drusus against him, perhaps, but for Drusus, not me. Perhaps we get our land back? Many things will change. But I will no longer rush to get you lot killed. I will consider you lot before my needs.'

'Lot?'

I smiled. 'Tudrus the Younger and his brothers. Others.'

He grunted. 'Gods. The Quadi. Fine. If your Drusus survives, we will follow him,' Wandal said with a gruff voice as if unsure. 'Lif? Your daughter. I would see her. I am sure she is prettier than you.'

'I saw her years ago,' I said and tried to remember her face.

'She walks now, eh?' Wandal said. 'And speaks!' He got up and picked up the plain iron helmet. I was staggered by his plain wisdom. She speaks?

He clasped me briefly and nodded at me. 'Let's rest for the night. We will break our legs out there on the mountain. We will bandage each other like we used to, eat their food and tomorrow, go and kill Odo.'

'Yes, Wandal,' I stated and left to rummage the bags of our enemies.

CHAPTER 36

Outside, a pale morning stunned us as we stepped out of the cave. There was a clear sky for a change, and it was promising to be a hot day. I squinted up the mountain's side. 'They must be far away. The damned raven is long gone,' I complained to Wandal.

Wandal pushed me aside and looked up, as well. 'There is a trail up there. It's rocky and gritty as a Jotun's face, but we will make it. Don't worry now, eh? We have to go up and see what's to be done.'

'Fine,' I agreed with misery. 'No horses?'

'The bear spooked them.'

I began to climb for where I had seen Odo's men the day before. I shook my head. 'Hopefully they camped for the night at least. Mad to try to ride up the mountain at dark.'

'Odo is mad,' Wandal said unhelpfully and hefted his ax and a shield, and some bows and arrows.

'Thank you,' I snorted. 'I hope that damned raven was a coincidence and led them someplace far.'

But it was there.

High above, still circling the peaks, running the winds between two high rocky formations, the raven was still there. And up there, high, near the bird sat Odo's troop. They were still, staring at the thing as the bird was flying higher and higher as if they had spent the day there, frozen in time. The crevasse split the road before them to right and left. 'Perhaps it was waiting for me?' I said with hope and some pride for the thought of such a divine messenger to take note of me.

'It's a damned bird,' Wandal huffed. 'Probably has a nest there, and the fools will rot staring at it. I ...' he began but looked astonished as I ran up the trail, clutching my sword. Even if Odo's men were an hour away at least, I felt too anxious to take it slow. Wandal ran after me and tackled me down. He looked after the riders flitting in and out of the trees upon the higher ground. 'Just wait. They will ride us down, eh?'

I nodded. 'The filthy bit of gristle is up there. Closer to Lif than I am.'

He squinted his eyes. 'The bird is keeping them busy for now. Armin said the road led to the left peak.'

'And Odo could not find this earlier?' I cursed. 'All he had to do is to ride up here and search until he finds the place.'

'The Cherusci guard the mountain,' Wandal told me while pulling me up. 'Now? With the war? Not so much.'

'Damned bird is just fluttering around,' I cursed. 'Surely it will have to go and find some carcass to peck at some point?'

'Let us hope there is something like that on the right side of the ravine.'

We climbed slowly, keeping to the shadows, constantly looking up. The bird was a spec, Odo's people were waiting patiently, with only Ansigar riding back and forth, trying to find out where the routes led.

Then the raven croaked, high up in the air and purposefully rode the winds to the right side of the ravine.

Wandal clapped my back and grinned. 'It's a damned nice bird. Now, let us go for they are leaving. We can pick up the speed, no? Don't alert them, eh?' We ran up, soon panting heavily, looking at a trail of men on a track leading through some woods for the right peak, trekking higher on the edge of the crevasse.

'So what are we looking for? Exactly,' I panted as I slid back some steps.

He shook his head. 'Woden's Plate is up there on the left. Somewhere.'

I was huffing as I climbed over small, man-sized rocks. 'How the Hel did they get horses up there?'

'Went around these, no doubt. Climb and bitch less!' he answered.

I nodded and huffed. 'Woden's Plate? Armin did mention it to me as well.'

He pushed at my rear; I pulled at him, and we cursed at some small rubble that nearly took us back down the route. 'That's where they sacrifice, you see, the ancient vitka. It is the secret place, very holy place, and few Marcomanni come up here. Only true vitka and völva know of it, people high in the knowledge of the gods and their servants. They come here, shed blood, mumble requests, and here they are closest to Woden. Armin says there is a spring there, running down to the roots of the great tree of Yggdrasill, and this is the place Woden hears men's prayers the quickest. Before it, a large stone, flat and smooth,' he said, and we reached the campsite of Odo. The land to the left looked inhospitable, but there was, perhaps, a small trail leading up it. Wandal nodded and pointed his finger that way. We began hiking for the left peak, leaving the gradually steepening crevasse on our right.

'And there Lok's blood must mix with Woden's Ringlet to undo all of our gods' creation,' I smiled. 'I'll just damned well slay the lot and bleed them on the stone.'

Wandal grinned back. 'With the number of people they have killed there, it is a wonder it has not happened accidentally. A family of Lok's bleeding on that dark hair of your family.'

'I guess it has to be a very special two people. One from each family,' I puffed. 'Certainly it has to be the third sibling of Lok's holy family.'

'I wish you had left when Tear offered you the chance,' Wandal laughed and cursed as he stabbed his toe.

'Then I would not have Lif,' I said and climbed over a fallen log.

The land opened up a bit, even if it was still terribly steep. We ran wildly and climbed unhappily for half an hour through rubble and dry mud, and we both cursed as we saw that on the side there was a track that was suitable for horses. We took to it. I felt lightheaded, strangely weak from the strain, my muscles were aching, but Wandal told me to keep going and so we did. Woden's Plate was a day's climb away. We had none

435

to guide us, but the route was suddenly surprisingly clear as we hiked by the great chasm.

'Ware!' Wandal said and pulled be behind a boulder. Far to the right, across the crevasse we saw men on dusty horses, going forward slowly. The crisp mountain air made things look brighter though the mountain was eerily silent, with some scraggly goats and thin, curious rabbits the only animals we could see around us. 'Come,' he whispered, and we went on.

'How far do you think they will ride out there?' I asked. He shrugged, too tired to answer. I squinted over the crevasse and did not see the raven. Down in the bottom, water ran slowly, and the trees above us were hardier and much smaller than the ones below. Was this where my little daughter was? I cursed Veleda.

Wandal grunted at me and clapped my shoulder. 'It is a good way to live, Hraban. They are not starving. They have peace and only when there are celebrations and vitka and völva disturb them do they have to worry about anything. Peaceful, near the gods up here. I like it.'

'She is just some few years old,' I told him morosely but decided he might have a point. With me, she would be dead.

The evening fell, and we sat down to breathe, to massage our feet, and I felt I had some fever. There was some wetness in the arrow wound in my side, and Wandal checked it, looking concerned. 'It will heal; you are a tough bastard,' he said grimly.

'We will be there tomorrow?' I asked him.

'Morning, if we sleep the night,' he confirmed though he sounded unsure. 'Armin said it would take one day to hike up there. We have been dragging our damned feet.' He waved for the higher ground, and we wearily got up, groaning in horror at the thought of some more walking. We trekked on in the fading light, and then while passing a very shallow spot between a craggy wall and the crevasse, we saw the raven. 'Look!' Wandal yelled, and pointed to the other side. There, finally, I saw the bird. It was circling around a stone, and men could be seen riding on it.

'You sure this is the correct side? Perhaps Armin meant for you to come from the east?'

'Why would he tell me to come from the east? Don't be tedious. We were at his hall when we spoke of this. How excited they are!' I saw Odo raise his hands in triumph. My heart froze in terror. I was sure they had found Veleda or a route to her.

But it was not a gesture of triumph.

But of rage.

'Wandal, look,' I said, and he nodded, sitting down easily.

'This side, Armin told me,' he noted proudly. 'And we came to the right way.'

The raven flew around the men on the other side, waving and weaving in the air, croaking, almost mocking them. After a while, the bird turned and flew to our side, over the crevasse. It fluttered over deep chasm, dodged thin trees, flying erratically until it headed uphill from us, finally sitting on a rock high above us. A shriek of manic hatred could be heard from across the canyon. I saw a man fall down to his knees, pushed by the spindly arms of Odo. It was Gernot who was pleading with the mad thing.

'No reason to hide, is there?' I said, and Wandal shrugged.

'I suppose not,' he said. He pulled his pants down, and the enemy on the far side froze as they witnessed Wandal pissing towards them, an insult of unparalleled magnitude. 'Gods, that feels good.' And I joined him, mocking Odo with my eyes, even if I could barely squeeze a dribble. Odo stared at us in utter stupefaction. He shuddered, slapped Gernot lazily once more and gave out soft, nearly embarrassed commands.

There were thirty men with him, and they turned around.

There we stood, as they passed back down at Odo's orders, their horses lamed by the rough route, many walking, strange men and odd women with weapons of all sorts. Odo saw me and ignored me, festering with anger. His men were filing after him. I noticed Gernot and Ansigar last in the line, guiding their horses morosely back the way they had come.

'Gernot!' I screamed. 'Gernot, my love!'

He stopped his horse, his hand covered with the red cloth.

'Time to give up the chase, or tomorrow I will kill you, brother,' I yelled. 'Ride away,' Ansigar looked at Gernot, who was sitting quietly on his horse.

Ansigar yelled back. 'Hraban! Tomorrow! Tomorrow it will be all settled. They shall be united! Lif and Lífþrasir! They shall wed over your corpse, and when your daughter asks who that fool was, I shall tell her he was a nothing. That is how she will know you!'

'Coming from a peasant beggar and a liar, I am sure she will figure out who is a nothing!' I retorted, but my eyes were guided to movement, for Gernot and Ansigar had not been last in the line. From behind a boulder, Ishild was riding forth, guided by two men. She sat on the horse, dirty, scuffed, and tired and she looked my way, her cheeks hollow. Somehow, the change in her made her look like Odo. She had been bright and happy, now she was fey and worried. On her lap, sat the boy. Lífþrasir, Odo's son, some six to seven years old. He was the one who was supposed to populate the world after it ended, with my daughter. He was a surprisingly good-looking boy, his intelligent eyes were regarding me with interest, his pale complexion a bit odd. But he had his father's eyes.

Ansigar glanced at her, touching her shoulder as she passed, and she shuddered. 'She still hates my touch, Hraban! If Gernot dies, she will learn to love it. See. She is not too ugly yet for me,' Ansigar called, laughing as his eyes settled on Wandal. 'Still following the liar?' Ansigar called out to Wandal. 'I'll give you an easy one, former friend.'

'You tried once. Try not to get lost on the road, eh? You were ever lost and afraid,' Wandal yelled back. Gernot looked down and away as if in shame as he guided his horse past Ansigar. 'Tomorrow we gut the lot,' he said with a dark voice as he pulled his pants up.

'I left him alive, once,' I said. 'The day I whipped him and took Gernot's hand.'

'I was there as well, eh? My mistake as well. I am sorry for Ishild. She seems ... gone?' he said.

I did not know and thought about it. 'She loved me once. She claimed it was so. Now she only cares for that boy. And perhaps Lif. She needs time to heal. Perhaps if we manage to free her tomorrow, she will heal again. She had spirit once, it might be there still, under fear and misery,' I said miserably, remembering the girl I had grown with. I had denied her love, for her family and my fear of them. She had slept with me once, tricking me for she had been jealous of Ermendrud, and there we were, fighting Lok's prophecy over our child.

'Yes, Hraban. Perhaps,' Wandal said doubtfully and threw me a blanket. 'We rest a few hours. They will not be here before tomorrow.' We slept that night. Wandal enjoyed the sleep of the dead, and I had nightmares of Ansigar raping Ishild, and I saw myself spearing him, ripping him apart, and I wished Cassia was there to lift my heavy heart. I saw Tear in my dreams, their mother, Lok's unhappy priestess; my former enemy crying over Odo and Ishild, and I felt wretched.

Someone important would die the next day.

Odo. Hraban. If things went very wrong, Veleda. And Lif would be Odo's. I woke up and stared at the sky full of stars. I spent a miserable night. Come morning we sped off.

We ran amidst wild patches of wheat and sparse woods along the tracks. Wandal was looking around carefully and finally grabbed me and pointed up. There, up high was a distant red rock like a finger pointing upwards, and around it grew ancient trees and wildflowers. 'Looks godly to me.'

'It's a damned rock,' I said, 'but I think that is it,' I surmised and pulled him along. We climbed a small hill with a mossy track in the middle, high stone walls stretching up on either side, fir trees adorning the near unseen route up. We came to the finger-like stone, wondering at it. It had been crafted and was not natural, and there were chisel marks around the stone. I walked around it, touching it gingerly. It seemed ancient, massive and totally out of place so high in the mountain, in the middle of an insignificant track. It was like an accusing finger of a Jotun pointing up at the gods. 'The old bird is no fool, is he?' I said, pointing at the raven sitting on a tree over a heavy, tall stone arch covered with vines. 'It is more than a rock, after all.'

'Armin said ...' Wandal began, but I nodded and cut him off.

'Look,' I pointed as the raven flew over the arch and disappeared. 'Let's run.'

We ran up the last stretch and entered the arch. The raven croaked somewhere ahead as if welcoming us. We walked through the small

439

tunnel, feeling trepidation at entering the holy place, but behind the arch, a small valley was revealed to us, and we forgot our fears. The place was a haven. Inside, green grass waved in a very gentle wind. Tall, yellow flowers were lining the high walls. The flowers looked like stars of uncanny beauty rising on the rocky pathways leading to the very top of the mountain. The bottom of the valley was serene and stone laden, and there was a large round rock in the middle of the valley with a suspiciously flat top. An ancient stall sat in the middle of the rock, yellow grass growing from cracks in the stone.

'Come,' I told Wandal, who shrugged and shook his head uncertainly.

'Gods live here,' he whispered. 'See.' He pointed to a small waterfall by the rocky wall, beyond the stall and the stone, that was surely Woden's Plate. The water was clear as ice, cascading down the smooth stone for a hole in the ground, and there was a sort of thunder-like sound coming from that hole. 'Gods listen to us from that hole. I am sure of it,' he whispered. 'Armin was right.'

'It's a waterfall,' I said tediously though there was a hint of uncertainty in my voice. It did look strange and holy. 'Let's check the stall and the stone. That is Woden's Plate.'

'Armin said the god ate there after declaring Midgard his,' Wandal whispered.

'Did he say what the god ate? Armin is just talking about echoes beyond time, and we are here for a purpose, not to see the sights and wonder at godly feasts. Lif is here, somewhere.'

'Don't see her,' Wandal said reverently.

'I'll not leave before I do,' I grumbled.

We walked down to the stone, and I ran my fingers across it.

Then I saw it.

At the edge of the cascading water, there was a small pool of water and beyond that, a small rise on the ground. On top of the rise, there was a wattle and mud house with a simple grass roof, surprisingly hard to spot. The raven sat on a rafter that was peeking from amidst the grass. Smoke was rising from a hole in the roof. Wandal clapped my shoulder as we hiked that way. Anxiety was making my legs weak as I walked. I prayed to

Woden for Lif to be there and Veleda as well and feared what would be revealed in the next few moments.

The hut was near, and we stopped in front of it. The raven crowed, and the door opened.

Veleda had grown.

Her eyes were huge and blue, her hair blonde as Ishild's, her face smooth, and she was wearing a white shift, her narrow hips having rounded a bit. She had been ten when I let her run from Odo in the Hard Hill. Now she was nearly a woman. She looked surprised though there was also resignation. She was not scowling, but she was not entirely happy to see us, and she took a deep breath. She looked at me, and then up at the bird and nodded to herself as she walked to me. She regarded me carefully. 'So, you came.'

'I came. What else is there for a man searching for his family?' I told her bitterly.

She smiled. 'It was always inevitable, I think. Did I not tell you we would meet one more time?'

'I could have died. Odo might have. Even you?' I said.

'Yes, but you are hard to kill, Hraban and because the Raven lived, all the events and players were pulled together here. It is so.'

'That is the raven,' I said and nodded at the bird that almost seemed like it was smiling.

'That is a raven that found the way,' she said. 'Woden's bird. But you were the Raven that fought his father the Bear and escaped Odo time and again. And now it has to be settled here.'

'I will fight for you,' I told her, gripping my sword's hilt. 'I will sacrifice my life if I have to.'

She smiled sadly. 'I hope it suffices. That is indeed a selfless act, but you are here for Lif, and that was selfish. No proper father or mother can be selfless when their child is in danger. We will see what you can do now. And if you fail? If he pours my heart's blood on Woden's Ringlet? Lok will be freed. Ragnarök will come, one day sooner than later. Cocks will crow, Jotuns will rise from slumber, Lok will raise the dead and gods will die. Your Lif and the boy will survive.'

441

'I know, Veleda?' I smiled. 'Please don't recite that crap anymore.'

'You do not believe in seidr or galdr, I know. Too many charlatans have ruined your child-like faith, but I see it. Just like I saw your Drusus dying.'

I shook my head. 'He is not dead.'

'Not yet,' she said sadly. 'He could have changed the world.'

Her words made me look away in rage, and I struggled to shake myself free of it before turning back to her. 'You said I owe you a life. Lif. You have her. You have her for my crimes and mistakes, and I did slay your caretakers. If you wish to know, your mother Tear is free and no longer part of the story. And now I want her back.'

'Adalfuns took Tear far to be happy,' she agreed with a smile. 'I know. Mother always hated her role in Lok's schemes. But there was the prophecy, and the family was mad with it, and so we had no choice but to play to the end.'

'How did you find this place?' I asked her.

'Lord Sigimer told me how to get here. He is the guardian of the Godsmount. Sworn to Woden like you are, Hraban. When Bero passed this way after Hulderic in the past, he married a relative of Sigimer. He married her, for Sigimer's family is from the north as well. You have heard this.' She glanced at Wandal, who bowed. She went on. 'They are your relatives and guard the mountain. They helped me get here. They provide us food. It has been coming even with the war.'

'Armin told me how to find this place,' Wandal said happily. 'So, Armin and you are related?' he asked me.

'Gods curse the whole damned family,' I spat and fixed an eye on the enigmatic little girl. 'I would have her. Stop stalling.'

'And take her where?' she asked me simply.

'I have settled most of my scores this summer. I swore an oath on a sword, and I want nothing more to do with this land. But she is my blood.'

'She would be very sad in your world,' she said with a small, pinched smile. 'You might have given brave oaths to be done with your meaner oaths, Oath Breaker, but I see your fight is only beginning. There will be enemies in your life if you survive here today.' I nodded and took off my helmet. I kneeled before her and looked deep into her eyes. She reached out before I said anything and ran a finger down the scar on my face as if to emphasize what my life was like. 'Perilous,' she whispered. 'Do not take her.'

I grasped her hand and spoke. 'Sadness is the way of the world, Veleda. Tell me, what do you believe in? You admonish me of dangers in my life, but is Lif safe with you? You will live in a world full of Romans and their enemies, and I heard from … Drusus that you take sides.'

She giggled. 'I helped Armin; that is all. They help me. And Lif will be mighty if she is not made Odo's slave,' she agreed. 'Her world will be full of dangers at times, but she will be loved by the people, and they will fight for her. Few Germani will love you, ever. Few Romans will.' She smiled and grasped my hand. 'I am her relative; she is not my hostage. But what I believe in, Hraban, is the future. A bright future for our kin, the free men, and brave women of the gods. I am a völva, and what my mother has, the sight, is given to me. I will be a woman, and then an old woman of power, and I will unite our people against those you serve this day. And the gods will push the Romans out, and I will be there. So will she. Lif will have a part to play in the future glory of the Suebi nations.'

'You have not seen Rome and her legions, perhaps?' I said with a knowing smile.

'Neither,' she said tartly, 'have you seen Rome. Legions are fine things, no doubt, but Rome will change. I see that, saw it in a dream. One day our people will travel the lands beyond the river. With sword and fire. Lif will be part of that, her children, and their children will be famous and mighty. I see these things. I also see I might die today, and all will fall to dust.'

I felt strange pride at her words and sighed. I rubbed my face as I stared at the girl and wondered at her many prophetic words. Lif will live on and in her children there will be glory? 'And if she comes with me? Should I survive this place.'

She shook her shoulders and hugged herself. 'Do not take her to Rome, Hraban.' I said nothing for a time, pondering her words. She stared at me, finally nodded and turned to the house. 'Lif!' she called out clearly, and I felt my knees shake. She turned to me and bowed. 'Enjoy this moment Hraban. Then prepare for a fight. I sense my brother is near.' I tensed as the door opened, but none came out. 'Come, Lif, your father wishes to see you. Meet him today, and then you will not see him again.' I still disagreed with that but said nothing as the door opened, and she came out.

There she stood, in a brown, small tunic, her hair a blonde, combed halo around her pretty face, her small nose perfect, the lips full.

She was alive and healthy.

I felt the tears coming as I went to my knees.

Veleda nodded at her with a smile and she took a tentative step forward, then another as I held out my hands for her. I remember her little fingers holding mine, her eyes as achingly beautiful on the night she was born. I remember everything, and there she stood, finally, uncertainly, shyly glancing at the bloody, ragged man in front of her. I cursed softly as I tore my helmet off, and her eyes went round as she saw the scar on my face.

'Lif, I am your father. Hraban. Come to take you home,' I said gently, glancing at Veleda, who did not react. Lif took a careful step forward and smiled at me tentatively, then she took my hand, and I pulled her carefully to me, her small feet dangling in the air. She giggled as my beard tickled her neck, and I saw Veleda smile at us with tears in her eyes.

Lif looked up at me, her round, huge eyes clear as the sky. She spoke, her high voice full of wonder. 'But I have a home. Are you going to come home with me?'

I smiled at her and said nothing, absolutely drunk on her face. 'I don't know, love,' I said and held onto her. She nodded and kissed me on the cheek. Somewhere behind us, horses were whinnying.

Veleda glanced that way and took out a wand, the mark of a vitka. 'Lif, it is time for you to go inside.'

'No, I want to ...' she started, but Veleda snapped her fingers, and she went, sulking, then singing as she happily found something to take her interest.

'Well, Hraban? What will you do now?' Veleda asked. 'You have seen her and found me.'

I pulled out Nightbright and my shield and grabbed my helmet. 'As I said. It was all meant to end here. I will kill him. And if I die doing that, then I will see you in the afterlife.'

Veleda shook her head. 'Is this your plan? You come here, and you aim to kill them all.'

'Yes, that is my plan,' I said. 'Are you of any use against your brother?'

She smiled sadly. 'I thought you said you didn't believe in spells?'

I spat. 'I hoped you would throw rocks, at least. Is that the only way in here?'

'I have a spell that is useful,' she said, and I rolled my eyes. She nodded impatiently and began to berate me, but then, somewhere, a cock crowed.

Wandal looked around. 'A cock? Is there a farm?'

Veleda shook her head heavily, her face pale. 'Three cocks will crow to herald the end of the world. It is not a cock from this world.' She pointed at the hole in the ground, a dark, slippery hole where the water ran. 'That takes one to the spinners of fates, Hraban. There, in the lands of the gods, Heimdall watches us. He is fingering his horn now, and the gods will be looking up from their merrymaking and meals. Lok is going to be free if I die, and the cocks know it,' she said and walked resolutely to the stone arch. We followed, and Wandal started to collect hand-sized rocks to his cloak, and then he carried them after Veleda. I went to the stone table and went to my knees.

I opened my arms and watched the sky.

'Woden,' I implored. 'Woden the Wanderer, oh wise Lord. Strong and savage, my god! Ever have you helped me in the time of need, and let there be fewer such needs in the future. Spare Lif Odo's attentions. Forgive me my ill choices, for I have been selfish, and foolish. You know this. You have seen me making a mess of things since Father came back. If one must die and a sacrifice is needed, then let it be me. Let it keep my loved ones safe.' I got up and heard distant yells and went to do battle for my daughter, her aunt, and the world. I pulled on my helmet. 'And if you don't want to hear me, you fucker, then go hump a goat,' I added, and he rewarded me with his battle rage.

CHAPTER 37

Wandal and I waited in the shelter of the stone arch. We waited patiently, staring down the mossy path, checking our shields, adjusting our armor. Wandal had collected even more sharp rocks at our feet, and I had helped him. We threw some downhill, gauging the range, and they rattled at the edge of the finger like stone. They would hurt the badly armored enemy but not stop them. Wandal laid a bow at his side and stuck arrows on the muddy ground. Winning seemed as likely as if we would try to stop the wind from blowing through the arch.

The horses could be heard somewhere down the hill.

'Thirty, eh?' Wandal asked. 'Did you count them?'

'Thirty, yes. We killed most in Gulldrum,' I told him.

'Wish I had seen that,' he said and pulled some hair from his helmet's eyeholes. 'Movement.' He was right. Down below, men were indeed gathering. The finger and trees were partly covering the path down, but we heardAnsigar scream at his people, we heard a grunt of pain as he hit a man and then, silence.

Until a horse neighed.

Odo rode up on a tired, bloodied nag, his red, dirty hair bouncing darkly as he regarded first the stone, and then he saw us. He said nothing for a time, and we obliged him.

'Is she there?' he finally asked, his voice strained.

'Ride up and we discuss it,' I yelled back.

He sneered at me. 'She is. And so are you. We are all here. You brought your hair as well.'

'I'll wear it proudly,' I spat, cursing I had not asked Wandal to shave me. 'Will you send your dogs running up so we can deal with them?'

'In a moment,' he said tiredly. 'Lif will be safe. I'll not lift a finger against her, no matter how much I despise you. Know this, and I hope it gives you comfort.'

'Feeling my sword in your gut will give me comfort, Odo. Come, this has been years in coming. Come on up,' I told him. 'You sister raping, murderous filth from Hel.'

He smiled thinly at me. 'Think you that I raped her? She loved me once. She was twelve and had a part to fill. It is the family tradition, you see. Lok's blood must be kept clean and our clan, Hraban, marries its own. You changed her heart. She was willing, she was at first.'

'She was twelve!' I yelled. 'That is filth!'

He shrugged. 'Then she fell in love with you. That was unexpected. It was unexpected you sired Lif. It is sad she had Lif with you, but she did. It is almost unbearable that Woden's blood will have a part to play in Lok's world, but it is my boy who will rule it.'

I threw a rock that startled his horse though it fell far short. He managed to calm it. 'She was terrified of you, and you raped a small girl,' I yelled at him. 'Lord of lies. Even your mother hates you.'

'Tear?' he asked. 'Zahar? She is well?'

'Never better,' I said. I picked up another rock and threw it with a grunt, hitting the ground next to him, again startling his horse. 'You will fail, Odo, to sap strength from our arms by inflicting despair with lies. That is your magic; tricks and lies.'

He looked at me calmly as his horse once more settled down. 'You have ever been afraid, Hraban. That is why we are here.'

I cursed him, but Wandal calmed me, and we prepared. Odo nodded and whistled. Wandal picked up the bow; I, a rock. Filthy, fey men and even women filed up to the path below us, looking up at us and the finger like stone before us. Odo ignored them. He was chanting, pulling his dark wand out of his tunic. Gernot dismounted next to him, not looking up, his spirit still dulled by what he had endured at Odo's hands. Ansigar pulled out a bow as he walked next to the milling group of enemies.

They were Lok's strange people. Old as time, their clan had led a miserable life in Gulldrum. Many were fur glad, some wore nothing but cloaks, shivering in the mountain air. They smiled or giggled, half mad, half serious, people who followed promises of Odo and Lok's chaotic edicts. Ansigar grunted at them, and they moved up, the ones with shields in the fore, chanting strangely. Odo was echoing them, and cursing us, his men taking heart in his presence. Odo's wand pointed at us, and I felt and saw Wandal flinching. 'Just lies, Wandal.'

'He is a vitka,' he said.

'He has no real powers,' I hissed.

'I hear they tortured Bero, and you saw and heard a goddess speak,' he grunted. 'And was Leuthard not Lok's thing?'

'Don't believe anything he says or does,' I insisted.

The sky seemingly darkened, and a sharp wind blew in our faces. I stubbornly shook my head at Wandal, and he prayed to Woden. I did as well, and my lord answered me as his rage filled every fiber in my body. I danced some steps before the advancing enemy, and they rewarded me as they shivered in fear. I felt the god's power, but I was also exhausted and hurt, and I feared the battle.

Lif was at stake.

'If you can, leave that one alive!' Ansigar yelled, pointing at me. 'Though we only need his hair.' He pulled an arrow and let if fly. It flew past us through the archway and rattled in the dark. The enemy charged with a ragged yell, their dirty feet stamping the ground.

'Throw your rocks,' we heard Veleda say. 'Go ahead. Fight and then, when you have to; run.'

I glanced behind. There she was. Veleda, her small hand making intricate gestures in the air, her wand dancing in the air. She sang, a strong song in a tongue I did not know, and our hearts filled with savagery. Wandal fired the bow, and the arrow reached down, piercing a shield and the man's forearm. He howled, and I threw my rock, which went wide. I picked up more and began to pelt the enemy, and Wandal fired arrows as fast as he could. One man caught a stone in his face, throwing him back senseless; another stone crushed a kneecap of a ragged-looking woman. An arrow took a man in the groin, and Wandal laughed savagely. Then his arrows were gone, and we picked up more and more rocks, throwing them wildly as Veleda sang at us. Our throws were true, many of the enemies hurt badly, despite the shields. They came on, slowly, trying to hold some semblance of a formation. Their eyes betrayed fear as their shuffling feet churned the ground from the finger to the archway, and we let fly the last stones, splattering a face of a boy and breaking the rib of an older, naked man, leaving him crying on the moss, rolling downhill, getting kicked by his compatriots jumping over him. I took my spear and threw it, and it hit the wrong man though happily one of the better armed ones, and he fell.

We picked up our weapons, my sword, and Wandal's ax and braced ourselves. I looked at Veleda. 'Go and guard her.'

She nodded and smiled. 'Fight well, Hraban. Fight long. As long as you can. Then run fast, and I will give you that one spell.'

'What do you mean?' I asked as Woden's song made me dizzy with bloodlust.

'Just fight,' she said and ran off. I cursed and then an arrow scratched my helmet, and I cursed Ansigar aloud. 'Bring a spear up here, rat!' I yelled at him.

'When you are down!' he yelled back. Gernot was following Odo, who was chanting, sweating, and trying to see the battle, his horse coming towards us, cautiously.

'Woden guard us, Hraban,' Wandal said, and I grunted in agreement as the enemy shrieked their hatred at our faces.

'If he does not, let Lok hump Odo's bones in thanks for all he has done.' I laughed and then we stepped forward, linking shields for the enemy was there.

They had shields, weak things, rectangular and oval shaped, ill cared for, and as we stepped forth, we smote ours at theirs, bowling them back over their friends. We stepped forward again, but not too far, stabbed, and hacked at the foe trying to get up. Their fallen got into the way of those who tried to get at us, and we stepped back to the arch.

But on they came, with no discipline.

Men died, blood flowed, and a huge man tried to rip the shield from my hand, but I cut his wrist open with a quick slash, and he fell away, his face white from the shock. We stood side by side; I was protecting Wandal with my shield, the arch doing the same for me to my right. We screamed and killed. They climbed over men who were down and bleeding, dead or just too afraid to attack. They pushed up relentlessly, Odo watching them. The fallen were grasping at our feet and ankles, tearing at our shields. Then, spears flew at us. Wandal was scratched on the side, another tangled in the hem of my chain shirt. I cursed and punched Nightbright in the eye of a young, vacant-faced man. 'Fight for her smile!'

'Do I look like I am idling? Eh?' Wandal panted.

A mad woman managed to push past me, and I impaled her neck to the wall next to Wandal, but at the same time, a man managed to drag my shield down and another behind him threw his cudgel. I felt stabbing pain as the spiked thing punctured my chest, and I fell, a man on top of me, trying to stab me from below the shield, repeatedly, like a single-minded, undead thing. Wandal hacked his neck, slammed his shield at another attacker and kicked the corpse off me. Then, Ansigar shot an arrow at him, and he yelped as it hit him in the shoulder, drawing a long wound.

I got up dizzily; we backed up, shields locked.

'How bad?' I asked, looking at the bleeding wound.

'Hurts, but I will manage. You?' he asked, panting in pain.

'I will kill a few more,' I said. We were guarding the arch ferociously, and the enemy had a terrible time coming at us. I yanked a spear off a man, kicked him back to his uncouth fellows and noticed Odo was close now, his wand held tightly, his knuckles white. He was cursing and casting spells, exhorting his troops, and Gernot was next to him, staring fixedly at me. I stabbed the spear at a man who dodged away and flipped it.

Then I threw it.

It flew fairly true, thrumming in the air as the ill-made thing careened towards Odo. The thin vitka opened his mouth to scream an order, but he closed it quickly as the spear came at him. The wand saved him, but his hand was mangled by a huge gash. He hissed, cursed and swore, and the enemy faltered. They took steps back, all eyeing Odo's pain. Ansigar screamed at his remaining fifteen men and women. 'Kill them! Push them back! Push, push, and we win!'

'Do it!' Odo shrieked.

And they pushed.

We stood grimly by each other, but we would not be able to hold them much longer. A cudgel finally broke my shield, and I discarded the broken thing. A hammer swung at me and hit my left arm, nearly breaking a bone, and I howled as I punctured the enemy eye. Wandal slew men left and right, but we were going back, back and soon, we would run.

'Come, Hraban,' he said, pulling me back as he lost his shield, and we exited the arch. We were startled near shitless when Veleda appeared, sang a sad note and tapped her wand at the side of the arch.

The arch fell in a grating rumble of stone and shrieks rang out. She grinned at me victoriously as the sides of the arch fell slowly over each other, and a huge cloud of dust billowed up in the air.

'Some mechanism?' I demanded, but she turned her back and ran towards the hut. We tried to follow her, but we were exhausted and stumbled along. Behind us, there were scrambling sounds, and we ran, but a spear flew in the air. I saw it come, but it hit Wandal in his back. He screamed and fell, and I turned to kill a woman who was running for him with a knife. I dragged him towards the hut as he was hissing in pain. 'Get up, you lump of fat.'

'Muscle, a lump of muscle,' he panted.

I pulled him up, hollering like the bear we had killed and rushed past Woden's Plate. We saw Veleda by the door, whispering to Lif, who was gravely nodding back at her. We got to them; I smiled at Lif, she smiled back at me, and then we turned to face the enraged enemy, some of whom were grievously hurt by the arch and the battle.

They climbed over the remains of the arch to the small valley, staring around in bewilderment. A horse made its way in through the slabs and rubble, Odo seated on it, the animal stumbling along precariously. They

451

saw us standing before the hut and slowly spread around us. Lif's eyes were huge, a bit scared as she regarded her paradise turned to a butcher's hall. Odo rode on, trailing blood, his face impatient, pained, and then ecstatic as he took note of the valley. He walked towards the great stone, taking his time, and finally dismounted and climbed the great stone platter and reverently walked to the stall while the enemy surrounded us.

He touched it and smiled.

He was at the top of his hill of dreams, closer to Lok than any of his family ever, at the very pinnacle of his life, and his eyes searched the valley feverishly, his hands stroking the stone as if sucking every vestige of Woden's sacred blessings he could from the rock.

Ishild rode up, for the arch had fallen to the side, leaving some room for a horse. A man was leading her, and the boy sat on her lap. She looked at me hollowly and with pity. Odo raised his arms high as his men surrounded us, weapons ready, Ansigar aiming an arrow directly at me. Odo pointed a finger at Veleda. 'Little sister? Will you come here?' Veleda shrugged, seemingly tired and uncaring and guided Lif aside and behind her. Veleda looked at Ishild, her sister, and she looked back. She did not move.

Odo spoke with a strong, irritated voice. 'Come now, Veleda. What is there to think about?' He turned to the stall and opened his hands to the sides. 'Oh, Lok! The herald of change, balancer of the gods. Many an age has passed, many a chance to set you lose, oh god of change! Now, you shall indeed be freed of the shackles constructed of your poor son's guts. Narfi's death will be paid back, for the age of vengeance is here. Be free! You shall be free! The time is nigh! The Nine Wolds shall tremble. Here, today, I, Odo the Faithful shall see it done. Rejoice, lord!' Veleda came to stand next to me. She still looked at Ishild carefully, their eyes meeting as if they were discussing, but with not words. They were sisters. Odo ignored us. 'We shall offer you blood, the blood of a third, heart blood of a great seer, the greatest in our time, that of my sister, Veleda! On a ring made of Woden's hair, we shall pour it, fouling the honor of the first men. Of Woden. See, Hraban of Woden is here, his hair the color of raven ...'

'You'll have to cut it first, you ...'

Odo continued. 'Long have we kept our blood pure. Now it is ready to populate the world!' he said, glancing at Lif in bliss, 'and long shall our children rule after. The circle has closed.' I stepped before the small girl to hide her from Odo's eyes.

'I said: it is not so easy to shear me, shepherd of corpses,' I bellowed.

'We will get it, nonetheless,' he hissed. 'Ansigar!'

He produced his bow, and around us the ten remaining enemy hefted their weapons. Wandal shuffled to cover Lif on one side and pulled at Veleda. 'Inside? Eh?'

Veleda shook her head. 'Cut the hair, Hraban,' she said.

'No!' I breathed at her. 'We will never obey him.'

'It will be all right,' she said and pulled my hand. 'For some reason you think it is your duty to thwart Odo. Nobody ever asked you to. Trust me. Cut the hair and give us some time.' I looked at her long and hard and growled until she nodded again. I kneeled, and she hesitated and then grasped a thick hank of my hair and cut savagely. Odo was watching and nodded at Ansigar, who put his bow down reluctantly.

'Well done, sister,' Odo chortled, near ecstatic with joy.

A long ululating call rang out. We all heard it, and whether it was a wild beast or truly a cock of strange worlds, a cock crowed the second time.

Odo bowed, his face slack with awe. 'Fjalar crowed first. He did so in Jotunheim, and we all heard it. The giants know; the time is nigh. And now, the Dead Voice; that cock readies Hel's armies so our lord can lead them! Only Kullingambi, the dark cock remains and then the gods must prepare for war. Heimdall's horn shall blow, the dead and the Jotuns shall sail, and the armies shall meet ...'

'Shut the Hel up,' I said, stealing his moment. He had been speaking feverishly, happily, and I could see why. Had not his family waited all eternity, ever since the birth of the land for this very moment?

'One more time shall the third cock crow,' Odo panted, his eyes glistening with heat, 'one more time.'

'Veleda,' I said miserably as Odo continued his speech.

'Yes, Hraban? I said do nothing,' she smiled.

'He needs my hair,' I whispered.

'Yes. And my heart,' Veleda confirmed. 'Who knows if it is so, and I doubt the Ragnarök is a quick matter.'

'He needs you,' I said heavily. 'I am sorry, Veleda,' I said and grabbed her, wincing with pain from my wounds. Wandal was shocked into inactivity; so was our foe as I sprinted towards the well with Veleda.

'Hold! Hold!' screamed Odo, leaning on the stall in terror.

The enemy ran for me. Wandal killed one as he ran after us, and we all raced to the well. An arrow chunked into my back, the chainmail saving my life, but I fell forward, Veleda falling from my arms. I saw her face was calm, near serene as she regarded me. I got up and grabbed her again, the enemy at my tail, and then I was at the edge of the abyss, Wandal covering me with a snarling face as I dangled Veleda over the edge.

Odo's face was white, and he trembled in impotent rage. The men around us dispersed as Ansigar pulled them back. Gernot was sitting near the hut, on his horse, looking at me. I had not noticed him riding in.

And Lif was near him.

I cursed and tried not to look that way. I sweated and trembled, for if I failed now, we would all fail. I called out to him. 'Leave, the bastard spawn of a misshapen god, for you are not welcome here. Take your curs, or her heart will go to the under lands without your ungentle, murderous knife touching it.'

He shook his head in denial, sputtering and trembling.

Veleda was calm as she regarded me, and I shrugged at her apologetically.

'Your plan has a flaw,' Odo called at me, and I saw Ansigar standing at the door of the hut, his bow loosely aiming an arrow at Lif, who was looking at us all with huge, bright eyes, her cheeks wet with streaming tears. Odo smiled happily. 'If I have no Veleda, then there is no need for Lif, either.'

I cursed them all. 'Go away and try again later.' I looked at my beautiful daughter as I contemplated a suicidal charge.

Odo looked up and then down and shook his head. 'No. You see, I do not wish to wait. I am selfish, Hraban. I will not wait, and there will not be another time, another age with some other fool standing here, doing this. I want the honor. Lok will not understand if I fail, of course, but then, I don't wish to lie. I want this, and I will have this or nothing. Now. Give her over, enjoy Lif's continuous well-being and just let the last cock crow.'

'Let me go, Hraban,' Veleda said, and I shuddered.

'I fail,' I told her, my eyes traveling to Lif. 'Again.'

'No. You are a father. But you will be sad. For I said no proper parent will be unselfish and leave their child to die. But there are improper parents. Those driven mad by their family.'

I placed Veleda on the ground. 'What?'

Odo's face relaxed, and he was nodding empathetically, his red, filthy hair bouncing. 'Come, Hraban. Do not look so glum. I might be merciful after this is done,' Odo said maliciously.

'You told me to trust you,' I told her back. She did not move. 'You told me I am a fool to think it is all about me. Why? And who is not the proper parent?'

'Fool you are and trust Ishild, rather,' she said sadly. 'Trust her, for she no longer is a good mother, and she is half mad. And trust your brother. And fight, after. Fight hard and you shall not be alone. They are almost here.' My eyes turned to Ishild, who was sitting on a horse, forgotten. The boy was there with her, and she was clutching him hard. Veleda continued. 'She would not do this if there were no Odo,' she told me. 'Remember that.'

'I don't understand,' I said.

She nodded at her sister. 'Ishild told me that. I remember it when I was but a babe,' Veleda said as I took reluctant steps towards Odo. 'Ishild always loved me. She said she would spare me if it came down to it. If she suffered enough and was brave enough. And now she has suffered enough and is brave with madness. It is not your selfless act that the prophecy spoke of. And happily for us, she is no longer a loving parent.'

I looked at Ishild's eyes, and she smiled at me sadly, and I understood what she was going to do. I could not stop her. And perhaps, I would not.

Ishild spurred the horse, the boy in her lap.

'Yaah!' she screamed as the horse charged forward, trampling a man reaching for it, and she cast a long, lasting look at me as she passed me. Then she screamed at her brother. 'I'll tell Lok your regards, Brother! He

455

will be so disappointed!' she yelled mischievously, sounding like the young, spirited Ishild again. Odo looked on, terrified as the steed carried his sister and son towards the well, the boy screaming on her lap. Then, her hair flying, she spurred the beast on to the slippery rock, then for the hole, water flying high. They fell on their side as the horse tried to stop itself, stumbling across the wet stone. It neighed in terror, Ishild gritted her teeth and kicked it, and they went forward into the wet hole and disappeared with no sound.

She was gone, and so was her son, the one who was to populate the world, and no cocks would crow for the third time.

There was a silence in the small valley.

The wind was blowing, and the mountain's stunning flowers seemed an unsuitable setting for a scene so terrible.

Odo began to scream thinly.

He screamed and screamed in abject hopelessness and ran for the well, his eyes huge and round. He looked like a dirty spider as he skittered around the well on all fours, crying, and even baying like a wolf. I pulled Veleda behind me as I retreated with Wandal, shoving him away from the edge as Odo got closer. I saw Ansigar was in shock and had relaxed the bow, and Gernot had guided his horse next to Lif and had picked her up to his saddle. Odo was on the brink of the hole, staring with mad eyes down into the abyss, crying and cursing, for he had lost his son, his sister, and former lover.

And Lok. He had lost his quest.

He whimpered, and cried, chanting and begging the gods to return the lost ones to the world, but that was not to happen. The raven that had guided us ruffled its feathers as if deciding that there was nothing more to see there and left.

Odo climbed slowly to his feet, his face a lank mask of shock. Slowly he walked to the well, holding his head, and after a while, he made a predictable decision. 'Kill the girl, Ansigar, kill it, and I shall slay my sister after all, and perhaps the world will end, even if there are none to rebuild it. Get Hraban's hair.'

456

'You are a mad dog, Odo,' I said and charged Ansigar, Wandal following me, hissing in pain. Ansigar gritted his rat-like teeth and turned to Lif, nodding at Gernot to push her down, but many things happened then.

Men rode to the valley, guiding their mounts over the stones and rubbles of the arch. Brimwulf was pulling an arrow from his saddle as grim Tudrus, Bohscyld, and Hund and three Batavi rode in, wielding spears and shields, axes and sword on their hips. They saw the enemy turning, only ten of them, and did not hesitate as they charged the foe. Brimwulf shot an arrow at one man, larger than most, and men began to die. Bohscyld jumped down from the saddle, Tudrus led the others as they formed a wall of wood and steel, tearing at the enemy who was coming at them singly or in twos.

I looked from Odo to Gernot, back and forth and Gernot, casually, pulled a knife with his hand as Odo was nodding with manic intensity. Gernot looked down at Lif, his eyes unreadable, then at me, and lifted his knife. 'No!' I screamed. I shook my head in denial and heard Odo laugh savagely at my distress.

Gernot dropped the knife to the ground and backed his horse away from Ansigar.

Ansigar pulled a cudgel, looking at Gernot in stupefaction. 'He is your foe! Hurt him! Kill the girl,' Ansigar screamed, gesturing at the little girl in his lap.

Gernot shook his head. 'No. I don't love Hraban. Never did. But he is my brother, my last kin, and I will not slay my niece for a mad dog. Be gone!' He spurred his horse at Ansigar, who retreated for the Woden's Plate.

I gazed at Gernot's relieved eyes and pulled Nightbright. I turned to run after Odo. He blanched, shaking his head in disbelief and fled, running with his spindly legs as fast as he could. A man got in my way, hollering incoherently as he swung his ax, and I stabbed him through, casually, grunting as I eviscerated him, his bowels falling to the ground. I yelled at Odo. 'All your threats are dust. Ishild, poor, mad Ishild died for you! I am loath to send you to her!' I cursed as I got closer. His eyes lit up with hope as I had hoped they would. 'But I won't hesitate,' I added and enjoyed perverse joy as his eyes filled with unfathomable fear. 'Your kin is dead! All of it.'

He cackled, despite his obvious fear. 'Gulldrum is dead. Not our kin! Lok is wise, Hraban. In the north? There are more! And they will find you, one day! Or your children. This game will play on!'

'Silence, you corpse,' I hissed, dancing after him.

I dodged as an ugly woman was running away from the fight with the Quadi brothers and Brimwulf shot her in the back. I stepped on her as I climbed the stone plate where Ansigar was grimacing at me, Odo behind him, his dagger shaking.

'Ansigar. No whipping this time. This time you won't get up until you reach Hel's sad gates,' I laughed. 'There Ishild will marry you, finally, and perhaps you will enjoy her rotten embrace.' Ansigar was licking his lips. Beyond the stone, I saw Bohscyld swing an ax so viciously at a man that his whole arm and shoulder flew in the air. There were but few of the enemy left, and I noticed Brimwulf eyeing Gernot uncertainly. He was sitting patiently on his horse, Lif with him.

The enemy ran.

The few, who could, skirted the terrible brothers and ran for the stone arch. There, a pair of savage dogs growled and ran at them, jumping at the fugitives, one tearing out a throat and another hanging onto a man's crotch. Hands, the bounty hunter, stood there with a spear as he received the last two. The spears flashed and clashed, and they died, crying at his feet. Odo saw all of this, his dreams crumbling, but he turned his malevolent face to me and pulled his wand.

'Fool, you are Hraban. There are others, I said. They will find her,' he said despondently.

I grunted. 'They will not find her, I will ...'

Odo spat. 'You will be famous. A lord. Easy to find. So, you will leave her with Veleda. To take her with you would doom her. You shall be a father, but no better than your own. You will miss her from afar.' I shook my head, but he laughed. 'Yes, you will. You will learn how to avoid your child, never to see her again.'

I cursed him and attacked them. I drew Nightbright back and charged, and Ansigar countered me, surprisingly bravely. He dodged and swung his cudgel back and down, scoring a hit on my arm, but I growled the pain away and with Woden's rage filling me, I slashed, slashed, and slashed until he fell on his back over the stall. I placed my foot on his throat and stabbed my blade in his belly, so deep it went through, and I laughed as I carved it up into his chest. He shuddered and finally died. I flicked the blade at my nemesis. 'Wait, Odo. Your turn, just give me a second,' I told the red-faced bastard, but he ran instead.

Brimwulf shot an arrow at him, missing, Hund sprinted for him, but it was Wandal who tackled the man on the ground. He held Odo, savagely twisting his hand, and I walked for them. 'I spared my father, Odo, for he is my father, and I will judge him when I know him better. But you? I know you well enough.' I charged forward, tore him from Wandal, pulled him to the edge of the waterfall. 'There, your sister waits. Your son. And your mother will cry,' I told him and rammed Nightbright through his belly. He huffed weirdly, hawking and sputtering, and I felt warm wetness on my hand as I sawed the blade back and forth, scratching his spine. I held him there and saw Woden's Gift on his finger. I hesitated, grabbed it and sighed.

I let go of it.

Then I pushed him over, and he disappeared, so quickly it felt I had never known the bastard.

With him went Draupnir's Spawn, and I crouched on the edge of the well, wondering if I had let it go deliberately. The Winter Sword. The Ring. All gone. Only Hraban was left.

I took a hand-sized rock and dropped it down the chute and it fell and fell, and I did not hear it hit the bottom. Perhaps it eventually hit the end of the worlds, bounced off the Yggdrasill's bark and rolled at the Wyrd sister's feet.

I held my head in sorrow for Ishild and flipped my helmet off.

I turned to Gernot as my friends gathered around us. Hands, the bounty hunter who had once worked for Father and then tried to capture Veleda, only to lose his heart to the chosen of the gods, went to his mistress. The dogs ran to lick my bloodied hands as I walked closer to Gernot. He looked at me calmly, not heeding or fearing the weapons pointing at him, his horse mimicking his master's mood, eating grass with no worry in the world. I stood next to him, and Lif smiled at me. I gestured at him, he nodded and put Lif down with his one hand, and I grabbed her, taking her to the side.

Brimwulf came next to me, sitting down, he smiled at the young girl.

'Pretty, like mine will be,' he said.

'She is pretty like her mother was,' I told him, and he held a hand on my shoulder as I let tears fall. Lif was talking to me happily, explaining how she played with rabbits, learned herbs and spoke with plants, and I could not help but think of Ishild.

Hands came to us as well, smiling his greasy, fat smile as he tickled Lif's chin, and I resisted an urge to gut him, but he had kept his word to keep Lif safe, and Lif smiled hugely at him, climbing onto his lap. I let her. 'Worry not, Hraban, I do not pretend to be her father,' he said. 'But I will brag about her, when she grows older, that it was I who found her father's band and guided them to save the day. I was going to find you, but you were involved with a bear, and I passed you by. I simply missed you. I saw the beast as we came up. Quite a monster. Lif will love you, but she will think you a fool, for she is very, very prudent.' I eyed Tudrus, who was laughing with Wandal, for they knew each other from our childhood. Wandal was in pain, and I knew our lives would ever be full of danger.

I nodded to myself. 'As long as she thinks of me as a father.'

Hund stirred near us, his customary smile hidden. 'Do you mean she is not coming with us?' He looked at me incredulously.

'She cannot,' I said, my voice breaking, longing and fear hurting me almost physically. 'Veleda was wrong and right, both.' I glanced in her direction. 'Mine is also a selfless act this day. And it kills me inside. She stays.'

Hands nodded. 'Say goodbye to her then. She will know you as a brave man' He scowled as he looked around. 'Though I will likely have to clean up your mess alone. Fenfir's ashen tail! You lot look almost as dead as the corpses!' He was right. Only Tudrus was unhurt, and the rest looked terrible. I got up, kissed Lif's cheek, and she squeezed my finger, unaware she had lost a mother, and a brother. And now, a father. I grabbed something from my belt.

'Give her this,' I said and handed Hands the ancient weapon, Wolf's Bane. The spear glittered in the air.

'Toothpick?' Hands asked as he looked at it. 'Old.'

'It was the spear of Aristovistus. King of the Suebi. Our ancestor. I cannot give her anything of my family,' I said. The ring was gone, gone with Odo, and I did not miss it, after all. 'It is a mighty, powerful artifact.'

'She will surely appreciate such a device. She will dress it up in a robe and put it to sleep every night,' Hands said with gentle mockery but bowed to my scowling face. 'Yes, she will have it. And we will tell her it's history, a fine one full of brave deeds, even if I have to invent some.' And so, Hands took her to Veleda.

I did not look at her again.

I gathered my gear, and Tudrus brought us horses. I mounted a gray, tired one and cast a last look around. I nodded at Tudrus, Bohscyld, Wandal, Brimwulf, and Hund, and the rest of my men, most half alive. I had kept my oath to Cassia and for that, I felt relieved. I sighed and shook my head.

I turned my face to Gernot and sighed. 'Well, weakling. Want to be a Roman?'

He shrugged. 'I have no hand.'

'Your remaining hand, brother, just gave Lif life. I will always remember Hagano's death. And the betrayals and danger you put us in won't disappear.' I rubbed my face and bowed to him. 'And I apologize for being a bastard when we grew up,' I said and held my hand out to him. 'We shall travel a long road and try to build bridges, eh?' I heard Wandal snort softly, for he alone knew Gernot's true color, but he had saved Lif.

He looked at my outstretched hand for a long while and finally took it awkwardly with his left hand. He followed us as we rode to find the Drusus.

CAMULODUNUM, ALBION (A.D. 42)

There is not much more to the story of my Winter Sword and the oath keeping of that summer, my Lord Thumelicus. Much has happened in Camulodunum while you rest, and we now have guards of King Togodumnus. I will later tell you how that came to be, but for now, we are safe. Safer than we used to be. I have been busy at nights, my Lord. You are nearly healed. You are awake much of the time, leaning your head back on the mattress, staring out of the open door listlessly.

You do not look like a man who will travel east across the waters and the length of Gaul to find Lif.

I spared you from the liar Claudius, perhaps, and abandoned my vengeance in Rome for you, but you have suffered greatly throughout your life and seem like a glum young man. You stare at me, occasionally, for you know who I am and what I have done.

In Germania, I am ever the Oath Breaker.

In Rome, they call me the traitor.

But I knew your mother, Thumelicus. I hated and loved and served your father and you will, I am sure, know my mettle in the end.

Wyrd, if you do not.

If the gods give us time, my Lord, I shall tell you what took place in Rome. For that is where we went. My father survived, so did Catualda, and we would meet them again. But most of all, I went to Rome and so did Armin, and there I learned much of the past of Maroboodus and did indeed understand him better. I never forgave him for Mother and Hulderic and his treatment of our family, but I understood some of his choices. Rome is a confusing land of lies and riches, and a man loses himself there easily enough.

I did.

As for that day, when the bloody group made its way down the mountain and the hills for the plains of Sigimer and the Cherusci, we still thought everything would be well. I thought of Ishild and the dead boy. I had dealt with Odo, killed Corinx, and Ansigar. Nihta lay dead. Father lived though his men were gone, and Catualda was out there to cause trouble for him. I was strangely happy with that as well. I had not killed kin, and I felt I had settled many of my scores.

I had given away the sword.

I had lost the ring.

Lif was safe.

I was both happy and sad and felt like I was living a new life. We rode wearily and stopped to buy food, to rest, and to bind our many wounds in a land filled with wounded men, owned by Segestes.

Segestes?

I sighed.

I would still have enemies, despite what I had promised Cassia. But perhaps, I would also have a family to chase the dark memories away. She was pregnant. So I thought when I rode from Lif that day, trying to forgive myself, unsuccessfully, the many deaths. There were so many. I had killed so many. Few men had ever slain so many people so young, but then, I had Woden's speed and his dancing spear on my side, and I had a talent for dealing death. I thought of dead, poor Ishild and shook my head. Of Fulcher. And his family.

Regret.

Regret makes one a husk of a man. In my mind, I saluted the dead. I blamed the wyrd, the sisters, and the world itself and told them I would see them in Asgaard, in the Hall of Woden, in Valholl as I joined the

Einherjar, the lords of the swords. There, none would hate each other, despite the battles and regret would fade, finally. Wyrd is a clever word. It allows the unhappy to find peace in their turmoil. Regret is to be buried behind honest toasts and happy songs and tears. Regret is for fools.

But I had one regret I could not forget.

I rode to find Drusus, knowing all my dreams might die with him.

The spear Father had thrown. The hasta had flown in the air, the magnificent aim near perfect, guided by malicious spirits. Drusus's happiness over the slaying of Sibratus, not seeing the deed. It all came together at the wrong time for the young lord. I failed. Had I not failed, had Drusus lived, the world would be a different kind of a place now. Happier, certainly, Rome worthy of admiration and less greedy. Perhaps Claudius, the most misunderstood of the sons of Drusus, would set it right one day, Lord Thumelicus, but I doubted it. The Republic was Drusus, and Drusus had fallen.

Father had been right. Drusus's injury was fatal.

Eventually, we rode to the former lands of Sigimer, aiming for the fords. My friends were chatting and laughing, exhausted and feverish from wounds. Tudrus was teasing Brimwulf he would marry Mathildis when he fell; Brimwulf was telling Tudrus that he would have to take care of a horrible brat as well. Bohscyld looked grim as usual, as he supported Wandal, who was weak with his wounds. Gernot was coming last, his horsemanship awkward. I sometimes looked at him, and he answered the look, with a sad smile. It would be a long road for any love to develop between us.

But he was my brother.

Thus, we rode for a few days, and the months of Lietha were ending as we trekked the lands of the Cherusci. We passed the battlefield, and the crows had shared a feast with wolves and foxes for there lay the cream of Cherusci and Chatti, Marcomanni as well, and who survived, was busily burning and burying their loved ones. They were a vast nation, they would fight again, but hunger and fear would be their unwanted companions that winter and Segestes would rule, despite his treason of Drusus. We rode over the rivers, and after the Buck, some Thracians found us. They were forlorn, and they told us Drusus was grievously sick. His leg had broken, had been splintered and cared for, but still it had festered. The legions had carried him south, towards Mattium, where a great camp was established in the former lands of Oldaric.

And he had been asking for me.

We rode fast.

We rode like the wind, forgot our misery and spent the hooves of our horses to ribbons. It took us two days in our condition, but finally, amidst the Hercynian wilds and near Castra Flamma, we found Roman horsemen, exploratores looking out for the Chatti and the southern Sigambri, and they guided us towards a Roman fort, a Castra Scelerata, the accursed fort, for it was clear to them Drusus would die. We found the castra, where the two legions stood watch. Patrols rode out; cohorts raided the countryside, quelling risings and it all looked ordinary. They were doing what they always did, made war, slept, ate, and trained.

But they also grieved.

Wandal looked alarmed as some more Thracian cavalry spotted us, demanding passphrase, and Gernot tried to hide his fear as well, but I gave one, an old one, and after I had told them to go fuck themselves, they understood I was a Decurion of 2nd Batavorium. The man leading the troop grinned at us. 'Hraban? Of the Batavi?' I nodded darkly, sick, tired, and angry. 'You are to go to the principia. As fast as you can,' he told me. We rode to the gates and dismounted, leading the beasts in. I gave my horse to a slave, my friends following suit, and we walked the long road to the principia tents, men of Drusus's official staring at us, for we were bloody, wounded, and hungry, our cheeks shrunk.

At the center of the castra was a building. Next to it was the praetorium, where the eagles and standards were held, and it was but a tent, but they had built a principia worthy of Drusus and the great hall was of wood, fine and well made, and around it, men were standing, keeping their heads down, some sitting in the dust. A pair of horses were held by a dusty man in a silk tunic, a tall man tottering with fatigue. I passed him and announced myself to the guards. To my surprise, old Saturninus came to me, looking me up and down. What he was doing there, I did not know.

He was going to say something but decided against it. 'Go in, Hraban,' he said simply and stood aside.

Then it hit me. *He would take over if Drusus died*, I thought.

I took off my helmet and entered the room. In the center lay my lord.

I have rarely seen a face so twisted in pain. His hair was plastered to his skull, and he was sweating in his tunic. His leg was uncovered as a medicus and a capsari hovered over it. There was a wound, a red and black wound where the bone had punctured out of the skin, and they were using vinegar to clean it and preparing to close the skin with a fibula, but the leg was so tender to their touch, Drusus howled. I watched away as he screamed and tears flowed from my eyes. Saturninus clapped my shoulder as the lord cried, and I saw another man sitting in a dark corner.

Then Drusus stopped screaming. I looked at him and saw he saw me, his eyes feverish. 'Hraban?'

'Yes, Lord,' I said, miserably.

'Drusus,' he reminded me with a grimace.

'I failed, Drusus. I failed to save you,' I said.

He shook his head. 'No. I failed and underestimated Armin once more. However, I did kill Sibratus. Was he a chief? Optima Spoila, Hraban. I managed that.'

'It was not Armin, Lord, who ...' I started, but he coughed hard, his breathing heavy.

He beckoned to a scribe. 'Make it known, that Hraban, this Germani of the 2st Batavorium is to be made a Roman citizen for his heroics in combat. Make sure of it,' he said, looking at Saturninus, who nodded uncertainly, eying the seated figure. Drusus dragged me closer. 'I will not be able to help your daughter, and I am sorry.'

'Think no more of it. She is safe,' I told him, and he smiled.

'Daughters, beware of daughters, Hraban. Roman daughters especially. All my children are going to be dangerous, my wife unhappy. If you can, help them,' he said ruefully.

'Lord, I am nothing without you,' I said, but he shook his hand, dismissing my protests.

'You are a warrior and a wily raven. A bastard and a champion. A Roman one now. No, I will not want to hear of betrayals. I do not wish to know why Hunfried sacrificed me. Perhaps it was Armin; perhaps it was someone else. Perhaps your father did his job, and perhaps he truly deserved to win. You know, I spoke to you about my dreams of the Republic, and I have enemies, even in my house, but it matters not now. My family does.' He was shivering uncontrollably.

'Cornix said Julia ...'

He shook his head and nodded at the man in the corner, who got up. 'My wife?' the man said harshly. 'Julia?'

Drusus pulled me still closer. 'Augustus, my stepfather did not do this. But that does not mean he won't hurt my family. You guard my family.'

'How Lord?' I asked, glancing at the man walking from the side for us.

'Tiberius?' Drusus said, weakly, and the man entered the light. *Gods, I thought, Tiberius is married to Julia now. He hated her, did he not?* He was a tall man, older than Drusus, his brother. His hair was stiff and short, his jaw was unshaven and strong, his face dirty, with lines of dirt where he had briefly wiped his face with a wet towel. His eyes were gray and his posture erect. A soldier.

So I met my future master.

Drusus grasped the man's hand. 'Make this man, and his men guardsmen. He has served me well. I want him to be close to my family,' he said, and Tiberius came next to me, looking at my eyes.

'What is that about Julia?' he asked again, with steel in his voice.

I bowed to him. 'Has your brother told you what is happening with Maroboodus and Segestes, Lord?'

He grunted. 'That they schemed to kill my brother for some woman in Rome? And you claim it was Julia? She is willful, unpleasant, angry, and crooked as a rich merchant; a whore, really, but she has little to gain from killing Drusus.' He emphasized the word "whore."

He looked hard at me, a backwoods noble of little consequence in the great game of Roman power. I gathered myself and stood my ground. I saw Drusus grin weakly, for had I not passed his scrutiny once? 'Her sons are to rule when Augustus dies.'

'To speak of the death of princeps,' he said very thickly, 'is a crime, Batavi.'

'Yet, lords die, and their sons take over. It is so even in Rome,' I said and looked at his Drusus with grief. He followed my look, and his face clouded with pain, and he nodded reluctantly as if unwilling to let go of murderous thoughts.

'And yes,' he allowed, 'perhaps she is planning for the death of lords, but I doubt she thought of it herself. Perhaps there are people using her, pushing her, hoping for her to shield them from blame. Perhaps,' he hissed, 'the whore is planning for dead lords and new husbands?' *He meant himself.*

I took a deep breath and said nothing. I did not speak of the son of Maroboodus, and if Tiberius knew of that scandal, he said nothing. He turned to look at me, his mind made up. 'He looks scruffy, dirty and savage. Germani Custodes Corporis has groomed men, and I have no authority to go around the usual recruitment methods, but surely I can try. But I make no promises,' he said, but Drusus grabbed his hand imploringly.

My lord was interrupted before he could say anything.

'That is the son of Maroboodus,' said a hateful voice as Antius walked to the room. 'The son of Maroboodus, a Marcomanni, Tiberius, and your father will want him. He must die, at Mamertine prison, or before, no matter his service. And he did fail to save your brother,' Antius said, silently, grinning at my face. 'His father threw the spear that put our Consul down.'

Tiberius removed his hand from Drusus's.

He turned to me, his eyes savage again, madness lurking inside the cold orbs. 'Is that so, boy? If it is, you will die here, today. Your men as well. We will crucify you upside down.' His calm demeanor cracked as the beast that was inside Tiberius reared his head. He was in pain, having ridden from Ticinum in Italy, over the Alps with the Rhaetian slave, breaking records to be with the brother he loved. He pulled out a sword, ignoring Drusus, who was trying to stop him.

I despaired and prepared to draw Nightbright. 'I also fought my father,' I told him evenly. 'Have been fighting him for years.'

'Antius is our enemy,' Drusus whispered.

Antius bowed. 'He is delusional, I am sorry, Lord.' Tiberius hesitated.

I snapped the scroll from my pouch to his hand. 'Here, Lord,' I said and bowed deeply to Tiberius. He scowled as if the thing was a leprous bit of meat and finally nodded, taking the scroll. Antius cocked his head carefully at the lord who was reading it, sweat on his forehead. Tiberius's eyes flashed to Antius, then to Drusus, and he kneeled next to his brother. They conferred for a time, and I kept my eyes turned away from Antius, a small, vicious smile on my face. *The bastard had never seen the scroll.*

Then, finally, Tiberius got up, slapping the scroll on his thigh.

'Hunfried will be found, and killed. Segestes will have explaining to do. Maroboodus will be found, in due time. I will take over the command of the Tres Gauls and lead the stricken men to slaughter all who resist Rome,' he told us softly, and I felt nearly sorry for Hunfried, who likely would suffer greatly for his treason. And as for Father? He had enemies. Tiberius nodded, making calculations. 'We will savage the Sigambri, the Chatti, and all the Cherusci, who will not submit. This will take place next year. As for this year? When I ride south with my brother, this man will follow me.' He nodded at me. 'He is a Roman citizen. His men are to be taken into the Germani Corpores Custodes, and thus, they are no longer of the 2st Batavorium. And I will be patron to the Batavi in any case.'

It was true. Tiberius would inherit the clients of Drusus, I thought.

'Lord ...' Antius began timidly, but Tiberius stepped forward and slapped the man in the face so hard Antius flew to his ass, his face a mask of pain and hurt.

Tiberius crouched before him. 'Paullus,' he hissed. 'Tribune Paullus. He wrote to you. Your name is in this thing!'

'I told him not to write my name ...' Antius began and went white from the face. 'I mean ...'

'I will see you crucified, Antius,' Tiberius laughed like a fiend. 'I wanted to do that to this man, and now I cannot get rid of the idea. Upside down, sideways, and the right way as long as the wood is slick with your blood. But first, I will have you questioned.'

469

Antius shook his head in denial as guards burst in to grasp him. He struggled in the doorway, his eyes on me. I lifted an eyebrow at him. 'Cornix is dead. He won't help you this time.'

'You sheep fucker!' Antius shrieked as they took him away.

Tiberius stepped close to me and lowered his voice.

He glanced at the doorway before he spoke to me again. 'I will speak with Antius, as said. We will bury Drusus in Rome, and I will war with the Germani next year. You will serve me, and when the war is over, the war my brother nearly won, you will follow me back to Rome for good. I have a great use for men like you. We will see who is to pay for this crime, and no sorrow ever inflicted on a man ... or a woman ... is going to compare to what I shall do to all involved.'

I saluted him. I would salute him thus for years to come.

Tiberius kneeled next to his brother. 'Now, leave us. All of you, for I would be with him alone. We grew up together, suffered and laughed as one, and I love him more than I have ever loved anyone, save for my first wife. I will see him on his way.'

So it was, Lord, that I became Roman.

I found Cassia at the medical tent. She was sewing a wound, and her eyes went wide as she saw me. The relief was such she punctured the wounded man's shoulder with the needle and led me out, leaving the man howling inside. She looked into my face, then to my hip and found no Winter Sword there.

'Where is it?' she asked.

I put my hands out and held her, she held me, and we rejoiced and grieved together for we were alive and she was pregnant. 'The sword will haunt its owner, but it is fine, for I hate the man.'

'Very well, Hraban,' she whispered. 'Are we done with this?'

'We will go to Rome. We will find who killed ... Drusus, and I will serve Tiberius. I am not saying our lives will be easy and full of joy, but I am now driven by you and this.' I put my hand on her belly. 'My Lif is safe. As safe as life allows.'

She wiped a tear from her beautiful eye and nodded. 'Thank you, Hraban.'

'Oh,' I added. 'You are now a Roman noble.'

'What?' she asked, and I laughed and cried, for I was both happy and sad. My oath was kept, my Winter Sword was gone, and we would have a new beginning.

Next morning, Drusus died, aged twenty-nine, Imperator and Consul, my friend, and the legions grieved, they still do to this day, and with him died any hope of Rome restored to a Republic. Like the last warmth of the sun on a chilly fall day, his last breath swept away all hopes of Senate once again ruling Rome.

Next day, Wandal brought me my horse, Fulcher mocked Brimwulf, the Quadi sharpened their weapons and Gernot stared silently at us. We rode to Rome, and I guarded Tiberius Claudius Nero, who walked behind the pier carried by grim legionnaires.

With the prisoners, came Antius. And there, as well, was Armin, the son of Sigimer. He waved at me from his cage, and I nodded at him. I went to him, and he stared at me in pain. 'I am not sure Thusnelda had this in mind when she asked you to help me.'

'I kept you alive,' I told him happily. 'She will appreciate it.'

He looked hard into my eyes. 'And if they strangle me in their cells?'

'I will beg they make it quick,' I told him.

'You damned thing,' he cursed.

'I think they will keep you. Segestes needs to be kept in check, after all.' I grinned.

He groaned and held his bound leg. 'Perhaps. Hopefully, they do not need a sacrifice to celebrate the death of Drusus. If I survive this, we will be back.'

'I am a Roman,' I told him brusquely. 'But perhaps you shall go home one day.'

'Roman you are, yes. And so shall Arminius be,' he laughed. 'But Armin will come back one day. And Veleda told me you shall come with him. And you will not be married.'

I said nothing to him, fear gnawing at my innards. I guided my horse away.

For many years to come, Lord Thumelicus, we had a deadly adventure in Rome, as Tiberius worked out who betrayed Drusus. And I became the sword of the terrible lord.

And that of his mother, Livia.

Hraban's stories will continue early 2016 with the book Snake Catcher

Thank you for reading the book.

Do **sign up for my mailing list** by visiting my homepages. By doing this, you will receive a rare and discreet email where you will find:

News of the upcoming stories
Competitions
Book promotions
Free reading

Also, if you enjoyed this book, you might want to check out these ones:

Grab them from my AMAZON HOMEPAGE

AFTERWORD

Hraban had decided on his course of action in Raven's Wyrd. He had given up on his dreams of becoming a warlord, a ring giver, and a Marcomanni noble with a rich hall, a thousand men saluting him with foaming ale horns, and poems glorifying his deeds. Once fame is gone, it is in the human nature to believe no further good of the person, but Hraban also learned his honor and love more precious than the fragile, passing fame.

His home was gone. So was his tribe.

But he had a new one.

He was to become a Roman by the grace of Chariovalda, the Batavi noble and the lord to them both, Nero Claudius Drusus, the most celebrated warrior and famed Republican, who loved the north. Hraban gave his soul to Drusus, who accepted Hraban gladly. Though Drusus had many enemies, Hraban adopted his dreams and would have served the lord to the end of his days. And he did though that end came far too soon. Serving Drusus was fine with Cassia and Hraban's remaining friends, for they too had seen so many die in Hraban's pursuits of vengeance and regaining his daughter Lif.

And so it is Hraban marries Cassia and gives her his oaths over the family sword, the Head Taker. To Cassia, however, it is the Winter Sword, cold and deadly, representing despair and an unreasonable drive for vengeance for Hraban and those who follow him. She asks Hraban to put their pursuits first, and so Hraban promises her to be finished with all his grudges the following summer and then he will abandon the Winter Sword.

Both Drusus and Hraban still had loose ends to tie in Germania.

In this book, most of those ends are tied, one way or another. Hraban fights for Drusus and himself, finds some very evil men, more evil than he ever was, and even helps his former foe Armin survive the turmoil of the Cherusci. He exposes the treason of Drusus's allies, and he finishes his dealings with the implacable Odo. He loses dear Lif though she prospers after.

By the end, the family's sword the Head Taker and the great ring Draupnir's Spawn are gone, perhaps for good. He did make a new enemy of the mighty Segestes and as for his father? They had a good, long talk.

Despite his oath to Cassia to turn a new page, the great man, Nero Claudius Drusus is dead. Hraban's best and brightest hope for a better life and a proper lord is gone to Hades.

Instead, he serves the infamously morose, coldly practical Tiberius.

And that is where the next book, Bane of Gods, will pick up.

While the deep woods and rolling hills of Germania are left behind for now, and Hraban marches for the splendor and filth of Rome, he will find life is complicated in the land of Augustus. He will have powerful, demanding allies, and a very interesting set of enemies in the imperial family, for where there is ultimate power, there are those who wish to possess it, and only one can truly grasp it.

The age of Drusus was brief, glorious, and decisive. He was loved, and he was feared and gods know if Rome would have been a different place than that of Tiberius, Caligula, Claudius, and Nero had Drusus but lived. And Germania might have been fully pacified, as well.

But it was not to be.

As for the wars of Drusus in Germania, it is clear there was a mighty push to pacify the restless lands. This was the Roman dream for decades to come until it was sullenly deemed impossible, and Rhine River was made the final boundary. During 9 AD to 12 AD, Nero Claudius Drusus fought hard to capture this land. He began relatively painlessly in the very north. Then he took on the Lippe River tribes, as it was in Raven's Wyrd. Finally, in this book, he suffered the battle of Arbalo with the Cherusci and turned south the years after. There, he apparently put to flight the Marcomanni, the Quadi, and then the mighty Chatti. The year after, he again went after the Chatti and came back to the lands of the Cherusci. It is said he reached all the way to Elbe River, even getting in touch with the Suebi Semnones living across from it. Strange, magical happenings, a völva, and his tired troops made him turn back and somewhere along the route, he fell from his horse and died from the injuries.

That felt unworthy of him. Instead, what Maroboodus was hoping to accomplish, all the dreams of Drusus and schemes of Antius and Segestes had to culminate in a mighty battle. There is, of course, no documentation of a great battle at this time, but it was needed for this work of fiction.

After Drusus had died, Tiberius took over the legions and partially pacified all the remaining tribes, though that, of course, was only a temporary respite from wars. Later on, Tiberius would turn against the growing power of the Marcomanni and Maroboodus, but that will be yet another book, for then Armin shall return home.

I hope you enjoyed the Winter Sword just like I hope you enjoyed the book 1, the Oath Breaker and the book 2, Raven's Wyrd.

I humbly ask you rate and review the story on Amazon.com and Goodreads. This will be incredibly valuable for me going forward.

Please visit www.alariclongward.com and sign up for my mailing list for information on the upcoming products and also find information on how I try to reward readers, for example by a competition where you can actually win once a month, should you find the time to place a review. I will also try to involve you, the reader in the future adventures by other competitions, where your ideas will be valuable.

Do sign up! And thank you.

Made in the USA
Lexington, KY
19 December 2016